Mystic Rising

Mystic Rising is a work of fiction. Any of the characters, organizations and events portrayed in this novel are either products of the author's imagination or are used fictitiously.

Cover art by Farras Raihan
Cover design by Devin Thornton

Trigger Warning: This novel contains harsh language, swearing and examples of bullying. Viewer discretion is advised.

Paperback ISBN: 979-8-218-31336-4

"To those who had inspired me to write, so that Mayu can run."

# Distortion

**I was crawling under the bushes** when one of the branches snagged my hair. I hissed at the sharp pain, but stifled down my cries, knowing a single sound could give us away.

"Mayu? Do you need my help?" Elizabeth whispered.

She crawled next to me. Her glasses hung crookedly off her nose, and small leaves clung to her twin braids. Elizabeth reached over my head and freed me from the branches.

"Better?" She said with a soft smile.

"Better," I replied, rubbing my head.

I turned ahead to an open field stretching from the bushes. Freshly cut grass swept through the air, but it was the chain link fence in front of us that caught my attention.

"And you're sure no one can see us?" Elizabeth said, following my gaze. She nudged her glasses up the bridge of her nose. "If we're caught—"

"We won't be," I promised, interrupting her. "Trust me, this is a blind spot."

I straightened my glasses and grabbed the loose part of the fence close to the ground. All it took was a few pushes for it to give way and open to a gap wide enough for us to crawl through.

Elizabeth turned to me, half smiling. "You've had a lot of strange ideas, but I think this might be the craziest."

I chuckled. "Would you rather sit in a library again?"

It was our favorite place to go during lunchtime, but since it was the last week of school, I convinced Elizabeth to try something different.

"Going to the library does sound nice," Elizabeth mused.

"But how often do we get to go outside, and it wasn't for practice?"

"Not as often as I'd like."

I flattened my stomach and slid under the stretch. Once I was on my feet, I held Elizabeth's hand and pulled her to the other side. My backpack, which she wore, got caught in the branches, but she managed to shimmy herself free and stand up.

As we brushed the dirt off our t shirt and shorts, Elizabeth plucked the twigs out of her hair and stared at the hole we'd just crawled through.

She grimaced. "We have to go through this again, don't we?"

We could have left through the school's back doors, but anyone could have seen us leave.

"At least we'll know what to expect when we head back," I said.

We stayed close to the fence, hidden by the trees as we made our way to the track field. As the runway came into view, I glanced over my shoulder to see Elizabeth slowing down. Her eyes fell on the empty school yard.

"Has the place always been so... big?" she murmured.

A month ago, this place was bustling with teammates practicing for the next meet. But with track season over and the school year ending, all the equipment was gone. The only sounds we heard were chattering birds and leaves shuddering in the rolling breeze.

"We had a huge clean-up after the last meet. So, it looks big without the high jump poles and hurdles lying around." I turned around and smiled at my friend. "Don't worry, you'll get to help us set up in high school, right?"

"Right..."

Next to the track field was a single runway with a sand pit at the end covered in a large blue tarp. Elizabeth stopped at the starting line, and I paced to the tarp. Worry, and excitement flitted in me as I lifted the corners and a smile pinched my cheek to see the pit was full of sand.

"We're good to go!"

As I spun around, I spotted them. Beads of light threading within the grass. They clustered around flowers and trailed up the trees. Some drifted with the wind and others moved in their own direction. A few, small ones were drifting towards me.

"Mayu?"

My breath hitched and the dancing lights scattered. They dashed into the bushes and tiny whispers fluttered from the leaves and rounded the track field.

"Mayu!" Elizabeth called again, snapping my focus back to her. The whispers faded and the string of light on the trees steadied into sunbeams. "Are you alright? You got quiet for a moment."

My stomach knotted. "Did you hear something just now?"

Elizabeth shook her head. "No, I didn't. Did you?"

I swallowed back, realizing that the lights and whispers weren't real. It was an aura, my mind scrambling to warn me a seizure was going to happen. Though lately, the auras seem to happen more than the seizures.

"Maybe we should head back..."

"It was a false alarm," I insisted, but Elizabeth seemed reluctant. "How about two jumps. Then we'll head to the library when we're done."

Elizabeth stroked one of her braids and stared at the runway. "Alright," she finally said. "Just two jumps."

As she returned to the starting line, I gave myself a moment to recollect my thoughts. Deep breaths to calm down and listen to the world around me. There were no strange whispers or moving lights. Just me, my friend and a runway. I fished for the stopwatch in my backpack and made my way to the sandpit.

"Are you ready?" Elizabeth called out.

"Ready when you are!" I yelled, waving the stopwatch.

She leaned back and her eyes narrowed on the sandpit ahead.

"Get set..." My thumb hovered over the start button.

At the sound of the beep, Elizabeth tore across the runway at breath taking speed. Her feet hit the take-off board with a loud clunk, and she sprung forward, arching in the air before plunging feet first into the sandpit.

"That was great!" I stopped the timer and hurried to Elizabeth. Her cheeks were flustered and sweat rimmed around her forehead.

"How far... did I go?" She panted.

I checked the take-off board and my smile widened. "Thirteen feet! On your first try too!"

Elizabeth's eyes lit up. She threw herself up and triumphantly shouted, "Finally!"

But her cheer erupted into a shriek when she fell back. I tried to catch her, grabbing her by her wrist and she pulled me into the sand. I landed on my stomach and Elizabeth suddenly lurched up and clutched her right shoulder.

"Are you hurt? I have band aids in my backpack!"

"It's fine!" She mustered, gritting her teeth. "I fell on it wrong."

Her tight grip loosened, and after a few deep breaths, she straightened her back and her pained expression relaxed. "Don't worry, I'm alright," she said, and her smile returned. "I can't believe I jumped that far."

I was still worried about her shoulder but decided to let it go for now. "Not bad for being out of practice. Imagine if you were at the last meet. You would've left the other team speechless!"

"I know," Elizabeth frowned, and her eyes lowered to the sand.

I knew it wasn't a good time to ask, but I had to know, "Why didn't you come to the last meet?"

Elizabeth rolled her shoulders and looked away. "I told you already, I was sick."

I would have believed her, except Elizabeth was a terrible liar. It was a big game and the last track meet of our year in middle school. She was excited about going and we practiced almost every day. Friday night, she called to make sure I was ready. She didn't sound sick or mentioned being unwell, so I was suspicious when her mother called the coach the next morning to tell her Elizabeth had caught the flu. I was even more suspicious when Elizabeth came to school on Monday, perfectly fine. No runny nose, sniffles, or a raspy voice. No matter how many times I asked, she'd tell me she was sick.

Elizabeth stood up and dusted the sand off her shirt and track shorts.

"How much time do we have?" she asked.

I checked my watch. "Thirty minutes, plenty of time."

Elizabeth helped me to my feet, and I gave her the stopwatch.

"Ready when you are," she said.

Smiling, I reached the starting line, patting the sand out of my hair. Pushing my glasses up the bridge of my nose, I leaned forward, locking eyes on the take-off board.

"On your mark!"

I bent my right leg and kept my left leg in place, ready to launch me when I heard the signal.

"Get set..."

The stopwatch beeped. I broke into a sprint a second too late and raced down the runway. My breath echoed, and my heart fluttered but I braced myself to make the jump.

As I struck the take-off board and a sharp pain wrenched up my leg, shattering my thoughts. Tumbling forward, all I saw was the sand pit before it flew into my face. At the cry of a familiar voice, I jolted up with a startled gasp, and sand caught in my throat. My head hurt, my legs ached and my ears rang as someone called out to me, soft and delicate like a bell.

I spun around to a girl running towards me. Her twin braids, and gentle brown eyes behind a pair of glasses were painfully familiar. Her name hung at the tip of my tongue.

"Eli...za...beth? What's going on?"

She stopped, her brows rose with shock, and... worry. "We're at the track field. Don't you remember?"

"We were?"

The memories were coming back to me. Slipping out of class when the bell rang, racing through the back exit doors, and crawling beneath the bushes. The gap in the fence, the floating lights and a distant cry from far away.

My ears twitched suddenly to a strange sound, and I jerked up to footsteps tapping on the runway. Someone was leaning over my backpack at the starting line. Her jet-black hair obscured her face, but she wore the same uniform we had; a navy-blue pleated skirt and a white blouse.

Elizabeth, craning her head to the side, uttered a familiar name. "R-Rosalina?"

Rosalina Evans flinched and, without saying a word, she took off with my backpack. Elizabeth darted after her. I pushed myself up, and though the ground was still swaying, I tailed behind my friend.

We chased Rosalina across the track field, keeping pace until she skirted to the open gate. Elizabeth and I were fast, but three years of tennis made Rosalina quick on her feet. She made sharp turns and sprinted toward the school's back doors, held open by her friends, Nara Jackson and Bethany Magdalene. The instant Rosalina crossed the threshold, her friends tried to close the doors, but Elizabeth grabbed the handle in time for me to rush inside.

"Give it back!" I shouted.

I reached for my backpack when I was close enough, but Rosalina jumped to the side. The suddenness of it caught me off guard and I tripped on my feet, trying to stop myself. I twisted back to Rosalina who was laughing at me with her friends behind her.

"Give it baaaack," Bethany moaned.

Elizabeth slowed down beside me. "Rosalina, this isn't funny."

"This isn't funny," Bethany repeated, mockingly.

"Aw, what are you going to do, Princess?" Rosalina sneered, tauntingly swinging my backpack. "Tell your single mommy on me?"

Anger flared in my chest. "Did you follow us outside?"

"Did you follow us outside?" Bethany echoed.

Rosalina retorted, "Don't act like you were supposed to be out anyway."

"Like you don't sneak out either?" I snapped back. None of the students were allowed to leave the school during the day, but that never stopped Rosalina and her friends from sneaking out to do who knows what.

Rosalina stepped back, her face twisted in disgust. "Ew! Have you been stalking us, you creep?"

"No one's stalking you," Elizabeth pressed. "Give Mayu her backpack."

"Give Mayu her—"

I glared at Bethany before she could finish her sentence. "Do you have anything better to say?"

She flinched, her lips puckered, and her eyes squeezed shut to force the tears out.

"Don't you yell at my bestie!" Rosalina yelled. She yanked the backpack away when I tried to grab it. "Stop trying to touch me!"

"Give it back!" I demanded.

"Why? What's in it?" A wicked grin crossed Rosalina's face.

She unzipped my backpack, and my stomach twisted when she shoved her hand inside. I reached for it again, but Rosalina jerked back. She pulled out one of our skirts and I could practically see the lie forming in her head.

"Oh my God, you were taking off each other's clothes!" She screamed and flung our uniforms across the floor. Nara and Bethany burst into laughter. Elizabeth quickly swiped our clothes and I chased after Rosalina again, fuming with anger.

"I knew you were a freak!" she cackled.

Enraged, I swung my arm for my backpack. As Rosalina yanked it away, she didn't notice my incoming hand until it snapped across her face. The slap rang down the hallway, and the laughter from Nara and Bethany fell to a deathly silence. For a moment, Rosalina's shocked expression mirrored mine.

Elizabeth and I took off, but a hand snatched the back of my shirt. The fabric tightened around my neck, cutting out my cries.

"Let her go!" Elizabeth shrieked. She charged after me, until Nara jammed her hands against her sides, shoving my friend hard against the locker with a loud thud.

My cries were cut by my shirt digging into my neck. Over my shoulder, Rosalina glowered at me, face beet red and her eyes darkened with rage.

"So, it's like that, then?" She raised her arm, and a hard slap whipped across my face. The pain scattered my thoughts. My mind was going in and out, but I remembered pleading to Rosalina to stop. She hit me again and again with manic blows while Bethany and Nara cheered her on. Next thing I knew, I woke up to pain pulsing through every part of my body.

Bethany threw a high-five at Rosalina. She approached me, and my trembling arms quickly covered my face.

"Yeah, that's what I thought," Rosalina spat. "That's what you get, freak!"

The girls turned to their next target, Elizabeth. She hadn't moved from the locker where Nara pushed her. Her head was buried in her knees, and her hands clutched her shoulders. Nara and Rosalina goaded her to get up. Bethany yanked her braids, and Elizabeth screamed for them to stop.

"Not so perfect now, are you!?" Bethany shoved Elizabeth again, and when she didn't rise, they laughed.

Rosalina laughed that awful cackle I heard every day when she insulted me. When I'd find hurtful letters shoved in my locker. When she stole my notebook and tore the pages out. Why did she hate me so much? Why did she have to devote three years to making me miserable?

At that moment, the realization struck me. I had been dealing with Rosalina for *three years*! Three years of insults to my face and rumors behind my back. Every day, I dreaded the next horrible thing she would do to me. No matter how hard I tried to avoid her, Rosalina would follow me.

*Did I want to deal with her in high school?*

A rush of anger flooded my thoughts, making everything seem unreal and dreamlike. Rosalina was about to walk away like she'd often do, flipping her hair over her shoulder as if nothing happened, until Nara saw me staggering to my feet.

Rosalina spun around and stomped toward me. Balling her fists, she hurled insult after insult until our eyes met. Her next words tore into a terrified shriek, then cut by a sudden crash.

The bell rattled, and I dropped to my knees, clasping my hands over my ears. Everything hurt, and I wanted to crawl into a ball, but I forced myself to walk on trembling legs toward Elizabeth. She wasn't moving and something red smeared the locker behind her.

Rosalina burst into an ear-splitting wail, drawing every student to her attention. A teacher broke through the forming crowd and ran to her first. She rocked back and forth, cradling her arm, howling how much pain she was in. As everyone turned to face me, Nara and Bethany quickly shouted, "Mayu, did it! She attacked Rosalina!"

• ● •

The teacher found my glasses on the floor along with my backpack. They helped me gather my uniform and Elizabeth's before sending us to the main office. I was sitting on the bench next to my backpack, listening to the adults whispering behind their computers. My leg was bouncing in place, and my eyes flickered between the infirmary and the principal's office next to it.

From the way Mrs. Evans was shouting, you would've thought Rosalina was the one beaten on the floor. It was an accident when I slapped her, but I didn't throw her into the locker like she claimed. Rosalina could have jumped back to make it look like I pushed her. It wouldn't be the first time she faked injuries to get her way. But how did she dent the locker? Would she hurt herself bad enough to bruise her back and shoulder?

The infirmary door opened, and Elizabeth stepped out, holding an ice pack on her head.

"I can hear her through the walls," she whispered.

"I think the entire school can," I grumbled.

Elizabeth eased beside me and flinched up when her back touched the wall.

"How bad is it?" I asked.

She winced. "It's fine. I hit one of the locks when Nara pushed me. It wasn't a deep cut."

*The blood stain on the locker and her shirt said otherwise,* I thought.

Mrs. Evans interrupted the office gossip as her voice exploded through the door. I guess the principal said something she didn't like because she was threatening to call her lawyer again. Sometimes I wondered if she liked hearing herself talk.

"Do you want this?" Elizabeth offered me the ice pack. "I don't need it, but the nurse made me take it."

I held it to my cheek where Rosalina slapped me, though the pain had already dulled away.

"I'm sorry you got hurt."

Elizabeth shrugged, twirling one of her braids. "What was I supposed to do, nothing? Not that I did anything to help."

"At least you tried." I leaned against the wall, sighing. "We should've gone to the library."

"Rosalina followed us to the track field. Do you think she'd leave us alone if we went elsewhere?"

She was right. With the kind of money her family had, you'd think Rosalina would do something better with her time, but she'd rather follow us to the moon if it meant ruining our day.

"You saw what happened to her, didn't you?"

Elizabeth shook her head. "I heard her hitting the locker, then screaming in pain. Nara and Bethany said you attacked her."

"I didn't!"

"I know you didn't. You wouldn't." Elizabeth paused. "Maybe she was trying to get you in trouble to—"

She perked up when the door to the main office opened. In came my brother, Ichirou, wearing a green flannel and jeans. He had to work an extra shift all year, and it showed on his tired face and unkempt hair.

He stepped to the side, holding the door open for Elizabeth's mother, Isabella Hudson. Dark brown hair hung over her shoulder like a rope, braided like her daughter's. Behind oval shaped glasses, her eyes narrowed as she marched up to the desk. At the sound of her heels hitting the floor, the adults clammed up like they just heard cathedral bells tolling for their funerals.

Elizabeth looked up at her mother but didn't say a word. I struggled to talk to Ichirou, but I could tell from his tired eyes he wasn't mad at me. Silence took over the office as the adults buried their faces behind the monitors. Even Mrs. Evan's rants halted, like she noticed the sudden shift in the air. One of the adults, a female secretary scurried to the principal's office and frantically tapped the door.

"She's here," she whispered.

A moment later, Mr. Shepard emerged from his office. He straightened his blazer and cleared his throat, motioning us inside.

Mrs. Evans's arm snaked around Rosalina and kept quiet as though she wasn't screaming a few seconds ago. Elizabeth and Ms. Hudson took the chairs in the middle, and Ichirou and I sat beside them.

Settling behind his desk, Mr. Shepard's weary eyes drifted between Rosalina, then Elizabeth, and me.

"I understand there has been history with you three, but this incident needs to be addressed," he began. "Rosalina told us she caught you sneaking outside, and I can see that neither of you are wearing your uniforms."

I hesitated to look up at him. My voice came out thin and weak.

"It was my idea to go outside," Elizabeth spoke up. "I wanted to try the long jump because I missed the last track meet, and I asked Mayu to come with me."

*No, Elizabeth wanted to go to the library. I led her outside and showed her the blind spot in the bushes.*

"We were going to come back before lunch ended!" I blurted out. "But Rosalina stole my backpack, and we ran after her."

Mr. Shepard's scrunched up face fell on Rosalina. "You left the building as well?"

"Are you calling my daughter a liar?" Mrs. Evans interrupted. "Can't you see this girl's statement is objectively false? I mean, why would Rosalina be outside during school hours? It makes zero logical sense." She held her hand up before Mr. Shepard could speak. "My daughter is a smart, gifted young lady who always follows the rules. Clearly, that girl—" she motioned at me. "—gets triggered when she sees a classmate more successful and accomplished than her, both academically and athletically. Rather than learn from Rose, she chooses to bully my daughter, and gaslights poor Elizabeth to take the blame for her messes!"

I pushed down the urge to yell at her. Like I would be jealous of a psycho like Rosalina. And I may not know what 'gaslighting' meant, but I'll bet my track shoes Mrs. Evans didn't know what it meant either.

"Doesn't this upset you, Isabella?" Mrs. Evans sneered at Ms. Hudson. Her angered voice melted into a slimy whisper.

"You raised your daughter so well, better than most single mothers could. I'd hate to see that effort go to waste, to see your sweet, intelligent daughter lose her chance at a good education 'cause of that girl."

"First of all, *Mayu* has a name," Ichirou said sternly. "And we're here cause, yet again, Rosalina can't leave my sister alone, despite the warnings and write-ups and meetings we keep having here."

"*Adopted* sister," Mrs. Evans scowled. My shoulders twitched. "Need I remind you that we're here because your *adopted* sister snuck out of school, then beat up my defenseless daughter!"

"Rosalina attacked me!" I shouted, tears welling up in my eyes. "She stole my backpack and called us freaks after touching our clothes!"

"Because you are!" Rosalina yelled. "And you hit me after I caught you making out with—"

"Enough!" Mr. Shepard barked. "We are trying to resolve this peacefully."

"There's nothing to resolve!" Mrs. Evans erupted. "And I won't have my daughter dragged to that girl's level!" she jerked up from the chair, pulling Rosalina by her arm until she was on her feet.

"I see what this is. My Rose was chased down and brutally assaulted, but you'll protect her attacker because her feelings got hurt. Some principal you are. If you truly care about the safety of innocent children in your school, you'll do what's right."

Mrs. Evans stomped to the door, then stopped and turned back, glaring at Ichirou.

"She's better off with a *real* family. Not raised by an irrational, and immature college dropout—"

"And you're such a shining example of 'mature and rational,'" Ms. Hudson's low, smooth voice had a calm fury that made my skin crawl. Mrs. Evans faced Ms. Hudson, and her boisterous pose weakened as if she'd seen the grim reaper.

"For all you have to say about Mayu, your daughter brilliantly reflects the spoiled brat who raised her."

"Excuse you!" Mrs. Evans barked, but Ms. Hudson cut her off.

"Spare your woes for someone who cares. But speak ill about my girls again," Ms. Hudson added icily. "And you'll have something to cry about, *Rebecca*."

At the sound of her name, Mrs. Evans scrambled out of the office, and Rosalina stumbled behind her. The way Ms. Hudson spoke made me remember why every teacher feared her. Sure, Mrs. Evans may have the money to make anything disappear, but it always felt like Ms. Hudson had the power to make any*one* disappear.

"I'm sorry for losing my composure there," Ms. Hudson said. "I'm sorry you had to hear that, Mayu."

I choked up as tears ran down my face. Ichirou wound his arm around my shoulders, and Elizabeth held my hand. A box of tissues moved closer to me on the desk. I looked up, meeting Mr. Shepard's sullen grey eyes. When I could speak up, Elizabeth and I told them what happened.

"Do you still think Rosalina did nothing wrong?" Ichirou asked. "So many people at this school have had trouble with her. And all these write-ups and call-ins only encouraged her to do worse."

Ms. Hudson said, sternly, "And if Mayu and Elizabeth are going to be expelled from high school for this fight, why not expel Rosalina for causing it?"

"Rosalina will face the consequences of her actions." Mr. Shepard said. I almost rolled my eyes at that old line. "But Lawrence High School has a strict policy that any physical altercations in their middle school will automatically decline their enrollment. I'm sorry."

"Even when they were hurt?"

Mr. Shepard shifted from Ms. Hudson's eyes. "It is the policy, ma'am. If your daughter truly feels unsafe around her, there are other private schools I know that—"

"No need," Ms. Hudson said suddenly. "Your attempts at addressing these issues made me realize I can't trust your word or any school you might recommend. I was going to inform you later about this, but I've enrolled Elizabeth elsewhere, so this doesn't happen again."

My eyes widened. Her words cut into me, much deeper than any insult Rosalina or her mother could throw at me. I turned to Elizabeth, and she had her head down and her hands knotting on the braids again. I thought back to the day. How Elizabeth was eager to go outside with me. Her somber stare at the track field, and the sadness in her voice. It all made sense. She wasn't going to be with me from the start.

• ● •

In school-suspension was the lightest punishment Elizabeth and I could get for sneaking outside. We had to spend the last few days in a small closet space of a room, with a long table and a window the size of a shoebox. We couldn't leave without being escorted by the teacher watching over us and asking to go to the library was out of the question.

Still, it was better than what Rosalina got—suspended for the rest of the year (what good that did), expelled from Lawrence High School and from what I heard, three private schools had rejected her. Somehow, everyone in class blamed Elizabeth and me for it. No doubt it was Bethany and Nara who spread that rumor, but I tried not to dwell on it. Our classmates had already avoided me after Rosalina told them my seizures were contagious, and this new rumor was no different. If there was one good thing about in-school suspension, we didn't have to be stuck in class hearing the gossip.

We spent the next few days in that small room playing board games, drawing, and talking about a fairytale inspired book series we had finished. We did pretty much anything we liked to forget we were going to separate high schools.

I finally asked her on the last day about the transfer. The teacher watching over brought our lunch trays and stepped out, leaving us alone. Between prodding the meal, a dry patty with a small pile of lettuce on the side, Elizabeth told me Ms. Hudson wanted to transfer her months ago.

My throat tightened. "Why didn't you tell me?"

"I didn't want to go to a new school again," Elizabeth replied. "Mom and I would argue about it whenever the topic came up. She finally decided to let me go to Lawrence High if I could keep my grades up but then... the fight happened."

Silence fell between us, and as though it was her way of changing the subject, Elizabeth asked, "What school are you going to?"

I rolled my shoulders. "My brother's old school."

"I hear it's not so far from your home. That's good."

"Guess so."

I didn't want to talk about it. I lost my appetite and stared solemnly at the table. If I hadn't convinced Elizabeth to sneak outside, we wouldn't be here. If I hadn't rushed to grab my backpack, Elizabeth wouldn't have gotten hurt, and we'd still be in class, making plans for what clubs we'd join in high school. Elizabeth knew me all too well, because she spoke up right as I was about to say it.

"You don't have to apologize. It had nothing to do with you. Mom wanted me in a school that was... right for me."

"I get it..." I got it all too well.

Elizabeth was a smart, straight-A student. She always came to class on time, took notes dutifully, and won the "Model Student" awards twice in a row, something that always got under Bethany's skin. Elizabeth should've gone to a fancier academy, one that looked like a castle hidden in the mountains.

When the last bell rang, a heavy dread settled in me. We gathered our bags and said goodbye to the teacher. She was a kind

17

lady, and she knew what was going on. She told us before we left, "You still have two months of summer with each other. And holiday breaks."

It cheered me up a little, but Elizabeth carried that saddened look as if the teacher's words didn't reach her. On our way outside, we passed by a bunch of students who were excited about being done with school.

"Ichirou, Hannah, and I were thinking about going to the mall tomorrow, the one with the huge bookstore," I said. "Are you interested?"

Looking down, she shook her head. "Mom wants me to stay home. We can go another time."

"Do you have any plans the day after tomorrow?"

"I'm supposed to visit my new school for orientation."

"What about next Monday?"

"I'm shopping with Mom for supplies."

"Can I come?"

"Sorry... Mom wants me to go with her this time."

I leaned forward a little, trying to catch her face. "What about next week?"

Elizabeth shrugged. "Maybe, I'll have to ask mom first."

We stepped outside, avoiding the sea of kids pouring out the main doors. I recognized Ms. Hudson and Ichirou's cars parked in front of the school. It hurt to say goodbye. My heart ached knowing it was the last day of school. We weren't going to rush to class in the morning together. We weren't going to hide in the library's maze and read whatever caught our interest. And we weren't going to cheer each other on at the track field.

I turned to Elizabeth, getting misty eyed and said, "You want to call me when you get home?"

Elizabeth, mustering a smile, said. "Promise."

# Voices

**I spent most of my summer at home,** talking to Elizabeth on the phone because it was all we could do. Her new school had so many orientations, campus tours and pre-placement exams that she was too exhausted to do anything else.

"I'm sorry. Maybe next time," she'd say, stifling a yawn.

That worried me the most. I couldn't imagine a school, private or not, that would take up her entire summer and leave her so drained. I asked Elizabeth a few times if I could come with her for support, but she insisted her school would only let students and their parents visit.

"Next time" didn't come until August. Elizabeth called me, in a livelier voice, apologizing for the cancellations and asked if we could spend the whole day together before the end of summer. I happily suggested we go to the aquarium on Saturday, the last weekend of summer vacation, and Elizabeth agreed to meet me there.

Friday evening, after I showered, I set out my clothes for tomorrow and turned on the alarm so I wouldn't wake up late. When night came, I went to bed an hour early, excited to see Elizabeth again.

·●·

I woke up to faint beeps, too steady and soft to be my alarm clock, and bright light in my face. I shut my eyes tight and shifted in bed when a dull pain throbbed in the back of my head. I hissed and reached back only to feel a sharp sting in my arm. My eyes flew

19

opened and I jerked up in an unfamiliar bed, surrounded by white walls.

"Easy there, sis!" said a familiar voice.

I jumped and turned to see Ichirou by my side; his hand quickly settled on my shoulder. He tried to reassure me, but my focus bounced from the IV standing between us, with a tube snaking into a patch attached to my arm to monitors beeping rapidly behind us.

Before I could ask, "what happened?" Memories of the aquarium broke through my foggy mind, and I almost threw myself out of bed, but Ichirou held me back.

"Hey, you shouldn't get up so fast! You're going to rip the IV out!" he warned.

"What time is it?" I cried. "I got to be at the aquarium by eleven!"

My head spun and the dizzying room knocked me back into bed.

"Take it easy," Ichirou said, calmly. The nausea faded and the rapid beeping started to slow down.

"What time is it?" I repeated. "What am I doing here?"

Ichirou paused, then said in a deep breath. "You had a grand mal seizure this morning. You were convulsing in your room and when you didn't wake up, I called an ambulance."

My voice was dry and cracked. "How long have I been here?"

"An hour. It's noon."

His words froze me on the spot.

"W-We were supposed to be at the aquarium by eleven."

"I called Isa and told her what happened," he said.

It was always odd to hear Ichirou call Ms. Hudson, 'Isa.' It made her sound less intimidating, although "Isabella" wasn't too far behind.

"She rescheduled the trip for another time."

"Can we call Ms. Hudson and let her know that I'm awake?"

Ichirou's gaze fell. "About that, Sanders wants you to get an MRI, so you'll be here for the whole day."

My heart sank. "What for?"

Ichirou stared at me, raising his brow. "You had your first grand mal seizure in two years. He wants to see if everything is alright in there." He tapped my forehead. "At least you're not hooked to a breathing machine for two weeks."

I knew he was trying to make me feel better, but it didn't make the news hurt any less. It would be my luck to have the worst seizure on the one day I planned to see Elizabeth.

After a moment of silence, I spoke up. "D-Did you tell anyone else... what happened?"

"What do you mean?"

I tugged on the edges of the blanket. "Did you tell Mom and Dad?"

Ichirou grumbled, "And what are they supposed to do? Yell at me about how I'm a bad influence on you, again?"

"... It could be different."

"They do this any time you're in the hospital. If I wanted to get lectured for 'not doing enough,' I would have gone to work." He leaned back, silent for a moment, then groaned, "I'll call them tonight, but don't expect anything different from them."

It was no secret that Ichirou didn't get along with our parents. When he was in high school, they argued with him about his grades slipping, getting into fights, and yelling at a teacher in the middle of class. Then one night when I was ten years old, Ichirou stormed out of the house and never returned. Our parents didn't speak to him for two years until they sent me to stay with him. The last time we were together was my middle school graduation and mom and dad weren't happy about the fight.

"I see Sleepin' Beauty has woken," a man called with a faint Cockney accent.

A doctor with short blonde hair stood against the open door. He wore blue scrubs beneath his white coat with a name tag attached to it that read, "D. Sanders."

"Hope ye feelin' better," he said. "The MRI is ready, but I'd like to do a basic checkup if that's alright."

Dr. Sanders first checked my face for discoloration and, thankfully, there wasn't. Next, he placed the cold stethoscope on my chest and teased me about relaxing my racing heart. When Ichirou mentioned I hit my head during my seizure, Dr. Sanders looked for any bumps or bruises.

"So far, there's nothing wrong with yer head from the outside," Dr. Sanders said, almost jokingly. "Let's see about the inside."

The MRI was in a separate room that had a big donut shaped machine and a long table for me to lie on. The technician gave me a medical gown to change into, and a blanket to keep myself warm during the scan.

As the mechanical hums filled the air with the start of the scan, I closed my eyes. Though the memories were hazy, I could recall waking up early and getting dressed before I heard something...

I jumped when a voice echoed from outside.

"What?" I called out.

"I said we were done," replied the technician.

Her gentle voice wasn't the distant cry I thought I heard. The humming stopped, and the light sputtered into darkness. The table slid out of the MRI and the technician helped me to my feet.

She noticed I was shaking and clinging to the blanket. "My goodness, you look pale."

"I'm a little cold."

"Good thing the MRI is over," she assured. She let me keep the blanket after I changed and I didn't hear that distant cry again.

●

Dr. Sanders returned with images he hung over the light box in the room. I saw what was supposed to be my brain, but it was the darker patches around it that made me tense up.

"What are those?" Ichirou asked. I waited with bated breath and braced for the news that haunted me my whole life.

"We're not sure," Dr. Sanders said, but quickly added. "They're not tumors or cancerous but I'll have to monitor them to be sure. So, Mayu may need to stay a week here."

I stuttered out, "A week?"

"Mayu starts school in a few days," said Ichirou. "Is there a way to treat this sooner?"

Dr. Sanders replied, "I can't start treatment until I know whether her epilepsy is hereditary or from an accident." His green eyes flickered between us. "Ye sure there's no medical records about the birth parents?"

I shook my head. I couldn't remember their names, or what they looked like. When I was younger, I used to wonder if they had ruffled black hair or blue eyes like me. Sometimes I wondered if I'm the right age because the orphanage couldn't tell if I was four or five years old. For all I knew, I could be thirteen instead of fourteen.

"It doesn't hurt to look anyway," Dr. Sanders said in a deep breath. "In the meantime, we'll continue the treatment as it is."

●

Spending the night in a hospital was nothing new, but I didn't enjoy being alone when it got dark. I begged Ichirou to stay with me for the night, but he had to go to work.

"You've spent nights at the hospital before," he reminded me.

"Not by myself! Not for an entire week!" I exclaimed.

"You won't be alone. There are doctors and nurses on the floor who can check on you, and I'll be here first thing in the morning before you wake up."

I sank back into bed, sulking. "What was the longest time you had to stay in a hospital?"

Ichirou paused and settled at the end of the bed. His gaze trailed to the ceiling as he pondered about it. "Six months in the Neonatal Intensive Care Unit. I was born too early, and I couldn't breathe on my own. Mom and Dad would take turns watching over me until they could take me home. The second longest was two weeks when my left lung collapsed in high school. If I remember correctly, you were sobbing by my bed."

My cheeks flustered. "I thought you were going to die!"

At the time, I didn't know a lot about pneumothorax. I knew Ichirou had weak lungs, so he couldn't do certain activities and easily lost his breath if he tried. The day he went to the hospital was the scariest moment of my life. Seeing him in a cold, white room, barely conscious, with tubes hooked to his chest would make anyone cry.

"What did you do for two weeks?" I asked.

"Sleep," he chuckled halfheartedly. "Then I got tired of that, so I read books, watched TV, and talked to you and Hannah until I recovered." He noticed my worrying frown and gave me a gentle pat on the head. "You don't have to worry about that. As far as I know, your lungs are fine."

"Did you have another attack after that?"

"I had warnings now and then, but the older I got, the less it happened. I hear seizures can lessen with age, so hopefully, this big one should be your last."

"I hope it's my last one."

●

My first night was uneasy. The room was dark and quiet, and Dr. Sanders wouldn't let me use the TV in case the lights triggered my seizures. TV had never triggered them before, but he wanted to be extra careful. So, instead of listening to old movies to fall asleep to, I bundled under the blankets and dozed off to the hospital bustle.

I don't know what time it was when my eyes snapped open. My room was dark, barely lit by a thin ray of light coming through the half-open door. A lump welled in my throat. Ichirou closed the door before he left, and Dr. Sanders wasn't supposed to see me until the morning. There shouldn't be anyone near my room.

I kept my eyes on the door when I slid out of bed. A nagging feeling in my head told me not to touch it, but I shut the door and darted back to bed. I dove under the blankets, curled into a ball and didn't move from that spot for the rest of the night.

●

Ichirou woke me the next morning for my MRI scan. The procedure was mostly a blur, and I went to sleep the instant I returned to my room. When I woke up around noon, Ichirou came back with Hannah Bastion, his girlfriend and our roommate. Both were in their mid-twenties, but Hannah's round face and soft umber complexion made her look like she was eighteen. Especially when she wore her work clothes, a red polo shirt, black pants and a visor that was engulfed by her poofy black hair.

"You have no idea how badly I wanted to see you!" Hannah pulled me into a tight hug, her shirt smelled of pizza sauce from her job. "My manager wouldn't let me leave until midnight. Are you feeling any better?"

"Better than yesterday," I replied. "How was work?"

"A pain as usual, but I got an early shift. And I snuck these out for you!"

She sat a small red box on my lap, and I held back my joyful squeal. They were my favorite desserts from Hannah's job, soft brownies and edible cookie dough rolled into four balls.

"Y'know you're not supposed to bring food to a hospital," said Ichirou, sitting beside my bed.

"Don't worry, we'll finish it before anyone notices," Hannah said, giving him an impish grin. "How long do you have to stay?"

I ate one of the cookie doughs and replied, "If nothing happens by tomorrow, I can go home before the end of the week."

"That's great! Home just isn't the same without you."

"You have me," Ichirou said, wounding his arm around her shoulder.

Hannah melted into his chest. "I always have you, but I want Mayu home too. And you sleep so much during the day, sometimes I forget you're there, Mr. Jumpscare."

Ichirou was about to protest but stopped because we knew she was right.

"You shouldn't stay up so late. Don't you start school soon?" I asked and realized how strange it felt saying that to my older brother.

Ichirou perked up. "Oh, thanks for reminding me..." He reached into a backpack he brought with him and pulled out a fat, manilla envelope. "We went to your new school to get your schedule and a few other things."

He gave me the envelope, and inside of it were thick stacks of paper, my schedule being the first page. Behind it was a letter congratulating me for enrolling into John Carter High School, rules about dress code, student assistants, and math homework. Lots of math homework.

*At least I'll have something to do.*

"What was it like going back to your old school?" I asked, sliding the papers back in the envelope.

"Horrible," Hannah grimaced. "Reminds me of my nightmares where graduation never happened, and I have to take a test while naked!"

Hannah and I shuddered. I've had three of those nightmares all summer.

"Wasn't the school renovated a few years ago? How does it look?"

"Like shit," Ichirou muttered.

Hannah elbowed his side. "The school looks nice. Better than when we went there. It's not that far, and you only have to take the bus. Not bad, right?"

I shrugged. "I guess so."

In truth, I wanted to go with Elizabeth to St. Laurel's Academy, a private school for rich girls. A month ago, Ichirou and I had gotten into an argument about enrolling me there. He told me the school was too far, and too expensive for him or our parents to afford.

Wanting to take my mind off it, I asked Ichirou and Hannah about their time in school. With an exasperated groan, they told me about the crazy events that sounded strange to be true. One year, during a late winter, someone set the school dumpster on fire. No one knew who caused it or how it started, but it left an ugly scorch mark on the building until it was torn down for renovation.

Another year, in spring, a kid's science project blew up at a fair and covered everyone in a sticky liquid that bleached their clothes. On their fourth year, Ichirou told me about a fight in his chemistry class where a student pepper sprayed someone, and the entire school had to be evacuated.

"You're making all this up," I said, shaking my head.

"Now you know why I always come home stressed out," Ichirou said. "Surviving for a day took a lot out of us."

"At least it's gotten better overtime," Hannah noted. "I remember when every first week of the year, religious protestors would surround the school, and officers used to search our lockers with dogs on Wednesdays."

My skeptical face melted into confusion, wondering what kind of insane asylum my brother was sending me to. "... I'll try to avoid anything suspicious. How hard could that be?"

Ichirou patted my head and smiled. "Ah, kawaii imōtoyo," He sighed, then his tone dropped. "You'll go crazy in a month."

The conversation about school continued into the evening. Hannah told me about her favorite classes, joining sports like the majorettes, the wrestling team and a Junior Reserve Officer Training Corps, which was like a military club. She was in the middle of a story where she spun a baton for a day when a nurse stepped in to remind us that visiting hours were ending. As much as I wanted them to stay, Hannah promised they'd visit me again in the morning.

"I'll bring you gifts and snacks tomorrow if you like," she said.

"More snacks, please," I whispered.

"Try not to start any trouble, Runt." Ichirou said.

"I'm not a Runt!" I pouted, crossing my arms at my old nickname.

"So, you say, Midget. I'll see you tomorrow."

My heart ached as they left. It was nice having them around, but I had to tell myself they would come back.

•●•

I woke up with a start to light streaming through the half-open door. I pulled myself up, ready to crawl out of bed when I glanced up. A pair of wide, grey eyes on a sunken, wrinkled face stared at me through the door. My sleepy mind erupted into fear. I screamed and scrambled out of bed, getting my legs tangled in the blankets.

A nurse threw the door open and rushed inside. Her brown eyes frowned with worry. "Is everything alright?"

"There was—" I struggled to catch my breath.

"Easy now." She rubbed my shoulders as another nurse entered the room. "What happened?"

"Someone was at the door!" My voice trembled. "I saw someone looking at me through the door!"

The nurses exchanged strange glances with each other. The brown-eyed nurse told the other to check outside. He returned seconds later, shaking his head.

"No one was near the door but us," he said.

The brown-eyed nurse turned back to me. "What did this person look like?"

I fumbled over my words. "I don't know. Wrinkled face and grey eyes. That's all I saw." My breathing slowed but I couldn't stop shaking.

"Maybe someone passed your room by accident," said the nurse, looking around. "We can call your brother if you'd like."

I gave her a small nod and took one of the blankets and wrapped it around my shoulders. I followed the nurse to a nearby station, and she let me use the phone to call Ichirou. He must have been working on an art project because he immediately answered before the first ring ended.

I sat in the waiting room until Ichirou arrived, wearing a pair of sweatpants and a green t-shirt.

The brown eyed nurse told him what happened and added, "It might have been a patient or a doctor passing by."

But Ichirou took one look at my uneasy face and asked for an extra blanket. We came back to my room and checked to see if anything was missing or out of place. Everything looked alright so far.

"Are you going to be okay with that?" I asked, sitting in bed. My room had a small couch in case visitors stayed overnight. Honestly, it looked too small for Ichirou to sleep on.

"I've slept in worse places," he said. "Besides, someone's has to make sure no one tries to come in again."

"What are you going to do in the meantime?"

"Finishing this." He pulled a sketchbook from his backpack and flipped through the pages of completed artwork.

There were detailed landscapes and character designs from a video game he was working on. He stopped at an incomplete sketch, and when I asked, Ichirou described the story as the pencil danced across the paper. That night, I dreamed about being a main character in his game, going on random quests in strange, different lands.

●

Ichirou woke me up on a bright Tuesday morning for the MRI. Dr. Sanders, who waited for us, had already heard about the strange visitor. Like everyone else, he said it was possible a doctor or a nurse was checking in on me.

"But you should've gotten a scan then," he added.

Ichirou and I stared at him, wondering what he meant.

"It's also possible ye might 'ave woken up from a seizure and it made ye see those eyes. I asked around, and everyone who worked that night said they didn't see anyone near your door."

I've had seizures in my sleep before and woken up to stars swirling above me and shadows crawling on the ceilings. Those eyes might have been another hallucination, and I felt dumb for getting scared and dragging my brother to the hospital at three in the morning. But if no one was near my room, who could have opened my door?

The scan went by quickly and, with lesser anomalies appearing in my brain, it was finally safe for me to watch TV. I settled on a channel that aired old and black-and-white monster movies. They were the only ones I could watch when I lived with my parents, and they used to scare me. I was terrified of the hoofed cyclops and radioactive dinosaurs, but as I've gotten older, I laughed at the silly-looking rubber costumes and watched the Claymation in awe, knowing a million frames could make still models come to life.

Halfway through a movie about a marsh monster, Hannah stopped by with more snacks from work. Knowing what happened, she asked about the scan and was relieved to hear about my recovery.

"I don't blame you for calling us so early. Hallucination or not, that's still a scary thing to wake up to," she said.

"The eyes might not have been real. But when I woke up last night, and the night before, my door was open."

"I could have sworn I closed it," said Ichirou.

"You did," I said. "Until someone opened it overnight. The weirdest part is that last night, the nurse said no one was near my door."

Hannah's eyes widened and she nudged Ichirou's shoulder. "This is like Ellie's locker!"

"Not this again," Ichirou groaned, crossing his arms.

My brows knitted together. "Who's locker?"

"It's an urban legend at the school." Hannah pulled the chair close to my bed. "It happened sixty years ago," she began. "It was a cold, quiet noon at Carter when a blood-curdling scream pierced the silence. Teachers and students flooded the hallway to see who or what could've screamed like that."

I gulped. "What did they find?"

"Nothing. The hallways were empty. The only unusual thing was a coat on the floor in front of an open locker. The name tag on the coat read, Ellie Wright, a sophomore who rushed out of the class an hour earlier, and some of the kids swore that she was the one who screamed. Everyone searched for her, but she was never seen again. It's believed that her ghost haunts the locker on the third floor. If you put anything inside, the door will open and toss the item out!"

"R-Really?"

"No!" Ichirou interrupted. "That school was so decrepit, everything fell apart, including the lockers."

"Babe," Hannah moaned. "I saw the locker open on its own with my own eyes."

"Did it opened on its own? Or did a latch break?"

"Does that mean the story's fake?" I asked.

"Of course! Seniors make up stories to scare any freshmen dumb enough to believe them. It was a rite of passage next to 'Senior Prank Week'."

"What about my door opening on its own?"

"Runt, I've been up all night and while you were asleep, a couple of doctors stopped by to check on us. That could have happened, and they forgot to close the door."

I wanted to argue, but I saw the bags under Ichirou's eyes. He was tired and so was I. I was tired of being in the hospital. I missed my bed, the apartment and walking around without nurses by my side. Stressing over a door of all things could trigger a seizure, and that would mean spending more nights in the hospital.

"Okay," I said, relaxing in bed.

Hannah looked up at the TV and joked about a character's bad acting, trying to lighten the mood. The tension disappeared and we spent the rest of the day making fun of the cheesy lines and the horribly made puppets.

My glasses disappeared the next morning. They weren't on the bedside table when I woke up, and I tore the sheets off my bed looking for them. Ichirou arrived with Dr. Sanders, and, after I explained why I was tearing my room apart, they helped me search for my glasses until Dr. Sanders found them in the bathroom sink.

"Are you sure you didn't move them?" He asked.

"No, I never got up or moved my glasses!" I cried.

Despite the panic in my voice, Dr. Sanders gave me another scan. The dark spots had faded, but he suggested I had another seizure that morning, one where my body moved but my mind was elsewhere. It used to happen, but I'd outgrew that part of my epilepsy years ago.

"I promise, ye won't stay another night over that," he said, but all I felt was frustration. I knew someone opened my door and moved my glasses. I wondered if they'd believe me if I wasn't epileptic.

With Ichirou leaving again for work, I needed something to do to take my mind off my glasses. I asked a nurse for a pencil and started on the homework. It was basic algebra, so it wasn't hard to do. I was halfway through the third page when someone knocked on my door.

"Mayu," Ms. Hudson called, her voice was gentle and deep. She stepped inside carrying a pink gift bag. "Long time no see."

My heart pounded. I shuffled the homework into the envelope and straightened myself. I wasn't expecting her to visit me.

She let out a small chuckle, "No need to tidy yourself up."

"How'd you know which room I was in?" I asked.

"Ichirou told me, and I wanted to drop something off for you." Ms. Hudson stepped inside, but my eyes were more on the door, wondering if anybody was with her.

"Elizabeth couldn't come today. I'm sorry."

I frowned. "Where is she?"

"Still at school."

I checked my watch and saw it was twelve in the afternoon on a Friday.

"She bought this for you."

Ms. Hudson gave me the gift bag. On top was a pink card covered in glitter, and a note inside written in Elizabeth's small cursive handwriting.

*"I found this at the bookstore and thought it would be fun to read. I hope you feel better soon."*

-Elizabeth

Covered in shredded, bright blue paper was a plush cat decorated in orange and black spots. It had bright green eyes and a collar with the name, "Hazel" on it. I was curious about the name until I found a book at the bottom of the bag. On the red cover was a calico cat balancing on a crystal ball. The title, written in silver calligraphy, read...

"*Witch Hazel*?"

"A new series Elizabeth got into. She asked me to buy a copy for you. Do you like it?"

I wanted to say yes, but only sadness stirred in me. Is that it? All I wanted was to see Elizabeth. The book was nice, but it couldn't replace my friend.

"Mayu, look at me."

I slowly met Ms. Hudson's gentle but stern gaze.

"I know that sulking face anywhere. Are you alright?"

"It's nothing."

"You're lying," she said softly. "You know I don't like it when my girls lie to me." Ms. Hudson stroked my hair and brushed my bangs aside, tucking them behind my ear. "I'm sorry she couldn't come today."

Tears blurred my vision. "Is... is Elizabeth mad at me? Did I do something wrong?"

"No, it was never you, I promise."

"Then why couldn't I see her all summer?"

Ms. Hudson bit her lower lip. "Elizabeth is going through some... things. But she'll tell you when she's ready."

I didn't understand what she meant. I wanted to press for an explanation when another knock at the door drew my attention to Dr. Sanders. He strode in, stopping to see Ms. Hudson.

"Didn't know you had visitors," he said. "Is everything okay?"

I wiped my eyes with the blanket. "I'm fine," I told him, but he kept a suspicious eye on Ms. Hudson.

"And, you are, ma'am?"

Ms. Hudson adjusted her glasses and glared at Dr. Sanders. "Isabella Hudson," she replied, sharply. "I'm a friend of the family."

"Did you sign in at the desk?" he asked in a demanding tone.

"Of course, I did."

She turned to me with a softened expression, and said quietly, "I have to go now. I'll let Elizabeth know you liked the present."

"Could she visit me soon?"

"I promise I will make arrangements so you can see each other again." Ms. Hudson pecked me on my cheek and left, casting an icy glare at Dr. Sanders when their eyes crossed.

"That was awkward," Dr. Sanders exhaled. His casual, friendly tone returned. "Now then, lass, where were we?"

He pulled a chair close to the bed and sat with a clipboard in hand. He began his round of questions: did I feel dizzy during my stay? Was I stuttering more than usual? I answered no, and he checked them off on the clipboard.

"Any problems with hearing?"

"No," I answered, shaking my head.

Dr. Sanders checked off another question on his list. "Ye should be able to go home soon. Do ye have any questions?"

I stroked the plush cat's ears and asked, "Have you met Ms. Hudson before?"

"Nope."

"Why were you talking to her like that, then?"

"Because that's how grown-ups talk." He answered with a kind smile.

I knew that wasn't true. Ms. Hudson never spoke to Ichirou like she wanted to hurt him, and Dr. Sanders hadn't spoken to any other adult with a menacing tone in his voice.

"How do ye know her?" he asked.

"Elizabeth—I mean, her daughter and I are best friends." I showed him the cat and the book. "She gave me this."

"How long have ye been friends?"

"Two years."

"Interesting. Ye know, there's an old saying that 'if yer friends with someone for seven years, it's guaranteed to last a lifetime.'" He rose from his chair, then added, "We'll call yer brother and ye can be discharged tomorrow. If another grand mal happens, come back here immediately."

After Dr. Sanders left, I held the cat like it was the closest thing to Elizabeth. I couldn't believe we'd only been friends for two years when it felt like we'd known each other our whole lives. We knew each other's favorite hobbies, favorite colors, and birthdays (or adoption day in my case) and we'd finish each other's sentences or talk in unison. We celebrated every holiday with each other and had so many sleepovers that Elizabeth's house had become a second home to me. So why couldn't I see her all summer.

•　●　•

I set my glasses on the nightstand and tucked myself in bed. I fell asleep to an old movie about travelers discovering a hidden world. One of the characters, a woman was talking to someone. Her voice shifted and dropped as though she were struggling to breathe.

"I can't... see..." she rasped in my ear.

I shot up in bed. The TV was off. My glasses were gone again, and the door was wide open. I leapt out of bed and slipped out of my room. An old woman with grey eyes turned the corner. The nurse at the station should've seen the woman walk by but didn't acknowledge her. My instincts told me to stay low as I shuffled past the desk and snuck down the hallway.

Walking through a hospital without glasses sucked. Large objects were fuzzy at the edges and details were a mesh of colors. I had to strain my poor vision to spot the old woman who seemed hazy in the bright hallway. Her thin, wavy hair, paper pale skin and the white gown reminded me of drifting clouds that would fade away as they passed by.

"Excuse me!" I called but she didn't answer. *Don't tell me she's deaf, too.*

I followed her to a dull grey hallway stretching toward a pair of metal doors. My legs suddenly stopped moving and my feet stayed rooted to the floor. I was half there, staring at the doors, and the other half was someplace else, some place... familiar.

*I've done this before.* I once stood in a long hall before a pair of doors, wearing a thin gown. A sour, metallic scent settled in the cold air.

The doors suddenly opened, snapping me back to reality. My mind scrambled, I jerked to a nearby corner away from the door. I covered my mouth to muffle my panicked breathing and listened to the old woman speak to someone in a low, raspy voice. A man responded in a hard tone with a familiar Cockney accent.

"What are you still doing here?" Dr. Sanders demanded.

A dozen questions whirled in my mind. Did he know the old woman? Why was he speaking to her so coldly, like he was talking to Ms. Hudson again? I tried to listen but all I heard were heavy footsteps drawing close to me.

My eyes darted wildly for a place to hide before landing at a niche tucked between a vending machine and the wall. As quietly as I could, I slipped behind the small space and clasped my hands over my mouth.

The footsteps, now closer and louder, came to a stop. I could feel Dr. Sanders' eyes on me and I was certain he could hear my heart drumming in my chest.

He took a deep breath, then exhaled, "I'm not leaving until ye come out, Mayu."

He waited and after a moment of silence, I crawled out of my hiding space and faced Dr. Sanders. His hands were tucked in his pockets.

"H-How'd you know it was me?"

"Lucky guess. Yer room was empty, and the hospital has cameras." He pointed to a black box in the corner of the ceiling with a clear, round lens trained on us.

"That old woman was the one opening my door!" I exclaimed. "She went into my room and took my..."

I turned to the hall. The doors were shut, and the old woman was nowhere in sight.

"Ye mean these?" Dr. Sanders pulled out my red framed glasses from his pocket. I stared, jaw hanging.

"I owe ye an apology. Our last patient, Deborah left us recently and forgot her glasses. She keeps coming back to look for her's and must have grabbed yers by mistake."

I blinked. "It would be nice if she told me instead of sneaking into my room."

Dr. Sanders waved his hand dismissively. "I had a talk with her and promised to find her glasses. Yer going to move to a new room. Turns out the lock was broken. Anyone could've walked in, and that's the last thing we need."

Relieved, I put my glasses back on and looked around. I could clearly see the sign hanging over our heads and make out the three black letters, "M" "O" "R" in all caps, before Dr. Sanders ushered me off the floor.

While we walked from one elevator to another, we talked about our day. Dr. Sanders told me his day was long and uneventful, and I rambled about the old monster movies I had been watching.

"Try not to stay up too late," he said as we stepped out of the elevator. "Yer brother told me ye were starting school next week. Excited?"

"I'm a little nervous," I admitted.

"Everyone gets the jitters when they're starting something new. Give it time and ye'll get the hang of it. For a clever lass like ye, high school should be as easy as crossing the street."

"Thanks." I looked away so Dr. Sanders wouldn't see me blush.

We stopped in front of my new room. It was smaller than my first room, with a breathtaking view of the city. My jaw dropped. I lived too far from the city, so I rarely got to see the buildings decorated in colorful lights or the cars flowing like twinkling lights on the highway.

Running around the hospital had finally caught up to me. I was starting to yawn as I watched a massive ship drift down the river. I crawled into bed and put my glasses on the nightstand next to the manilla envelope and *Witch Hazel*. Dr. Sanders must have had one of the nurses bring them to my room. With my glasses secured and the room locked, I curled under the blankets and held the plush cat in my arms.

Shadows dancing off the corridor walls haunted my dreams. I was walking toward the open door, leading to darkness. The drifting cold air carried a scent of something familiar like metal drenched in water. I hesitated to move and then a voice from the darkness called out to me.

# Presence

**"Hey!"**

I turned from the street to a girl standing next to me in the bus shelter. I must have been lost in thought because I didn't notice her or the other five kids behind her. The clothes she wore, a white button up, khaki capris and tennis shoes made me wonder if she was going to the same school as me.

"Can you move back a bit," the girl asked.

I shifted to the edge of the bench, thinking she needed to sit down. The girl stood in front of the bus shelter and held the phone over her head, tiling it toward her to take a picture.

"Excuse me," I said nervously. "Does this bus go to John Carter?"

"Uh, yeah," she answered, keeping her eye on the phone. "Are you going to Carter's?"

"I am!" I said, my shoulders perked up. "What about..."

The girl snapped the picture and turned to the other group, talking to them as if she didn't hear me. I wasn't sure what to do next, so I leaned back on the bench and continued to wait for the bus. That is, until I heard someone say, "Who dresses up like that?"

My stomach tightened. I glanced at the group to see their eyes fall on their phones. But the instant I turned to the street, the whispers rose.

"Is she going to church?"

"Who wears a skirt nowadays?"

"She must be new. I haven't seen her before."

"I think she can hear you."

"And?"

36

I lowered my head, my hands tightened on my skirt. I wanted to call Ichirou to see if he could take me to school. But I knew he would tell me to wait. He and Hannah spent a week teaching me how to catch the bus on my own, and drilled me on which bus to take, which stop to get off on, and how early I'd have to wake up to get to school on time. At the time, I felt so confident in taking the bus alone, but as the whispers and giggles continued, all I wanted to do was go home.

Moments later, the bus arrived, making a loud grumbling approach to the shelter. I grabbed my backpack that sat next to me but before I could stand up, the other kids swarmed in front of the shelter. The bus eased to a stop, and they flooded inside when the door opened.

I was the last to climb aboard. I swiped my pass and found a seat by the window. There were twelve people on the bus and most of them were students who stared at their phones or talked to each other. The girl sat with her friends and completely forgot about me, which was a relief to me. I was anxious enough going to school on my own. I didn't need a bunch of eyes following me on my way.

As I watched the houses pass by, it started to sink in that I was on the bus by myself, going to high school on my own, surrounded by strangers. My heart raced but I kept my eyes on the window, hugging my backpack.

At the next stop, the students rose from their seats as a massive building that towered over the houses came to view.

The way Ichirou talked about the school, I always imagined it to be a rundown warehouse with boarded up windows and graffiti sprawled across old, worn walls. Nothing prepared me for this pristine ivory white building with wide windows reflecting the bus coming to a stop. The name "John Carter High School" was etched over the open doors.

My jaw dropped.

I got off with the rest of the students and followed them across the street. I hurried inside, eyes widened with excitement until a bright light stung my vision. I slowed down, and my eyes squinted through the light to make out a few red tiles on the linoleum floor, then noticed the bright red lockers lining the walls and students in red polos walking in and out of red door frames.

*This school really liked their colors.*

I stepped away from the crowded side of the hall to let my eyes adjust. Lawrence Middle School was passionate about their colors, but they never went as far as to put navy blue and gold tiles on the floor.

I pulled my schedule out of my backpack to see where my classes were. I read the room number when the hall burst into an ear-splitting ring. I jerked back, letting out a startled cry and looked up to see the school bell directly above me.

A dozen heads turned to me, and the commotions fell silent. I clutched my backpack and paced down the hall, keeping my head down so no one would see the red rushing to my cheeks.

My English class was on the first floor and as far as I could tell, all the students were girls. The teacher writing on the blackboard was a towering, mid-toned man, though he looked like he could have been nineteen or twenty. He had dark, unkempt hair that reached the back of his neck and bangs over a pair of striking amber eyes.

"Can I help you?" he asked.

The hairs on my neck bristled.

"Um, are you..." I glanced at my schedule, then back at him. "Are you Mr. Penn?"

"Nah, I'm Ethan LeiDoff. Ms. Penn's over there if you're looking for her." Ethan nodded to the teacher's desk in the back of the room where a woman with blonde hair waved at me. Ms. Penn had a round, childlike face and bright blue eyes behind her glasses that made her look like she could have been a student instead of a teacher.

"You must be Mayu," she said, cheerfully. "I heard you were at the hospital last week. Hope you're feeling much better!"

I thanked her in a small, squeaky voice.

"No need to be nervous," she smiled. "If you need any help you can ask me or Ethan. He's my assistant."

"Like a teacher's assistant?" I asked. Ms. Penn nodded. "I didn't know high schools had one."

As soon as I said that I remembered one of the papers in the envelope mentioning assistants. I guess I was too busy with my homework and worried about my glasses to read the letter.

"A lot of public schools hired assistants four years ago," Ms. Penn said. "Yours didn't have any?"

I shook my head. "I went to a private school."

"Oh," she looked surprise for a moment. "Well, assistants like Ethan help are like second teachers. If you need anything, don't be afraid to ask either of us."

I thanked Ms. Penn and sat at one of the desks closest to the board. Ethan finished writing on the board just as Ms. Penn began her lecture on a short story. I found a textbook sitting in the basket beneath the chair and read along. But there was a nagging feeling that I was being watched. I looked up and Ethan quickly turned to the board when our eyes met. He never looked at me again, and I was certain he was trying his best to avoid eye contact with me for the rest of class. I wasn't sure which was weirder but decided not to think about it.

My next class, Physical Science, was down the hallway from English. There were boys and girls sitting at tables instead of desks. The walls were sea green and had posters about Newton's Law, the periodic tables and other stuff about physics. I didn't see an assistant, but found a large, burly man with bulging muscles and a buzz cut sitting behind the teacher's desk. "Mr. Baryon," was etched on the bronze sign in front of him.

"New here," the teacher grunted, sounding more like a command than a question.

"Yes sir," I mumbled.

I gave him a letter Dr. Sanders wrote, explaining why I was absent, and another by Ichirou, summarizing my medical history. It didn't seem like Mr. Baryon read them because he took one look at it and returned it to me along with the textbook for class.

With the book in hand, I made my way to the first empty chair I found. There was one girl at the table who noticed me before I said anything. She was probably my age, maybe a year older. With her flawless, pale face, straight dark hair and a book in her hand, she made me think she would spend her free time immersed in a library.

"Is anyone else sitting here?" I asked, pointing to the empty chair.

"No," the girl answered softly.

I pulled the chair out and found a student ID on the floor. It had the girl's nervous smile, and her name printed beneath the image.

"Marietta?" I said, reaching for the ID. The girl lifted her head from her book. "Is this yours?"

She gasped, "It is! I was using this as a bookmark!"

"It must have slipped out." I handed her the ID and sat beside her. "Your name is really pretty."

"Thanks, but you can call me Mary." Mary tucked her ID between the pages of her book and closed it. "What's your name?"

39

"Mayu," I told her.

Mary's eyes widened. "Huh, one letter difference. What are the odds?"

I looked at her confused, then realized she was talking about our names. "That is strange." I gave her a small smile. "Are you a freshman?"

Her brows pinched. "This is a freshman only class."

"Oh, right," My cheeks burned, but I tried to laugh it off.

Mary and I decided to work together on our assignment. She shared her notes with me, and we answered simple questions in the textbook.

I don't know who long it was before I noticed the other girl. I was searching for a definition in the book and my eyes caught a deathly pale face staring back at me. Dark circles curled beneath her weary eyes and her mousy brown hair slumped over her shoulders. I jolted back in my seat, grabbing Mary's attention.

Before she could ask, the bell rang, prompting everyone to get up and leave. My head swiveled back to the girl but she was suddenly gone.

"What's wrong?" Mary asked, looking worried.

My throat tightened. "Was there a girl here a second ago?"

"What girl—" Her eyes snapped to the empty chair, and I saw the color drain from her face. "Oh... *she* was here?"

"Who is 'she'?"

"That was Sarah Blaine," she answered in a low voice. "You don't want to talk to her. Nobody talks to her."

"Why?"

"She's got a lot of issues up there." Mary tapped her head a few times for emphasis. "You're better off not knowing her. And its best not to talk to her."

That didn't feel right. "Are you sure?"

"If you saw what she did last week, you'd stay away from her too."

Mary stood up and hoisted her bag over her shoulder. She seemed eager to leave, like she was worried Sarah might appear again. Now, eager to leave, I walked with Mary into the hall. We stayed together until we had to part ways at the stairs. Mary headed to her class on the second floor and I made my way to the third floor.

Algebra in room 330A, and I found every number except for it. I wandered up and down the hallway until the late bell rang and students herded into their rooms. I swallowed back my panic and looked for someone to ask. The doors were closing, and the floor emptied by the second.

Was there a typo in my schedule? I checked again, walking toward the stairs and jumped at the sound of a loud, metallic crash. I spun around, seeing no one except for an opened locker with its door swaying on its hinges.

"H-Hello?" I called, looking around.

No one responded.

At that moment, I remembered the creepy story Hannah told me. My eyes scanned from wall to wall, then landed in front of the locker.

Its inside was aged and rusted, and a sour smell peeled off it's walls. I backed away, and almost let out a scream at the first person I bumped into.

The man flinched, holding his hands up. "Easy there, Miss! I didn't mean to frighten you."

"S-Sorry," I panted. I looked up at the man as he towered over me, and my heart skipped a beat. He looked like a porcelain statue come to life with flowing black hair parting in bangs between his thin, ice gold eyes.

"Have I seen you before?" he asked, his low smooth voice rung in my ears like a cello. My voice cracked.

The man's brow furrowed as his attention shifted to the open locker.

"Yours, I'm guessing?"

"It was already open." I stammered, feeling butterflies in my stomach.

The man stretched his arm out and closed the locker with ease, cutting off the cold, strange air.

"Sometimes the locks are faulty. They don't always stay closed," he said. A thin smile broke his icy stare. "Might I ask, why are you in the hallway? The late bell has long since rung."

My shoulders relaxed but my heart was in somersaults. "I-I was looking for my class."

"What's the number?"

"330A. Are you a teacher?"

"I'm an assistant," he offered his hand. "My name is Cedric Turner. Most people call me Mr. Turner. And yours?"

"I'm Mayu Hinamori." I shook his hand and gasped at the icy touch.

"I do know you!" He exclaimed, softly. "You have Algebra with Mrs. Bean, correct?"

I checked my schedule and found the teacher's name. "How did you know?"

"I'm her assistant. Your name is on the roster and when I heard about your stay in the hospital, I made a packet of homework for you so you wouldn't fall behind."

*So, he's who I have to thank.*

"Mrs. Bean was convinced that you transferred schools. She called me silly for sending you homework in the first place. How was it, by the way?" Mr. Turner motioned for me to follow him.

"It wasn't too hard," I admitted. "My math teacher taught basic algebra earlier this year."

"Then you have nothing to worry about. We teach the basics for the first two weeks and if you understand most of it, the rest of algebra should be easy to work on."

We stopped in front of a classroom door at the top of the steps. I remembered passing the room on my way upstairs, but the open door covered the number, 330A, so I didn't see it. Mr. Turner let me in first, and I was greeted with students sitting in rows of desks. Math equations and problems covered the entire whiteboard.

"You're late again, Cedric. Did you have another meeting?" A woman grumbled.

I turned to a short round woman staring at us from her desk. The name on the plaque read: Amarella Bean.

She sneered at me. "Do you need anything?"

Mr. Turner said, "Remember the student you thought transferred? I ran into her in the hallway."

He patted me on the back, ushering me close to Mrs. Bean's desk. I held my backpack to my chest, hesitant to meet her beady eyes.

"Your last name is Hinamori?" She asked.

"Yes, ma'am," I replied.

"I understand you were in the hospital all week."

"Yes ma'am." I showed her the letters and gave her the packets of homework.

Mrs. Bean set my work aside and skimmed the letter. "Ichirou? Let me guess, you're his daughter?"

"Sister," I corrected. "Did you have him in your class?" I knew it sounded stupid, but I always heard that Ichirou and Hannah's teachers were nice and used to tell silly jokes before class.

"Of course, I had him junior year," she paused for a moment. "Why is your brother signing this? I need your parents' signature."

"Ichirou is my caretaker for the time being." I said, warily.

She paused for a moment. "Fine, I'll write you in."

"It's nice to meet—"

"Take your seat. You're already behind."

"I'm sorry!"

I sat close to the board and was already feeling the exhaustion set in. I was grateful math went by without trouble and happy to know I had lunch after it. I got up shortly after the bell rang, and it kept ringing. My legs stayed rooted in place and the classroom pulled away.

"Are you alright?" A deep voice rang in my ears.

I spun around and found myself standing upright in class and staring at a worried Mr. Turner.

"I... I am," I managed, regaining feeling in my legs. "I'm alright, now."

"Are you certain?"

"Yes," I insisted. I needed to walk off the aura.

After thanking Mr. Turner and saying goodbye to Mrs. Bean, I maneuvered through the sea of students and joined the line forming in the cafeteria.

A wide plated glass that took up an entire wall, giving students a good view of the neighborhood. I got my tray of food and hurried toward an empty seat near the window. But as I got closer to the table, a girl threw her backpack over the seat next to her. She shot me a dirty look and I turned away. I searched for a seat but in the end, the only place I could sit was a lone table near the exit door, far from the window. My heart sank. So much for a good view. That bothered me more than the dried meal I ate.

Unlike Algebra, Gym was hard to miss. The first thing that caught my attention were the bright red words, "GYM" sprawled across the two doors. They opened to a long inner corridor of windows, leading to another pair of doors.

Laughter and clamor bounced off the Gym. On one side, students threw themselves at each other to snatch a basketball. Careful not to run into anyone, I weaved around them to a man watching them. He wore red sweatpants, a plain white shirt and a name tag, "Mr. Trouse" attached to it.

Without looking at me, he said, "Go to Ms. Bloom," and pointed to a woman on the other side of the room.

There, students surrounded the volleyball net and standing near the bleachers was an older woman in similar sweatpants but with a red jacket over a white shirt. Her curly blonde hair piled on her head like cotton candy. When I told her my name, her eyes lowered to the clipboard in her hand.

"There you are," Ms. Bloom said and wrote a check mark next to my name. "Where are your clothes?"

"My what?"

"Your clothes for gym. You didn't bring any in that backpack?"

"No?" It didn't occur to me to bring them. "I'm sorry..."

"No worries," Ms. Bloom said. "You can sit at the bleachers for now. Make sure your bring proper clothes next time."

"Yes, ma'am..."

I hiked to the higher seats, hoping to get a better view of the gym, when I spotted Mary at the top of the bleachers, still reading her book.

I waved at her. "Hi Mary!"

She looked up from her book and waved back. "Long time no see!"

I hurried toward her, relieved to see a familiar face. "What are the odds of us having gym together?"

"It's rare, but it happens," said Mary. "Freshmen aren't supposed to have this class until junior or senior year. I think someone messed up our schedules."

*That could explain why I don't have a history class.* "Won't we get in trouble?"

"Don't think so. I've been here all week, and no one's said anything. Besides, I hear having senior elective classes this early will look good on your resume."

I sat next to her and noticed she was reading the same book from earlier. Curious, I tilted my head toward the cover and read the title. "Anthology of Shakespeare?"

Mary's cheeks reddened. "It's for my English class. Have you read his plays?"

"I've seen a few movies and some plays and ballets," I said and got a warm feeling in my chest. Elizabeth liked musicals and theatre. Sometimes we'd reenact our favorite scenes.

"Got a favorite? Mine is a Midsummer's Night Dream."

"Mine too!" I exclaimed, smiling. "It's not Shakespeare but Swan Lake is one of my favorite ballets."

Mary's face brightened. "I can't believe it! What are the odds I meet someone who likes plays?"

"It's rare, but it happens," I repeated. "I take it you forgot to bring your gym clothes too?"

Mary glanced, sheepishly, at her blouse and skirt. "Actually, I'm skipping out on purpose." Her gaze fell to the students below. "My first week here, everyone treated me like I was a dumb kid because I'm fifteen. The teachers told me they were playing around, but it's hard to tell when they call you 'freshman' all the time."

"But Mary sounds prettier than 'Freshman.'"

"Tell that to those seniors," she sulked.

I had an idea. I jumped to my feet and cleared my throat, noticing Mary's curious look.

"For sweetest things turn sourest by their deeds..." I began. "Lilies that fester smell far worse than weeds."

Mary's face lit up. She quickly opened her book, and her eyes fluttered across the pages until she stopped at a scene.

"All that glitters is not gold!" She recited with passion. "Often have you heard that told. Many a man his life hath sold! But my outside to behold."

"Bravo!" I cheered, giving her a round of applause.

Mary took a graceful bow. "I'm learning about it in class. Do you want to read A Midsummer's Night Dream?"

"Sure!"

Before we knew it, gym class had turned into a theater duet with Mary and me acting out the lines from the play.

Mary offered to walk with me to my last class. She had study hall, which was another senior elective, except the classroom was the school library and her 'teacher,' the librarian didn't mind if she was late. Her classmates were mostly seniors that spent most of their time on the computers.

"You're lucky, having two senior electives!" I sighed, wistfully.

"I know. The library has its own courtyard, so if I want, I can read beneath the gazebo, surrounded by flowers like a real fairytale!"

I looked at her skeptically, "Are you sure this isn't a secret garden?"

"I'm serious!" Mary insisted. "I'll have to show you one day. It feels like you've been pulled into another world!"

We continued down the busy hallway until a familiar number caught my attention, Room 309, Art. Small drawings the size of cards decorated the doorframe and between that, paintings and sketches hung over the lockers like a mini art museum. I peered inside and saw portraits of landscapes decorating the walls.

"Guess that's my cue." Mary seemed a little sad. "See ya tomorrow."

"Later."

As the bell rang, I hurried inside the art room. Students sat in three long tables, sketching random items lined up at the table like a yard sale. There were hour glasses, seashells, old clocks, geode cluster, you name it.

In front of the chalkboard, was a man in his thirties at his desk. Mr. Eisele was the name on the bronze plaque, and he told me I could sit anywhere in the room. It didn't take long to find his assistant. Afterall, she was the only person out of uniform. Leaning back on one of the chairs was a finely tanned girl with wavy dark hair. She wore a long-sleeved white shirt, jeans, and combat boots. She was the only assistant I met who had a lanyard with her name on it.

### Teacher Assistant: Lutea Hillenbrand

"Loo-tee?" I said, raising an eyebrow.

"You're close," she said, playfully. "It's 'Loo-teh-ah,'"

"Loo-teh-ah," I repeated.

"There you go!" Lutea praised. "Are you new here?"

"Yeah. My name's Mayu." We shook hands and Lutea's grip was like an iron vise.

"Hinamori? I heard you were at the hospital last week. Good to see you on your feet."

"Likewise," I paused. "Wait, I mean—"

"It's okay," Lutea snickered. "Did you need any help?"

I looked around, noticing everyone sketching. "I don't know what I'm supposed to do."

"We're workin basic shapes by drawing whatever's around us," Lutea explained. "Can you draw?"

"A little bit."

"You're off to a good start!" she beamed. "Have a look around, see if there's something you like."

I wandered around the room. There were pastel portraits of a forest, animals sketched from charcoal, and a blend of watercolor paint to make a deep blue sea full of fish and other creatures.

A round, hollow shell caught my attention. It fit in my hand, rough on the outside, but its inside was smooth and gleamed a different color under the light. I returned to Lutea, still marveling at this shell.

"You like that one?" She asked.

"What is this?"

"Abalone. I found it at the Orkney Isle last summer."

"Orkney?"

"A group of islands near Scotland. I was visiting with my dad. Do you travel?"

"I've been to Japan a few times and waited in airports in Toronto and Beijing." I sat across from Lutea and noticed small scars on her shoulders, partially covered by her shirt.

"Got any favorite spots in Japan?" Lutea asked.

"The countryside," I answered. "I don't like the city noise and bustle so much."

"I get it. I'm not much of a city person myself."

Lutea and I talked about what we liked about the countryside through most of the class. I got to know her more than my classmates. Before the final bell, everyone packed up their supplies and lined up at the shelves. Following their lead, I slid my artwork inside the drawer. I returned to the table for my backpack when I noticed Lutea was staring at the window.

"Mayu," she said to me, "Do you take the bus by chance?"

"Yeah—" I said and spotted the bus as it turned the corner, making its way to the school. At that moment, I remembered Ichirou and Hannah's final warning: If I missed the first bus, I had to wait another hour or two for the next one. The bell rang and I darted through the door, throwing my backpack over my shoulder.

# Tension

**The bus was crammed with students by the time I got on.** The loud clamor bombarded my ears until they hurt, and my stomach twisted at the stifling musk inside. Every seat was taken and there was hardly room to stand in aisle.

I quickly turned back, figuring an hour late wouldn't be bad compared to this. However, the door had already closed, and the bus lurched forward. I quickly grabbed the sweat covered handle and braced for a very uncomfortable ride home.

My arms were going numb by the third stop. Sweat rolled down my neck and the suffocating heat made my head spin. Still, I managed to keep a tight grip on the handle when the bus jerked to a stop and everyone standing in the aisle tumbled over each other like dominoes.

After a few students got off, everyone shouted at the driver, hurling foul names and demanding he'd slow down. While I had to agree with them on the last part, I could only grip the handle when the bus lurched forward, knocking everyone back. Through the commotion, I heard my street's name from the speaker, and I reached for the yellow cord that hung over the window. At the sound of a bell, came an uproar of aggravated moans before the bus jerked to an abrupt stop.

I squeezed through the crowd and jumped outside, taking deep breaths as if I was holding it in for a long time. The bus pulled off and I could still hear the shouts and curses as it continued down the street.

*I have to ride that all year?* I shuddered at the thought of it, and my sweat-soaked blouse that clung to my skin.

Now, more than eager to change clothes, I crossed the street, passing the bus shelter I waited in that morning. Behind it, tall hedges wound around the small townhouse called Union Circle. My home was the first one I saw where the familiar blue curtains behind the patio door came to view.

On my way, I heard a soft mew coming from a sprawling oak tree that stood in front of the apartment. Tucked between its roots was the world's fattest cat with orange and brown spots decorating her white fur and wide green eyes that stared at me.

My smile rose. "Hi Tuna! Did you miss me?"

Tuna's little mews rose to warbling yowls as she trotted toward me. She brushed her head against my ankle and began to nibble at the corner of my shoes.

"Come on, I was only gone for a day," I said, though I missed her more than I was willing to admit. Tuna stared at me and her with wide, hungry eyes, melted away any sternness I had for her.

"One moment, I got to put my stuff away first."

Tuna circled around my feet when I unlocked the door, though I had to dance around her to slip inside before she could follow me. As much as I wanted to keep her as a house pet, Ichirou was allergic to cats. Any trace of fur would have him break out in hives.

I dropped my backpack near the door and went to my room, embracing the fresh, indoor coolness. Everything from the wiped table, vacuumed carpet and artwork hanging neatly off the walls were clean.

After I changed out of my uniform to a simple shirt and shorts, I heard my phone ringing in my backpack. I returned downstairs and answered the call, knowing it was Ichirou checking on me.

"Ya home yet, Runt?" he asked, lull ambient music played in the background at his job.

"I made it in one piece," I said.

Ichirou chuckled. "Let's keep it that way. How was school?"

"It wasn't too bad."

I went to the kitchen and warmed up a small plate of leftover casserole and told him about the new school and meeting the assistants.

"It's about time. A lot of schools were getting assistants long before I graduated. I wished we got them sooner."

Someone called Ichirou's name in the background, pulling him away from the phone. Ichirou told them softly, "I'll be there in a moment," before returning to me.

"Duty calls?" I guessed.

"Yeah," Ichirou groaned. "Have you had any warnings today."

I squirmed in place. "Sort of, but nothing happened after that."

Ichirou didn't reply. He was probably thinking about what I should do next. Warnings could mean a potential seizure, and another visit to the hospital.

The same voice came back, calling Ichirou's name again more firmly.

He let out a deep sigh. "I'll see you tonight, Runt. Stay downstairs until we get home and keep the phone near you."

"I will. Have a good day."

"No promises."

Ichirou hung up, and the music cut off to silence.

I wanted to call Hannah, but knowing her job was against using personal phones, I texted her that I was home.

With the casserole warmed up, steam billowing off the melted cheese, I took the plate outside and sat on the concrete slab of our "porch." Tuna circled around me, meowing excitedly for a bite.

I'll always remember the day I found her, scrawny, with a shoestring tail, and gobbling up a half-eaten tuna sandwich near the dumpster. She was too weak to run, and her raspy, mews were heart breaking to hear, I couldn't help myself when I snuck small portions of food and sandwich meat to her.

At first, Ichirou was upset when he found out about Tuna. Allergies aside, he was worried about the food sitting on the porch for other animals or insects to find. He told me I had to be with Tuna when she ate and threw away what she didn't finish. Hannah would take her to the vet for checkups and as long as I cleaned up after Tuna, she could stay near the apartment.

"One little piece wouldn't hurt, right?" I muttered and scraped a small spoonful of casserole for Tuna. "Careful, it's still hot."

We ate together, but Tuna slurped hers up, then looked at me for more.

*Maybe one more piece...*

If Tuna had smaller spots on her back, she would've resembled the calico from *Witch Hazel*. I wondered if Elizabeth thought the same thing when she found the book. Then I wondered if she was still reading *Witch Hazel* or finished it. Elizabeth could go through a novel in a day if she was interested in it.

With a delightful purr, Tuna licked the casserole clean, then laid on the sunbathed porch, satisfied with her meal. I sought the chance to slip into the apartment. Using the phone hooked to the wall, I called Elizabeth's home and Ms. Hudson answered in a firm, professional voice.

"Isabella, speaking."

"It's me," I told her. "How are you doing today?"

"Peachy as usual," Ms. Hudson said, dropping the professional voice. Though she could be terrifying, I knew Ms. Hudson enough to hear a smile in her voice. "Ichirou told me you started school today. "How was it?"

"It was alright. I got lost, though."

"You too, huh? Elizabeth has gotten lost a few times at her new school as well Strange since she has been visiting the campus all summer."

"By the way." I nervously twisted the hem of my shirt. "Is she back from school yet?"

"She didn't tell you?" Ms. Hudson asked, mildly surprised. "Elizabeth is staying in the school dorms for the semester."

My fingers froze. "She never brought it up."

"Elizabeth figured it would be easier to focus on her studies if she stayed on campus instead of commuting."

My words stammered out, still shocked by the news. I always thought Elizabeth would live in that large house forever. "When will she be home?"

"I told her she should spend the first few weeks in the dorm, then we can talk about plans for the weekends. I'll let Elizabeth know you called and will keep you updated on those plans."

"Thank you."

"Anytime." Ms. Hudson hung up, but the phone stayed in my hand. I tried to imagine Elizabeth living away from home and wondered why she didn't tell me. Tuna pawing at the door, mewing for another plate of casserole, interrupted my thoughts.

∴

It was around nine when Ichirou came home, his old black mustang parked in front of the door and Hannah's blue hatchback pulled into the parking space next to him. Hannah was the first out of her car, carrying two pizza boxes in her way inside.

I pulled the sliding door to let her in. "How was work?" I asked.

Hannah let out a low groan and dropped the boxes on the table. Ichirou walked in and closed the door behind him.

"It was rough," she answered, tiredly. "Seems like every pizza we made walked out the door free because every customer had a complaint about it."

She threw herself on the couch and snatched the visor off her head, messing up her curls.

"Do you need anything while I'm in the fridge?" Ichirou asked. He was in the kitchen bringing out plates for the pizza.

"Scotch and a two-year vacation," Hannah said. "How about everyone else? Had a good day?"

"Same old, same old," Ichirou replied. He brought a glass of water to Hannah, and he sat at the table.

"Mine was interesting," I said, joining Ichirou.

I started at the beginning with the bus shelter, meeting the assistants, Mary and the teachers. Upon hearing Mrs. Bean's name, Ichirou's eyes widened, and Hannah sprung up with a worried look on her face.

"Mrs. Bean?" Ichirou repeated. "Short round lady who sounds angry all the time?"

"Uh huh..."

Hannah's jaw dropped. "She's still there? She should have retired by now!"

"More like fired," Ichirou remarked.

I lowered my head. "She did come off as strict, but is she a bad teacher? Ichirou passed her class."

"Barely," he scoffed. "I had to switch out of her class, or she would have failed me out of spite."

"Why would she do that?"

"Because she could," Hannah answered. "Did she give you a syllabus?"

I leaned back in the chair for my backpack and pulled the syllabus out along with the homework. Hannah left the couch and read it with Ichirou. Their faces twisted with worry.

"I know, it's a lot of work," I said.

Hannah snorted, "That's the least of your worries. She'll tell you to work on an assignment, then when you turn it in, she'll act like she gave you more and fail you for not finishing it."

"What!"

"She's done it before," Ichirou said. "I should have known something was up when you got all of that homework last week."

I gulped. "Maybe she mellowed out... Any chance she changed over the years?"

They laughed.

That night after taking a shower, I sat on the floor in my room putting my homework and textbooks in my backpack. My eyes fell on the plush cat on the pillows and the book on my nightstand. Then I heard a knock at my door.

"Who is it?" I asked.

"Who do you think, Runt?" Came the reply. The door opened and Ichirou stepped inside. "Try not to stay up late tonight?"

"I know."

"Are you ready for your second day?"

"More nervous about Mrs. Bean. Are you sure she hasn't changed?"

He sat on the bed and his shoulders relaxed. "I never saw her as someone who lets things go, but it's possible she might have since I was there. It's been... ten years?"

"Seven years, babe!" Hannah shouted from her room.

"She might have changed," Ichirou continued. "But if she gives you trouble, you can always switch out of her class."

"Alright..." I zipped my backpack, and I felt Ichirou's hand on my head before he ruffled up my hair.

"You did good on your first day. So why do you still have the 'mope of doom' on your face?"

"I wish Elizabeth would have gone with me."

"Did you talk to her today?"

"Ms. Hudson said she's living in the dorms now."

"Isa let her go?" His voice rose in a small shock. "Must be a good school if she trusts them with her daughter."

"The whole summer she always talked about orientations, but never mentioned the dorms or staying in them," I paused. "Ms. Hudson says she isn't mad at me... but it's like she doesn't want to tell me anything anymore."

"Maybe Elizabeth wanted to get used to her school first." Ichirou stretched his arms. The tiredness of work was starting to settle. "Even best friends need time away from each other."

"We've been away all summer!" I reminded him. "How much more do I have to wait?"

"For as long as you want. She'll reach out to you when she's ready and instead of sulking about it..." Ichirou propped himself up and straightened his back. "You should go to bed. Don't stress yourself too much over this."

He left, wishing me a good night and Hannah did the same, calling good night to us from her room.

I tucked myself in bed and set my glasses on the nightstand. My racing thoughts, keeping me from falling asleep. After fifteen minutes of tossing and turning, I sat up, turned to *Witch Hazel* that sat on the nightstand and read the first chapter.

⠂●⠂

The next day, I partnered with Mary for a small group project. Sarah was at the table, nodding off to the paper in front of her. Mary tried to pretend she wasn't there until I suggested that Sarah could join us. It was a group project after all. But Mary glared at me like I uttered a curse.

"What's wrong with—" I turned to Sarah and jumped in my seat when I saw hers was empty.

My head whipped back and forth but there were no traces of Sarah ever being here. Everyone continued class like she didn't exist.

"She does this all the time," Mary said, as if she read my mind. "You'll get used to it."

"How does she do that?"

"It's best not to question it. Like I said, Sarah isn't right in the head." Mary said, looking warily at Sarah's chair.

"She seems to keep to herself."

"Sarah wasn't always this quiet. On the first day of school, Sarah had a mental breakdown in the middle of class. She was talking to herself, repeating the same word, getting louder, and then she told us to leave her alone. No one said anything to her that day."

I couldn't imagine Sarah talking, let alone screaming.

"If she scares you, why don't you change seats?"

Mary shifted in her chair. "Mayu, look around you. There's nowhere to sit and no one here wants to sit with Sarah."

I scanned the room and saw she was right. There was never an empty seat beside ours. But that only raised another question; did anyone see Sarah leave?

"Don't you think it's strange that she just... disappears without making a sound."

Mary shrugged. "You're better off not worrying about her."

*Hard to do that when she sat across from me*, I thought. But I could see Mary getting uncomfortable with Sarah, so I let it go.

Shortly after the bell rang, I headed to Algebra where I saw Mr. Turner standing in front of the open door. He was greeting the students and handing them small pieces of paper as they headed inside of class.

He noticed me and smiled, "Good morning, young miss. Enjoying your second day?"

"Can't complain," I said, still thinking about Sarah. "What are you doing with the papers?"

"Mrs. Bean assigned seats to everyone." He gave me one of the small papers with my name scribbled in red ink. "You're sitting in C-11."

I read the note curiously. Ichirou and Hannah never mentioned Mrs. Bean having assigned seats in her class. I walked inside and saw the once spaced-out desks lined up in three straight rows. I glanced back at the hastily drawn "C-11" on the paper and found row C close to the window. My new desk, "C-11" sat at the back of the room, farthest from the white board.

"Mayu, please take your seat," Mrs. Bean's voice rose behind me. I jerked around and saw her sitting at her desk.

"And place your homework here when you come in," she added, tapping her red pen against the bin beside her.

I did so but Mrs. Bean immediately took my homework. She flipped through the pages as if looking for something. I was worried she would ask about an extra assignment I didn't know about.

"Mrs. Bean," I said in a small voice. "Am I supposed to sit back here?"

She glared at me as though I'd asked if the sky was blue. "That's your seat until the end of the year. And no—" she cut me off before I could speak up. "—you can't move elsewhere. Now, can you sit where I placed you?"

I reluctantly took my seat. At the sound of the bell, Mr. Turner closed the door and flicked the light switch, leaving the class in the dark. Mrs. Bean left her desk with a small remote in her hand. She pushed a button, and the smartboard lit up with a faint hum, yet I couldn't see the notes sprawled across the wall.

The students in front of me were too tall to look over, and the notes were hard to read when I leaned to the side. I was lost in numerical nonsense and incomplete definitions until I finally gave up and raised my hand. Mrs. Bean didn't notice, but I kept my arm up, straining it before she finally acknowledged me.

"Cedric, go see what she wants," she told him, and Mr. Turner approached me.

"I can't see anything," I whispered to him.

He whispered back, "There's an empty seat up front. You can move up there for today."

Relief washed through me until Mrs. Bean bellowed "No one is allowed to switch seats!"

Mr. Turner returned his attention to her. "She is struggling to see the board from here. If only for today, can she sit at the front?"

"Then there'd be no point in having assigned seats if anyone can sit wherever they want!"

*Who pushed her out of bed today?* I raised my hand again and cleared my throat. "Can you slow down a bit?"

Mrs. Bean's beady stare fell on me. "We're on a tight schedule and have a lot to cover. I can't afford to 'slow down' because you don't want to pay attention!" She huffed and flipped to the next slide. "Cedric, since you're there, can you pass out today's assignments? They're on my desk."

Mr. Turner breathed in through his nose. He muttered a soft, "sorry," to me before going to her desk. Mrs. Bean continued the lesson like nothing happened. I was more lost in my notes with no clue what was going on until a hand nudged my shoulder. I was so focused on trying to see the board that I completely forgot that I was sitting next to somebody.

"You want to copy my notes?" My neighbor whispered.

His scruffy dark hair grew past his chin, barely touching the red headphones resting around his neck, and bangs covering the right side of his face. He slid his notebook close to me. His handwriting was messy, the words smudged, but he had every equation, terms and example written there on the page. I glanced at Mrs. Bean talking and changing slides, then quickly copied the boy's notes. I was on my second page when I asked for his name.

"It's Aiden," he answered. "Aiden Keihana."

"That's a nice name." My voice cracked and heat rushed to my cheeks.

"You think so? What's your name?"

My face grew hotter as the words tumbled out of my mouth. "It's—My name's—"

"Mayu, are you writing this down?"

I flinched. Mrs. Bean was staring at me from the smart board.

"Well? Do you have all of this down?"

My voice was wedged in my throat.

"At ease she is paying attention," Mr. Turner assured from the next row.

"Oh?" Mrs. Bean jeered. "So, you can see the board. Then why were you complaining you couldn't moments ago? Why do I hear you talking?"

I shrank in my chair.

"Why don't you back off," Aiden grumbled.

"Excuse me?" Mrs. Bean snarled. "What did you say?"

He said loudly, "I just wanted to help."

The tension swelled in the air.

"Well then," Mrs. Bean said. "Since you're so helpful. Do you want to trade places with me?"

Aiden didn't answer. He twirled the headphone wires and it irritated Mrs. Bean

"While you're at it, take those headphones off. Or leave, since you like to break the rules so much!"

Without pause, Aiden grabbed his backpack and stomped out of the room, slamming the door behind him.

"Real mature..." she muttered.

*There goes my friend*, I thought and realized he left his notebook behind. Suddenly, at the corner of my eye, the smartboard sputtered out, and the room darkened. I gasped as murmurs filled the air.

"Did the smartboard go out again?" Mr. Turner asked. He quickly opened the shade and daylight returned to the room.

"It's still running, I can hear it," Mrs. Bean replied. "The screen's not working!"

She fidgeted with the smartboard's buttons, then grunted in frustration. "Never mind, everyone can work on the chapter. We were at the end of the slide anyway."

Everyone groaned. We opened our textbooks, but my face scrunched up as I read the problems then looked at the notes.

"Mrs. Bean," I called, raising my hand. "These examples don't match the problems."

She scowled, "If you would have paid attention, Mayu, you would have—"

"I don't understand it either," said a boy in row A.

A girl, in the mid-section of row B, stuttered, "Y-Yeah, what does this mean?"

Mrs. Bean turned her glared to Mr. Turner.

In a deep sigh, he marched to the board, and wrote the examples perfectly clear and easy to read. Though Mrs. Bean was trying to rush him, Mr. Turner took his time breaking down the problems until everyone could solve the assignment. When class ended, I went to see Mrs. Bean who was grading papers at her desk.

"What do you want, Mayu?" she asked, keeping her eyes papers.

"Can you move me to the front desk tomorrow?"

"Are you telling me what to do?" she accused.

"No. I couldn't see the board. That's why Aiden was helping me."

"It looked like you were bothering him. I get it, you were absent for a week, but you shouldn't make other people do your work for you."

"I wasn't—" I stopped myself. "Why did you move me in the back?"

"I read your doctor's note and saw you staring off into space yesterday. You're not sitting anywhere near my board so you can have a seizure in my class."

"That's not how—"

But Mrs. Bean interrupted me, "You of all people should know that lights and colors can trigger epilepsy, since you have it. That's why there's warning signs in movies and video games, not that most kids pay attention to it anyway, but I expect you to."

"My seizures aren't—"

"Most teachers wouldn't care about your condition. So, I'm going out of my way to look out for you. Remember that. If you want your grades up, then do tonight's homework." She set the pen down and gestured to the door. "I have another class to teach, so if you don't mind..."

I left with a frustrated sigh and made it to the stairs when a familiar voice called out.

"Hey, Mayu!"

I spun around to see Aiden leaning against the locker, waving at me. Since we weren't in a dark room, I had a good look at the boy who helped me. He had the sun touched complexion of an islander with a bright, playful smirk.

"Were you waiting for me?" I asked.

"I left my notebook behind," he said. "Do you still need it?"

"A little, but I can give it back."

"Don't worry about it. I have a good memory," he replied with a small chuckle. "I'm only taking notes because she grades it."

Mystic Rising

I was unsure if I should take it, but regardless, I slid the notebook into my backpack. "Thank you."

"I don't know what her problem is today. She had an attitude last week, but nothing like that." He readjusted his headphones though there was nothing wrong with them, as far as I could tell.

"I don't think she likes me," I said.

"Doubt she likes anyone here."

The classroom door opened, and Mr. Turner stepped outside when he saw us.

"Thought I heard you two out here. I have something for you," he said.

Aiden and I stared at him, and he gave us a handful of papers with the notes and more detailed examples printed on it.

"I made the notes this morning and Mrs. Bean put together the slide," he explained. "I didn't realize she would make the examples so vague. I'm glad I printed copies in advance."

"It would have been nice if you gave us those instead."

Mr. Turner lowered his voice. "Mrs. Bean would rather you copy off her slides."

"Guess I can return the notebook," I said to Aiden.

Our conversation was cut short when Mrs. Bean roared from the classroom. "Cedric, what are you doing?!"

Aiden and I quickly split off. It was when I made it downstairs that I realized he couldn't see the board, so how was he able to copy off the board.

* ● *

I saw my first fight in school the following day. I was heading to English, and a crowd of students gathered near a door, holding their phones out. A few students jumped away as two girls tumbled on the floor. I staggered back, my mouth hanging with shock at the girls beating each other. Cheers and whoops rang in the air.

"Everyone gets back to your classes!" a voice shouted over the commotion.

One of the assistants, a dark-skinned girl with long, jet-black hair skated past me, demanding everyone to leave. Ethan raced behind her, and he pried one of the girls off the floor. She was thrashing in his arms, kicking and screaming at the top of her lungs.

Ethan kept his grip on her and spoke loudly but firmly in her ear, "Stop it! That's enough!"

The other assistant ushered everyone away from the fight when I froze up. My body stiffened and my heart raced at a sharp viciousness stirring in the air. The girl on the floor twisted in a low crouch, bending her knees before she launched herself at Ethan. Screams tore through the air as everyone rushed down the hall. Caught in the tide, I felt elbows strike my arm and shoulders hit my face, nearly knocking off my glasses. A pair of hands dug into my rib and sent me hurtling into a locker.

Stars flew across my vision. My legs weakened and I sank into the floor. The stampeding students turned into fleeting shadows and their stomping shoes softened to approaching footsteps. Screams dampened to silence where a single voice echoed in my ear. "Are you alright?"

My eyes squinted at the stinging light and my hazy vision struggled to make out Ethan's figure. Harsh, dark red lines crossed his cheeks, his hair was a bit disheveled, but what caught my attention and kept my mind from fading were his eyes. The familiar amber burned a fierce gold, like blazing coal.

Then I blinked and the fire was gone.

"How many fingers am I holding up?" Ethan held up two, but I didn't answer.

"Your eyes...What happened?" I winced at a jolt of pain in the back of my head.

"You got knocked over pretty hard," Ethan said. "C'mon, I'll take you to the infirmary."

He wound my arm around his shoulder and gently lifted me up, though he was so tall, he could have carried me with one arm.

We rounded a few corners on the first floor and Ethan stopped in front of a door with a sign hanging off a hook that said, "Infirmary." Ethan opened it, revealing what looked like a small waiting room. It had a wooden bench against the wall, a painting of purple flowers above it and another door that led into the infirmary. The instant I stepped inside, a faint sweet, woodsy smell hit my nose. I took a deep breath, eying the vase on a desk and a cabinet full of medical supplies that faced a row of beds lined against the wall.

Sitting next to one of the beds was a plump olive toned nurse in lilac scrubs, dabbing a cotton ball on a girl's face. I recognized her from the fight and my body cringed at the nasty scratch across her face. She had a large padded bandaged on her forehead and I hate to imagine how gruesome that wound looked.

"Another one, Ethan?" the nurse called, keeping her attention on the girl.

He told her, "This one got pushed and hit her head when everyone was running away."

The nurse waved her hand for me to sit on another bed. She patched the girl's face with a bandage, then checked on me, touching the spot where I hit my head. It stung a little, enough to make me wince but, aside from that, I didn't feel dizzy or sick.

"No bruise or blood," the nurse muttered, though I wasn't sure if she was talking to me or herself. She asked if I had any medical conditions and I told her I had epilepsy and showed her the medical band clipped to my watch.

"Wearing a bracelet would make it easier for people to notice it," she said.

"My watch helps me keep track of time in case I have a seizure."

"Are you on any medication?"

I shook my head. "They don't work on me anymore."

The nurse looked at me suspiciously. She probably thought I made it up so I wouldn't take my medication. It wouldn't be the first time.

"I see."

The nurse went to her desk and returned with a bag of ice for my head. However, she wanted me to stay in the infirmary just in case I had a delayed seizure from the impact.

Before he left for class, Ethan told me he'd let Ms. Penn know what happened.

"Remember, if you're feeling sick, dizzy or sleepy," he started.

"Head back to the infirmary," I finished. "I know."

The nurse would check on me and the other girl every few minutes. Then, after an hour of nothing happening, she let me leave first when the bell rang, signaling the end of the second period.

The day could have gotten better. I spent algebra pretending I wasn't copying Aiden's notes. It was easier said than done when Mrs. Bean was watching me from her desk. After lunch, I met with Mary as she was leaving her class. We walked to the gym room and the first thing we noticed were the bleachers folded back and a volleyball net occupying the extra space. Unlike the previous two days, everyone had to wear their gym clothes and participate in class—no exceptions. So, it was my first time going to the locker rooms.

The bright fluorescent lights and echoing chatter brought back my headache. I ducked from a tube of deodorant flying over my head and choked on a cloud of body spray. Mary found an opened stall and someone behind us shouted, "Move!" We jumped back as an older girl sped into the stall and slammed the door in front of us.

"One minute left!" Ms. Bloom announced. Her voice rang off the walls and the girls scurried out of the locker room. Mary and I stood dumbfounded, surrounded by clothes and hygienic products sprawled across the floor.

"You think Ms. Bloom will notice if we hide here?" She asked.

I sighed. "We're the only freshmen here. She'll notice."

We didn't enjoy gym one bit. Mary tripped over her shoes, trying to save the volleyball, and when she served, it somehow bounced off her hand and hit her face. When it was my turn, my stomach sank with dread. I thought back to how Hannah played, and I lightly tossed the volleyball, brought my hands together, and swung my arms. It soared over the girls' heads...

And into Mr. Trouse's face.

My apology came out in a squeak among the laughter. Mr. Trouse let me off with a warning and tossed the ball back to us. Cheeks burning, my shoulders shrank when I slipped to the back of the team, wishing I could hide in the locker room for the rest of the year.

·●·

"Played volleyball today?" Lutea guessed, sitting beside me. Another thing I didn't like about that sport was how sore I was after the game. "You can take a break until your arm's a little better."

"I'm already a week behind. I need to catch up."

"You can't get much done on sore wrists." Lutea leaned back on the chair, lazily rocking it back and forth. "Take it easy. Try to draw something simple."

I held the pencil, rotated my wrist and added light strokes to the shell. I was lost in the art piece, listening to the idle gossip floating class, feeling the warm breeze through the open window.

Then the dull creaking chair snapped with a loud pop. A defeating crash brought my attention to Lutea as she hit the floor.

I jumped out of my seat and hurried to her. "Are you okay!"

"Still active," she grunted, sounding more annoyed than hurt. What was left of the chair beneath her was broken pieces and bent legs.

Worried students gathered around us before Mr. Eisele broke through the formation.

"Did the chair break again?" he asked.

"Second one," Lutea pushed herself up, and looked down at the broken pieces. "I shouldn't have leaned back so far."

Mr. Eisele brought a large trashcan to Lutea and helped her throw the pieces away. The other students guessed that she had an old, flimsy chair, hence why it broke. They decided to check on their chairs, but I couldn't take my eyes off Lutea.

Anyone would have been sore or limping, yet she shrugged it off and pulled up another chair to sit in, as if she simply tripped over her feet.

"You're a lot sturdier than I thought," I blurted.

I caught a glimpse of a small scar near Lutea's neck, but she shifted her long-sleeved shirt, and the scar disappeared beneath it.

She chuckled halfheartedly. "This is nothing. I've fallen off a cliff before, so it's going to take more than broken chair to keep me down!"

She smiled but couldn't shake off this uneasiness about her, like she wasn't telling me the entire truth.

At the last bell, I hurried to the bus before it was taken over by the student stampeding inside. I held on to the handlebar, bearing through the heat, the sweat and voices shouting in my ears. It was at the third stop when two voices rose through the usual clamor, and the commotion quieted down.

*Just three more stops*, I told myself, tightening my grip on the handle. *You'll be home in three stops.*

A sharp bump on the road knocked me into one of the students. I braced for an earful of angry insults, but the panicked shrieks erupted from the center of the bus. Students frantically shoved past me as someone shouted at the driver to stop the bus. I peered ahead, tightening my grip and saw, to my horror, two students grappling and shoving each other against everyone else.

*Oh no...*

Someone shoved me back and my grip slipped from the handle. Panic took over as I frantically grasped for something to hold on to. Suddenly, the bus screeched to a stop, and everybody toppled over each other. Everyone cried and pleaded to get off, and when the door finally opened, I bolted through the crowd, shaking off the hands grabbing my clothes and backpack, trying to pull me into the pile.

I tumbled out of the bus with five other students. Staggering to my feet, I caught my breath and gulped in lungfuls of air. My glasses were knocked aside, my shoe dangled off my foot and my backpack hung off my shoulder. Students were hurtling curses at the bus, throwing backpacks, rocks and bottled water as it sped down the road.

I swiveled from side to side, seeing the unfamiliar houses that surrounded me and school was nowhere in sight. Students walked away, using their phones to call someone prompted me to dig my phone out of my backpack. I fit my foot into my shoe and straightened my glasses as I called the first person who could help me.

"What's up, Runt?" Ichirou said.

My voice trembled. "Where are you?"

"I left the complex. Where are you?"

"I-I don't know..."

"What do you mean, you don't know'? Aren't you on the bus?"

"They kicked me off."

"How—" Urgency rose in his voice. "Where are you now?"

I saw a street sign nearby. "I see Jefferson Street."

"What's around you?"

I spun around for more details. "I'm standing in front of a red house—There's a stop sign at the corner and a small apartment across the street."

"Stay where you are. I'm on the way!"

I felt lightheaded, then numbed in my hands. I squeezed my phone and choked out my brother's name.

"Mayu? What's wrong?"

My eyes darted at the houses, then the street that stretched forever under the vast, blue sky.

"A-A red house," I stuttered. "A blue car. Bus signs."

"Keep talking to me!"

"Red house, yellow house, white house, black roof, blue car, beige truck..." It made little sense saying it out loud, but all that mattered was that Ichirou heard it and I could hear myself saying it. "Red house, yellow house, white house, blue car…"

I didn't realize another voice was repeating my words until I stopped talking. "Red, yellow, blue," it continued, wistfully.

I spun around, thinking someone was mocking me, but no one was there. Chills crawled down my spine and my heart raced. The voices were close yet seemed to fade in the rustling leaves.

"*Red house, yellow house, blue car…*"

I tore my attention from the tree and stared at the street for Ichirou's car. I gripped the phone to feel it in my hand. I spoke to Ichirou to hear my voice and his.

"I see you right now!" he said, sounding distant, like he was a few feet from his phone.

Faint music spun around me, but I forced myself to ignore it. To ignore the singing from the flowers. To ignore the movements in the grass and the dancing changing lights.

I jumped at the car horn blaring the sounds away and Ichirou's old black car pulled up near the curb. The engine switched off and Ichirou rushed out of the door.

"I'm right here. Look at me," he pleaded, clasping my shoulders.

I closed my eyes, took three deep breaths and opened them. It was me and my brother on the sidewalk. The ground stopped moving, and the sky wasn't pulling away from me. The trees weren't watching me, and the flowers stopped singing.

"I'm fine now," I said after a short breath.

I was still shaking when I held his hand and he walked with me to his car. I sank with relief into the worn leather seat and welcomed the cool air blasting through the vents.

"So, how did you get kicked off the bus?" Ichirou asked. I told him about the fight. "Were you hurt?"

"I banged my head during an earlier fight."

Ichirou checked on my head when the car stopped at a red light. I told him I was fine and reminded him to pay attention to the light, which immediately turned green.

"Did fights happen on buses when you went to school?" I asked.

"I've seen fights at bus stops, but never on the bus. I didn't think kids were that crazy."

"I thought things calmed down."

"Compared to when I went there, it did." He paused. "Next time you don't feel comfortable taking the bus home, call me or Hannah and one of us will pick you up."

"Don't you two have work, though?"

"I pass your school to go to work anyway."

"Okay." I thought about taking the later bus. I would have to wait another hour, but I hope it wouldn't be as bad as overcrowded students.

"By the way," Ichirou said. "Do you have any homework from Mrs. Bean?"

I let out a loud moan and slumped into the seat.

"I'm going to take that as a yes."

# 5

# Chance

**Mary wasn't in class that Friday morning.** At first, I thought she might have been late, so I sat at the table, ignoring Sarah sleeping across from me, and copied notes off the board while I waited.

*She might have been absent.*

But as moments passed, the anxiety picked at my sides. Memories of the fight flickered in my mind, and I wondered if something had happened to Mary. Was she safe? Is she in the infirmary? I paused, shook my head and buried those thoughts in my schoolwork.

During class, Mr. Baryon stood in front of the board and spoke about Isaac Newton and the laws of motion. It was hard to pay attention because a few girls at a table next to mine wouldn't stop whispering to each other.

"This is so boring," one of them moaned to her friend.

"Right?" The friend agreed. "No one cares about some old dead guy. Like, who's going to use this crap in the real world?"

It was typical gossip, though I wished they were quieter. A different girl replied, and her nasal voice with a lazed drawl sent ice through my veins.

"Yeah, only losers with no life care about this stuff."

My shoulders stiffened. My mind reeled back to middle school, to Rosalina behind me, whispering to Bethany and Nara. Their eyes searing into my back as they followed me in the hallway, hurtling insults every day, throwing objects or flashing lights in my face.

*She can't be here*, I thought, gripping my pen. *She shouldn't be here!* A small part of me reminded me to breathe and steady my racing heart. *Deep breaths, Mayu. Take deep breaths. You've been in school for a week. If it was Rosalina, wouldn't she have said something by now.*

The giggles continued. I drew another deep breath and slowly turned to the voice, to see the nightmare that I would have to face again for another year. Without Elizabeth.

It wasn't Rosalina.

Her fair complexion and braided, brunette hair didn't resemble Rosalina. But her voice was so similar, I would have been shocked if the two had never met.

*I hope she wasn't a Rosalina fangirl or something.*

Mr. Baryon cleared his throat. "Could someone explain to me what I just discussed?"

The classroom murmur fell silent. Everyone shifted awkwardly in their chairs as Mr. Baryon scanned the room, waiting for an answer.

"Anyone?" he prompted. "Does anyone know the first law of motion?"

I slowly raised my shaky arm and dozens of eyes trained on me.

"The first law is an object in motion will stay in motion unless acted upon by an outside force. The second law is that an object not in motion will stay in place until it's influenced by an outside force as well."

"Correct!" Mr. Baryon praised and repeated the definition to the class.

But the Rosalina clone gossiped to her friends, "Look, a loser in her natural habitat." Giggles rung around me.

"I didn't know physics was so funny, Victoria," Mr. Baryon said, turning to the girls. The class quieted again. "Come on. Why is 'an old dead guy' such a joke to you?"

After a moment of silence, the Rosalina clone, Victoria, shrugged. "I dunno."

"*Sir,*" He demanded.

"I dunno, *sir,*" she added with a repulsed look.

"Hmph, figures," Mr. Baryon turned to the rest of the class. "Newton's Third Law is that every action has an equal, and opposite reaction. For instance, the more Victoria decides to mess around, picking on others, she might find herself back here in the same grade next year."

Victoria pouted and shot me a dirty look. I retreated to my notes. Mr. Baryon passed out the assignments and woke Sarah up when he gave us our papers. Though chatter filled the class, an uneasy silence loomed at my table. It was strange not having Mary around, but stranger to see Sarah in class for more than a minute. Mr. Baryon returned to the table and tapped her shoulder, and her tired eyes fell on the paper in front of her. She couldn't be that bad of a person. I got out of my chair and moved to the empty seat next to her.

"S-Sarah?" I said, softly.

She jolted up with a start. Her dark eyes widened like a deer caught in the headlight. Her uniform, a white blouse and knee-length skirt were covered in wrinkles and looked too big on her.

"Do you mind if I sit with you?" I asked.

Sarah slowly shook her head.

I slid into the seat and shared my notes with her. "Um... Do you want to work on the questions together?"

She gave me a hesitant nod. I inched closer and read the questions to her. For the first time, I heard her speak in a small, quivering voice.

"Why are you talking to me?" she murmured.

I paused for a moment. "I don't see why I shouldn't."

"You don't know—"

A paper ball bounced off Sarah's head.

"No sleeping in class, short bus," Victoria hissed, and her friends laughed.

Sarah lowered her head, burying her face in her arms. I turned to Victoria and felt the anger flare in my chest. She was exactly like Rosalina, and the last thing I needed was another version of *her* in high school.

"Would you stop that?" I said and the laughter at the table stopped.

Victoria's voice sharpened. "Why don't you mind your own business!" she shouted. "Go back to reading your textbook, little girl."

"Victoria," Mr. Baryon warned. "Do you need to be moved to another table?"

"We aren't doing anything! They're acting crazy! She's—"

A loud shriek peeled from the table as Victoria fell off the chair and hit the floor. She was groveling and holding her arm. A nauseating wave rolled over me as her friends rushed to help her up. I saw Rosalina crying on the floor, cradling her arm. Whispers formed around me and their eyes bore into my back.

"Someone pushed me!" Victoria howled. "Someone put their hands on me!"

"How? Nobody touched you," said Mr. Baryon.

My head swayed.

At the sound of the bell, I snatched my notes and backpack and hurried out of the classroom. I spotted Sarah darting past me with a wide, frightened look on her face. No, I didn't want her to think I hurt her too.

"Sarah!" I cried.

She weaved through the passing students and vanished behind the windowless door of the girl's bathroom.

Mary told me no one ever goes to the bathroom on the first floor and when I dove inside, I quickly found out why. The smell of body spray and stale cigarettes slammed into me with the force of a swinging door. The stalls lined next to the sink were riddled with graffiti. And the ceiling hung high over my head, spotted with mysterious dark stains. I would have left the bathroom if I hadn't heard sobbing coming from the back.

I followed the sound and found Sarah pressed against the wall, hunched over and shaking.

"Sarah?"

"G-Go away!" she whimpered.

Cold air began to pinch my face. "Sarah, what happened to Victoria, I didn't touch her! I swear!"

Sarah slammed her hands against her ears and was rocking back and forth. "Please stop! Stop talking so loud!"

"O-Okay," I whispered. "D-Do you need help?"

"Go away!" Sarah roared. "Leave us *ALONE*!"

I bolted out of the bathroom and raced down the hallway. Never had I rushed so quickly to Algebra and when I got there, I dropped into my seat.

"What happened to you?" Aiden asked.

"I don't know," I panted. "I'm not sure if I want to know."

"Wanna elaborate?"

"Mayu!" Mrs. Bean shouted, making me flinch. "Do I need to remind you there's no talking in my class?"

She brushed past me on her way to the smart board. Looking around, I realized Mr. Turner was nowhere in sight. I jotted in my notebook, *'Where's Mr. Turner,'* and passed it to Aiden. He wrote something beneath my question and slid the notebook back to me.

*'They're having a meeting. There weren't any assistants in my last two classes.'*

We ducked down when Mrs. Bean turned back to the class. Throughout the lesson, she would say things to me like, "I hope you're paying attention to this, Mayu," or "make sure you're writing this down, Mayu." It felt like I had to hold my breath for an hour. Moments before class ended, Mrs. Bean passed back our graded homework. She tossed my homework on my desk, red Xs crossed over all my answers.

"That's not right," Aiden whispered. He showed me his homework, and our answers were the same, except he had check marks over his, and the number "99" drawn over his name. I had everything right.

"Why did she fail you?"

"I don't know."

At the end of class, I turned to Mrs. Bean at her desk. I guess there was one benefit to having her sit behind me.

"Don't you have other classes to go to?" Mrs. Bean said, exasperated.

"This is my lunch period."

"Maybe you should go before the lines get too long."

I didn't move. "Why did you give me a bad grade?"

"Because you should have answered the question. I didn't need to see the work."

"But the assignment said, 'show your work.'"

"Yes, as in show me your answer."

"Aiden showed his work, and you gave him a better grade."

"Why are you looking at other student's work? Focus on yourself instead of worrying about everyone else."

"So, should I show you my answers instead?"

Mrs. Bean groaned, "Mayu, in case you haven't noticed, my assistant isn't here today, and I have a lot to do, including getting ready for my next class."

I bit my lip and pushed down my anger before swiping away from Mrs. Bean. "That attitude won't change your grade, Mayu!" she yelled.

Aiden was leaning against the locker, notebook in his hand. On our way to lunch, I told him what Mrs. Bean said.

"That's the stupidest reason to fail you," he said. "What does she have against you?"

"I don't know," I grumbled.

We stopped by the cafeteria door, making sure we weren't in the way as the other students passed us.

"Try not to let her bother you," Aiden said. "I bet she's like this because Mr. Turner isn't here today. He'll be back tomorrow and she'll be back to scowling at you."

71

"I'd rather not have that either," I said, though I knew he was trying to make me feel better. "But I hope you're right."

Aiden left for his class, and I joined the students lining up at the cafeteria. It was hamburger day, and I was lucky enough to grab the last burger before the complaints broke out behind me. I sat at my usual table where, for the first time, I had company. Two girls were chatting with each other, but I doubt they cared that I was there.

I was about to bite into my burger, wanting to forget about my morning, then a loud bang silenced the cafeteria clamor. Grunts and shouts came from two boys tackling each other to the floor. Everyone swarmed around them before a security guard could pry them off.

*Not again,* I thought irritably.

And then things got worse. The girls' conversation somehow turned into a shouting argument. As fast as it started it quickly stopped after one of the girls slapped the other.

I jumped back in shock as the girl lunged at the other, yanking chunks of hair and scratching her face like an animal. Students circled around us, whipping out their phones to record the madness. I couldn't take it. I shoved through the wall of people and raced for the exit. I took a swift turn around the corner and slammed into Lutea.

"What the—" she exclaimed as I hit the floor. "Oh crap! I'm so sorry! Are you alright?"

The blow knocked me back and pain throbbed across my head.

"Ow..." I hissed, looking up at her. "What's your head made of?"

"Not iron. Why were you running?"

A shriek brought our attention to the cafeteria. Lutea's kind eyes sharpened with a sternness that I've never seen before.

"Wait here," she said and hurried upstairs.

I stood against the wall with bated breath as everything quieted down. After another agonizing moment, the door opened and Lutea emerged with one of the girls. My head spun when I saw the blood. She was gasping in between sobs, her hand covered her nose and mouth, but the blood trickled from her wrist down to her arm.

"Let's get you both patched up," Lutea whispered, patting the girl's back.

Thankfully, the infirmary wasn't far from the cafeteria. Lutea entered with the girl and called out a name, "Caritas." The same plump nurse who helped me, lifted her head from her desk. Her eyes widened with shock at the bloodied girl and then she noticed me behind them.

"What happened *this* time?" She cried.

Lutea gave her a quick explanation about me running into her after a fight broke out in the cafeteria. Caritas immediately tended to the girl. She drew a cloth from the cabinet and used it to stop the bleeding, then bandaged her face. Next, she checked on me. I didn't have any injuries, but she gave me another small bag of ice.

"You need to start coming to school with a helmet," Caritas mumbled.

"More like body armor," I added, jokingly.

The door opened again, and a security guard stepped in with a boy I recognized from the first fight. His cheeks were swollen and blood trickled from a cut over his eye.

Caritas sighed, "Busy Friday, I see."

"Do you need help?" Lutea asked.

"No need," she replied, shaking her head. "Nothing I can't handle."

"Do I need to stay?" I asked her.

Caritas pursed her lips. "You can sit outside. Lutea are you busy?"

"Kind of but I can spare a few minutes," she said.

Lutea motioned me to follow her. I held the ice pack to my head with one hand, slung my backpack over my shoulder and we sat at the bench to give Caritas and the others privacy.

"Are you going to watch over me?" I asked. "Head injuries trigger seizures but it's almost rare for me."

"You can't be too careful," Lutea said. "But I've been meaning to ask if you were doing alright this week."

I looked at her curiously, wondering where this was coming from.

"You always look tense and worried when you come to art. Don't tell me Gym is that intense."

"Only if they make me play volleyball." I chuckled softly.

I never realized how much I had on my chest until I started talking to Lutea. How I couldn't stand Mrs. Bean, the gossiping girls, Sarah popping in and out of nowhere, and the fights happening everywhere I go.

"Someone told me high school would be as easy as crossing the street. Now, I'm wondering if he meant crossing a busy road."

"Probably," Lutea huffed. "Believe it or not, it used to be a lot worse. Pure pandemonium every hour."

73

"'Pan-demo-nium'?" I repeated slowly.

"A fancy word for 'chaotic.' On my first day here, I subbed for a class after a teacher I was supposed to assist walked out on the job. The same year, a school admin got dragged into a fight with a student and the kid body-slammed him into a table. Broke the table and the admin's spine in two places."

I cringed. "Sounds like something Ichirou went through."

"Ichirou?"

"My brother. He was a student here several years ago. He told me all about the crazy incidents. Believe it or not, he also had Mrs. Bean as a teacher." I paused. "I wonder if she had some sort of grudge on my brother. Maybe that's why she hates me."

"It's not just you," Lutea said, bluntly. "Mrs. Bean hates everyone, especially assistants."

"How come?"

"She claimed students wouldn't learn if someone 'did their work for them.' But too many were failing her class en masse, so she was forced to get one."

"She was that bad?"

"Yeah, and she went out of her way to make herself difficult to work with. Two assistants lasted a year before they switched to a different class. Cedric was the only one who volunteered to assist her, knowing she would continue to fail any student for petty reasons."

"Yeah, even for doing their homework." I grumbled.

"Tell you what, the library is right around the corner. I can take you to see Cedric if you like."

"Really?"

"I got time, do you?"

I peeked at my watch and grinned. "Got fifteen minutes to spare."

Lutea stood up and nudged the infirmary door wide enough to let Caritas know we were leaving.

"Be careful, out there!" she yelled back.

"We will!" Lutea and I said at once, paused and looked at each other before snorting into laughter.

We headed down the hall until Lutea stopped in front of a pair of doors. A yellow paper taped to the window read, "assistant staff meeting, DO NOT ENTER" and scribbled beneath it was, "unless you're the librarian."

"Usually, we don't let outsiders in, but I think we can make an exception," Lutea said in a low voice. She drew a set of keys from her pocket and unlocked the door.

I was going to ask Lutea what the meeting was about, but she held her finger over her mouth and opened the door with a low, dull creak.

Mary has always told me the library was its own world, a peaceful place where she can sink into stories and weave through the labyrinth of shelves. I thought she was exaggerating until I stepped inside, and my heart stopped at the sheer size.

The hanging lights dimly lit the towering shelves and narrow aisles. Murmurs and whispers filled the room from the people gathered at round tables. Printers hummed and keyboards clattered as fingers tapped the tablets and pens scratched across papers. There were unfamiliar faces, and a few I knew like Ethan and Mr. Turner.

"Lutea," a voice called from our left.

I turned around and the first thing I noticed was a young man's half shaved, ghost white hair and dark clothes. He wore a black shirt, baggy cargo pants and combat boots. "Teier" was printed on the lanyard he had stitched on his shirt.

"What took you so long? Marie was about to send someone to find you," he said.

"I had to help security break up a fight," Lutea explained. "Is Cedric busy at the moment?"

"A little..." Teier's head lulled to the side, catching my gaze. His grey eyes grew comically big and darted wildly between us and the assistants.

"Lutea, students aren't supposed to be here!" He hissed through his teeth.

"I know, I know." Lutea stepped back, holding her hands up. "But she needs to talk to Cedric. It's Mrs. Bean."

At the sound of her name, Teier's stiff shoulders went slack and the urgency in his eyes evaporated. Even his voice dropped into mild annoyance.

"Say no more, I'll get him," he moaned and walked to one of the tables. I wondered if he was one of Mrs. Bean's previous assistants.

"Should we look for Mr. Turner too?" I asked, glancing up at the shelves. The thought of exploring the aisle had me itching to walk around and discover how big the library was. It was like another building was attached to this already massive school.

"Best if we wait here," said Lutea. She leaned against the wall with her hands in her pockets. "The meeting is still going, and I don't want you to get in trouble for being here."

"What is this meeting about, anyway?"

Before she answered, she waved back as Mr. Turner approached us.

"Can you help Mayu with her homework?" Lutea asked him.

Mr. Turner blinked. "This isn't the best of times."

"I know but..." she turned to me. "You should let him see it."

"What did she do this time?"

"This," I said and showed him my graded homework.

"I leave class for one day..." Mr. Turner grumbled under his breath. "Why did she fail you?"

I told him why and he pinched the bridges of his nose and let out a heavy sigh.

"Showing your work gives you extra credit," he said, returning my paper to me. "This is an inexcusable reason to fail you. I'll have a talk with her after the meeting."

"Do you think she'll listen." Lutea asked. "Mayu might be better off changing classes."

"I already thought about it," I said. "But I'd have to wait for a few months to do it."

"Mid-October," Mr. Turner corrected. "Though I might have a solution for the time being. How do you feel about tutoring after school?"

I cocked my head to the side. "What?"

"Next week, we will be opening a club gathering after school. It's where you meet and get to know the assistants. I'm considering opening a tutoring session. You're not the only one struggling with their classes."

"I thought the school already had tutors."

"They do. But the difference is if you give Mrs. Bean your papers with my signature, as proof that I looked at your work, she can't lower your grade out of spite. How does that sound?"

He took my widening smile as a yes and returned to the meeting, coming back a moment later with a green half-sheet of paper. Beneath a decorated emblem, the word Assistants Meeting sprawled across the paper with a letter at the bottom.

*"Congratulations, dearest scholar, on being invited to the Assistants' Meeting where you can engage and socialize with the assistants of John Carter High School. We offer tutelage, field trips*

*and other activities. Our meetings are Mondays through Fridays from 2:30 to 4:00. If interested, please sign the bottom, and bring it with you to the meeting at the library after school. If not interested, return the slip to an assistant. Have a nice day!"*

*-Marie Naiad.*

"Assistants have to sign it," Mr. Turner explained. "But it is optional to have a parent or guardian sign the papers."

That evening, as the setting sun peered over the complex, I sat at the table, jotting down math questions and examples in my notebook. Hannah had finished taking a shower and washing the smell of pizza sauce out of her hair. In the kitchen, Ichirou was cooking a dish he made at his job—grilled salmon with vegetables and shrimps. Though this was our normal Friday routine, the hectic school days made me miss the simple sounds of home. Better than screaming, cursing students and bells going off every hour.

My vision glazed over the numbers, so I gave myself a short break, taking off my glasses and letting my eyes rest for a few moments. Before starting on my homework, I reread the letter again.

*Naiad*, I thought. The name sounded familiar though I couldn't place where I've heard it before. I flipped the paper over and saw empty slots for personal information like my name, address, school ID number, and emergency contact. At the bottom were three signature lines.

"What'cha looking at, Runt?"

I glanced at Ichirou as he set a small plate in front of me.

"Something I got from Mr. Turner," I said and gave him the invitation to read.

"Are you going on a field trip?"

"No. It's a club meeting."

"And you need a permission slip to join?" His brow rose suspiciously. "Hey, Hannah!"

"Yeah," she called coming downstairs with a towel wrapped around her wet hair.

"Have you ever heard of this club?" Ichirou showed her the letter. They stared at it and exchanged uneasy looks like something was wrong.

"It probably started after we graduated," Hannah said. "What's it about?"

"It's where you meet the assistants after school. But Mr. Turner wanted to tutor me there." I could practically see the gears working in their heads.

"Why do you need an invite?" Ichirou asked. "Isn't tutoring open for everyone?"

"Mrs. Bean won't fail me if Mr. Turner signed my homework," I said, noticing the skeptical look in Ichirou's eyes. "Didn't you have to be invited to clubs?"

Hannah answered, "The ROTC was the only meeting where you had to fill out an application. And you're kicked out if your grade was lower than a C."

"I thought you wanted to join the track team," said Ichirou.

"If sports in high school are anything like middle school, you're suspended or taken off from the team if you have a low grade."

"She's right," Hannah agreed.

"Can you sign it?"

Ichirou held on to the invitation. "Let me think about it."

If there was one thing I loved about Fridays was spending the night in Hannah's room. The lilac walls were decorated in paintings and artwork that she'd done over the years. She never believed you were too old to have toys, so her bed was buried under a mountain of plushies. My favorite was Bosco, a large teddy bear she won at a carnival last summer.

I snuggled against Bosco and finished my homework while Hannah drew at her desk. Ichirou, who preferred to work in silence, stayed in his room to finish his projects. Hannah didn't mind a little noise as she had a movie playing on her laptop. She helped me whenever there was a problem I didn't understand. If I ran out of graphing paper, she had extras in packets. If I needed double checking, Hannah triple checked my work.

By midnight, I finally finished my homework. All thirty pages. Numbers and word problems swam dizzily in my head and all I wanted to do was sink into Bosco and let sleep take me away.

The door knocked and knowing it was Ichirou, Hannah answered, jokingly, "We're not interested."

"Is anyone tired yet?" he asked.

"I'm still up. Mayu's about to pass out, though."

"No... I could stay up..." I propped myself up on my elbows, trying not to look as tired as I felt.

"Come on," Ichirou said, gathering my papers. "If you're going to pass out, go to your room. Hannah needs her bed, too."

I crawled out of bed and readjusted my glasses. I said goodnight to Hannah and carried my textbook and homework when Ichirou gave me the green half-sheet paper. On it, I saw his signature under Mr. Turner's.

"Try not to lose it."

# Welcoming

**I was so excited to see Mary in class again** that I practically ran to our table to give her a hug.

"Wow!" Mary laughed. "I didn't know you missed me that much."

"Class wasn't the same without you," I said. "Where were you last week?"

"I had three exams coming up and since the library was going to be closed, I stayed home to catch up on my notes."

"That makes sense." Sometimes, Ichirou and Hannah would stay home to cram for their exams, so Mary doing the same didn't sound odd to me.

"By the way, I heard you talked to Sarah," Mary said in a low voice. Her somewhat stern look gave me a feeling she caught me doing something wrong.

I shifted awkwardly and glanced at the chair across from me. Sarah never came to class, but one could never tell when she was going to appear out of nowhere. And after Friday, I wasn't sure if I wanted to see her again.

"I tried to help her," I admitted. "I followed her into the bathroom, and she yelled at me to go away."

"At least you weren't hurt. I hear she can get violent if you get too close to her. Next time, keep your distance from her."

*Easier said than done.*

I caught a glance of Victoria talking to her friends at her table. No insults or paper balls thrown at anyone, but if she was anything like Rosalina, it was only a matter of time before the teasing started. It would be my luck to be in the same class with a Rosalina clone.

"What else did you do?" Mary asked.

I told her about running into Lutea, going to the library and talking to Mr. Turner about the Assistant's club meeting.

Mary's voice lifted. "When is it happening?"

"Today," I said and showed her the invitation.

Mary fawned over Mr. Turner's signature. "It's so elegant. I hear he's the most attractive assistant in the school. Do you think so?"

My cheeks warmed up. "I can't disagree with that."

Mary read the letter, then her wistful eyes narrowed. "What is this?" She pointed at an emblem. A knotwork pattern shaped like a shield that wound around a flower at the center.

"Isn't that the school emblem?" I asked.

I pulled out my schedule, and we compared its emblem to the invitation's. Carter's was a simple line drawn shield with the school's initials "JC" inside.

"Maybe it's a decoration," I guessed. "I don't recognize the flower."

Mary shrugged. "They sure went out of their way to design it for tutoring. I didn't think you needed one. You're already a smart person."

I blushed at her compliment. "Mrs. Bean would say otherwise."

Mary shuddered, having heard the horror stories.

Speaking of algebra, I dreaded coming to class until I learned that Mr. Turner was teaching for the day, while Mrs. Bean graded papers at her desk. His smooth voice flowed through the room like music to my ears, and his elegant handwriting across the board (in perfect calligraphy, no less) made me ashamed that I couldn't copy his style. When the time came to start on the assignment, I opened the textbook and used the letter to mark where to stop.

"What's that you got there?" Mrs. Bean grumbled, towering over my desk.

My shoulders tensed up as I gazed at her. "Wh-What do you mean?"

"That green note doesn't look like it belongs here. What is it?"

"Mrs. Bean," Mr. Turner called. His attention remained on the smart board. "She's not bothering anyone, and she is taking her notes."

"I saw her looking at it and wanted to know what it was."

I was about to protest, but when I saw everyone's eyes on me, my confidence drained.

Then Aiden spoke up, "I have one too."

He pulled out an identical paper from his notebook and showed it to Mrs. Bean. "Mr. Turner gave it to me last week."

"What for?" Mrs. Bean swiped my invitation from my desk. The way she pinched the side of the paper, I thought she was going to tear it to pieces.

"I've never heard of this club meeting before. And there's no one here named Marie Naiad." Mrs. Bean's head whipped back to Mr. Turner. "Cedric, why are you giving these to students?"

"It is an after school-meeting for assistants," Mr. Turner answered calmly. "I was going to let you know, since I need to leave early today."

"But the library's closed after school."

"Not to assistants." His gold eyes flashed as he faced Mrs. Bean. "You have your answer. Now, can we continue the lesson, Amarella?"

Soft gasps rose around the room. I thought Mrs. Bean was going to explode. Instead, she reeled back at me like I had something to do with Mr. Turner's response.

"You are going to put this away and focus on your actual work."

She tossed my invitation, and Aiden caught it before it hit the floor. Mrs. Bean stomped back to her desk.

I mouthed the words, "Thanks."

He replied with a playful smirk.

Mr. Turner tapped the marker on the board, bringing everyone's attention to him. "Does anyone know the answer to this?"

A few students raised their hands, including Aiden, and with the questions answered, the tension quickly lifted. However, something did nag at me, and it wasn't Mrs. Bean's death stare digging into my back. Rather it was what she said.

Not that I would ever admit it out loud, but Mrs. Bean was right. The library always closed before the last bell. Ms. Penn made that clear when she encouraged everyone to do independent reading for extra credit. I believed Mr. Turner, but doubt set in when I asked him about it after class. He simply told me, "Be at the library after school."

"Did you know the library closed after school?" I asked Aiden, walking with him after class.

"Somewhat, but I'm not worried about it," he said.

We stopped next to his classroom, and Aiden leaned against the lockers next to the door. "If the assistants are going, it should be opened to the people they invite."

"That makes sense," I peered into the classroom and spotted the white-haired assistant, Teier at the board. "I didn't know you were going to the meeting. Do you need help with class?"

"No, I need help to relax. Apparently, I stress myself out too much and it shows."

He toyed with his headphones and looked up at the lights. I held my chin, pretending to inspect him.

"No grey hairs, but you look awfully exhausted. You might want to get some sleep."

Aiden chuckled, "Tell that to my little sister."

The late bell rang, startling me as the sound burst in my ears. I didn't think I was going to get used to that.

After Aiden went to class, I headed to the library, too curious about the club meeting and when it would happen. I pulled the library door open and embraced the scent of aged papers and polished wood. The peace of soft whispers and clattering keyboards brought me back to Lawrence Middle School with Elizabeth.

I stepped inside and stopped to someone clearing their throat.

"Looking for something?"

I turned to a middle-aged man with thick grey hair, wearing a zip up sweater, standing behind a tall, circular desk.

"Um, are you the librarian?" I asked. I couldn't be too sure—for all I knew, he could have been a teacher.

In a low, gentle voice, he said, "Oh, no, I'm holding the fort while the old man's away. He sure likes to take his time." He smirked, and I giggled at the joke. "Anything I can help you with?"

I told the librarian about the meeting and showed him the invitation. He reached for his glasses hanging around his neck and read the letter with a raised brow.

"I knew the assistants were talking about starting a club," he said and returned the letter. "Maybe it's in the room next door. Most after-school activities happen in the classrooms."

My heart sank. "Oh... okay."

"If I see an assistant, I'll ask 'em about it."

"That's okay, I can ask one in my class later," I assured, but was a little worried about the meeting.

I spent the rest of the period exploring the library. Idling around the shelves, I counted the number of covers decorated in flowers, and titles that started with 'a court, a trial, or a ballad of.' And books written by authors named Claere, Claire, Clairie and Clare.

As I turned to the next aisle, something fluttered at the corner of my eye. I turned to the windows, where I found a gazebo outside, clad in ivy and surrounded by potted plants. Mary did mention there was a courtyard in school. My eyes fell on a slim black door wedged between the windows. But it didn't open when I pulled the handle.

"Guess it needs a key..." I muttered.

I went to the computers when a musky scent wafted over me that I could only describe as old pages. Aged books with faded titles filled the shelf from top to bottom. There were leather covers ebbed away by time, and fabric covers that had long since lost their color. I leaned toward one book and read the title.

"This area's off limits."

I jumped back and spun around to see the librarian right behind me, carrying a large box of printer papers.

"S-Sorry," I said, stepping away from the shelf. "How come it's off limits?"

"Those books are the oldest things in this school," he explained. "They're delicate and I've had kids sneak back there and do..." he rolled his hand like I was supposed to finish his sentence.

I stared at him, not sure what he was talking about.

"Be more careful around this area."

The librarian returned to his desk, and I sat at one of the tables to start on my homework. After lunch and gym, I visited the library again with Mary. I looked around to see if there were any signs of an after-school meeting, but everything remained the same.

"How are you getting home tonight? Are you catching the bus?" Mary asked.

"Ichirou is supposed to pick me up." I replied.

"Mind if I take you home?"

I looked at her.

She added, "I was invited to the theater club today. If our meetings end at the same time, would you like to get a ride from my dad? I don't want you to be stranded again."

Mary sounded like she wanted me to come with her. So, I told her I'd let Ichirou know I was going with her.

In art, Lutea's (new) chair was empty, and she wasn't anywhere in class. I asked Mr. Eisele where she was, and he told me she went to the library at noon. My brow arched. I would have seen her at some point or passed by her on the way. Maybe she took another route...

It was hard to concentrate for the rest of the class and when school ended, I hurried to the library, worried that nobody was going to be there. The lights were on, but the doors were locked. Worried, I stood on my tiptoes and peeked through the windows.

It was still empty.

My heart pounded. *Where is everyone? Did I come too early? Was it in a different room?* But then I noticed movement coming from the back of the library. I tapped the window like my life depended on it and somebody stopped. Ethan emerged from the shelves and jogged to the door.

He unlocked it and pushed it open. "Hey, how's your head

Ever since the fight, my head injury has become somewhat of an inside joke between us.

"It's alright now," I replied, anxiously. "Is the meeting happening now? Is it in the library?"

"Yes, and yes," Ethan said and let me in. "Try going through the back doors. It's much easier."

The library was too quiet for my liking; the computers were off, the tables were empty, and the librarian was nowhere to be seen. I hesitated to walk with Ethan as he approached the tall shelves, obscured in shadows.

He glanced at me over his shoulder. "What's wrong?"

"I thought this area was off limits," I said warily.

"Only during school hours. Don't worry, nothing's going to jump at you." He gave me a gentle pat on my head. "It's going to be okay."

Ethan walked ahead. The air was cold, and the smell of old papers grew stronger the further we went. I hurried to his side when he turned the corner, and I saw light stretching across the floor. Voices rose nearby but one, soft and chime-like sounded louder than the rest.

"Welcome in! Have a good time!"

I stopped in front of a decorated wooden door with a glass pane, but my focus was more on the girl seated on the desk. Streaks of platinum in her long blonde hair parted between her bright green eyes. Her clothes, a dark pleated skirt and tie fixed around a white blouse would have made her look like a proper student, but the large headphones she wore seemed out of place. They were black with a pair of butterfly wings sticking out of the cups. I'd never seen headphones like hers and wasn't sure if she could hear anyone through them.

"Are you a new member?" The girl spoke up and I realized she was talking to me.

"Yep," Ethan said, and he nudged me toward her. "This is Min. She's our receptionist here."

*Receptionist? What kind of school club needs a receptionist?*

"You were able to come here, so do you have an invitation?" Min asked.

"Oh, right!" I took off my backpack and found the invitation crammed between the textbooks and journals. I showed it to Min and her eyes flew across the letter.

She smiled. "Pleased to meet you, Mayu. I hope you have a good time!"

I opened the door, my breath hitched at the fresh, cool air that chased away the stale pages, and the commotion pouring through the door. There was friendly clamor, and booming laughter from the round tables where assistants and students sat. Shelves lined the walls full of books and plants that sprouted in round jars, and garlands hung off the exposed beams.

A scent, savory and spiced, drew me to platters of food at a table. There were slices of fruit arranged on a tray, a large bowl of salad with the greenest leaves and diced vegetables. Half-moon meat pies the size of my hand filled the platter, golden fried cakes with a honey sweet scent covered another, and at the center, a cauldron with stew bubbling inside.

My mouth watered and my fingers twitched a bit, anxious to grab something or everything.

"Feel free to take whatever you like," Ethan said as though he read my mind. He passed me a plate, then reached over my shoulder to fill his.

"You better save that for everybody else," Lutea scolded Ethan from one of the tables. His mouth was already full when he mumbled out an answer. I heard him say along the lines, "see ya!" before he veered to one of the tables.

Lutea rolled her eyes. "We spent two hours prepping the food, and he's already scarfing it down."

"My brother always says to trust the food the chefs will eat." I picked up a plate and, following Ethan's lead, I grabbed one or two of everything until I had my own hill of food.

Lutea chuckled, "Leave Ethan unchecked, and he'll inhale an entire buffet."

"Hey!" Ethan protested and I heard his voice cut into small rounds of coughs.

A different girl sighed. "Ever heard of chewing your food? You got canines for a reason."

Lutea checked to see if Ethan was alright (he was), and I walked around, looking for a place to sit. I counted a dozen students and maybe thirty assistants, but the room didn't feel overcrowded. I spotted Aiden at one of the tables and joined him, careful not to drop the meat pie and honey cake.

"Hey, you made it!" Aiden said. "I was worried you wouldn't show up."

"I was afraid there wasn't a club here. Thanks for helping me in class."

"I tried my best." Aiden blushed and he looked away. "Can you believe she tried to find this place?"

"No kidding!"

"Mr. Turner saw her sneaking around the front doors. Guess she wanted to see if it was 'school appropriate' but he convinced her to leave."

"What does she have against this meeting?"

"Who knows? Maybe she hates fun."

I finished the meat pie and salad, then dug into the cake when a woman spoke up, quieting the commotion. "May I have your attention please?"

Everyone turned to a table where three people sat. There was Mr. Turner, a dark-skinned man with tied back locks and a tanned woman whose wavy hair flowed passed her green, shoulder length dress.

Standing in front of them was a woman with shining dark hair, wearing a powdered blue knitted dress, dark leggings and knee-high boots.

"Good afternoon, my young scholars," she announced. Her voice was light, almost childlike. "I am Miss Marie Naiad, head of the Assistants' Meeting as of four years from now."

My eyes widened as I recognized her name from the letter.

"It's nice to meet fresh faces this year. Welcome back veterans, good to see you're still alive, and congratulations seniors, you're almost done."

Everyone applauded and some of the students cheered about how they missed her.

"Yes, yes, I missed you too." Miss Naiad brushed back her hair. "Before we get to the fun stuff, I want to lay down some rules."

87

"I hope she doesn't take all day to explain," Aiden whispered to me.

"Don't worry Aiden," her voice projected across the room. "You'll have time to hear the rules and have fun like everyone else."

Aiden's face turned bright red.

"You know her?" I asked.

"No," he squeaked.

"Number one!" Miss Naiad began, holding up her thumb. "While we are open to potential members, we are strict about who we let in. If you have parents or guardians coming to pick you up, they will have to wait outside until you come to them, or until the meeting is over—whichever comes first.

Number two!" she continued, extending her index finger. "We have various activities in our group such as tutoring, gaming, reading and artwork. Have fun, but don't get out of control. If it's so loud that I can't hear myself think, that means we are too loud, capiche?"

Everybody nodded.

"And number three. There's no need to be afraid to be yourself. And if you're nervous about introduction, you can start with getting to know us and your fellow assistants."

Every assistant raised their hand and Aiden, and I went to Lutea's table. Five students asked her where she was from, what her favorite animal and color was.

"Europe, I think," Lutea said, her head crooked to the side. "I like reptiles, dragons and my favorite colors are purple and turquoise!"

"How old are you?" A girl next to me asked.

Lutea pondered, leaning back in her chair. "I'm not entirely sure," she said. "But I might be somewhere in my hundreds."

Aiden's eyes widened and the girl's brows came together.

"Yeah right!" I exclaimed in laughter. I've heard this joke a bunch of times from Hannah and Ms. Hudson. "You don't look a day over nineteen."

Lutea smiled brightly, "Aw, thank you!"

Then a man's deep voice chortled from the other side of the room, "Don't flatter her. Her head's big enough as it is!"

"Tora, don't be mean!" Lutea chided back. From the light tone of her voice and the laughter radiating in the room, I realized it was playful banter between assistants.

Lutea asked about us and the girl next to me spoke up. Her name was Gabriella Caraballo and she lived with her father and grandmother. She liked to fly and was part of the honors program. Next was a boy, Lucas McKnight and everyone thought his last name sounded cool.

"I get that a lot," he said in response.

Fitting enough, he came from a family of knights and could trace his history as early as the Middle Ages.

"I guess it was common to have your last name based on your job," Lucas said with a shrug.

"Especially if it's a family business," Aiden remarked.

"Where are you from?" I asked him.

Aiden replied, "From the Eastern Pacific Islands. My mom's a story writer and my dad's a metal worker. I have a sister, Kaiah who goes to college and my little sister, Natia just started kindergarten."

"What brought you overseas?" Lutea asked.

"My dad was following a job after it changed locations. I've lived in a lot of cities and been to different schools. So far, I think we're staying in this area for a while. At least until Natia goes to college."

"Do you miss your home?" I said, suddenly.

He gave me a meaningful look. "All the time. My family upholds a tradition to go back every summer. Do you travel?"

"Not as much. I used to visit Japan to see the cherry blossoms every spring."

"Used to? You don't go anymore?"

My heart sank. There were a lot of reasons the tradition ended. Ichirou leaving, and me moving out of our parents' home.

"I'm sorry if that was too personal!"

I shook my head. "No, it's okay. One of the reasons I don't go is because it's gotten so expensive to travel."

"Ain't that the truth!" Lucas groaned.

"Tell me about it," Aiden agreed.

Another student chimed in, and it was at that time, I got up to get something to eat. On my way to the table, I couldn't help overhearing Ethan explaining where he came from. He lived in a cabin, deep in the woods with his family. He's the oldest of three siblings and they hunt together every night except during a full moon.

"Why the full moon?" a student asked, and I was curious to know as well.

"Hunting during a full moon is too cliché," he said. "It's an inside joke."

I would have asked about the inside joke, until I found Mr. Turner at another table.

"Long time no see," he said. "Enjoying yourself so far?"

"Yeah. When you said this was a club meeting, I wasn't expecting this."

"We do what we can to make everyone feel welcome. Do you have your homework with you? I'd like to look at it."

I almost forgot the reason Mr. Turner invited me. As much as I needed his help, I wanted to explore the room more and meet more people.

"I'll be right back."

I returned to the table where I left my backpack and took my homework to Mr. Turner. He quickly read through my answers.

"How come you don't grade the work?" I asked.

"I've tried to, but Mrs. Bean is paranoid that I might replace her."

"Can assistants do that?"

"It happens if a teacher is no longer available." Mr. Turner drew a pen from his pocket and in one swift motion, his signature appeared over my name. He did the same to the other pages. "That should do it."

"That's it?" my voice cracked, and my eyebrows came together at the signature. "I thought you were going to tutor me."

"You're doing better than you think. All your answers are correct, however," he added. "I still plan on tutoring if you have any questions. Come back tomorrow and we can start."

"That would be great!"

Relieved, I returned to my table, where Lutea was playing cards with Aiden and another group of kids. It looked like a game I used to play with Ichirou. I joined and never realized I could have so much fun being at school.

• ● •

But before I knew it, Miss Naiad announced that the meeting was ending. I checked my watch and was shocked to see it was already four. It felt like the meeting had started hours ago. All the food was eaten, and the students helped the assistants clean up before leaving.

I said my goodbyes to the assistants and Min on my way out and followed Aiden and the other students to the back doors and we went our separate ways. I walked to the school's main doors where I found Mary sitting by herself, reading a book.

I called out to her, "Hope I didn't keep you waiting!"

She looked over her shoulder. "Not at all," she said, closing the book. "How did the meeting go?"

"It went well. How was yours?"

Mary was about to answer, then a musical chime blared from her bag. "One moment, my dad's calling."

She pulled a bright pink phone from one of the pockets. She tapped the screen, turning off the chimes and spoke to someone whose low gruff voice could be heard from the other line.

Seeing her on the phone reminded me to check mine. I pulled it out of my backpack and my eyes widened at the missed calls and messages from Ichirou. How come my phone didn't go off during the meeting?

I texted Ichirou, *"No, I didn't get kidnapped. I didn't turn my phone off. The meeting just ended. Mary is giving me a ride home. Is that alright?"*

He replied, *"Call me if anything happens."*

"Okay, we're on our way," Mary said. She tapped the phone, ending the call and stood up. "My dad's waiting outside. Ready to go?"

"Yeah," I said.

I pushed the door open, and waves of the late August heat flooded inside. Parked on the street was a sleek black car and a man dressed in a blue shirt in the driver's seat. He had dark hair like Mary, with grey stripes near his temples, a perfectly shaved face and a pair of sunglasses that hid his eyes.

"Dad, this is my friend, Mayu," Mary said to the man. "Can you give her a ride home? She doesn't live that far from here."

Her father grumbled something which, according to Mary, meant "Yes." She opened the passenger door, and the cool air pulled me into the cold leather seats. In a low voice, Mr. Brown asked where I lived, his hidden gaze stared at me from the rear-view mirror. I gave him my address, and his brow rose above his sunglasses.

"Union Circle? You live in the college complex?"

"Seriously?!" Mary twisted around in the passenger seat to face me. The car had pulled away from the school. "How did you end up living with college students?"

91

I answered, tucking my head in my shoulders, "My brother and his girlfriend are going to college."

"And your parents are okay with that?"

"They made me move in with Ichirou."

Mary's jaw dropped. "Lucky you! You're practically living on your own."

"Not really. Ichirou can be more like a second dad than a brother at times."

"So, Mayu," Mr. Brown began, dragging my name. "Do you plan on going to college around here?"

"I never put much thought into college, yet. I wanted to wait until my third year."

"Thank you!" Mary heaved, throwing herself against the seat. "See Dad, not every freshman has college on their mind."

I had a feeling this was an ongoing conversation.

"Marietta," Mr. Brown stressed. "All I'm saying is that you can't read books and daydream forever. You need to think about your future."

Mary pouted, "What if I don't want to go to college?"

"Then what will you do after high school."

"Travel and explore the world, or something."

Mr. Brown groaned.

I shrank in the seat while they debated about college and tuition. Before I knew it, Mr. Brown had pulled up near the sliding door.

"Thank you for the ride." I said, trying not to sound too eager to leave. I slid out of the car and headed to the sliding door.

"If you ever need a ride back, let me know before school ends," Mary said.

"I will."

I waved goodbye to Mary and the car drove out of the complex. The instant I walked inside of the apartment, I was hit with the spiced scent of curry and sauté garlic coming from the kitchen.

"Welcome back, Runt," Ichirou announced. "Dinner is almost ready. Do you want a small plate?"

"Yes?" My answer came out more like a question.

The carpet had been vacuumed, and the TV screen and table were clean of dust. In the kitchen, Ichirou was standing in front of the stove, stirring curry in a pan.

"Did you stay home today?"

Ichirou shook his head. "My chest started to hurt on my way to class, so I drove to the hospital to get it checked out. It was a warning, but I called off work to be safe." He noticed my face change from curious to concern. "I'm fine. Spices clear my lungs up."

He wasn't sickly pale, or talking in a raspy voice, but it didn't stop me from worrying about his health.

"Let me know if you need any help." I said, then carried my backpack to my room.

"By the way, Elizabeth called not too long ago."

"Okay." It took a moment for Ichirou's words to register and when they did, I raced back to the kitchen. "When did she call?!"

"I think it was half an hour ago—she's not home!" He added before I could grab the house phone. "Elizabeth called from her dorm."

"Did she give you a number?"

"I asked, but she said she'll call back."

The joy in my chest evaporated. I slumped on the chair at the table, wishing I could have spoken to Elizabeth. But I would have missed the meeting I had gone straight home.

Ichirou set a plate of rice and curry in front of me along with a small bowl of salad.

"She'll call you back," he promised. "Elizabeth sounded a little sad when I told her you weren't home yet. She asked how you were doing."

"What did you tell her?"

"I told her you were fine. But she could ask you herself."

"Thanks," I said, feeling a bit better. "And thank you for the food."

"Anytime, Runt."

I dug into the meal, and when I finished, I heard Tuna mewing outside. She was on the grass, paws tucked beneath her, and her wide bright eyes trained on me.

"Ichirou..."

"Give her a small bowl," he said.

With that, I jumped out of my chair and skipped to the kitchen. Since I arrived home later than usual, I wanted to give Tuna something special to make up for it. I pulled some sandwich meat of the fridge and made her a small dish with slices of turkey, smoked ham and drops of fish oil for flavor. Finally, I topped her meal with a frozen shrimp from the freezer. I stepped back with my hands planted on my hips, admiring my creation.

Ichirou stared at it, eyes trailed up and down like a judge in a cooking show.

"In my personal experience working with only the finest of dishes," he started, and opened a cupboard over the stove. Ichirou pulled out a tall, dark green bottle of wine. A present from his job after working there for a year. "I'd recommend mademoiselle minou a fine Zinfandel if one wishes for a generous tip."

My pride dissolved into laughter. "Shut up."

Still, I carried the dish with one hand like a fancy waiter carrying an entrée to their customer. I set it on the grass and Tuna scarfed it. She licked off the fish oil, then bit into the meat when the scrape of the sliding door interrupted her. Her fur bristled, and she darted to the oak tree.

Ichirou stepped outside with his own plate.

"I think she still hates me," he said. "She hissed at me earlier when I came home."

"Well, I'd be mad if someone hosed me while I napped."

"She was on top of my car. She could have dented it."

"Are you calling Tuna fat!"

"She's one shrimp away from bringing down the tree, Runt." He sat beside me. "You can tell which branch she likes to sit on."

"Rude!"

He snickered. "So, are you feeling better?"

For a moment, I almost forgot what he meant. "Yeah. I know she'll call back, eventually."

"Good. I don't want you sulking over that and forgetting the entire day again."

"I know."

"How was the meeting."

He shared his portion with me while I told him about it, the members and the assistants. By the time we finished, the house phone rang. Ichirou went to answer and called me over.

"Told ya so," he murmured, giving me the phone.

My voice fluttered with excitement. "Hello?"

Elizabeth piped up, "Hey! I hope I'm not bothering you."

"You're never bothering me!" It was a relief to hear from her again. "How have you been?"

"I've been hanging in there. I can't believe we haven't spoken in weeks."

"I know!" I continued the conversation in my room. There was so much to tell her and so much to hear from her. She was shocked when I told her about the fights and fawned over the assistants.

"My school doesn't have those!" She exclaimed.

Elizabeth told me all about the classes she had, and I noticed we had a similar schedule, minus history.

"Is gym a senior elective at your school?" I asked.

"We have gym every year. It gets more advanced for each grade. I hear we do field exercises in our fourth year."

I scoffed, "Is your school training for the Olympics?"

"It would not surprise me."

What did surprise us was that we didn't join the track team yet. I told her track season didn't start until spring at my school. It was yearly at Elizabeth's school, but she wanted to join choir club instead. I thought it was fitting for her since Elizabeth had such a beautiful voice.

"I have good news!" she piped up. "Do you have any plans on September, twentieth?"

My face scrunched up, then I smiled. "Not that I know of. Got any plans for your birthday?"

"I'll be home all weekend, starting Friday. Would you like to spend time with us...Hello? Mayu?"

It was like all my dreams had come true at the same time. I screamed "yes!" and jumped around the room, like I'd won the lottery. "Why can't it be September already?"

"I know," she moaned. "Mom says she can pick you up. Would that be—"

I didn't hear her next words as a strange soft voice filled my ears, making me freeze on the spot.

"Hello? Are you there?"

I blinked, finding myself back in my room. "Huh? What—did you say?"

The words echoed in my head, then faded as Elizabeth spoke up.

"...Are you okay?" she asked. "Have you had any seizures?"

"Not recently."

I listened for that voice again and checked the windows. The sky had darkened with a violet haze on the horizon.

"It's gotten so late," I said.

"It has—it has!" Elizabeth shrieked. "I haven't started on my homework! I'll call you back tomorrow. I promise!"

"Y-yeah."

"Next month?" she repeated.

"Next month..." I agreed.

We ended our call after that. I sat in bed, clutching the phone. My chest tightened and my heart raced.

# Inquire

**I set the phone on my nightstand and counted the seconds on my watch**, dreading the numbness that would wash over me and cast my thoughts away. When distant traffic met my ears, I let out a shaky breath, relieved to know a seizure wouldn't happen. But uneasiness stirred in my chest.

"Mayu?" Ichirou called. The stairs creaked as he hurried to my room. "Are you okay? You got awfully quiet for a moment."

Not wanting to worry him, I lied. "Yeah, I got off the phone. Elizabeth invited me to a sleepover for her birthday. Can I go?"

"I don't see why not. But are you sure you're okay?"

"I am."

He gave me a skeptical look, then sighed, "Alright. I'm going to put the food away. I left a plate for Hannah, so if you want seconds, this is your last chance to get it."

"Got it."

Ichirou left my room, and I let out a relieved breath of air. As excited as it was to see Elizabeth, all I could think about was the voice. It was one thing to hear strange noises. It's another when the same sound returned. What could it mean? I should've told Ichirou, but he'd call Dr. Sanders and that would mean another trip to the hospital. Another scan and possibly more nights spent in a cold room.

*What if I can fix it myself?*

I sprang up from my bed and tiptoed to the bathroom. The mirror over the sink opened to a medicine cabinet full of cough syrups, and allergy medications, but what caught my attention was a bottle of small purple pills used to treat epilepsy. I used to take them twice a day and wouldn't have a seizure or sense an aura for weeks.

At first.

One day, I woke from a daze, hours after taking my medication. It worried me a little, but at the time I didn't put too much thought into it. A week later, I snapped out of another daze with no memory of what I'd done moments before. When I told Ichirou about it, he watched over me to make sure I took my medicine. He finally believed me when I had a seizure shortly after. I was in and out of the MRI and given different dosages, but with my seizures worsening, Dr. Sanders took me off the medication.

I wondered if I needed time off before taking them again.

*One way to find out.*

• ● •

Tuesday morning, I went to the bathroom to take my medication. Holding the pill in my hand, I berated myself for not telling Ichirou yesterday. It would have been one more thing for him to worry about and if the voice was an effect of a seizure, all I had to do was take the medication. I flushed the toilet to make my bathroom trip sound convincing, then used the running water from the sink to swallow the pill.

The rest of the day was normal overall. Mary and I finished our classwork, then I copied Aiden's notes while Mrs. Bean passed our graded homework. She must have been upset about Mr. Turner defending me because my paper was scribbled in red ink and a large "0" was scrawled over my name. I pushed down the urge to turn to her desk, knowing Mr. Turner would help me later.

And he did.

At the sound of the last bell, I hurried to the library, going down a set of stairs near the back of the school. There were fewer students, and it ended next to the library's back door. It truly was an easier path.

Min cheerfully greeted me at the clubroom's door, and the welcoming air pulled me into the room. I wandered around the tables, saying hello to assistants and students as I searched for Mr. Turner.

"Looking for Cedric?" said Miss Naiad.

She sat at the table with three girls, and a set of decorated cards laid out before her. Her chin rested on her hand as her hair swept over the side of her face. Miss Naiad pulled a card delicately between two fingers, her eyes flickered between the image on it, then me.

I stuttered, "Ma'am—Miss Naiad. Do you know—"

A soft laughter leapt from her. "No need to be formal. And there's no need to apologize either, little star."

My voice seized before I could say 'sorry' or call her ma'am again.

"Cedric is upstairs if you need him."

I blinked several times. "There's an upstairs?!"

Miss Naiad laughed again. "You didn't notice? It's been behind you the whole time."

Shocked, I turned around, taking in the clustered stones on the shelves and plants sprouting out of terrariums, stopping at the set of stairs reaching toward a raised floor. I climbed the steps, wondering how a classroom could have a second floor.

Three tables sat in front of a blackboard, facing Mr. Turner. I joined the students at one of the tables who had the same homework as I did. It didn't take long to realize we had Mrs. Bean's class at different periods, and it was clear I wasn't the only person she was giving a hard time to.

Mr. Turner began the lesson. He went over the formulas and examples, then drilled us until we could solve the problems on our own. We couldn't use calculators because Mrs. Bean had said one day, "why should I give you cheat codes for math? In gym, you don't pass because you wear gym clothes!"

But with his help, we didn't need calculators. I could focus with no one staring at me, and the math that seemed so difficult to solve in class was easy to figure out. If we had questions, even if it sounded silly or repetitive, Mr. Turner answered with such enthusiasm, I wished he was my algebra teacher instead.

After finishing our work, much faster than we would in class, Mr. Turner ended the session by signing every page. He said he wouldn't put it past Mrs. Bean to fail any work that didn't have his signature on it.

With tutoring over, and plenty of time to spare, I grabbed a plate of food and joined Aiden at the table with Lutea and the other members. We played games, spoke to each other and overall, had a good time.

For the next few weeks, I slipped into a steady routine. I'd take my medication in the morning, write notes with Mary in class, sketch with Lutea, hang out with Aiden during the meetings, and talk to Elizabeth as soon as I was home. I considered telling Ichirou and Hannah about the medication but seeing them struggle to adjust to school and work, I decided against it. Besides, I hadn't heard any weird voices or felt an aura so, maybe the medication was working. What they didn't know couldn't hurt them, right?

Before I knew it, it was September. The sleepover was on my mind so much, when I asked Mary to borrow a pen, I accidentally called her Elizabeth. I stopped myself, but Mary's confused expression told me she caught my mistake.

"Can I borrow a pen, Mary?" I asked, weakly.

"Sure." Mary handed me a spare pen from her bag. After a moment of awkward silence, she spoke up. "So... who is Elizabeth?"

"She's my best friend. We went to the same middle school."

"Does she go here?"

I shook my head. "Elizabeth goes to a private all girl's school called St. Laurel's Academy."

"Wait, you're friends with one of those rich girls," Mary whispered, her face was scrunched up. "Let me guess, she's a bit entitled? A little snobbish?"

"None of the above. Elizabeth's very nice."

"Oh, really?" Mary's hair swept over her eyes, hiding her expression, but I knew something was bothering her.

"Are you okay?"

She tucked a strand behind her ear, but her focus stayed on the book. "Back in junior high, there were a ton of girls who were accepted into St. Laurel's. They claim it was through merit, but really their parents just had deep pockets. They were all the same—rude, loud and obsessed with anything trendy. I always kept to myself, so I could never fit in with them. It would have been nice to have someone to talk to back then."

I nodded, understanding what she meant. "Are things different now?"

"Seems to be," She faced me with a small glimmer in her eyes. "I have you and the whole theater club. Its going to take time getting used to."

"It always does."

"That reminds me," she muttered. "If you have time, would you like to come to theatre club with me? It would mean so much if you were there."

My chest ached. As much as I wanted to, there were the tests to worry about. "We can do it after the exams, promise?"

"It's a deal."

In algebra, Mrs. Bean passed back our homework from the previous week, and she sat my homework upside down on my desk. Dread knotted in me as I lifted the paper, and my heart sank at the bright red "60" over my name. After class, I went straight to Mrs. Bean at her desk.

"What do you want now?" she grumbled.

"What's wrong with my homework? Why did you give me a sixty?"

"It's what you earned. Don't demand a better grade. You got to work for it like everyone else."

"But my answers were right, and I wrote them on the paper attached to it."

"Why was this on a separate sheet where it could get torn off?"

"I tried to write on the paper, but there wasn't enough room."

Mrs. Bean rolled her eyes. "I've said this a million times to write on your paper. Do you have a hard time listening? Or do you only listen to Cedric during your… meetings?" She sneered at the last word with revulsion.

Mrs. Bean never mentioned in class or in the syllabus about writing our answers on the same page.

"Mr. Turner only told us the answers need to be readable."

"And whose class is this exactly? Cedric's or mine?" Mrs. Bean sat up in her chair, locking her hands together. "Come on, tell me."

I glanced at Mr. Turner, who was writing math problems on the smartboard.

"Answer the question," she growled. "Whose class do you think this is?"

Gritting my teeth, I grounded out the word she wanted to hear. "It's yours."

"Exactly. I'm the teacher. I give the assignments and the grades. Cedric is an assistant. I don't care what a grown man does at your little club meeting, but in this class, you listen to me. If I say write your answers on one page, don't run to Cedric. Don't cry to Aiden. Do what you're told to do."

I glared at her.

"Don't get upset 'cause you can't have your way. Assistants aren't supposed to have favorites, anyway. They can lose their jobs that way, and if Cedric leaves, his signatures won't matter. Keep that in mind next time you want his help."

I pushed back a rising urge to scream and stomped out of the classroom. Aiden waited by the locker, toying with his headphone wires.

"That bad, huh?" he asked with concern. I didn't answer, but my expression must have given it away. "Don't let her get to you."

"Easy for you to say. It's not your grades on the line." My back pressed against the locker, my knees weakened and the anger in me vanished. Tears welled up as I slid onto the floor.

Aiden kneeled in front of me. "Look at it this way, sixty is still a passing grade and I hear you can change classes in October. So, you don't have to deal with her for long."

I shrugged weakly. October felt so far, and September started a week ago.

"Tell you what. Lucas and I are having a gaming event at the meeting. Y'know, relax before the exams and we could use an extra player."

"I'd like that," I sniffled. "Aiden, do you get tired of writing notes for me?"

A soft smile rose on his face. "If I had an issue, I would have told you. And have you heard me complain?"

"N-No."

"Then there's no problem." He stood up and reached for my hand. The warmth rushed through me as he pulled me to my feet.

"Holy crap, you're light as a feather!"

He laughed with such radiance a small laughter fluttered from my chest. After the bell, Aiden left for his class and I headed to lunch, drying up the remaining tears.

·•·

A thing about me and video games. My parents banned it from the house because of my seizures, but truth be told, I can play games if they don't have a lot of flashing screens or changing colors. Ichirou owned a few fantasy games, and he'd let me play as long as he was watching over me. One could never be too careful.

Fortunately, the game wasn't flashy. It was a single player fantasy game where the character had to fight colossal monsters.

Aiden and I joined Ethan, Teier, and Lucas in a small part of the room where a couch surrounded a big screen TV.

We took turns beating the monster. One was more difficult than the other. When it was my turn, I struggled to keep the character from losing their grip. The monster got me a few times, and I almost handed the controller to Aiden, but he cheered me on. I tackled the beast and after a few slips, the character plunged the sword into the monster, and I leaped off the couch with a cheerful cry.

"You put up a good fight!" Aiden held out his open, sweaty palm and we slapped our hands together in a firm shake.

"I appreciate it," I stuttered. A lightness knocked me off balance.

"Do you need to sit down?"

"Yeah." I stepped back and waited for the dizziness to wear off.

The meeting wasn't as crowded as it had been on my first day. Students and assistants were reading upstairs, conversing at the round tables or bunched up on the couch. What did the room used to be? I'd seen large lecture halls but never one at the back of the library or had its own stairs leading to another floor.

I passed by a few assistants, and my eyes caught one with brown, furry ears pointing out of her messy hair. It reminded me of cat ears on a costume. Then, when I almost bumped into an assistant, I thought I heard a hiss from her direction. I stepped through the door when Min called out to me.

"Are you leaving early?" She asked.

"No," I said, shaking my head. Min had what looked like a lot of homework on her desk. "I'm getting some fresh air."

"I didn't think that'd be a problem there."

It didn't' occur to me until she mentioned it, but you would think the room would get stuffy with so many people and food inside. Yet, the air always stayed cool and fresh, despite not having a window.

"Min, do you always sit by yourself?" I asked.

"I prefer to be alone. It's easier for me to do my studies."

"You're always sitting here. Do you ever leave?"

"It's my job to greet members as they come and go. And I leave around the time Miss Naiad does."

I stared at Min's glowing face. "Min...are you an assistant?"

For the first time since I met her, Min's welcoming face dropped. "What do you mean by that?"

"I never see you anywhere but here. I don't think I saw you during the meeting in the library. Where did you come from?"

Min hesitated. "I... uh, I'm Miss Naiad's assistant!"

"Miss Naiad is a teacher?"

"Y-Yeah!"

"What does she teach?"

Min squirmed in the chair. She sounded exactly like Elizabeth all summer. How hard was it to answer a question?

"Never mind," I turned to leave when Lutea stepped out of the room.

"Wondered where you went," she said.

"You were looking for me?"

"You seemed a little out of it in art. And Aiden told us you were dizzy after the game. Is everything alright?"

"I am," I said. "I just have a lot on my mind."

"Is this about Mrs. Bean? Cedric heard everything she told you."

"How could he? He was on the other side of the room."

Lutea was silent for a moment. "For what it's worth, he spoke with her after you left. She shouldn't have said those things to you."

I sighed, "Whenever he talks to her, she still takes it out on me. I think... I think I need some time alone."

"You don't look like you want to be alone."

"I do."

"...Okay."

●

Mary was at the main door, reading when she noticed me.

"You're here early. How'd tutoring go?"

"I skipped it," I said, guilt creeping up in me again.

"I hope everything is alright...where are you going?"

I stared at her, holding the door open. "Huh?"

"Mayu, dad isn't here yet. I texted you when you were in art that he was running errands, so he'll come by a little later."

I checked my phone and Mary's message was the first thing I saw. "Sorry, I'm not used to texting anyone other than my brother." I noticed Mary had asked me for another favor. "Did you still need help with a scene?"

She perked up. "Yeah, I was in the middle of reading it."

For the past few days, I had been helping Mary rehearse her lines for class and the theater club. She would give me her book, and no matter which scene I read aloud, Mary could recite the next lines. We were rehearsing long enough to finish a play and that made me check my watch to see it was almost four-thirty. I stood up, peeked through the school door with worry when Mr. Brown's sleek black car never appeared on the street.

"Mary, how late did you say your dad was going to be?" I asked.

"He should have called me by now." Mary set her book down and dug through the messenger bag, shuffling between journals and textbooks. Her brows pinched and her hands darted from the bag to its pockets.

"What's wrong?"

"My phone's missing!" Mary yelped. She flipped the bag over, dumping its contents in a small pile on the floor. Panic surged in her voice. "Does this thing have a hole in it?"

I looked around but didn't see Mary's flashy pink phone. "Where was the last place you had it?"

She pondered it, brushing her hand through her hair. "Dad texted me when I was in the library. I don't remember using my phone in the auditorium."

"Maybe it's still in there," I said. "There might be some assistants who can help us."

Mary scooped her books in her bag, and I slung my backpack over my shoulder. We headed to the library's backdoors but didn't open when I pulled the handles. When did they lock it? I stood on my tiptoes and peered through the window, and the library was completely dark.

*They left already?* I thought.

"See anyone?" Mary asked.

"No." I tugged the door handle again. It rattled and clanked like something was loose but didn't open. "The assistants must have locked this before they left..."

"I didn't see them leave through here," Mary pointed out. "Did they go through the front door?"

"That's locked too," I said. "There might be someone inside. If we wait for them now—"

"Mayu, I need my phone now," Mary pressed.

"How are we going to get in?"

"Well," she looked away, tucking a lock of hair behind her ear. "I sort of know a shortcut."

Mary turned around, and I followed her down the hallway to the main doors. She rounded the corner and, after passing a few classrooms, Mary stopped in front of a door propped open with a janitor's cart. No one was around to see us sneak inside.

"Mary, what is this?" I asked.

The room had tiered seats leading down to a podium. Definitions of words that I'd vaguely heard of covered the blackboard. My eyes locked on a wide window where the gazebo stood, draped in a curtain of vines.

"This is English Advance Placement," Mary said. "Sometimes my teacher lets us read outside and recite our lines under the gazebo."

"But I thought we were going to the library," I said, confused.

"We are. The courtyard connects to the library, and the keys work on all doors."

Mary circled to the teacher's desk and pulled one of the drawers open. Rustling papers and clanking metals filled the room, followed by jingling keys hanging off a ring in Mary's hand. Realizing what she was doing, I adjusted my backpack and hurried to a slim black door near the teacher's desk. Mary unlocked it with a dull clack, but it felt like we were pushing against a wall of bricks.

I grunted, "What is this thing made of?"

"You got me," Mary strained. "My teacher makes it look so easy when he opens it."

As the door widened, the scent of plants and blooming flowers rushed into the classroom. Mary and I slipped outside and paused to catch our breath. I jumped at the loud click and whipped back to the closed door.

"Don't worry, it locks on its own," Mary explained. "As long as we have the key, we won't be stuck inside of the courtyard."

Mary was confident about it, so I tried not to worry about it.

The courtyard looked like a secret garden. Butterflies leaped off the coneflowers, and yellow daises lined the walls. Birds peeped through their nests and little houses with leaves for walls and a flower bulb for a roof.

"You read here all the time?"

Mary smiled. "Amazing, isn't it? I heard the assistants helped make this courtyard."

"They certainly went out of their way..."

Our footsteps echoed off the winding cobble stone path leading to an identical door, coated in moss with thin roots clinging at the edges.

"Doesn't look like this has been used in ages," I murmured.

"Weird, since this key works on both doors," Mary said. "When you told me about the assistant's meeting, I thought it was going to happen here."

"I thought the same thing, but I realized the courtyard would be too small for so many people," I said.

"So, they have it in the library?"

"Sort of. It's in a big room at the back. I can show you if you like."

"I still need to find my phone first."

Mary unlocked the door. A sharp screech tore from its hinges when it opened. Covering my ears, we hurried inside, and the carpet softened our footsteps. The loud click cut the sound of nature behind us, replacing it with a deafening silence.

# Shift

**The sunlight barely touched the tables** near the shelves, leaving the library cloaked in shadows. Our nervous breaths echoed as we looked around. Then Mary asked the obvious question.

"Where are the assistants?"

I stared at the old, tall shelves. "They could be cleaning in the other room."

Miss Naiad made sure everybody cleaned up before the meeting ended. She said she would "tan our hides" if we left a paper ball on the floor. But wouldn't we have heard movement or the assistants leaving the room?

"I'm going to call your phone," I said and dialed Mary's number. At the first ring, loud musical chimes broke the silence. We darted to the old shelves, following the ringing until a small, bright screen flashing on the floor caught my attention.

"Found it!" I cried, snatching up the phone, before the ringing came to a stop.

Mary exhaled with relief. "Thank you so much! I don't know what I'd do without this."

"Good thing we found it here." My smile started to fade away as I felt the shadow of the old shelves looming over our heads. "Why would your phone be here?"

Mary followed my gaze. "I go through here to get to the theater club, it's much easier than taking the front door."

"Oh," I said, feeling like an idiot. Here I thought the back door was a secret route that only the assistants and the members knew. "Does that mean you've met Min?"

"Who's Min?"

"She sits at a desk outside of the meetings."

Mary's crooked brow matched mine. "That's odd, I've never seen a girl at a desk or a room back here."

"I can show you. She's not that far from here."

But Mary looked hesitant. "Maybe another time, we got to go back. Dad could be here any minute."

"Sure. We'll probably run into Min, anyway."

As I said that, something Min had mentioned came back to me. She was always at her desk before the last bell, which wasn't far from the back door. Mary couldn't have missed her more than once or ran into an assistant on her way out of the library.

That was when a thought occurred to me, did I run into an assistant after school? They were always at the meeting no matter how early or late I was. Lutea would stay in art until the last student left, yet somehow, she would be in the clubroom before me.

How come I never noticed that?

I snapped out of my thoughts when I realized Mary hadn't spoken up. I circled back to the aisle, now empty as if she was never there.

Worry surged in my chest. "Mary? Where'd you go?"

I called her phone, but instead of a dial tone, a dead silence met my ears. I paced down the aisle, my hands trembled as I called her again, yet my phone and the library stayed quiet. I rounded the shelves and shouted Mary's name, until I came to a stop in front of Min's empty desk and the clubroom door beside it.

I would be so excited to go to the meetings, so eager to get my homework done and spend time with my friends that I never paid close attention to the door itself. The glass didn't show the room, but a solid black entrance drawing in the air like the mouth of a cave. A knotted pattern carved into the wooden frame trailed up to a symbol of wings sprouting from four arrows that pointed in different directions.

"This isn't real," My breath shortened. "This isn't real..."

I stumbled back, feeling a horrible, itchy shock creeping up my spine. I had to leave. I had to get out of here! I whipped around but the shelves pulled away and the floor lent up. My body lurched back, and a cold force crashed into me. Darkness flooded the library and muffled the scream before it escaped my throat.

A crashing boom and a jolt of pain wrenched me awake to strong currents pushing me down. Crackling light flashed around a dark mass, and a deep, hollow roar bellowed in my ears. My heart raced, but I couldn't move. My throat rippled, but I never heard myself scream. My eyes rolled back as my thoughts drifted.

Specs of light danced in my blurry vision as hushed leaves and bird cries met my ears, bringing me to wakefulness. My movements were sluggish when I rolled to the side, my joints ached, and my limbs felt like I was dragging wet sandbags through mud. A typical feeling after waking up from a grand mal seizure.

The medication didn't work after all. I should have known better. The dreadful sensation I felt was an aura, and it caused me to see the strange markings on the door.

"Mary..."

A chime-like bell drew me to a cluster of leaves where I found my glasses on the ground. A butterfly was perched on top of them with bright blue wings, as if they were glowing. Reaching for my glasses startled the butterfly, and it took off, its wings let out the same chime as it fluttered toward the trees.

Parts of my brain must have been waking up, I thought. I put my glasses on, and my vision cleared up as I slung my backpack on my shoulder. I sat up slowly from the bed of leaves, noticing the sprawling roots leading to the stone wedged into the tree. It was terribly aged and caked in moss, yet I could still make out the strange symbols carved across its surface.

My brow furrowed, my mind asked if I was hallucinating. A few threads of sunlight broke through the thick leaves above, revealing more standing stones circling the tree.

A hard lump swelled in my throat.

"M-Mary!" I shouted and the leaves burst into applause, stifling my shaking voice. I heard claws skittering and movements shuffling through the tall grass. Chirps, yips and shrieks leaped across the canopies. Crooked branches groaned over me, some locked together with other massive trees.

I jerked back and let out an echoing shriek when the ground gave way. I quickly caught myself before I fell and spun around to see what I stumbled from. They were old stone steps, half engulfed wiring plants and shuddering grass.

Falling leaves drew me to the trembling branches. Small animals darted in different directions as the air rumbled, before I registered the ground shaking beneath me.

My first thought was an earthquake, until I realized the pebbles chipping off the stones, the branches raining down on me, and the rumbling drawing closer as the shaking grew stronger.

There's no promise that anything capable of making the forest shake would be friendly. I frantically searched for a place to take cover in. A colossal tree with a hollowed-out trunk caught my attention and I scampered toward it. I barreled through the shrubbery, crawled beneath the hanging vines and tucked myself at the back of the cavity.

Spiders scattered from the crevices and dust trickled over me as booming voices rose with the approaching tremors. I heard voices shouting in another language, wheezing breaths and knocking hooves beating the ground.

"Keep your eyes sharp and have your flares ready!" a woman commanded, her voice was deep and brute. "Fan out for anything that doesn't look like it belongs here."

A few grunts answered and the trembling continued down the path.

"Whatever opened a gate this far out is clearly not of our world!"

"It could have been a sudden activation. Or the gate didn't properly close," a young woman said, and her familiar voice made my heart skip a beat.

Lutea.

Questions raced through my mind. I covered my mouth to hide my panicked breath and listened to their conversation.

"What is this?" Lutea murmured. "A... backpack?"

My heart stopped. I was so scared, I didn't realize my backpack slipped off my shoulder. I sat frozen in the tree, my mind raced between staying hidden or revealing myself.

"So, something did come through!" the brute woman snarled. "We must proceed with caution!"

"Hang on," Lutea pleaded. "There might be something inside that can tell us who this belongs to."

I shifted to peek through the leaves when a branch beneath my feet snapped, and the loud, dry pop halted the movements.

I pressed my back against the tree, shuddering at the insects crawling down my shoulder. I hoped if I stayed still and quiet, no one could hear me, but it felt like everything heard my loud, pounding heart and shaky breath. Footsteps rounded the tree, and a pair of hands parted through the leaves.

"Mayu?" Lutea's voice was a mix of shock and confusion. "I-Is that you?"

Hesitant, I opened my eyes to see her kneeling down.

Her eyes widened, "Oh gods, it is you!"

I struggled to say her name but realizing it was my friend, I crawled out of the tree and threw my arms around Lutea's waist and buried my head on her shoulder. Her hand gently stroked my head and patted the insects off my clothes.

"It's okay, I got you," she said, softly. She carefully slung my backpack on my shoulders. "How did you end up here?"

"Library," I stuttered out. "Mary and I were...were..."

My voice wedged in my throat when an olive toned woman peered around the tree. She had long, black hair braided over her shoulder, long slanted ears and a pair of fierce, stormy grey eyes. At first, I thought she was extremely tall until I noticed the sheening black fur on her waist, covering four knobby thin legs, and shiny hooves embedded in the ground.

Lutea called my name again, but my eyes stayed on the woman and the people crowding around us. Half humans with the lower body of a horse, carrying sleek silver bows and quivers strapped around their broad shoulders. It was one thing seeing centaurs in movies, but it was another having them stare at me, hands curled around their bows and hilts of swords.

"What is a scholar doing this far out?" The brute woman's demands came from the first centaur. "Why is she staring at us like that?"

"Melanippe," Lutea called to her. "This one isn't from here."

The centaur, Melanippe stared at me, then her eyes suddenly sharpened. She unslung a bow from her shoulders, and I shrieked at the arrow aimed at me. As if on cue, the other centaurs had their arrows drawn or raised their swords until Lutea quickly turned her back to me and stretched her arms.

"Don't shoot!" she commanded. Then she glared at Melanippe. "What are you doing!"

"She is not from here!" Melanippe roared. "She must be the anomaly!"

"She's not—I know her from school. She's not going to harm us!"

"You knew she could do this?"

"No!"

"All the more reasons to take caution with this one! She's a threat for all we know!"

"For all we know, something could have brought her here. Lower your weapons," Lutea repeated sternly. "Let Galumine sort this out."

Melanippe held her glare, then in a sharp sigh, she slipped the bow around her shoulder.

"Aposýromai!" She commanded and the centaurs lowered their blades but never sheathed it.

Lutea breathed out, but I stayed, frozen to the ground.

"You're going to be okay. Let's take a moment to—"

She never finished her sentence. I felt her hand on her shoulder and a sudden flash of light blinded me. My back cracked against the ground on impact, and loud booms thundered around me. Lutea dragged herself up from the underbrush a few feet away from me. Two centaurs hurried to Melanippe who was on the ground. Before I could move, my heart seized up as a dozen arrows were aimed at me.

"Move, and we fire!" a centaur hissed.

My voice broke.

Melanippe's trembling legs pushed her to stand, looking taller than before. Her thunderous eyes shot at me as if she was about to strike me at any second.

"You cursed child!" she bellowed, rearing up on her hind legs. "What did you do!"

I bolted from her and the centaurs exploded into chaos. I swerved from slamming bodies and ducked beneath swiping arms. Someone snatched me by my backpack and lifted me off the ground until my arms slipped through the straps.

I wounded around the trees and charged toward a narrow gap when something whistled past my ear, forcing me to stop. An arrow was buried deep in the trunk where my face would have been, its fletching shuddered inches from my face.

"Mayu!" Lutea screamed.

My body acted faster than my mind could. I whipped around, seeing Lutea one moment before my foot slipped on the ground. The world flipped and a sharp pain burst in the back of my head. I tumbled into a ditch and looked up to Lutea standing above me with her back turned.

"Stop firing!" She shouted.

She swung her arm and pieces of arrows rained on me. Panic forced me to my feet, and I ran as fast as my legs could carry me.

112

The muddy ground caught my shoes, and I tumbled down a mossy slope. Branches struck my face and roots caught my ankle, knocking me down. But I dragged myself up and ran until the voices grew quieter.

The instant I stopped, my muscles cramped up, my knees buckled down and I collapsed on the grass, panting out of breath. I laid on my back and listened for the hooves, but only heard soft chimes, gentle brushes from leaves and streaming water. The warm breeze carried a potent scent of the forest, that I could taste it.

"It's all real, isn't it?" I muttered in a deep breath. "All of this is real."

My shirt was ripped and covered in mud, my shoes slipped off and my knee-high socks were torn apart. If I wasn't so exhausted, and frightened, I would have been impressed with how far I made it bare feet in a forest. I patted the dirt off my blouse and skirt, and felt my phone in my pocket.

I didn't care how it stayed inside, nor did I know who to call. The screen lit up and a wave of relief crashed in my chest. Tears watered my eyes, and I pushed the first button, nine—

A sharp light burst in my hand, blinding me. I shrieked and tossed the phone away. I rubbed my eyes and the second I realized what I did, I quickly reached for my phone and found it charred, its screen cracked and burnt beyond recognition.

"No!" I scooped up the pieces, hoping the phone could somehow work in its state, but there was nothing I could do to fix it. My mind raced on what to do. My only means of contact were in pieces and it was only a matter of time before the centaurs caught up to me.

I don't know how long I sat there before a soft bell rang in front of me. A sparkling blue butterfly crawled over the remains of my phone.

*This couldn't be the same one*, I thought. *Could it?*

"Are you ...following me?" I asked. The familiar chime met my ears and almost cried in relief. The butterfly leapt from my phone and landed delicately on my trembling hand.

"You were there when I woke up here. Can you help me?"

With the flap of its wings, the butterfly took off, soaring to one of the trees. I followed its darting movements, balancing over the roots until it vanished beyond the leaves. I listened carefully for the chimes, straining my hearing when somebody said, "Fine creature, isn't she?"

"Ah!" I jumped back, losing my footing and fell in a pile of bushes. The phone and its pieces flew out of my hands. "Ow…"

A woman chuckled. Her voice was soothing, nothing like Melanippe's. "Didn't mean to startle you."

An outstretched hand reached out to help me, but it was the markings that caught my attention. Circular patterns swirled around her dark wrist, shimmering like light rippling off water as it trailed up her arm and crossed her face, disappearing beneath waves of soft, snow-white hair. My eyes narrowed at a pair of rigid horns crowning the side of her head.

"Be not afraid," she spoke smoothly. "I am here to help you. To guide you out of here."

I hesitated at first, pulling back for a second before my hand settled on hers. The instant we connected, brushes of air swirled around me. The mud on my face dried and flaked away, and the leaves untangled themselves from my hair. Water droplets wiped away the grind and my clothes mended themselves back together. I even felt my feet slide into my shoes.

"Good as new!" she cheered. "Hard to believe one so small is the anomaly I've been hearing about. You are more like a griffin cub who fluttered too soon off her nest."

I stared in shock. "How did you do that?"

"Would you believe… magic?" She chirped with a playful grin. "I am relieved you weren't hurt. All of that running and not so much as scratch." She pulled away and straightened her back. "Now that you're cleaned up, Mayu, you can follow me with no problem befalling us."

The leaves near her slipped away, revealing a winding path, but my feet stayed rooted to the ground.

"H-How do you know my name?" I asked, timid at her appearance, but in awe with the path that opened before her.

"The trees have heard you and Lutea. And word travels fast around here." She walked ahead, her off-shoulder dress trailed across the ground.

My attention still focused on the woman's face. There was something familiar about her and then it hit me.

"Wait, I know you!" I blurted, and the woman stopped "You came to the club's first meeting…You were at the table with Miss Naiad and Mr. Turner."

I thought it was her. I would have remembered someone with horns, white hair and glowing tattoos on at the first meeting, though.

"Quite observant, aren't you, little cub," The woman mused. "My true form can be overwhelming to many children, so I chose to hide it under illusions. I am Galumine, Keeper of Erehwon."

"Erehwon?"

She pursed her lips. "Ever hear tales of mystical worlds of sort? Agartha, Shangri-La or Tir na nog?"

"I have. B-But it's not real... right?"

Galumine's eyes showed no hint she was joking. "You were chased by centaurs, yet you doubt the existence of other worlds?"

"I'm still trying to believe centaurs chase me!"

"Fair enough." Galumine moved down the weaving path, creaking branches bowed to her presence and the plants on the ground parted before her.

"In truth," she continued. "Erehwon is a world much like the lands of legend you've heard about. It is a home where those you call 'mythical creatures' are as real as the earth and skies. You've met them before."

I mumbled, "No offense, but I'd rather not meet another centaur."

Galumine frowned. "I am truly sorry. Melanippe and Lutea were sent to apprehend you under my orders, so I take full blame for what happened. However, I was not referring to them. You've met them before you came here. I believe some are in your class."

I looked up at her, taking in the markings on her face and the horns glinting under the sunlight. She gestured to an opening tucked between two trees drenched in moss and vines, but her words hung in my thoughts.

Then two voices came from beyond the trees. One was Melanippe spilling out apologies after apologies to someone. Remembering her fierce glare and booming demands, I wouldn't have imagined her speaking softly.

I turned to Galumine. Her eyes, warm and gentle, reminded me of my days in primary school, where I was holding my mom's hand because I was too scared to leave her side.

"They will not harm you." Galumine promised. She led me into a clearing of grass that brushed against my kneecaps. Curtains of water flowed through small channels and spilled from arching ruins into large ponds. It was so still and clear, it reflected off the garden of old, cracked pillars dressed in greenery.

Melanippe's voice drew me to the side. She was apologizing again, and someone responded. Sitting on an overturned pillar,

Lutea was consoling her. Without thinking, I ran to her, calling her name.

"Mayu!" She caught me in her embrace again. "I thought we lost you! You're not hurt, are you?"

"No. What about you?" My eyes fell to the holes torn through her white shirt and pants, but there wasn't a scratch or a drop of blood on her.

"It's okay, I'm alright—no, don't run!" She grabbed my arm before I could run from Melanippe. But she looked ahead, her legs bent forward as she kneeled and pressed her arm across her chest.

My brow furrowed until she said, "Mistress," and I realized, as I turned around, she was speaking to Galumine. "Forgive me, I didn't mean to lose her from my sight."

"At ease. You did what you could, my friend. How are the others?"

"Everyone has returned to their positions, awaiting my command, but..." Melanippe steered back to me. "With all due respect, I'd like to know what is going on before I leave."

Lutea spoke up first. "Mayu must have fallen through the door in the library. But it should have closed by the time everyone left."

"Not always. Not entirely," said Galumine. "However, no one should have been in the library so late. What were you doing there, Mayu?"

I stammered, explaining how Mary and I snuck into the library to find her phone, and a rush of fear came over me.

"What happened to Mary! She disappeared when we tried to leave!"

"No, you did," Galumine stated. "The spell placed on the invitations works so only those who signed it, then returned it to Min, can find my gates. Anyone else would simply see a regular library while it's active. Once closed, the gate will disappear."

My voice lifted. "So, Mary's alright?"

"Most likely, if she is still looking for you."

"I need to let her know I'm okay!"

Melanippe interjected. "We need to know how you crossed over!"

"Is it really a big deal?"

"It is a great deal!" she shouted, immediately calming down when Galumine raised her hand.

"What my friend means is that the space between worlds is dangerous. Usually, we'd use spells or relics to traverse safely from this world to yours. So, it's unusual that someone with no

116

protection crossed over intact. But... it would seem you don't know how it happened, either."

I shook my head.

"What should we do?" Lutea asked.

"I say she stays here under watch until we find answers," Melanippe suggested. "It would be a risk to let her go."

"She has family and friends that are bound to look for her. Keeping her here would be risky too."

Galumine stared at me, like she was looking into my thoughts. "You wish to go home, don't you?" she asked.

This was too much to take in. Everything I wanted to say and ask came out in stutters. "I do, but I want to know what's happening here. Why am I here? What is here?"

"We will find answers in time. But not now. Your friend has waited long enough."

Galumine raised her arm and water poured over the arch. Through the rippling waves, I saw the library bled into view.

"The gate to your world will remain open so long as I allow it."

"Miss," said Lutea. "Can I go with her. I'd like to make sure she is home and given what's happened, she may need someone to talk to."

"You may," Galumine said, softly.

Lutea stood beside me and managed to smile. "Are you ready?"

Despite my uneasiness, I gave her a small nod. I'll admit, I found myself holding Lutea's hand on our way to the entrance.

"It's okay, I got you," she whispered.

I stared at the library, recognizing the aisle leading to the clubroom door. Knowing this, my hand tightened around Lutea, bracing for what's to come. I stepped forward and the clamor of nature fell silent. I was standing on the carpeted floor, surrounded by walls of vintage books.

"Never gets old!" Lutea gasped. "You did good, Mayu. Are you feeling okay."

I choked on my words. "Is this real? The centaur, the forest and Galumine, all of this is real?"

Her smile faded. "There's nothing to fear from us we're—"

"I had an arrow shot at me! A woman with horns told me I was in another world and that the assistants are mythical creatures!" my voice trembled. "A-Are you?"

Lutea stayed silent.

I stepped back, my heart raced in my ears. I tore my gaze from Lutea and ran to the back doors, gripping the handles and yanking as hard as I could, making a loud metallic clunk that echoed across the library.

"Mayu," Lutea called quietly and concernedly. "Do you want to talk about this?"

"I'm fine." I pulled the handle, but the door stayed closed. "I need to find Mary."

"You don't look fine to me."

"I am!" I wrenched the door handle again, but it wouldn't open!

"You're not supposed to pull it." Lutea nudged the door open. "Are you okay?"

I stared at her, arms trembling and palms sweating. My thoughts screamed at me to run away, but all I could do was utter a shaky, "No..."

Lutea said with a deep sigh, "I know, you've been through a lot. I won't stop you if you need to get away from us."

I wanted to talk to her, but at the same time, she frightened me. They all did. I didn't want to be in the library anymore. I didn't want to think about this anymore. Lutea gave me such a caring gaze that hurt me when I pushed the door aside and walked away. Bright lights and vibrant red lockers stung my eyes but felt all the more real.

"Mayu!" Mary exclaimed, racing down the hall from the school's main doors. Her appearance made my heart leap into a pounding sprint.

"What happened to you?" she cried. "I thought you left me the library!"

"I wouldn't! I... I couldn't find you."

"How? You were right behind me."

"How long was I gone?"

Before Mary answered, something buzzed in my skirt. Confused, I reached in my pocket and my eyes widened, seeing my phone in one piece. It was good as new, smooth without a crack and the screen was beaming with Hannah's number. I answered and her angered voice blew up in my ear.

"Where have you been!" She yelled. "Why haven't you been answering your phone?"

I pulled the phone away. "I'm sorry, I'm at school right now."

"Well, do you want a ride? I'm in front of the school."

Apologizing to Mary, I pushed the door opened and a heatwave slammed into me. I hurried to Hannah's blue car and apologized to her once I was inside.

"You're fine," she insisted. "What happened? You didn't pick up for almost an hour."

I stuttered, feeling my mouth turn dry and cottony. My vision blurred and Hannah's voice grew distant, drowned out by a different voice ringing in my ears.

*Can you hear me? Can you hear my voice?*

# Confrontation

**Ichirou and I arrived at the hospital the next morning.**

While waiting in the lobby, my mind was piecing together what happened yesterday. Hannah told me I had a seizure in her car; my eyes were vacant, and I was mumbling something under my breath, then I woke up at home, drained of energy and sluggish until nightfall.

My memories were hazy at first. I remembered sneaking into the library with Mary, but details of the forest broke through the daze and the centaurs, Galumine, Lutea and her words surfaced back to me in almost perfect clarity.

"Hinamori?" A nurse called.

Ichirou and I stood up and followed her through a maze of hallways into one of the rooms. Moments later, Dr. Sanders arrived and promptly gave me a checkup. He put the cold stethoscope on my chest and asked the usual questions: have I been feeling sick or dizzy? I told him I felt lightheaded after playing a video game at school.

"Are they teaching game design?" He asked jokingly.

"It was after school," I corrected, smiling.

Dr. Sanders continued his questions, asking if I've been stuttering more than usual or lost my sense of balance lately? I answered 'no' and then he asked if I was taking any medication. Biting my lip, I told them I was taking my old prescriptions after hearing a voice in my head. I could see the confusion on Ichirou's face while Dr. Sanders wrote something on the clipboard.

His brow arched with interest, "As I recall, your medication didn't work, and you often hear voices when an aura hits. Why is this one different?"

"Because it always came back," I answered.

"When did you first hear it?"

"I think I heard it last time I was in the hospital, then again at school, last week and yesterday."

Rather than ask why I didn't bring it up before, Dr. Sanders jotted more notes on the clipboard. "What would this voice say?"

"'Can you hear me?' 'Can you hear my voice?'" Repeating those words aloud raised goosebumps on my arms. "Then... I had a weird dream last night."

"What was so weird about it?"

I said, lowly, "I wasn't sure if I was dreaming or not. I was lying in bed and there's a shadow standing over me."

"Was it the shadow who spoke to you?"

"No, it didn't say anything. It only moved closer as the voice spoke." I felt Ichirou's hand stroking my back and my shoulders stopped trembling.

Dr. Sanders sat in silence, tapping the pen against the clipboard like he needed a moment to absorb it all. Four years ago, he told me he worked with other patients with epilepsy and different conditions that made them hear voices or see imaginary things, so whatever I said should have sounded normal to him. Except the way he leaned back in his chair to take a breath made me wonder if this was weird for him to process. He asked a lot of questions about the voice and the shadow; did they threaten me? Did I recognize the voice? I shrugged and told him it only asked if I could hear it.

"Did it sound like a boy or a girl, man or woman?"

"I don't know. It sounded like it could be a boy or a girl. Or both."

"Androgynous, then," he muttered. That must have been his last question because he set the clipboard aside and told me to be ready for a scan.

The MRI went by quickly, but it took Dr. Sanders a long time to return with the results. In the patient room, I sat on the bed, toying with a string that was coming off my old t-shirt.

"So, when were you going to tell me about the medication?" Ichirou asked. "I thought they didn't work anymore."

I took a quick glance at him before my eyes fell back to the floor. "They worked at some point."

"...until you had a seizure and Sanders took you off of it. Runt, I know you can hear me." I stopped fidgeting with my shirt and looked up. Ichirou had his eyes on me, and his arms crossed over his chest. "Out with it. What's going on?"

I nudged my glasses to my face, feeling the guilt gnaw at me "I wanted to see Elizabeth again and was worried I'd have another seizure like in August."

Ichirou was about to say something, when Dr. Sanders shimmied through the door. "Sorry, the printer jammed," he said and sat in the rolling chair. He hung the pictures against a lit wall and the room went silent. There were two dark patches on my brain. A sliver of dread swelled in me. My hands closed tightly around the ends of my shirt.

"Good news, they are not tumors," Dr. Sanders started. "You can put that thought to rest." He looked at me, and I didn't realize it scared Ichirou until both of us sighed in relief.

"So, what are they?" Ichirou asked.

"And that's the strange news. There's no sign of injury and they're not harming the brain. When we were monitoring your MRI scan, the shapes appeared and faded away. I'll have them re-examined. If we find anything, you'll be the first person we call."

That didn't help. It was never good news to me if a doctor didn't know what it was.

"Aside from that," Dr. Sanders rotated the chair and sat down, meeting my gaze. "It doesn't take a doctor to know when someone is under a lot of stress. You're more tense than before. Having problems with your friend?"

I squirmed in my seat, wondering what to tell Dr. Sanders. "I have a math teacher who's been giving me a hard time."

He snorted, "It's always the math teachers. Anything else?"

I shook my head.

"Sounds like you're under a lot of stress, which can trigger a seizure. As for the dream, you may have experienced sleep paralysis. It's not unusual, and it's commonly associated with stress as well. Have you been running track again?"

"Track season doesn't start until winter. We only play volleyball and basketball in gym." I told him.

"Exercise a bit and play some sports to take your mind off things." Then he added in a firm voice. "And stop taking the medication. You should have thrown those out a year ago."

Ichirou and I nodded.

We left the hospital, and Ichirou detoured to one of the fast-food restaurants nearby. I scolded him lightly for going there, shortly after leaving the doctor's office.

"Dr. Sanders said I needed to eat healthy food," I reminded him.

"One fry won't kill you," Ichirou teased. He ordered a burger and fries, and I got a salad bowl and a yogurt parfait. The drive was mostly quiet before Ichirou spoke up.

"Runt?" he said. He had a drink in one hand and steered the car with the other. "I'm not mad at you for taking the medication, but you didn't have to keep it a secret."

"I'm more worried about the things in my head."

Ichirou placed the drink in the cup holder and focused on driving. "Like he said, he'll have someone else look at it."

"What do you think those things were?"

"I know about as well as you do. Sanders could be right about the stress causing it. You haven't seen Elizabeth in months, and you have Mrs. Bean, of all people. She's nothing but a hassle. That could mess with your head, and make you hear things. So, take it easy for now until the results come back."

Ichirou pulled up to the apartment to drop me off before he went to college. It was my idea to stay home. Hannah had gone to class and Elizabeth was still in school and wouldn't call me until five. For the next hour, I sat at the table, nibbling on my salad, and writing my homework. It wasn't something I liked to do in my spare time, but it kept my thoughts busy.

When I finished, I sat on the porch to relax my mind. I hoped Tuna would visit me. Sometimes she'd sleep under the bushes in front of our apartment or hunt around the dumpster for mice. Though I caught some movements between the leaves, they turned out to be squirrels. They raced up the oak tree where birdsongs echoed from the branches.

Those sounds paled in comparison to the orchestra of life from the forest. The oak tree looked like a dandelion compared to the behemoth trees that towered over each other. It was a scary thought knowing another world exists elsewhere, and the creatures there were as real as the people around me. But the people around me weren't entirely what they seemed to be, either.

I needed answers.

I went inside the apartment, closed the screen door and headed upstairs. Ichirou didn't mind me using the desktop in his room, but I had to stop by my room to grab a sweater first.

Ice Bear used to be Ichirou's nickname because he always kept his room cold and dark like a cave in the arctic. He says it helps him breathe but Hannah and I could never figure out how he could sleep like a rock when his room was like a second freezer.

Even with the sweater on, I shivered upon opening the door. Thin rays of light peeked through the black curtains, tracing across the queen-sized bed. Between that taking up most of the space, and the books stacked on the floor, there was little room for me to walk to his desk. How Ichirou never trips over anything here is beyond me.

I sat on the chair and turned on the monitor, then searched through the mural of sticky notes on the wall for the log-in password. There were numbers and to-do lists, random sketches and photos of Ichirou and Hannah on their various dates. My cheeks burned when I spotted my ten-year-old self, an old photo from picture day. I had straight, shoulder length hair, bangs that covered my forehead and a pair of round, silver glasses too big for my face.

I muttered, shaking my head, "I can't believe he still has this."

My eyes fell on a green sticky note beneath the picture. "Password" was written on it, along with a string of numbers and letters.

"Worth a shot." I typed it in and logged in at an instant.

I looked up "Erehwon" and clicked on the first article about it. Erehwon was used to describe a place of mythical beings found in different cultures at different times. In some beliefs, it was called the Isle of Demons, an island shrouded in mist, that appeared in the human world every century. It was said to be home of ferocious monsters, but in another paragraph, it was called the Sheba Garden, a beautiful world where fantastical creatures and immortals lived, and those immortals would offer blessings to chosen humans.

Other names included Lemuria, Tir Na Nog, Axis Mundi, Mahoroba, and Mount Olympus. That last place sparked a memory about centaurs being part of Greek Mythology. So were nymphs and... *naiads*! I slapped the side of my forehead, remembering the naiads were water spirits in the lore. But... would a naiad call themselves Miss Naiad? Better yet, were the assistants immortal beings?

I left the article and typed in "school assistants." After all, how did immortal beings end up working at a high school? I tapped the search bar and shock coursed through me when my school's website appeared in the first results. I browsed through the page and clicked on 'historical events.'

There were black and white photos of the school's construction over time, and a portrait of a stiffly suited man with slick back hair, standing proudly in front of a bricked school building named John Carter, but it looked nothing like the school of glass I was familiar with. Beside the pictures, a paragraph detailed the school's history from its construction in the thirties by a man, John Carter, its first established football team, to its renovation several years ago. Only one sentence mentioned the assistants' helping students graduate, but there was nothing about where they came from.

I left Carter's website and scrolled down when a sentence, 'List of John Carter's Missing People' caught my attention. I clicked the link, and a lump welled in my throat. There was a history of people vanishing in or around the school, whether they attended as students or worked as staff. Many were labeled runways or elopers, but a lot of friends and relatives of the missing people said they were not the type to run away.

Their names and faces were listed in chronological order, and the first person made me tense up: John Carter, the founder himself. A month after he built the school, he and his personal assistant, another well-dressed man with slick dark hair, vanished while surveying the building. It was possible the men went missing around the same time, and despite months of searching, there were no clues of their whereabouts. To this day, their case has remained open.

I slowly scrolled through the other names and photos, my heart tightened as I spotted a familiar name, "Eleanor 'Ellie' Wright."

Friday, October thirteenth, a sophomore student rushed out of her classroom in distress. Moments later, students and staff on every floor heard a blood curdling scream, believed to be Eleanor, but she was never seen again. Her case was still open.

Knowing this urban legend used to scare kids turned out to be real, including the scream made my skin crawl.

I left the site to focus on the assistants and clicked on the first link that mentioned the Assistants' Program. It was established a decade ago with the goal of having alumni from private schools tutor students and aid teachers in public schools. There was a name of one of the private high schools, St. Ignatius, but when I looked it up, I found thousands upon thousands of schools that shared the same name. Sighing, I typed the assistants club meeting and a couple of words, "vanishing," and "club" crossed my vision.

"The Assistant Program's Vanishing Club." Instantly, I clicked the link and a chat room opened before my eyes.

**Ama98**: Has anyone ever heard of the Assistant Program? A bunch of teachers or students come to public schools. They sit in class, helping everyone out. I couldn't find their website, so I thought I'd ask here.

**KrimsRo506**: hey @ama98. i know what program your talking about it started at my school a few years ago. i heard they graduated from St. Ignatius, but there's thousands of those schools with the same name hard to tell which one they're from. Very suspicious.

**5JenaMori13**: Hi, I saw this post and I wanted to reply. Thank goodness, I'm not alone. The same program is at my school too! Maybe they came from all of those schools. Though, I didn't see any of their sites mentioning them.

**Ama98**: wow. That's strange. Ever thought how weird some of the assistants are though?

**KrimsRo506**: yeah, i know exactly what your talking about. They almost fooled me at first by being nice. But I know they couldn't be good ppl statistically speaking no rational human is ever nice without motive it makes no logical sense. They were up to something, and I was proven right one day.

**Ama98**: What do you mean? @Krim

**KrimsRo506**: i was following an assistant down a hall. i tried to follow her because she was going to the restricted area in my school. but when i got there, she vanished. then, on my way back, i swear i heard her voice echo in the hallway. she appeared in my class, asking if i was alright, acting as though i didn't hear her ten seconds ago. i tried to expose but my teacher took her side and told me to leave her alone.

**5JenaMori13**: That is weird. What about you @Ama98? Had anything weird happen?

**Ama98**: Well, has anyone ever heard of the Assistant's Club?

**5JenaMori13**: I only heard rumors about it though. It's when the assistants meet up with a handful of students from the school. It used to be an open invite until two years ago, they changed it invite-only at my school.

**KrimsRo506**: don't you find it odd that they changed it to invite? makes no sense unless they're hiding something.

**Ama98**: From what I heard, it ended quickly after an incident at a different school. I had a friend who went there and they said something happened. But they can't remember much and no one made a post about it.

**KrimsRo506**: sounds like a cover up. want to hear something weirder? my friend was invited in the meeting a month after the year began, but no one can find it. it's in school, but i have no idea where it could be.

**Ama98**: Did you talk to your friend about it?

**KrimsRo506**: no. i know they must have done something to him. my friend used to be quiet and always listens to me, now he's outspoken, but all he tells me he's been speaking to the assistants. but not what they did to him.

**5JenaMori13**: That sounds suspicious.

**KrimsRo506**: i don't trust them. they're hiding something and i'm going to get to the bottom of this. I said too much. if you don't hear from me, they probably did something to silence me. stay strong. the truth is out there.

My eyes stung when they blinked. I exited the site, feeling sick inside like someone was watching me in the dark, or behind creaking walls. Then I jumped at the sudden flutter against the window. I had enough. I turned off the computer and rushed out of the room.

I felt safer being surrounded by sunlight as I went downstairs. I was about to sit on the porch but stopped at a pair of green eyes peering through the bushes. My heart leaped when Tuna trotted toward me. Her soft fur rubbed against my ankles, then she flopped to her side. Seeing her fat belly jiggle like a furry water balloon made all my fears feel so distant.

The next day, Ichirou drove me to school, and I sat stiffly against the seat, dreading to see the assistants again.

"Last chance," he said when he pulled up at the curb. "If you don't want to go, I can drive back home."

A part of me wanted to stay home but I knew I couldn't skip school for the rest of the year. I gripped the car handle, my thoughts yelled at me to take the chance. *Ask him to take you home.*

"If I need to come home today, can I call you?" I asked.

His brow rose. "I'll be here as soon as possible. Make sure you're at the door by then."

"I will."

"Take care of yourself, Runt." Ichirou patted my head and messed with my hair.

I was about to fuss about it until I noticed the dark rings under his eyes.

"What are you staring at?"

"You need to sleep more."

•●•

I couldn't shake this uneasiness stirring in my chest, like something bad was going to happen. I could feel the assistants looking at me, their whispers drifting over my head as I passed by them. "She's the one who crossed over." I kept my head low, and hurried to the next class where I could talk to Mary and pretend things were normal.

"Where were you yesterday?" she asked, jotting notes into her journal.

"I had to see a doctor," I said.

"Did you get sick again?"

I shook my head. "It was a checkup."

"Does it have something to do with your epilepsy?"

I looked at her.

Mary lowered her eyes at my watch and pointed at the medical clip with her pen. "I saw it a week ago. I didn't think you wanted to bring it up, but when you panicked, I thought you may have been having a seizure or something."

My shoulders relaxed. "I don't bring it up so often. Had a lot of bad experiences."

"Don't worry, your secret's safe with me," she promised. "By the way, what happened at the library?"

I tensed up. "I... I was...I got lost."

"Lost? At the library?"

I wracked my head for an answer. How would she react if I told her about the other world?

128

"When I have seizures, it's hard to tell what's real and what isn't. I panicked."

"I think I get it," said Mary. "That sounds rough."

"Tell me about it."

My eyes flickered, and I almost jumped in my chair in fright. It was easy to forget Sarah sat in front of me, especially when she was so quiet.

"After school, I'm rehearsing a scene from Othello. If you can, would you like to come to the theater club with me?"

I glanced back and Sarah was gone again, along with the uneasy air around her. "Yeah... sure."

As if my day couldn't get any worse, I completely forgot about the algebra test. Weeks of studying and memorizing formulas blanked out of my mind overnight. I tried to focus, but there was something about Mr. Turner idling around that broke my concentration. Was he human? Did he have a monstrous form hiding under that kind face? I peered over the desk as Mr. Turner walked past me.

"Keep your eyes on your paper, Mayu!" barked Mrs. Bean from her desk. My eyes darted back to the test. Was Mrs. Bean human? She could have been a mean old troll or a nasty evil witch. I shook my head and focused when the bell suddenly rang.

By the time I arrived in art, I was anxious to talk to Lutea more about Erehwon and the assistants. The look in her eyes told me to wait. I spent the entire hour thinking about what to ask Lutea while sketching a broken watch. When the last bell rang, I met Mary at the door.

"I thought I was going to wait forever!" she moaned. "Theater club starts in a few minutes."

I glanced at Lutea over my shoulder. "I'm sorry, but would it be alright if you go ahead without me? I'll come to the auditorium later."

Mary's smile dropped. "Seriously?"

"I need to talk to Lutea. It'll only take a few minutes."

"Promise?"

I paused. "If not, then I can meet you at the auditorium when I'm done."

Mary's eyes darted over my shoulder, before she nodded. "Fine."

I returned to the room and closed the door.

"Since you're here, I have a present for you." Lutea tossed a glass bottle to me, and I caught it before it hit the floor. The bottle was cold to the touch.

I yelped at her, "What if I dropped it!?"

"It won't break," she assured me. "It's completely shatterproof."

I examined the bottle, staring at the clouded pink liquid inside. "What is this?"

"Polypop. Shake it and it changes into one of three flavors. That one has kiwi, strawberry and pineapple. My friend told me to give you a welcoming present."

A million ideas filled my mind to the brim. Was the drink some sort of magic potion or deadly venom? Would it grant me superpowers or change me into a monster?

"It's completely safe," Lutea said.

I slowly popped the cap open. There was a faint scent like sweetened nectar. I took a sip and shivered at the cool, tangy taste of pineapple. Curious, I capped the bottle, shook it and gulped down the biting, sour kiwi. One more shake, and I tasted sweet strawberries.

"Good?"

"Mm-hm!" I nodded and capped the bottle, wanting to save it for later. Looking at her, I felt terrible about leaving her at the library.

"How did your day go?" she asked.

Lutea dragged a large garbage can to her and tapped the dustbin against the rim, emptying it of pencil shavings and shredded paper.

I leaned back on the table and gently swirled the Polypop. "It was ...strange, almost dreamlike." I confessed. "Everything's the same, but it's like everyone I know are strangers."

"It's because no one else knows," Lutea said. "None of the teachers and students know about us or Erehwon. The only exceptions are the club members."

I slipped the bottle in my backpack. "None of the assistants are human? Not even you?"

"Not even me," she echoed. "But we're still the same people you talk to every day. And we'll still be the same people you talk to tomorrow."

I clenched the hems of my shirt and asked, "What are you? You look like everyone else, but what can you do?"

Meeting my eyes, Lutea straightened herself and rolled her wrist, gesturing for me to come closer.

"It'll be easier for you to see it."

Though hesitant, I approached her until we stood face to face. Lutea brushed her bangs aside, tucking them behind her ear. There was a mark on her hairline, shaped into letters or shaped I'd never seen before. It was pale compared to her tanned complexion, like an old scar. Easy to miss if I didn't look hard enough. Without thinking, I almost touched it before I quickly pulled back.

"Sorry!"

"It's okay," she said, gently.

My hand was shaking but I touched the scars. Her face was warm, yet firm like polished marble. The marks had a slight indent like someone carved them onto her skin, then smoothed them over by...

"Is this clay?" I asked, taking a step back. "Are you covered in clay?"

"I'm made of stone." Lutea untucked her bangs and they fell over the scars. "Have you heard of a golem?"

My mind went back to old movies I used to watch, and books I read with Elizabeth. "They're living statues, right?"

"Yep. Animated with enchantments, brought to life by a spell. I'm the only one of my kind who looks human enough to pass for one."

My face fell to her arms, noticing small, harsh etchings on her elbows and wrists. I brushed my thumb against the scars that looked the most recent.

"These were from the arrows. You were trying to help me... and I ran away."

Lutea broke into a small chuckle, "Can't say I blame you. If I didn't know Melanippe, I would have run too."

"But you were hurt!"

She shrugged. "I'm a lot tougher than I look. And I can't feel pain."

I had a lot of questions circling my head. "If you're a golem and centaurs are real, then what is Galumine?"

Lutea's expression softened. "Someone who took us in. You may know our kind as mythical creatures, the supernatural or cryptic monsters, but for the sake of simplicity, we call ourselves mystics. The world you fell into is our home, though at some point we used to live here, among humans."

"What happened?"

"A tale as old as time." She stared at the houses below. "Humans hunted us down, out of fear, or for power or fame. Naturally, we fought back, but that didn't stop the persecutions and conflicts. So, we hid ourselves, disguised as humans or shrouded in hidden worlds.

As our existence faded to mere legends and works of fiction, we began our venture into your world. To learn from humans. To walk among them. Unnoticed, but safe. It's possible you may have passed a few mystics in your life and never knew."

My mind reeled at the thought. "If you wanted to fit in, why did you become an assistant? Why come to a school, of all places?"

"We don't work primarily at schools. Galumine wanted us to help the community and show we're capable of living peacefully with humans. We offer aid in shelters, do volunteer work around the city, and help children and teachers as assistants. There will be humans who aren't afraid of us, and who want to understand us more. That's why we made the meetings to get to know each other."

"What made me qualified to join a meeting like yours?"

"Cedric took a risk, but he saw you needed help with class. Inviting you was the only way he could tutor you."

Why did I feel like Lutea wasn't telling the whole truth? I was about to ask her when she made a strange look, and her head tilted to the side. "Is that your friend at the door?"

Mary was trying not to make it obvious, but I caught her peeking from the corner of the door's window. I grabbed my backpack and opened the door.

"I thought you went to the theater club," I said to her.

"I know," Mary replied. "But I realized I never told you where the auditorium was. I was worried you might get lost trying to find it. Are you done in there?"

"Yeah," I said, nodding.

"That's good. The meeting has already started, but we can be a little late."

Mary tugged my wrist and pulled me away from the room until we were downstairs. The auditorium was on the first floor, not too far from the school's main doors.

Mary pulled on the door, opening it to a massive auditorium. Red and white lights beamed on the stage. Several people gathered in a circle and welcomed Mary as we joined. I sat between Mary and a blonde girl who introduced herself as Katie.

"Are you a new member?" she asked me.

"She goes to a different meeting," Mary replied before I could answer. "But she wanted to come here."

"I'm taking a break," I added.

The meeting began with simple stretches and after the club president passed out scripts to the members, I climbed off the stage and watched from the seats. Between the scenes, I remembered the PolyPop in my backpack. It was as cold as when I caught it. I took another sip, my cheeks pinched at the taste of strawberry kiwi and a pineapple aftertaste.

"Hmm, this is good."

# Splinter

**"Mayu? Are you up yet?"**

My eyes fluttered to the sound of tapping in front of me. A doorknob twisted and turned before it opened. In front of me stood a woman in a large, pine green shirt, a pair of track shorts and a cloud of poofy black hair. Her name surfaced in my foggy mind.

"H-Hannah?" I winced at the sunlight peeking through the blinds in my bedroom. I covered my face, and my arm ached from my backpack hanging off my shoulders.

"Are you okay?" Hannah asked.

I didn't answer. I stared at my feet planted on the floor and noticed I was wearing my school uniform. I thought, '*When did I get out of bed?*'

"Hannah! Is she awake?" Ichirou called from downstairs.

Hannah leaned back and replied, "Yeah, but I think she had another seizure!"

Footsteps raced upstairs and Ichirou emerged from around the corner.

"What happened?" he asked.

When my voice returned, I responded softly, "I... I don't know. I was standing here and...I don't remember getting up."

"You must have had a focal seizure." Ichirou brushed his hand across my forehead, pushing the bangs aside so he could check on my face. "Did it end?"

"Looks like it," said Hannah, holding her chin as she inspected me. "You're not pale...Maybe you should take your medication again. This is the second seizure in a week."

"They don't work on me anymore," I said.

"And I threw her medication away the other day," Ichirou added. "Her non-motor seizures come and go on their own. It's the spasm or a black out we should worry about." He turned to me. "Are you sure you want to go to school?"

I didn't see a reason not to.

"I can go," I said, then readjusted my backpack. The straps were digging into my shoulders.

Hannah protested, "She should see the doctor again. Last time I checked two seizures within a few days weren't normal for her."

"I can't take any more days off school, and I can't stay home for every seizure I have."

"And I'm driving her to school," Ichirou said.

Hannah bit her lip. "Fine, but if anything happens, call either of us."

"I will," I said and followed Ichirou downstairs.

I stepped outside and the bird's cries tore through the air and my throat tightened at the foul, gagging scent wafting up my nose.

"What is that!" I yelled, covering my ears.

Ichirou jerked back with a strange look on his face. "Wha-Why are you shouting?"

"Is everything alright?" Hannah said.

I spun around to see her standing by the door.

"Don't you hear the birds up there?" My hands lowered, and the chirping stopped. "And why does it smell like garbage around here?"

"You mean the robins' nest?" said Hannah. "They've been here for years. You're now noticing that?"

"And I hate to break it to you," said Ichirou. "But this place always smelled like trash. We live near the dumpster, remember?"

It was my least favorite part of the complex, but the smell was hard to notice unless you were close to it. Now, it was like someone moved the dumpster in front of our door and I wanted to go to school to get away from the smell.

I spent most of the ride insisting that I was alright until Ichirou turned on the radio. I lurched into a ball and slammed my hands in my ears as rock music pounded through the speakers.

"Why is it so loud!" I wailed.

Ichirou lowered the volume. "Runt, it was at a ten. What's going on? Why does noise hurt you today?"

"I don't know. Everything's so loud. Even the light is loud. How was *that* possible?"

"Sounds like a migraine. I get those a lot. There should be something in the glove compartment you can take. It's over the counter stuff, not prescriptions."

As tempting as it sounded, I've never taken medication for migraines and didn't know how it would affect me.

I groaned, shaking my head, "No, no more medicine, no more pills. Do migraines go away?"

"They do, but it'll feel like eons before it settles."

I leaned into the seat and closed my eyes. I gave my temples a small massage and it dulled the pain.

Ichirou said, "I'm going to change the station. I promise it won't be as loud as the song."

The car slowed to a stop, and he switched stations from music to the news. While the talk show host reported the weather, I remembered bits and pieces of what happened the previous night. Mary's cheerful goodbye after her dad dropped me off at home. Sitting on the couch, reading *Witch Hazel* and sipping the last of the PolyPop, then talking to Elizabeth. After that, the rest of the night was a blur.

I was going to ask Ichirou if anything happened last night when the host spoke about a car fire.

"Gasoline was discovered around the vehicle that was set on fire on Jefferson Street at three in the morning. Though witnesses claim they saw individuals flee the burning vehicle, it is unclear if this was an accident or an act of arson."

"That's the street you picked me up from," I said, opening my eyes. The light was no longer stabbing into my vision. "This happened last night?"

"The night before," Ichirou corrected. "Someone threw a Molotov cocktail on a Hummer. I'm surprised you haven't heard about it."

"No one talked about it in school." Or perhaps I heard about it, and it didn't register. My thoughts were still processing the assistants being mythical beings.

"What's a Molotov cocktail?" I asked.

"You've seen it in movies and shows," Ichirou replied. "It's those glass bottles with a flaming cloth at the end. A makeshift bomb."

"Why would somebody make that?"

"Why would anybody make that?" he grumbled. "By the way, do you have to go to that club meeting today?"

I was hesitant to answer. I wasn't sure if I was ready to go back there yet.

"If you do, make sure your friend can take you home. I don't want you out on the street again."

"I know." I stared ahead, watching the roof of my high school rise above the trees as we drove closer to it.

"I'm sure Elizabeth doesn't have to worry about being kicked off the bus or burning cars."

"Looking forward to the sleepover?"

I chuckled halfheartedly. "I think something would be wrong with me if I wasn't."

•   •
●

The migraine ebbed away by the time I was in school. In English, I was reading *Witch Hazel*, when Ms. Penn told us she needed to leave the room to answer an important phone call. The girls' faces lit up, as her leaving meant Ethan would be in charge. As soon as Ms. Penn was out the door, the girls pulled their desks together in a circle. The metal legs scraping against the floor tore me out of the story and the whispering, which rose to loud clatter, didn't make it any better.

"How's your head?" Ethan asked, sitting in front of me. His eyes startled me. They used to be dark brown, almost black but now they were bright, amber and gave off a wild edge to it. Then I remembered Lutea's words, *the assistants aren't human.*

"Are you wearing contacts?" I blurted.

Ethan pulled back a little, surprised at my question. "I was, then I took them off. They get uncomfortable after a while."

"My brother says the same thing," I said. "Do you wear glasses too?"

"I can see fine without contacts." Ethan tilted his head to the side and his eyes narrowed at my book. "*Witch Hazel.* Is it good?"

"I hadn't finished it yet, but I like it." I wanted to ask what he was and what he could do. Should I ask him right now in class where anyone can hear us?

"What's the book about?"

"It's—" My shoulders tensed from the desks scraping the floor and I noticed Ethan's face tightened in pain.

I continued in a soft voice, "It's... about a girl who learns that she's a witch, so she tried to cast her first spell, but it ends up turning her into a cat."

"That's unfortunate," he remarked. "Does she turn back into a human?"

"Not yet," I said. "But Hazel gets to see how different her neighborhood is through the eyes of a cat."

"Sounds interesting." Ethan adjusted himself in the chair. "My sister likes cats and I think she'd like to read *Witch Hazel*."

"Does your sister go here... or work—" Another sharp screech pierced my ears, and I quickly covered them.

Concerned, Ethan whispered, "one second," and stood up. I didn't know what he was doing until he turned off the lights near the door. The buzzing in my ears stopped and the other girls glanced at the ceiling.

"Sun's enough light for us," Ethan told them. "And tone down on the noise. Ms. Penn is still outside."

"Okay," one of the girls said, and the group continued their conversation in a lower voice. Ethan returned to the desk in front of me. "Better?"

"A little."

"You'll get used to the noise overtime."

"Like I don't have enough problems."

"Speaking of which," Ethan muttered. "Have you been feeling different lately? Y'know, since you crossed over?"

I bit my lower lip and thought about the seizure and my migraine. "Why are you asking me?"

"I was told to keep an eye on you. Orders straight from the Miss herself."

"Did you have to make it so obvious?" I shifted in my seat, certain that one of the girls was whispering about us.

"Nah, I was also wondering why you always sit by yourself."

I glanced to my left and realized what he meant. There were only fifteen students in my class, who were all girls, but Ms. Penn had extra desks because her other classes had more people. The girls always sat together, and I was the only person sitting three empty rows away from them.

"I don't think I'd get along with them," I said.

"Why is that?"

I murmured, "They remind me of girls who would tease me. They're popular in the hallway, always loud and they talk about other people from different classes."

"Welcome to high school," Ethan scoffed. "Drama will happen no matter where you go, and you're only listening to one half of the story. The girls here are much nicer than you think."

"For now." I turned to the next chapter but didn't read it. "They'll find a reason to make fun of me, eventually."

"Funny you would say that. Those girls asked me to check on you." I stared at Ethan. "You've been here for over a month and haven't spoken to anyone. They were worried if you had trouble making friends."

"I have friends."

"In this class?"

"I talk to you."

"Then talk to them," he insisted. "Come on. It's my job to make sure no one makes fun of others. Promise."

After a few seconds of staring at Ethan, I relented. "Fine."

"You seem… different," Aiden said to me in the hallway. We had gotten out of a grueling hour in algebra, where Mrs. Bean wanted us to work on the harder chapters without talking or asking for help. The hallway clamor filled my ears, but like Ethan said, I got used to it enough to talk to Aiden while we wove through passing students.

"What do you mean?" I asked.

Aiden shrugged, toying with his headphone wires. "You were absent Monday, and you looked a little tense during the test yesterday. And you stopped coming to the meetings."

"You noticed that?"

"We sit next to each other. I know the test was hard, but I thought Mr. Turner was helping you."

"He was." I said, walking down the crowded steps. "I wanted to take a break from studying."

"Is that why you left the meeting early?"

I nodded, knowing it was going to be hard explaining the whole reason to him.

"I may not be great at giving advice, but if you want to talk, preferably someplace quieter, you can ask me. Okay?"

"You know any places with fewer students?"

"I may know one or two… that isn't the library."

"Then it's a deal," I said, and the bell rang.

"And that's my cue." Aiden stopped at his classroom and said over his shoulder. "Hope the day goes well."

"You too!" I said, a tingling warmth fluttered in my cheeks.

•  ●  •

Mary and I headed to Gym, changed clothes and followed the older girls to the floor. The first thing we noticed were the bleachers laid out for everyone to sit in, and no volleyball nets.

"What's going on?" I asked Mary.

"You got me. Maybe we're going to do real exercises."

*What kind of exercise?*

We sat in the first row, and I looked around, overhearing the seniors and juniors guess what we were going to do. Someone said we might do an exercise routine while others said it was a free day and contemplated leaving class early.

A loud metallic thud brought our attention to an open door near the bleachers. Ms. Bloom emerged, hauling a cardboard box full of red and blue straps and Mr. Trouse followed, dragging dozens of red rubber balls packed inside of the net. My insides seized up, my heart pounded hard and fast, knowing exactly what we were going to play.

Dodgeball.

"If your strap is blue, you're on team blue," Ms. Bloom announced, bringing the box to the center of the gym floor. Mr. Trouse untied the net and set the balls in a neat line behind Ms. Bloom. "If it's red, you're on team red. Red is to the right, Blue is left. The strap has a clip so you can wrap it around your waist. You have a minute to pick a team starting..." she stared at her watch. "Now!"

Students scrambled to the box, and eagerly swiped a strap and raced to opposite sides of the gym. The box was almost empty by the time I grabbed the blue strap, then turned to Mary and the red strap in her hands.

She frowned, "You don't want to be on the same team?"

"We could be in the next game."

Back at Lawrence, the gym teacher would let players switch teams in new rounds.

"Yeah, but wouldn't it be better if we were together?" Mary implored.

Sighing, I traded my blue for a red and we joined the rest of our team. I didn't know anyone's name, but I recognized the volleyball players on team red and a few students who played basketball. Then I looked at the members in team blue and my stomach sank. The girls were the hard throwers who took volleyball seriously. And the boys had a habit of slamming into each other when they played basketball.

Mr. Trouse stood at the center. He gave out the rules, which weren't that different from the rules in Lawrence: if you're hit by the ball, you're out. If you catch a ball, the thrower is out, and you can bring a member back to the floor. If the ball bounces off the floor and hits you, it doesn't count. You can hit anywhere on the body, except for the head.

"Any questions?" Mr. Trouse demanded.

Everyone shook their heads and said "no." As the teachers left the centerline, I stretched my arms and legs to prepare myself, and saw the other students do the same.

*At least I can put my track skills to use*, I thought.

"This is going to suck," Mary moaned. She stood against the wall and the dread was clear on her face. "Are you going to play?"

"Don't have much of a choice, do we?" I told her.

"Ready?" Mr. Trouse yelled.

Silence flooded the room. All eyes were on the balls. My knees bent as I leaned forward. It's like track, think of it as track...

"Get set..."

I lifted my knee and arched my back, gearing to run on cue. At the shrill of the whistle, footsteps thundered across the room. Rubber balls snapped in the air, shouts and cries ran rampant from both teams. I reached for a ball when a fair boy swiped it off the floor. His arm reeled back, ready to throw and I dropped down, feeling the wind rush over me.

I jumped to my feet and turned when something happened. Time seemed to slow down and the hair on my neck stood on end. A heavy pressure rolled up my spine, growing stronger. I ducked as the ball flew over my head and landed in front of me. I spun around and lurched to the side, dodging another ball that almost hit me.

I ran to the wall, and my back hit the padded surface. My chest was heaving, and my legs were shaking. But more importantly, what was *that* feeling?

"Mayu, how did you do that?" Mary squeaked. I didn't think she left her spot. "You took off so fast—and you dodged the balls without seeing them!"

"Reflex?" I panted. "Used to...run track."

141

Members in team red leaped to the side to avoid getting hit. A senior girl hurled a ball but the same fair boy in team blue snatched it mid-air. Another boy in team red jumped over the oncoming ball, dove toward one on the floor, and threw it, hitting a girl in team blue on their back.

Swallowing my fear, I pushed my glasses back and sprinted for one of the balls rolling on the floor. The sensation came back, and without thinking, I threw my hands out. A stinging pain rushed from my palms, and I staggered back but the ball was still in my shaky hands.

"Nice save!" Someone cried.

A girl from team red rejoined us. My body lurched back as a ball soared past me. A familiar shriek caught my attention. I found Mary on the floor, a dodgeball rolling away from her.

"Mary, are you—ah!" I shrieked to the pain of a ball striking me from behind.

Across the gym, one of the boys was mocking my scream, making it sound more dramatic than it was. I glared at them, then turned to Mary.

"Are you hurt?" I asked, helping her up.

"My head," she groaned. "That boy didn't have to hit me so hard."

We sat on the bleachers, and Mary was still holding her head.

"Does it hurt?" I asked.

"I'll live," she replied. "But this game is so unfair. Everyone is bigger than us and, of course, they're going to pick on the only two freshmen in class."

"We can ask Ms. Bloom to leave."

Mary huffed, "She'd probably make us stay…"

We continued to watch the game. Most of team red's wins were lucky shots and catches, but it was the fair boy in team blue I couldn't take my eyes off. He moved as swiftly as the wind, snatching the ball and throwing it with such force, whoever he hit slammed into the floor.

"Damien, not too hard!" Mr. Trouse barked.

Ms. Bloom blew the whistle, and the first game went to team blue. Mr. Trouse gave us a ten second break, then everyone hurried back to their teams. We weren't switching members like I thought.

Rather than race to another ball, I stayed behind with five other teammates and watched. Team blue threw their dodgeballs at the same time team red picked theirs up. Luckily, not a lot of my teammates were hit. Some dodged, a few caught the balls, and the rest scampered away.

When I saw a ball soaring toward no one, I leaped and caught it in my arms, then jerked to the side as another ball rushed past me. I ran back to the wall with the ball in my hand when a girl—one of the juniors nearby cried, "over here!"

Knowing what she meant, I tossed the ball to her, and my eyes widened when she bowled the ball, and it hit one of the furthest players near the wall. Red and blue had six members on both sides, but team blue had more dodgeballs. Team red scattered. I lurched to the side and ducked for cover. Mary swerved behind me, yelling, "Watch out!" I turned and saw the ball coming before it smashed into my face.

The whistle shrilled again and again, and the gym room quieted to whispers. I stared at the blurry ceiling, pain flared across my face. Members from both teams surrounded me until Mr. Trouse rushed to my view. He held my hand and pulled me to my feet. I patted my face and before I could panic, one of the girls brought my glasses to me. I put them on, getting a good look at everyone staring at me. Mr. Trouse, still holding my hand, narrowed his eyes to the medical band attached to my watch.

Before I knew it, he pulled me to the side.

Ms. Bloom paused the game to remind everyone not to hit anyone in the head. I don't remember what she said next because Mr. Trouse had me sit on the bleachers far from the other player to ask about the medical band.

"Why didn't you mention this? You could have gotten hurt!" he scolded.

I told him about the doctor's note I showed to Ms. Bloom on my first day. I guess she never told Mr. Trouse. He went on and on about consequences and other stuff I had heard since primary school. I told him my old gym teacher knew about my epilepsy and still let me play, and I was on my school's track team, which helped control my seizures. Mr. Trouse tapped his foot against the floor and gave me a stern warning: if someone hit me on the head again, then he would ban me from playing dodgeball.

I returned to the floor and found Mary sitting in the bleachers with the other members.

"What was that about? Why did he pull you to the side like that?" she asked.

"He saw my medical band." I took off my glasses to check for scratches. Ms. Hudson had bought stronger frames for me and

Elizabeth when we joined the track team, and luckily, everything stayed in one piece.

"He didn't check on me when I was hit in the head," Mary said in a pouty voice.

"If I'm hit in the head, it can trigger a seizure," I explained. Though that rarely happened to me.

"I'm sure that ball gave me a concussion."

"You should tell Mr. Trouse or Ms. Bloom. They'll probably let you sit through the rest of the game." I put my glasses on, and my vision cleared up.

We continued to watch the game when someone called out to us from behind. It was the brunette, toned junior who found my glasses.

"What's your name?" she asked.

"I'm Mayu," I replied.

"I'm Becky-Tran." She offered her hand to shake. "Are you two doing alright?"

"Yeah."

"More or less," Mary said.

"Great! We're planning on taking Damien out first. Do you want to help? We're good throwers, but we could use someone who can dodge and catch."

"I'm great at catching!"

"I think I can do that." I rotated my shoulders as though shrugging off the pressure.

"Great!" Becky-Tran looked at me. "I overheard that you used to run track. Ever did a hurdle or long jump?"

I answered yes and the whistle blew, signaling us to return to the floor. Ms. Bloom realigned the balls, and Mr. Trouse had his eyes on me when I rejoined my team. He announced to the class it would be our last round and told us to have fun. Yeah, I didn't think we could have fun playing with Damien.

Team red's formation was more aligned than the last two games. Once the whistle blew, I swiped a ball and slipped back before another could hit me. I raced to Becky-Tran and tossed the ball to her. She swung her arm, hurling the ball across the gym and striking a boy in team blue. We repeated the same routine and managed to knock off four players. Mary passed the ball to Becky-Tran, and I jerked to the side when she threw it toward a girl in team blue. It was about to hit her when Damian jumped in the way and caught it.

Becky-Tran cursed under her breath before jogging to the bleachers.

Mary and I traded nervous looks. Without her, all we could do was dodge. Mary and two more members were hit. I ducked from one of the balls and felt another flying toward me. I could have dodged it. I knew I could, but I didn't. I opened my arms, and the ball slammed into my chest, crushing the wind out of me. I kept a firm grip on it and turned to the bleachers where I locked eyes on Mary.

If she were Elizabeth, I would have called her back. Sure, we weren't the best at playing dodgeball, but we would have fun no matter how many times we were hit. I shook myself out of the daze and called Becky-Tran back to the game.

She dodged one ball, grabbed another, and threw it at one of team blue's players. Our team was down to three, while team blue had four left. Still, I was impressed we had gotten that far. My team members were lean, and taller than me—They were easy targets for Damien.

I remembered when I used to run track, my coach would always call me the team's "Little Bullet" and it gave me an idea.

Becky-Tran and another junior threw the balls at Damien. He maneuvered from the ball and caught two in his hands as I sprinted toward him. I snatched one of the balls and charged at him. Damien was so focused on the other members, he didn't see me coming until it was too late. I swung my arm as hard as I could, and the ball smacked against his shoulder. The final whistle blew, ending the game.

"Nice one," Damian laughed.

His eyes were hazel green, with slit pupils like a snake, and glistening scales peppered around his neck and shoulders. My voice caught my throat as he patted me on the back and jogged to the boy's locker room.

The girls from team red swarmed me. Hands patted my shoulder, and compliments followed me to the locker room. My stomach fluttered and my cheeks burned. Who would have thought I'd get so much praise over a game? After giving Ms. Bloom my red strap (which I forgot I had on), I made my way to one of the stalls. Mary had stepped out, already wearing her uniform.

I furrowed my brow; she would always wait for me so we could take turns changing clothes. Some of the girls could be territorial about certain stalls.

"Mary?"

"What," she said with a sharp edge in her voice.

I flinched. "Is something wrong?"

"Nothing. I'm fine."

That didn't sound like 'nothing.' I followed Mary to her locker. She yanked it open and grabbed her bag. One of her books fell and I reached for it when she snatched it off the floor. I didn't understand why she was upset. She was alright on the gym floor, so what happened?

"If there's anything bothering you—"

Mary slammed the locker shut and the startling noise bounced off the walls. "How come when a ball hits the back of my head, I'm fine, but when your glasses get knocked off, the whole gym stops?"

"I was hit in the head too," I reminded her.

"And why was it okay for those girls to praise you but ignore me? They treated me like they always do, like I don't exist." She pulled away, rubbing her eyes. "You didn't notice it, did you."

I stammered, "We wanted Damien off the floor."

"Is that why you called Becky back... and not me?" she choked. "Does a stupid game matter more than me?"

"Wait!" Despite my legs shaking, I tried to catch up with Mary, but she stormed out of the room, far from my reach.

# 11

# Omen

**Becky-Tran and the other girls warned me to slow down** as I hurried from the locker room. Having already changed into my uniform, I turned the corner and caught Mary's messenger bag vanishing behind the gym's closing door.

"Mary, wait!" I cried.

I bolted into the hallway and stopped myself from nearly crashing into a group of passing students. I gave them a flurry of apologies, then jogged down the hallway. My head whipped side to side to find Mary, but it was as if she had vanished into thin air.

Then, I remembered the next place Mary would go and headed to the library. I was so focused on finding her, I barged through the doors. The loud thud drew in the attention from the students at the computers, assistants by the shelves, and the librarian at his desk who eyed me curiously.

"S-Sorry," I stuttered.

I lowered my head, averting my eyes from everyone's gaze and idled around the tables. Mary wasn't near the shelves or the computers, though she preferred to read her book in the courtyard. And like that, I spun around to the windows, but the gazebo was empty. I bit my lip in worry, wondering where my friend could have gone.

Then the bell rang.

By the time I reached the third floor, I was tired from dodgeball and running to the library. My legs were trembling, and the dizziness made the floor sway. I stopped in front of Art class to wipe the sweat off my forehead when the door opened.

"I was wondering where you went," Lutea said, stepping out. "Did you walk Mary to class again?" Her cheery expression suddenly changed into worry. Lutea could always tell when something was wrong. Then again, I didn't exactly have the happiest look on my face.

"Mary's mad at me," I murmured.

"Oh no." She sighed through her nose, pulled back and widened the door. "I have to run a quick errand, but do you want to talk about it when I come back?"

I gave her a small nod and walked into class. The instant I sat down, too exhausted to draw, I rested my head on the table and thought about what happened in Gym. Not about Mary, but how I dodged a ball without seeing it. Had I always been that way? I doubted it, or I would have dodged every paper ball Rosalina threw at me. Ethan warned me about side effects from crossing worlds. What if sharp reflexes were one of them?

My thoughts were interrupted by a student who asked, "Is that girl with the glasses sleeping?"

Curious, I lifted my head and glanced at the students sitting far from me. They noticed me but went back to talking to each other. Prenting that I didn't hear them, I got up and grabbed my drawing from the art drawer. Turning around, I noticed I sat at least three chairs away, and it reminded me of what Ethan pointed out in English.

I always kept my distance from my classmates and never spoke to anyone beside Lutea. They never bothered me. Most of the time, they talked about the newest trends, the latest shows and movies, but none of them ever caught my interest.

Until someone talked about the car fire last night. My ears perked up, and I sat down, I listened to the conversation. It turned out, a boy lived on the same street where it happened and saw someone standing on the roof.

"Why didn't you record it?" a girl next to him asked.

"I was going to," the boy replied. "But when the car blew up, they were gone!"

"Did they use a bomb?"

"They threw a bottle at it, the ones that explode."

"A grenade?"

"No, it has a flaming cloth at the end."

"You mean a torch?"

"No, it's—"

"A Molotov cocktail," I interrupted. "It's where you put gasoline in the bottle and..." My voice faltered when I noticed my classmate staring at me as if I could have made the bombs myself.

"O...kay?" one of them said.

"Never mind." I sank into my chair and buried my burning face in my drawing. I wished I had never opened my mouth.

Moments later, Lutea returned and sat across from me.

"Sorry, didn't mean to take so long," she said and scooted closer. "So, what happened to Mary?"

"Lutea, can I ask you something?"

"You already did but ask away," she said with a small grin.

My eyes flickered to my classmates, who quickly moved to another topic. "H-How do you talk to people?"

"You start by opening your mouth and saying words."

I snorted, "No, not that. How do you get people to like you?"

"I'm not sure what made me the expert in that."

"You always know what to say to everyone. And they like talking to you."

Lutea pursed her lips. "Well, you have to feel comfortable being around people, but it doesn't happen overnight. It takes time and practice to build that kind of confidence."

My heart sank. I wasn't the greatest at talking to people.

"Believe it or not," Lutea continued. "I used to be quiet like you. It took me a while to get out of my shell. It didn't help that I had to be an impromptu teacher. But do you know what I learned?"

"What?"

"Everyone is drawn to those who share the same interests as them, like kindred spirits."

"Is that what makes people popular?" I asked.

Lutea said, waving her hand dismissively. "I wouldn't worry about trying to be popular. Too much trouble for what it's worth. But if you focus on what you're passionate about, you'll eventually draw in the right crowd, or they'll come to you. You know the saying, birds of a feather..."

"They flock together," I finished. Now that she mentioned it, I had befriended a few people like Aiden and Mary because we liked similar things. Or so I thought...

"Lutea," I said. "What would you do if you had a friend who didn't like what you liked?"

"Does this have to do with Mary?"

I told her what happened in gym but left out the parts about Damien. That was another topic I needed to discuss later.

"Now I can't find her to apologize."

"Apologize for what?" Lutea shrugged. "Having fun?"

"For making her feel bad. Making her feel... left out"

"Mayu, tell me something," Lutea leaned closer to me. Her voice softened. "Do you like going to theatre club? Be honest."

I shifted in my chair, and my eyes fell to the table.

"Do you feel left out when she's acting with the other members?"

I shook my head.

"So why should you apologize for doing something you like?"

"I don't know...Because it made Mary feel bad."

"Last time I checked, friendship didn't come with a contract. If Mary told you she didn't like old monster movies or *Witch Hazel,* would you agree with her because she's your friend?"

"No."

"It's okay if friends like different things. And you can still connect with her from other similar interests. You don't have to like or dislike everything because it's what Mary wants."

"Should I tell her that?"

"You can't find her, and she might be upset. Give her a few days for her to calm down."

"Okay." I rested my head, letting my bangs fall over my face.

"Hey, for what it's worth..." Lutea lifted my bangs and met my eyes. "...anyone who can shrug off a dodgeball to the face has my utmost respect."

I didn't tell Lutea, but I went to theatre club after class. Mary might have been mad at me, but I hoped we could talk to each other. Elizabeth and I rarely had an argument, but the few times we were upset with each other, one of us would apologize later that same day. Maybe Mary was the same.

I stopped in front of the auditorium and slowly pulled the door open. A low, creaking moan drew the members' attention to me from the stage. Mary wasn't there and the members didn't look surprised to see me. I shook the awkwardness off my shoulders and walked down the aisle, approaching the club president who sat at the edge of the stage.

His eyes lifted when he recognized me.

"Hey there...Miyu, was it?" he said, kindly.

"It's Mayu," I squeaked, then cleared my throat. "Have you seen Mary today? I can't find her." I didn't have the heart to tell him about our argument.

The club president's expression softened. "Sorry, she texted me she wasn't coming today. Not feeling well. She didn't tell you?"

A lump formed in my throat. "No," I said in a small voice. "She might have texted me too, and I didn't check yet..."

"Most likely," the club president agreed, though I had a feeling he knew I was lying. "Would you be interested in staying? You can use Mary's script in the meantime."

"Thank you, but that's alright."

It was weird enough going to theatre club without Mary, and it would have been stranger to join the meeting when I barely knew the members.

For the next few moments, I wandered the school as it emptied, no longer looking for Mary, but unsure where to go. It was almost three in the afternoon when my phone buzzed in my pocket. I checked the inbox, and my eyes bulged at the sudden flurry of messages. All of them immediately appeared, despite the time telling me the messages were sent an hour ago.

*Did I pass a dead zone?*

The messages were from Ichirou and Hannah, asking if I made it home or was still in school. I could go home. Maybe reading *Witch Hazel* or finishing my homework would take my mind off the day. I saw the main door at the end of the hallway but in the corner of my eye, I recognized the back doors to the library.

My stomach fluttered.

A new message came from Ichirou, asking again if I was home.

"What the heck," I whispered and replied, 'I'll be home later.'

I stuffed the phone in my pocket and pulled the door open. Like an old habit, I followed the familiar path around shelves, and, after a few turns, I found Min at her desk. She was holding a book in one hand and a white Styrofoam cup in another.

"Welcome back, Mayu!" She called out. "How's your week going?"

My eyes trailed to the door, and I was relieved to see a room and not a vast stretch of darkness.

"I'm fine," I answered. "How about you?"

"Can't complain," Min chimed, specks of light glimmered through the wings of her headphones. "We had an interesting card game with Miss Naiad. Almost nobody could beat her."

I always thought the wings were fake with lights installed to give it a flashy look. But the more I focused on Min, the more I noticed how they swayed despite there being no wind, and the haze of gradient blue in her eyes, almost like an insect's.

"Oh, that must have been fun." My shoulders sank. "Min...I'm sorry for how I talked to you."

"No worries! Members usually don't engage with me outside, so your questions caught me by surprise! But if there's anything you'd like to know, feel free to ask!"

"Since you offered..." My eyes trailed to the cup in her hand. "What are you drinking?"

"This?" Min asked with a perplexed expression. "It's nectar that I got from home."

"Is it good?" *Of course it's good, stupid. Why else would she drink it?*

"To me it is. It's very sour to others." Min uncapped the cup and offered it to me. "Would you like to try it?"

I shrugged. "Why not?"

The nectar was honey gold and had a dizzying sweet smell to it. "Here goes," I said and lifted the cup. The sharp sourness pricked my tongue and stung my ears. I winced as it went down and left a sickly-sweet taste in my mouth.

"I take it you don't want seconds," Min said, stifling a laugh.

I returned the cup. My face puckered at the sourness across my lips. "I think that sip gave me a cavity."

"If only you could see the look on your face."

She held the cup, and a black, thin fuzzy string darted from her lips and dipped into the nectar, as though she were drinking through a straw. My mind was so clouded by a sugary fog, the next sentence slipped out before I could stop myself.

"Are you really a butterfly? How can you drink that?"

Her tongue slipped back into her mouth. "You answered your own question. Everyone who drinks this says it's too sweet or sour, and someone spat it out one time."

I felt better knowing that I had kept it in. "If that's your tongue, then how can you speak?"

"The same way you can speak. A tongue is still a tongue."

"I've never heard butterflies speak like you."

"You have to listen carefully. Our voices are small and delicate, easily carried by a breeze." Min pulled off her headphones, and I discovered the wings were grafted on the sides of her head where her ears should have been.

"I was losing feeling in them." Her wings fluttered as she stretched her arms.

Out of curiosity, and hopefully, for a simpler answer, I asked, "Do you listen to music or are those headphones a disguise?"

"Both!" Min said, her cheeks dimpled. "I like songs that have a nice low base to them. But I prefer techno over anything else. It never fails to get me out of a bad mood. I heard that your world has a market called a... music store?"

"You mean electronic stores? Last I checked, they sell music and other stuff like headphones, movies and games."

"I'd love to visit one someday, but I can't handle myself in crowds yet. I'll turn into a butterfly if I get too nervous."

She gave a whole new meaning to 'butterflies in the stomach.' "Are there more butterflies like you?"

A bit of sadness crossed her face. "It's me and my sister," she said, somberly. "You've met her before."

"I have?"

Min smiled again. "Do you remember a blue butterfly in the forest?"

I gasped, "That was your sister?"

"Her name is Mei-Mei, and she wouldn't stop talking to me about how you knocked Melanippe off her hooves!"

My face warmed up. "And here I thought I scared everyone."

"No one scares me more than Mei-Mei. She'll sit in a room full of vampires and will tell me all about the embroidery decorating the blackout curtains." Min feigned an exhausted sigh, her hand splayed dramatically across her forehead before she erupted into laughter.

"I'm surprised you came back. I was worried we might have scared you away."

"It scared me at first," I admitted. "But after talking with Lutea, I understood it better. And you're still the same Min I met on my first day. I don't see why it should change the way we see each other."

"Does this mean you'll come back?"

"I never thought about quitting."

"Then, by all means," Min gestured to the door.

The moment I opened the door, cool air brushed against me, carrying a faint scent of cloves and spices. Maple leaves, and yellow flowers wrapped around the exposed beams and hung loosely off the bookshelves. I spotted Aiden at the tables, playing on a game console and Gabriella was reading a familiar red book. My eyes widened at a pair of bronze wings wrapped around her legs like a blanket. Next to her was a girl with deerlike antlers sprouting from her auburn hair.

"Please refrain from staring," Miss Naiad's voice was in my ear.

I spun around. The first thing I saw were her eyes, one was bright molten gold and the other icy blue like arctic waters.

"These kids get that enough as it is at school in disguise," she whispered. "No need for them to feel this way here."

My words fumbled. "I didn't mean to. No one looked like this before. What did I miss?"

"Clearly a lot, dear. Everyone felt comfortable putting down their disguises in safety. That is the purpose of our meetings, after all."

I glanced at the kids, recognizing a few with extra or sharpened appendages. *So, my classmates aren't human, either.* I thought.

"Some are human, though with mystical qualities of their own."

I whipped back to Miss Naiad.

She grinned. "You must keep an open mind. Start talking to them. Most of us don't bite, anyway."

Her hand settled on my back and nudged me forward. What should I do? What should I say? I turned to Miss Naiad, but she vanished.

"She does that a lot," Lutea called from my left. "You'll get used to it."

She stood by the bookshelves, hanging up a stream of orange and yellow leaves and Ethan was on the other side, doing the same.

"I thought you were going home today," Lutea said.

"I had nothing else to do," I confessed.

"You came here out of boredom?" Ethan said accusingly, though I knew he wasn't serious.

"Better than being bored at home."

I stepped back, letting Ethan hang the streamers. My brow furrowed at the gold acorns tucked between the leaves. "Isn't it too early for the fall?"

"Fall is in a few weeks," Lutea said.

"And the members voted on decorations based on a certain book," Ethan gestured to one of the tables where Aiden sat along with Gabriella and a girl with the antlers. My eyes widened at the red book next to her and the silver, cursive writing wound around a cat on the cover.

Excitement cracked through my voice. "You read *Witch Hazel* too!"

Gabriella jolted in shock, and her wings ruffled. "It's one of my favorites. Have you read it?"

"I'm in the middle of it." I sat across from her, next to Aiden. "I wondered if the spells in the book were real."

"Why don't you ask our witch herself?" Lutea motioned ahead. Miss Naiad was sitting next to me, shocking the life out of us as we jumped in our seats. She was quiet like Sarah!

"Must you shout every time?" Miss Naiad groaned. She had the book in her hand and her finger flipped through the pages. "What would you like to know?"

I was still shaken from her appearance to ask.

Aiden cleared his throat, "Can someone turn themselves into an animal if they haven't used magic?"

Miss Naiad mused, never taking her eyes off the pages. "Transformation spells are the oldest, possibly the first spell in history. There are so many ways to conjure it, it wouldn't be too surprising if one used the spell by mistake." She snapped the book closed. "Interesting read."

I blinked. "Did you read the whole story?"

"I did."

"That fast!" Gabriella stuttered.

"Yes. Credit where it's due, the author did thorough research in witchcraft, but some parts are a little embellished."

"What parts did they embellish?" I asked.

"You don't need to wave a wand and speak Latin to use magic," she explained. "Spells are intuitions brought forth by focus, and wands direct the spells to manifest. But with enough practice, any witch can cast through thoughts alone."

"Can you cast the spells from the book?" Gabriella asked. I was curious about that, too.

"Depends." A gleam flickered in Miss Naiad's eyes and a snake-like grin crawled across her face. "What spells would you like to see?"

I thought about it. "There's a spell in the book that lets you float. Could you cast something like that?"

"Too easy!" Miss Naiad tapped the table and a cool rush of air pulsed through us. Gabriella's wings shuddered and my arms became light and weightless.

"What the!" I shrieked.

Gravity lost its pull on me. My legs lightly kicked in the air as I laughed and rolled back to touch one of the garland leaves. Aiden bent his knees and propelled himself to my side.

"You're a real natural!" I chuckled.

"It's just like swimming." He smiled, until he leaned back a little too far, and somehow lost balance in the air. "Holy sh—"

"Language!" Miss Naiad scolded.

Moments later, a loud tap rang from the table, and a heaviness lulled me down. The instant my shoes tapped solid ground, it felt like gravity had stitched my feet back to my floor. Feeling lightheaded, I, along with the other members, stumbled toward the chairs.

Aiden moaned, holding his head, "It's like I got off a roller coaster."

"First times are always rough," Miss Naiad said. "Any other spells you would like for me to demonstrate?"

After the laughter calmed down, an idea came to my mind. "I read that crystals could calm your thoughts and make you astral project."

"It depends on the crystals. For instance." Miss Naiad rolled her wrist and opened her hand. In her palm were cloud white and peppered stones glimmering in different colors. Aiden, Gabriella and I leaned toward the gems in awe.

"By themselves, moonstones can't do much, but imbued with a witch's magic, it can project the dreams of whoever holds it. Anyone bold enough to share their dreams?"

I stared at the stone, wondering what my dreams would look like. What would everyone think if they saw it? Aiden, Gabriella and I exchanged nervous looks.

Then I turned to Lutea and Ethan. "Are you interested?"

Ethan shook his head. "I was up all night. No sleep. No dreams."

"Can golems even sleep, Lutea?" Gabriella asked.

"I tried once," Lutea replied. "Tora called me a 'constipated statue.' Though it looks relaxing when he sleeps…"

Ethan stared at her. "You watch him sleep?"

"Someone has to make sure he does!"

Aiden cleared his throat. "I'll go. It's not like I had any embarrassing dreams."

Miss Naiad passed him a moonstone. Specs of light danced from Aiden's hand. Then stars appeared over our table. They twisted into the shape of circles, triangles, and squares full of numbers and decimals. Square root equations, fractions and decimals trailed off to an endless row of 9s.

"Aiden!" Miss Naiad commanded. Aiden shook out of his daze and the fog of math faded kind of like... a dream.

I slowly turned to Aiden. "Got a lot on your mind, huh?"

He gave me a halfhearted shrug. "I was cramming for an exam all night..."

Gabriella went next. She held the moonstone and sunlight beamed from it. A plume of pink clouds swirled around the table, bringing a cool breeze that ruffled the leaves above. Gabriella confessed she hadn't flown in a while.

Anona, the girl with antlers, held the moonstone and my head lulled to the heavy rain tapping against a roof, a train rumbling by carrying an echoing horn with it. Voices of different people in Anona's life drifted by; a teacher's lectures, lines from a movie she watched, and a girl whispering the words, "do you want to go out?" Anona's face flared up and she dropped the gemstone.

It was my turn, and I was eager to see what would happen. My fingers kneaded the gemstone, taking in the rainbow colors dancing off the surface. Nothing happened at first, then cracks jolted across the stone and sparks of thin blue light jutted from it. Before I could say a word, a deep and hollow wind roared in my ears and shook my table. Fire whipped across my vision and the smell of wet wood and gasoline chased away the room's sweet pine. Then I heard it, those familiar words that sent shivers of dread through me. *"Can you hear me?"*

I jumped with a start, my heart hammering in my chest until I realized I was still in the clubroom. The moonstone clattered against the table. It was in one piece. Lutea's hand was on my shoulder as I caught my breath. She and Miss Naiad asked if I was alright, but I couldn't muster an answer.

Lutea pulled me to a table furthest from Miss Naiad and the other members. From the worrying looks on Ethan's face and the eyes that followed me, my heart was pounding. Did I do something wrong?

Lutea pulled out a chair from one of the tables and sat in front of me. "That voice we heard; do you know anything about it?"

157

That's it? I raised my brow at her question. "I hear it now and then in my head whenever I feel an aura. Sometimes it can happen in my sleep. It's another side effect."

Lutea's face scrunched up. "That voice sounded too clear to be a side effect. Have you ever spoken to it?"

"Why would I talk to it? It's all in my head?" I insisted. Lutea's stern expression worried me. "...right?"

"Even in the Mystic world, it's unusual to have a voice speak to you in your thoughts and dreams. It might be dangerous."

My heart raced. "How can a voice be dangerous?"

"It can threaten you, make you to do something you're not comfortable with or tell you something that isn't true. That's why I'm curious about the one we just heard."

"I don't know anything about it. What do I do if it speaks to me again?"

"One of my friends, Chitose can help. She isn't here but I will tell her about this voice. She might know what to do. In the meantime, we can stay in touch in case it comes back."

Lutea pulled her phone from her pocket, and we exchanged numbers. "You can call me any time of the day or night."

"At night? Are you sure?"

"Remember, I don't sleep."

After the club ended, I was back at the bay of bright red lockers when someone called out my name.

"Mayu? Mayu, wait!"

I turned around.

Aiden caught up with me. "Do you have a way to get home?"

"Yeah," I said, then stopped when I remembered Mary's dad wasn't coming to pick her up. "I—I'm taking the bus."

"By yourself?"

I looked around the hallway. Everyone was leaving in groups. I was the only one waiting for the bus.

"Mind if I wait with you?"

My cheeks flustered. I didn't see the harm in having someone waiting with me, and Lutea's warning worried me so much, I would've been lying to myself if I said I wasn't afraid.

"Don't you have a way home?" I asked.

"I usually call my sister to pick me up. Are you doing alright? You looked pretty... upset after we left."

I wasn't sure how much Aiden had heard. I wanted to talk about it, but wasn't sure where to start: my seizures, the voice or the dream.

"I'm fine."

Aiden didn't look convinced. Before he could say something, I saw the bus coming down the street and got on as soon as it arrived. It was almost empty, except for two adults who didn't bat an eye when I idled towards a seat by the window. Without overcrowding students and loud voices in my ear, taking the bus felt different and a little terrifying.

I answered the phone as soon as I was home, and relief washed over me when I heard Elizabeth cheery voice on the other end.

"That was fast, were you waiting by the phone?"

"I just came back from school." I said, dropping my backpack beside the couch. "How was your day?"

"It was super busy. I've been studying and tutoring for an exam so much, it feels like my eyes are about to roll off!"

I laughed. "Didn't think you needed a tutor."

"Oh, no, it's not for me. It's for Suzanne."

"Suzanne?"

A girl's voice soon flooded my ears from the other line. "Hey, hey, hey friend! Are you Mayu? Lizzie told me so much about you. It's nice to meet you, well, hear from you, but I hope we can meet each other in person one day!"

"Hi...?" She sounded like someone put her on fast forward and left her like that. "Are you Suzanne?"

"Suzanne Watson. But you can call me Sue. Everyone calls me Sue. Well, except for Lizzie."

Lizzie? I thought Elizabeth didn't like being called Lizzie. She told me it didn't sound right to her.

"Suzanne!" Elizabeth cried. "I needed to talk to her about the sleepover."

Suzanne groaned. "Can we come to the sleepover too?"

"Maybe next time."

There was a shuffling before Elizabeth spoke again. "I'm sorry about that."

"Don't worry," I said. "Your roommate sounds nice."

"Thank you!" Sue cheered in the background.

"She sure is," Elizabeth laughed. "Anyway, I wanted to check and see if you were alright. I've heard there were a lot of vandalisms in your neighborhood."

"A lot of people were talking about it at school," I said, leaning against the wall. "But other than that, the complex has been peaceful. I didn't know about these events until today."

"Still, it's a little concerning. If you don't feel comfortable taking the bus, Mom said she could pick you up from school in case Ichirou or Hannah can't. She doesn't like the idea of you going home by yourself."

A fuzzy warmth blossomed in my chest, knowing Ms. Hudson wanted to help. "She doesn't have to do it. It's not like I've taken the bus home before."

"Didn't you tell me you were kicked off the bus?"

"Oh…"

Elizabeth's voice softened. "Please, promise you'll be careful. I want to see you in one piece."

"Yes, Mom!" I moaned and Elizabeth laughed.

Suzanne called out to Elizabeth, but I couldn't make out what she said. Next thing I knew, Elizabeth's laughter faded. "I'm sorry. I have to help Suzanne with her homework. I'll call you tomorrow. Same time?"

There was so much I wanted to talk to her about. Every story swelled for attention, ready to burst if I didn't say it. *Speak up, Mayu.*

"Sure. I'll talk to you later," I said.

"Stay safe," Elizabeth said, and the phone clicked to silence.

I held the phone, my thoughts reeling with everything that happened, dodgeball, Mary's argument, and the dream and the voice.

$$\bullet \; \bullet \; \bullet$$

Branches cracked beneath my feet, and the dry snaps rang in the cold, still air heavy with an odd, yet familiar scent like copper drenched in water. Dread filled my heart and the urge to run away was all encompassing, but the voice was already in my ear before I could take the first step.

"*Why do you run?*"

Its whispers reverberated around me. I opened my mouth, feeling my lungs freezing, and gasped between clattering teeth. "Sh-She told me you were dangerous."

"*Dangerous?*" it repeated. "*How am I dangerous?*"

A deep, guttural snarl curled up my spine. Burning eyes on bristling black fur caught my gaze. Its muzzle peeled back revealing sharp canine teeth. A shriek leapt out of me as it lunged forward, its jaws snapped the air where my neck would have been.

I ran through the frigid air and uneven ground toward an ember haze at the horizon. The faint glow framed around a towering figure. His face was deathly pale, and blood red eyes locked into mine.

"*They* are the dangerous ones..."

The flames' sharp glow dulled to soft light beaming through the blinds. Feeling the solid floor beneath my feet, and the air, still cold, having no metallic scent, I let out a sigh of relief. It was just a dream.

As my eyes adjusted to the dark, my brow furrowed at the computer on my desk when I never owned one. I turned to the bed, and my heart leaped in my throat when I found a stranger sleeping in it. His arm rested over his face and the other settled on his chest. The drowsiness wore off as I recognized him, and fear settled in its place. This wasn't my room and the stranger in bed was my brother.

# Ethereal

**I jerked back, bumping my ankle against a stack of books** on the floor and it toppled with a raucous thud. I almost yelped until I slapped my hands over my mouth. Ichirou slept like an undisturbed stone, letting out small moans as if it were any normal night.

I pulled my trembling hands away, feeling a grainy texture between my fingers like dust. But it was too dark to see what it was. I rubbed it off my shirt, then tip-toed over the books towards Ichirou. The carpet straining under my feet did little to disturb his sleep.

"I-Ichirou?" I whispered, tapping his shoulder. His eyelids twitched and he stirred a little. I sucked in a deep breath and shook his shoulder.

"Ichirou!" I yelled.

He shot up as if he was doused by cold water. His head swiveled from the wall to me.

"Geez, Runt!" he shouted, jolting back. He took a moment to catch his breath. "What are you doing here?!"

"I don't know," I said in a quivering voice. "I woke up standing here."

"What do you mean? You don't remember getting out of bed?"

"No, I was..."

My head spun as memories of the evening pushed through my foggy mind. I was on the couch, talking to Elizabeth then doing my homework or... was I reading? When did I fall asleep? When did I change into my night clothes?

Mystic Rising

I rubbed the side of my head. "Ichirou, what was I doing when you came home?"

He groaned, "I had to work late so I came home around eleven. You were already sleeping in your room by then."

My stomach sank. "The last thing I remembered was talking to Elizabeth. I didn't feel tired."

Ichirou's grumpy face softened. He pulled himself out of bed and left the room.

"Where are you going?" I asked, on my way out.

"Checking around," Ichirou whispered. He nudged Hannah's door open and peeked inside. Aside from soft, deep breaths from Hannah, her room was quiet. Ichirou gently closed the door.

"Do you think I had another seizure?" I whispered.

"Maybe," Ichirou whispered back. "You've wandered around during your seizures before."

He headed downstairs and I followed. I never liked walking around the apartment at night. It always felt like there were too many spaces covered in shadows and too many strange noises from places I couldn't see.

"Wait," I said, something clicked in my mind. "The other morning, I woke up standing in my room."

"Do you remember going to bed before that?" Ichirou asked.

"Yeah, but I don't remember getting out of it."

He let out a deep sigh, "We may have to call Dr. Sanders about that."

Ichirou approached the patio door and drew the curtains aside. Shafts of moonlight outlined the cars, the grass and the tree, but something else must have caught Ichirou's attention. He immediately unlocked the door and pulled it open. The dead silence was filled with the sound of distant, wailing sirens.

A hard lump pressed against my throat. "Ichirou?"

"Stay inside," he demanded.

I froze beside the couch. Dread knotted my chest, my mind panicked at the thought of something lunging at Ichirou from the tree or between the cars. He made it to the grass and picked something up. My eyes narrowed at the white frame in his hand.

Ichirou turned around, when he looked up. "Runt, did you open your window?"

"No?" My voice cracked with fear. Ichirou returned to the apartment and closed the door. In his hand was a dark mesh stitched inside the square white frame.

"Is that window screen?"

163

"This is your window screen," he corrected.

Fearing the worst, Ichirou tossed the screen on the couch and rushed upstairs. My hands trembled when I locked the door, before hurrying after him. We reached the top of the stairs when Hannah emerged out of her room, tired and cradling a stuffed bear in her arms.

"Babe?" She moaned, drowsily. "Why is everyone up?"

"Mayu's window is open," Ichirou told her. "Did you hear anything unusual?"

Hannah's sleepy, half-closed eyes popped open. "Was someone trying to break in?"

"We don't know," I replied.

We hurried to my room and found my window pried open; moonlight shone across my bed through the raised blinds.

"Where's the screen?" Hannah asked.

"On the couch," said Ichirou. "It was outside like someone pushed it out."

He gripped the window to close it, but it was jammed to the frame.

"Did you open it?" Hannah asked me.

I shook my head and told her I woke up in Ichirou's room with no memory of falling asleep. "Did I do anything yesterday?"

"You went straight to your room shortly after I came home. I assumed you were going to sleep."

I chewed my lip, wracking my brain for an explanation. A focal or absence seizure could explain my memory loss, but I would have woken up moments after it happened, not hours. And if I had a grand mal seizure, I would have woken up on the floor, exhausted and dazed.

"You could have been sleepwalking," Hannah suggested. "I have a friend who used to wash dishes and cook in his sleep."

"I've never—" my voice seized up as the hairs on my neck stood on ends.

A deep, rippling howl tore through the silent night. An icy shiver traced down my spine, but as abruptly as it came, the howl faded, taking the noise of the night with it. No crickets chirped, the movements in the bushes ceased, even the tree froze with bated breath. Until a loud bark broke the silence. Small yips and yowling soon followed as if every dog in the neighborhood suddenly woke up.

Hannah spoke up first. "Was that a wolf?"

164

"There aren't any wolves here," Ichirou insisted, but I could hear a small tremble in his voice.

She gave him a wide, scared expression. "I used to live near the woods. That's a wolf, and it sounds close."

"It sounds big." I said, stepping away from the window. Memories of the beast in my dream rushed back to my mind.

Ichirou hopped on top of my desk and pushed his weight against the window while Hannah helped him pull it down.

"We should check around the apartment," Hannah said. "Make sure everything is locked.

"I already did," Ichirou grunted. "But I'll check again."

I jumped at the snap of Ichirou's fist pounding against the window. "This screen can only be pushed from inside, so I think—" he hit it again. "You could be right—" then again. "About Mayu sleepwalking!"

Ichirou pushed down and I covered my ears from the tearing screech coming from the window, before it stopped with an abrupt snap.

"I'll fix the screen tomorrow," Ichirou exhaled, then tugged the strings that released the blinds. "The best we can do for now is keep the window locked. Runt, are you going to be okay sleeping in here?"

"No," I said, rubbing my ears. "I don't feel comfortable right now." Especially after the howling.

"Mayu can sleep in my room for the night. And I can use the air mattress," Hannah said.

Ichirou looked at me. "Are you okay with that?"

"Better than sleeping in here," I confessed.

Ichirou double checked every lock in the apartment while Hannah pulled an old air mattress from her closet. She placed a lumpy grey rug next to her bed, flicked the switch and soft hum filled the room as the mattress steadily rose into the shape of a large pillow.

I grabbed my phone from my nightstand and returned to Hannah's room. I crawled into her bed, engulfed by the plush toys. Lutea told me to reach her in case anything weird happened. I thought the dream, the voice and waking up in my brother's room qualified for that.

*I heard the voice in my dream again.*

"Who are you texting this early?" Hannah asked, hovering over my shoulder.

I snapped the phone close. "No one."

"Uh, huh," she dragged then a small mischievous grin pinched her cheeks. "You were texting your boyfriend, Aiden, weren't you?"

"He's not my boyfriend!" I protested. "I don't even have his number."

"Sure, you don't."

Hannah stepped over the ballooning air mattress and pulled out an extra blanket from her drawer.

"First buildings are broken into, then cars are set on fire, and now wolves. Here I thought the fireworks going off in the dumpster was crazy."

"How long has this been happening? I only heard about the car catching on fire yesterday."

"Hard to say," Hannah yawned. "Buildings have been vandalized every year by attention seekers. This is a little extreme, though it wouldn't surprise me if torching a car was the latest trend. Makes you wonder who the real animals are."

I slipped under the blankets and turned to the blinds covering Hannah's window. Thinking about the wolf, I remembered a detail I read in a book about them. If one of their members was lost, they would howl to their pack to find them. But that only raised a worrying question about the wolf we heard: How many more were out there?

"I hope the wolf wasn't too close..." I said, softly.

"They typically don't like being around people, so it might have run back into the woods."

The door opened and we looked up to see Ichirou peering inside. "Apartment's clear and no boogeyman in sight." he said it so casually, I couldn't help but giggle. "Everyone all tucked in?"

"We are," Hannah said in a teasing voice. "Mayu was texting her boyfriend."

"He's not my boyfriend." I pouted.

"You shouldn't be on your phone right now. Put it away or turn it off," Ichirou said and closed the door. With the light banter gone, Hannah slipped under the blankets and frowned at the time on her clock.

"I can't believe it's already four in the morning," she moaned. Hannah usually had to be up around six.

"I'm so sorry."

"You don't have to apologize."

"Sorry..."

"Stop apologizing and go to sleep." She pulled the blanket up to her shoulder. "And stop texting your boyfriend."

I joked, "Fine."

Between burrowing in the soft blanket that smelled faintly of lavender and being surrounded by plush animals, sleep came almost instantly.

My eyes fluttered open to a low buzzing in my ear. Realizing it was my phone, I fished it from under the pillow and checked my messages. The screen dimly lit the toys when I read Lutea's reply.

*What did it say? What happened?*

I texted back. *Can't talk now. In Hannah's room. Don't want to wake her.*

Hannah shifted in her air mattress. She moaned and turned to the side, facing me. The phone buzzed, but I waited for several long seconds before I read Lutea's reply.

*Talk to me as soon as you're in school.*

• • •

Rumors of strange noises from last night circulated in class. One of the girls in English, Janie, said she woke up to a wolf howling outside and her usually quiet dog was awake, growling at the front door. Another girl, Catherine, claimed she heard loud booms coming from the woods, "like a cannon was going off!" Ms. Penn told her it could have come from the trees falling as a few blocked one of the roads on the way to school.

"Then what made the trees fall?" Janie asked, worry clear in her voice.

Ms. Penn went silent.

I stayed quiet during the conversation, worried about something else. What were the odds I'd dream about the woods the same night these events were happening. What danger was the voice trying to warn me about? Everything sounded mystic enough for me to ask an assistant, but Ethan was absent.

Physical science was no better. Sitting next to Mary was more awkward than I hoped. I had to force down the urge to speak to her, and when I wanted to, I shifted my gaze to Sarah who was asleep the entire time. Mr. Baryon woke her up a few times, then she dozed off the instant he walked away. I'd seen Ichirou and Hannah pull all-nighters, but I had never seen someone so sleep deprived, they looked like a corpse ready to collapse.

After the bell, I braced for Algebra when a familiar voice called out to me through the crowd.

"Hope you don't mind if I borrow you," said Lutea.

I smiled, "Not at all—"

I caught sight of Mary as she brushed past us. Not even a glance before she rushed for the stairs.

"Still not talking to you?" Lutea asked.

I shook my head.

"Give it time. For now, why don't you come with me to the assistant's lounge, if you want to talk about last night."

"There's an assistant's lounge?"

Lutea's smile returned. "If teachers can have one, why can't we?" She turned to the stairs.

I tailed behind her but before we headed there, we stopped by at algebra. Mr. Turner stood by the door, his tied-up hair was slightly unkempt and faint dark circles hung beneath his eyes, making his white complexion stand out more.

"Did anyone sleep last night?" I asked.

"Afraid not," Mr. Turner replied. "I take it you're going to be with Lutea for today? Do you have a pass."

Lutea answered. "Wrote it before I picked Mayu up. Can you sign it?"

He yawned, "I will as soon as Mrs. Bean signs it."

At the sound of her name, Mrs. Bean stalked to the door, puffing up her chest.

"What do you want my signature for?" She scowled.

"It's for an emergency," Mr. Turner told her. "She needs her note signed by an assistant and a teacher."

"Why?" she demanded. "Does she need to leave immediately?"

*Why do you care*? I thought. *It's not like you wanted me in class to begin with.*

Mr. Turner gave Mrs. Bean the pass. Her nose wrinkled as if he had given her a handful of garbage.

"I don't know what this is about," she said sternly, her eyes flitted between Mr. Turner and Lutea. "But I will make sure the admin hears about assistants pulling students out of their classes. I hope you know you're preventing them from getting the education they need."

Mr. Turner rolled his eyes. Lutea took the note, and I couldn't be any happier to leave Mrs. Bean. I could still feel her eyes digging into my back.

"I almost forgot how much of a pain she was," Lutea mumbled. "I can see why you needed help."

I strolled down the hallway, my hand grazed absentmindedly against the lockers.

"Why does Mr. Turner let her do this?"

"Trust me, if he could, he would do more to help that class. But Mrs. Bean cares more about wanting him gone, than *educating* her students," Lutea said, mocking the word 'educating.'

*Horrible*, I thought.

I stopped in front of the same rusty locker with its door hanging open. One would think someone would have fixed the latch or used a lock to keep it closed.

"Speaking of Cedric," Lutea said beside me, coming to a stop. "Since you're coming back to the meeting, are you going to let him tutor you?"

I closed the locker and gave her a half-hearted shrug. "Mrs. Bean told me he could lose his job if he picks favorites."

"Oh, please!" Lutea scoffed. Her reaction confused me before she explained it. "Mrs. Bean is always looking for a reason to get rid of Cedric. If all it took was his signature on a student's homework, he would have been gone day one."

"He can help me?" I dragged out the words, realizing how easily I believed Mrs. Bean, of all people.

"Of course! He would love to teach you again."

Embarrassment couldn't begin to describe how I felt. My face melted into my hands to hide the heat rushing to my cheeks. I couldn't say my next words aloud, much less in English.

"Aho ga-ru desu..."

"Not sure what you said, but... it happens to the best of us? In any case, we should head to the lounge. And you can't see it if you keep covering your face."

I groaned and reluctantly lifted my head.

We arrived at the second floor and stopped in front of a door that had a bronze plaque beside it with the word, "HOME EC.," etched on it. Through the window I saw blue walls and round tables with one or two assistants each. Lutea pressed her lanyard against the sigh, and after a small beep sounded, she opened the door.

"Welcome to the assistant's lounge," She announced proudly.

Bittersweet coffee hung over the lounge. Small talk circulated from the assistants conversing at the round tables. Few sat alone at the counters or with company at the couches.

I was speechless at first. "Did I just walk inside of a café?"

Lutea laughed. "You should have seen the principal's face after we remodeled it. We wanted to do the same for the teachers' lounge, but they were against it."

My eyes widened. "Why? If I was a teacher, I'd love to come to a lounge like this every day!"

"That was the ongoing problem," another voice joined us from behind.

I spun around to find a dark-skinned girl at the table. She reminded me of a goth person. She wore black laced gloves, and a frilled skirt held up by a pair of suspenders, fishnet leggings and combat boots that reached up to her kneecaps.

"Can't teach if you don't want to leave," the girl spoke, her sterling green eyes sent a shiver down her spine. Then I realized I'd seen her before. She was the assistant who helped Ethan break up the fight and was often by his side during the meetings, though I hadn't learned her name.

"Mayu, this is my friend, Chitose Yumekui," Lutea introduced. "I told her about the dream and the voices."

*Yume Kui*? I pondered. *Her surname's Dream Eater?*

"It's nice to meet you," I said to her.

Chitose's eyes flickered in my direction, and I blinked a couple of times when I noticed they were brown.

"I've seen you in the meetings but it's nice to meet the Anomaly in person."

Her brown eyes changed to grey, then it changed again to another color. The harder I focused, the more tired I felt.

"So, what's going on with the dream?" Chitose asked. "Lutea told me you heard a voice speak to you."

My eyes fluttered open, and I was suddenly awake. I pulled up a chair and sat with Lutea and Chitose, shaking off the sleepiness. I noticed a board behind the counter with a long list of names and days on it. Most were checked off with "Xs" and I noticed an empty slot next to Ethan's name.

"Is Ethan alright?" I asked, Chitose followed my gaze. "He assists my English class and wasn't here today. Is he sick?"

"He was working last night but should be back tomorrow." Chitose replied.

"He has a second job?"

"Something like that." She sat up, straightening her posture. "So, tell me about this voice."

I told them what I saw in my dream and what the voice warned me about, before waking up in Ichirou's room.

Chitose's blue eyes melted to lilac as worry settled on her face. "Was that it? Were you holding something?"

"I wasn't," I said. "But I heard a wolf howling the same night I dreamt about a beast. I remembered being in the woods, the same time I heard about trees falling on the road this morning."

"Do you think what you saw in your dream and what happened is related?" Lutea asked.

"I'm not sure," I said. "It feels like it."

"Or it could be your mind incorporating events into your head," said Chitose. "Dreams are so abstract, having consistency in them is the most unusual thing to happen. Right now, the only consistency is the voice."

"Do you know what it is?" I asked. "I know I shouldn't have spoken to it, but it sounded like it wanted to warn me of something dangerous."

"Yet, you woke up standing in your brother's room with no prior memory," Chitose reminded. "It sounds like the voice is an ethereal being that's testing its control on you. Last night might have been its limit."

My chest tightened. "Why me?"

"Most Etherians, like ghosts or fae seek something from the mortal world, but it needs a mortal body to interact with it. It might have unfinished business or craving a simple joyride."

I recoiled. The thought of being used like a toy felt wrong in ways I couldn't describe. "Don't Etherians need the person's permission before possessing them?"

Chitose snickered, "You watch too many movies. The polite ones ask." My heart started to race when her cold silver eyes melted into a haunting green. "We don't need your permission to control your body."

My heart stopped.

"Hey, I asked first."

Lutea cleared her throat. "Chitose, what can you do about it? Can you investigate her dreams?"

"I don't sense anything in you now. Whatever was controlling you, left," Chitose said. Then she looked down at my watch. "Does that come with an alarm?"

I replied, feeling my throat drying up. "It does. Why do you ask?"

"The voice had appeared twice in your dreams. And twice you've woken up in odd places. This implies the entity doesn't have

171

full control yet if it can only take you in your sleep. But if you had a way to wake yourself up at night, maybe it'll leave you alone."

"Has that worked before?"

"Etherians prefer hosts with vulnerable minds. They won't put any effort in possessing someone who can fight back."

I shifted awkwardly in my seat, processing that I was talking to a spirit or whatever was in that girl's body. But the alarm didn't sound like a bad idea. Better than none, I suppose.

"My break is about to end," Chitose said. "Good luck, Mayu. I hope this all works out."

"Wait, what?"

"Mata Ne!"

Wisps of smoke peeled from her body, smelling faintly of charred plants and ash. I lurched back and she vanished, leaving behind an empty chair where she once sat.

"I should have warned you about her first. Chitose can be a bit excentric when meeting new people," Lutea said quietly. "Are you going to be alright?"

"I wasn't sure what to expect." I brushed my hand through my hair, taking in everything I heard. "Do you think this plan will work?"

"It doesn't hurt to try. And you know who to come to if you need help."

"I know." I straightened my back and stared at my watch. "Any chance you know how to set up an alarm?"

She narrowed her eyes on my watch, her brow arched, and her head tilted to the side. Then Lutea stared at me and shrugged.

·●·

The old librarian greeted me at the door. I gave him a kind hello, then looked for a place to sit. I found a table close to the window, but someone was already there, resting his head against his wrist. Though his bangs covered his face, I recognized the red headphones on his neck.

I moved closer to the table. "Aiden?"

He sprang up with a start, his hair clung to the side of his face and drool trailed down his chin. Surprisingly, his bangs still covered his right eye.

"Mayu?" His voice slurred. "What are you doing here? What time is it?"

"It's twelve-o-two," I said, sitting in front of him. Aiden relaxed and sighed in relief. "I didn't mean to scare you. You looked awake from where I stood."

His left eye widened. "I was asleep?" He rubbed his cheek and glanced at his arms. "Y-You didn't see anything strange, did you?"

"Do you talk in your sleep or something?"

"I don't think so," Aiden mumbled. He patted his hair down to its somewhat messy style. "Are you feeling better?"

I stared at him, narrowing my eyes. "Huh?"

"Sorry for prying but I overheard Lutea asking to excuse you from class earlier."

Aiden was no stranger to the mystic world, but I didn't think he should know about my sleepwalking or the voices, yet.

"Oh, I needed to talk to her about something, so we went to the lounge, and now I'm here."

"So, you're skipping class," He grinned. "Aren't you a rebel in the making."

"No!" I said, my blushing cheeks rose. "I had reasons to skip Mrs. Bean."

"Same," he remarked. "Got a headache and Mr. Turner had to convince her to let me leave."

"I bet your head's feeling much better, huh?"

"Getting away from her certainly helped. Two of her least favorite students leave and she acts like it's the end of the world."

"You do seem to leave her class the most. And aren't you supposed to be in Physics, right now?"

Aiden scoffed, "Announce it through the P.A why don't ya. And I don't see you in a hurry to class."

"Jokes on you. This is my lunch period."

"Fine, fine, you got me," he chuckled. "Before I left, Mrs. Bean mentioned docking grades for anyone who leaves her class early."

"Of course, she would."

"Not to worry, Mr. Turner always has our backs." Aiden drew the blue notebook from his bag and cleared his throat. "To thy lady," he announced, boldly. "I present to ye, thy scrolls of algebra in aid against thy ghastly ghoul."

I burst into laughter, curling into my seat. I covered my mouth but couldn't stop the giggles slipping between my fingers.

"I know it's lame," he said, his face reddening. "My teacher made us talk in Old English for extra credit."

"It suits a knight like you. You're always 'Aid-en' me."

Aiden snorted. "I thought I was bad with puns. Since we're doing this, 'May-u' do the honor of returning that tomorrow?" His face twisted into a disgusted look. "That sounded way better in my head..."

"You'll get the hang of it." I said. "Do you know how to turn on a watch alarm?"

"You don't know?"

"Not anymore."

It used to go off twice a day when I was on my medication. When they stopped working, Ichirou turned off the alarm, but I never asked him how he did it. Looking back, I wished I had. I could have asked Ichirou to change it again. He's heard me say crazier things about my seizures, but "turning on an alarm to stop a voice in my head from possessing me" would be the strangest.

"I can try it," Aiden offered, eying my watch. "Can I get a closer look at it?"

Rarely had I taken my watch off, and it felt strange not having it around my wrist. As I passed it to Aiden, something bright flickered in the courtyard, grabbing my attention. I froze. Aiden turned around as the lights bunched against the window.

"The sprites are getting more active by the day," he said, his gaze returned to me.

My insides tensed up. "Sprites? You can see them?"

Aiden's eye narrowed. "Moving lights, yes. You thought you were the only one who could see them?"

My eyes fell on my watch. Aiden noticed the medical clip, and he gave me a knowing, understanding look.

I whispered, "Small voices and floating lights are symptoms of an aura—a warning before I have a seizure."

"Are you sure that's a symptom?"

I looked up at him.

"Mayu, the assistants are mythical creatures. A small portion of students here aren't entirely human, and we meet in a magic room run by an actual witch. Is it hard to believe that floating lights could be more than just...symptoms?"

"My brain scans say different," I insisted.

"Sometimes there are things science can't explain yet." Aiden left his seat and turned to the courtyard. "If you want to be certain, do you want to see them up close?"

"Them?" I repeated. "How?"

We grabbed our bags, and I was about to approach the librarian when Aiden asked, "Where are you going?"

I turned and replied, "We need a key to get into the courtyard."
Aiden motioned me to the door. "Watch this."

I returned and saw Aiden's hand ball into fists. He lightly tapped the door in a fast, arrhythmic pattern, then we heard a loud, hard click from it.

I stepped back. "What did you do?"

He answered quietly, "I let them know that we're here. Ready?"

Aiden pressed his hand against the door, and it eased open without a groan to be heard. The late summer warmth rolled inside, filling the library with a scent of flowers.

My mouth hung. "This thing weighed a ton before!"

"Only if you go in with the key. If you knock to the fae, they'll take the weight off the door."

Aiden let me go first.

I couldn't shake the feeling that we were being watched. From where, I couldn't tell. Was it from the ivy vines clinging to the walls? Did it come from the tree slouched over a bench? Or the sunburst yellow flowers rimmed around the gazebo?

I caught the orbs of lights bobbing over the petals. I recited the names of the flowers, the colors, then I forced myself to look past the light, straining my vision to see a tiny, wispy body. Their hair flowed like thread of a spider's web. Faint and quick, yet soft as a feather brushing against my arm.

"This is…" I choked out.

The sprite floated off my hand. Tears pricked my eyes as they bounced from the primrose to the coneflowers. They peered at us through the vines, and floated toward the flowers, carried by rays of sunlight between the trees.

"Still think this is in your head?"

I spun around to Aiden. Beads of light bubbled off his hands and floated to the vines above. "You got a visitor."

I looked up and my hands cupped a fluttering flower bud. Insect legs sprouted from the buds and a small round face with compound eyes beamed back at me. The petals on their backs waved gently like wings.

"I'm not… fading," I said, then realized Aiden could hear me. "I'm sorry!"

"Not so loud," Aiden whispered. "You're a giant compared to them."

I whispered the softest apology I could muster to the fairy. Its petal wrapped around its trembling body. I lowered my hand to the potted plants. The bulb waddled toward the stem and burrowed itself in the soil.

Walking along the path, I took in every sprite around us. Water sprites were clear, their bodies shimmered fragments under the lights and they left little wet spots on the wood where they walked. Light sprites rode the sunbeams to the gazebo, and they moved like fireflies in the shadows beneath the leaves.

"What did you mean by fading?" Aiden asked.

I joined him on the bench in the gazebo.

"When an aura hits, I fade into a seizure," I tried to reword it so it would make more sense. "Have you ever watched those sped up videos of stars moving as the earth rotates, but the ground stays perfectly still?"

"Yeah."

"Sometimes, my aura is like that. Except the sky and the earth are moving and I'm not. No matter how hard I want to move forward, I fade into the background."

"That sounds terrifying. Are you feeling it now?"

"No."

A Light sprite sloped in my hands, their bodies were warm to the touch, and it danced merrily to the vines, bringing sunlight to its leaves.

"Aiden, if the fae are real, why do I always have a seizure when I see them?"

"I'm not a doctor, so I'm guessing here. If seizures affect the brain, maybe it unlocks certain abilities that you've never had before, like seeing fae and other spirits."

I stared at him, curiosity written all over my face.

"My parents told me humans used to see and interact with mystics. There was a time when we had abilities like them. Telekinesis, clairvoyance, mind reading and so on."

I was skeptical about the last part. "Then how did we go from having powers to having none?"

"The answer's right in front of you," he said, showing my watch to me.

My brow wrinkled.

"We wanted more than what we were capable of, so we made anything and everything that could fix all our problems with little effort. But the more we relied on that, the less strength we put in our own powers, and it slowly faded overtime."

We watched the wind sprites dance around the hanging leaves, twirling them in a small breeze.

"A lot of people can see or hear the fae but they either ignore it, look for some scientific explanation or assume it's all in their head."

"What made you realize they were real?"

"I've always known." Aiden met my eyes. "Can I show you something? Promise me you won't panic?"

I broke out in a nervous laugh. "You're not going to change into anything, are you?"

"You have my word."

He sat up and brushed his hand across his face, pushing the bangs aside. A twinge of shock ran through me. He almost looked like a different person but was still Aiden. His left eye was earthly brown with hints of green around the iris. Then I saw his right eye, a solid pale green, like sea foam breaking on the shore.

"You're...blind?"

Aiden let his bangs sweep over his clouded eye. "When I was two, I got sick and came close to dying. There was nothing doctors could do, and my parents prayed for a miracle. They told me a being of light appeared before them. It wasn't a sprite but something more... archaic and obscure. It heard their prayers and told them it could save me, but in return, it had to take something."

"It took your sight?"

"That was the tradeoff," Aiden said, shifting up on the bench. "Honestly, it could have taken any part of me, so I got lucky... sort of. After I recovered, I could see the fae much clearer than before, like my other senses had heightened to make up for the loss of sight."

"I can't imagine how confusing that was."

"Unbelievably so," he huffed. "At first, I thought everyone could see them. It wasn't until I was nine that I realized it wasn't the case. My parents and Kaiah can sometimes sense them. Natia has acute awareness, which is normal for a five-year-old."

My eyes drifted to the surrounding flowers and floating lights bumping against the windows.

"Does it get... easier?" I asked. "Being part of this world."

Aiden paused. "Eventually. It also helps that there are more people like us. Makes the world feel less lonely."

I almost forgot he had my watch until he gave it to me. "Hold the button to set the alarm, then use the button on the opposite side to change the time you want."

"Thank you." I fixed the watch on my wrist. We sat in silence, and I found myself getting closer to Aiden, wanting to take away that inch of space between us. I wanted to talk to him more, yet I preferred the silence as we watched the fae go about their day.

Like every good dream, the shrill bell cut the moment short.

"Off to class we go," Aiden said.

"Unfortunately," I added.

Aiden left for the door. I gathered my backpack and noticed a couple of fae on the bench. They were dressed in purple petals and covering their mouths while their shoulders shook up and down almost like they were giggling. One of them leaned into the other and pecked them on the cheek.

"He's just a friend," I hissed through my teeth and hurried to the open door.

We left the peaceful courtyard, left the silent library and joined the students as they passed through the noisy, crowded hallway.

"Have a safe trip to class," said Aiden.

"You too!" I said. "And don't skip yours anymore, you hear me!"

Aiden smirked. "Jokes on you. This is my lunch period."

# Phantom

**My ears were ringing**. Whips of heat flew in my direction and fire splattered against the trees, igniting the leaves into a burning inferno.

"*Run!*" The voice cried out. "*Run, now!*"

I took off from the fire and retreated into the darkness. The heat choked the air out of my lungs and the smoke burned my insides. I could *feel* the smoke burning. Through my blurry vision, I could make out a familiar face. His ice gold eyes landed on me, now flared with rage. His pale face illuminated by the fire. I scrambled back, unable to let out a scream before he lunged at me and a sharp pain twisted into my chest.

I woke up in a cold sweat in my bed, feeling only the fabric of my pajamas bunched under my fist. There were no fire or smoke and the pain in my chest quickly faded.

*It was just a dream.* I thought, sinking into the bed.

"Just a dream," I croaked. My throat ached, feeling like sandpaper. Then I remembered the ringing and I quickly checked my watch. The alarm had gone off, but it didn't wake me up.

*That's alright.* I heard it in my dream and woke up in my bed.

I put my glasses on and squinted at the morning light streaming through the window. Ichirou fixed the screen while I was in school and, thankfully, it looked like no one tried to break in or out. One less thing for me to worry about. I crawled out of bed and changed into my uniform when someone knocked on my door.

"Mayu, are you up?" Hannah called.

"I am." I fastened the buttons on the blouse then opened the door to see a worried look on Hannah's face.

179

"Is everything alright?"

"I wanted to see how you're doing. You scared us last night," she said.

Last night? "What do you mean?"

"You were sleepwalking. I heard an alarm go off around three and saw you leave your room. Your eyes were half open, you didn't answer when I called your name. You just... went downstairs."

"I... I didn't hear you. What was I doing downstairs?"

"Ichirou and I followed you to the screen door. You were fumbling with the locks like you were trying to get out. And then you collapsed until Ichirou caught you. He had to carry you upstairs."

I paused, trying to process her words.

"I think you should get this checked out," she continued.

Before I could say anything, Ichirou called out from the bottom of the stairs. "Is she up, Hannah?"

"Yes, I am!" I called back.

Hannah asked, "Should you go to school?"

"I'm fine now," I said. Staying home wouldn't fix my sleepwalking anyway. I slipped on my backpack and hurried past Hannah, but I couldn't ignore how concerned she looked.

On the way to school, Ichirou and I listened to the news on the radio. Another fire had broken out near the woods. My stomach stirred, thinking about the fire's heat, the suffocating smoke, and those gold eyes.

"Runt, are you okay?" Ichirou asked.

"I don't know," I said.

"Want to talk about it?"

I shrugged, but figured there wasn't any in it, I told Ichirou about the dream.

"You keep dreaming about the fires because that's all you've been hearing," he said and turned off the radio.

"Hannah told me I was sleepwalking again."

"Yeah, you almost left the apartment." He turned the corner, only to discover the fallen tree blocking the road, so he took another route, keeping quiet on the way to school. That worried me.

"Ichirou?"

"You could have left the apartment last night. You don't think you're going to do the same when you're at Elizabeth's?"

"What?" Those words tightened around my chest. "What do you mean?

180

"Until we figure out why you're sleepwalking, I think you should postpone the sleepover."

"But I'm trying to stop it!" I cried.

"How? Is that why you had the alarm turned on?"

"I thought it could wake me up. I heard it in my dreams."

"You still didn't wake up."

We pulled up at school, but I didn't move.

"Don't make us reschedule," I begged. "I'll do the dishes tonight."

"Runt…"

"I won't ask you to look at my homework!"

"Runt."

"I'll go to bed early—"

"Mayu!" Ichirou shouted. Silence filled the car before he added quietly and firmly, "We'll talk about this later at home."

"But—"

"Later. Go to school. Now."

I yanked up my backpack and stormed out of the car and into school. It wasn't until I was walking down the hallway, eyes stinging beneath the fluorescent light, that I realized Ichirou had a point. What if the voice came back when I was at Elizabeth's house? What if I did fall and hurt myself. Or left the house? I didn't want to cancel the sleepover, and I didn't want to spend another night at the hospital. I needed answers.

Instead of going straight to class, I went to the infirmary. Caritas wasn't Dr. Sanders, but it wouldn't hurt to ask her about sleepwalking. Maybe she knew how to treat it and if not, I could talk to Lutea or Chitose.

On my way to the infirmary, the voice's words came back to me. Someone was dangerous, and it wanted me to run away. Slowing down in front of the infirmary, I clenched my knotting stomach. Nausea settled over me as the beast and the pale man with golden eyes flickered back into my thoughts. Why did those eyes look like—

My nose wrinkled at a sharp, wet and metallic scent spilling through the infirmary's half-open door. I heard hushed, yet frantic voices from inside and someone grounding out in pain.

I eased closer, peeking inside to see the stools had been upturned, and dark blood stained the floor and one of the beds. Chitose was on her knees, holding someone's hand, but it didn't take long to recognize Ethan on the floor. My eyes lowered to his back, and I covered my mouth, masking my shock at the deep gashes torn into his skin. His glazed eyes stared up at the ceiling, only to squeeze shut in pain.

"Of all the places to bring him, why here?!" Caritas hissed. She dropped to her knees beside Ethan, partially covering my view of him.

"This was closer to where we were," Chitose told her. "If we went home, he would've bled out before he could heal."

"This is a school's infirmary! I only have so many supplies."

"These will have to do." Mr. Turner said, carrying gauzes, a white cloth, and a bottle of alcohol, but it was the needle in his hand that sent a shiver down my spine.

"Ethan, we're going to have to stitch the wound closed, so bear with us."

Chitose tightened her grip on Ethan while Caritas held him down by his legs. Mr. Turner got closer with the thread and needle in one hand and a bottle of alcohol in the other.

Ethan's eyes shot open with agony, and he bucked on the floor, but Chitose and Caritas forced him still. Caritas spoke to him in a soothing voice, but he seemed to be in too much pain to hear her. I didn't know how long I watched, but when it was over, Ethan's chest rose and fell, sweat pooled down his forehead and his glazed, amber eyes turned to me.

I jerked up and raced to the hallway. I held my chest, my heart thudded heavy and hard in my ears.

No matter how much I didn't want to think about it, or how hard I tried to drown my thoughts in reading, I couldn't stop wondering if my dreams were connected to the events around the neighborhood.

Ms. Penn was writing questions on the board when the door opened, grabbing her attention. Ethan stepped inside with his neck and left arm wrapped in gauze and his right arm hung in a sling.

"Oh my God, what happened to you?!" Ms. Penn yelped.

"Were you attacked?" Janie asked.

"Did you get into an accident?"

Curious, I lowered my book and looked at him.

"I fell down some stairs," he said flatly. "And through a window."

The room exploded with the girls calling Ethan a liar.

One of them shouted, "Yeah right, what *really* happened!"

"Alright, that's enough, leave him alone," Ms. Penn urged. "You still need to finish your passage."

The girls moaned.

Ethan approached my desk, and I froze. The hairs on my neck bristled and my heart skipped when he caught my gaze.

"You're two rows apart again," he rasped.

I stuttered, "No, I'm..."

My head turned slowly to the left and sure enough, two empty rows sat between me and my classmates.

With a sharp sigh, I gathered my backpack and moved to a desk closer to the girls. For the next ten minutes, everyone was reading, but it was hard to ignore Ethan's wincing when he moved around the room.

"I'm fine," he insisted when Ms. Penn told him to see a doctor. "Don't worry, I'm going to be okay."

No one believed him. Then, almost like the girls and I read each other's thoughts, we offered to assist Ms. Penn. Catherine read aloud, then the next girl volunteered to do the same. Another girl wrote on the board while I passed the papers around. Ms. Penn was impressed and suggested we should be assistants when we were older. It was a funny thought until I looked back at Ethan and his bandaged wounds. It made me wonder what assistants had to deal with when they weren't helping teachers or breaking up fights at school.

"Are you sure you're going to be okay?" I asked Ethan after class.

Even shifting in his chair was painful for him. "It could be worse," he whispered. "Don't worry, I heal fast anyway."

"Take it easy. I don't want get hurt any more than you are."

"You and me both." Ethan winced.

Rather than ask him what happened, I told him to take it easy and went to my next class, hoping he'd feel better.

It was another awkward day in physical science. Mary was reading another play as I sat next to her, and Sarah was fast asleep. I kept to myself, jotting down notes and working on my assignment when Mary said, "hey" in a low voice.

I looked at her, confused. Then gave her a similar response. We returned to silence before I finally asked, "Are you still mad at me?"

Mary faced me. "I thought you didn't want to hang out with me."

I snorted unintentionally. "Over a game? Why would I leave you for that?"

She rolled her shoulders. "You seemed to have so much fun with them. And you picked that junior over me."

"Mary, I wouldn't forget about you in one class. You're my friend. I see you more than Damian or Becky-Tran."

"I realized that too," she sighed. "I don't know what came over me. I can't believe I got mad over a boy."

"It happens."

"Do you want to work on the assignment together. I missed that."

I smiled, "Sure."

Mary set her book down and pulled out her journal. We shared our notes, read the question on the paper and looked for the answer in the textbook. For a moment, it felt like things were going to be normal again.

Mary and I jumped to a loud scream coming from our table, bringing the classroom commotion to silence. Sarah was wide awake, hands clutching the back of her head. Her teary eyes darted to Victoria, who stood at her table with a shocked expression on her face.

"Why did you pull my hair!" Sarah yelled, voice wobbling.

"What, I didn't do anything!" Victoria snapped. "Do what, don't go crazy on me."

"You pulled my hair!"

"Victoria," Mr. Baryon called from his desk. "Do you need to change seats for today?"

"I did nothing!" she protested. "Why should I move? She's the one acting crazy!"

Victoria dropped into her chair and crossed her arms in a huff. Sarah rubbed her head, stifling her cries as tears rolled down her cheeks. Seeing the other girls snickering at Sarah and mocking her, struck a chord in me. I stood up and walked to Sarah, ignoring Victoria's angry glare.

"Hey, do you need help? Do you need to see the nurse?" I whispered.

Sarah didn't respond. The back of her hair was tousled with strands strewn around her chair. I happened to glance up at Victora and noticed similar hair strands clinging to her capris.

She shouted sounding almost offended, "What are you looking at!"

I bit my lip, fighting the urge to respond.

"Yeah, that's what I thought!"

"Victoria, change seats now," Mr. Baryon.

"But I'm not doing anything! These crazy girls keep acting up!"

I ignored her and turned back to Sarah. She stopped crying and her trembling shoulders settled.

"Sarah?" I whispered.

An iciness in the air pinched my cheek, and a new voice, cold and hollow, floated around me.

"Don't do it...please" Sarah murmured. "You'll only make it worst."

I stepped back, then jumped to a scream erupting from Victoria's table.

Victoria twisted around, holding her hair. Her water eyes landed on me. "You think this is funny!" she bellowed.

I said, confused. "What are you talking about?"

But she stormed to our table, only making it a few feet when she tumbled forward and fell clumsily in front of me. I jumped back to see her friends throw accusatory glares at me. Before I could speak up, I froze upon seeing the girl towering over Victoria.

No one reacted to her, as if they couldn't see her. Her body was translucent, her long, ink black hair slumped over her face, but the tightness in my chest told me she could see me too.

I bolted out of the classroom, not caring that Mary or Mr. Baryon were calling my name. I stopped to catch my breath and jumped at the school bell ringing. My thoughts were racing. I took another deep breath when Sarah rushed by me.

"Sarah!" I called, catching up with her. "T-Tell me you saw her too, didn't you?"

Her eyes widened and her lips quivered. "I—I don't know what you're talking about."

"You were telling her to stop, not me," I said. "Did she push Victoria?"

"No! Leave me alone!" she yelled and hurried down the hallway.

Just as I was about to catch up to her, Mary called out to me, hurrying to my side.

"What happened back there? Why did you run out of the room like that?"

"I..." I turned back to the hallway and Sarah disappeared again. "I...wanted to help Sarah..."

"But you left before she did. Mayu, I know you want to help her, but you have to stay away from her."

"What was I supposed to do, let her get picked on again?"

"No, I wanted you to..." Mary's voice stopped, and then she gasped. "Oh no..."

The hairs on my neck rose and I spun around, catching Victoria before she shoved me against the locker. She arched over me, eyes burning with rage.

"You friends with that freak?" she snarled. "Did she pull my hair?"

Tears pricked the corner of my eyes. *Don't cry*, I begged myself. *Don't cry. Don't cry.* I couldn't stand looking at her face, but I didn't want her to think I was afraid of her.

"She didn't," I mustered. "But you shouldn't have done it either!"

Victoria sneered, "What're you gonna do, snitch on me?" She pushed me against the locker again and stormed off.

*Don't cry. Don't cry.* I rubbed my arms again and again. *Don't cry. Don't cry. Don't cry. Deep breaths. Don't cry. Deep Breaths.*

Mary's hand rested on my shoulder. "What did she have against you?"

My body shook so much, I could barely get the words out. "I was trying to help her."

"Why?" Mary pleaded. "Why are you so quick to defend her? Didn't she shout at you in the bathroom? Didn't she tell you to go away?"

Her words snapped something in me. I stopped trembling and whipped around with anger in my voice. "Don't you think she doesn't want to be treated like an outcast all the time?"

Mary stepped back, but her expression softened. "I know you want to help her, but Victoria could've hurt you. Whatever Sarah's dealing with, it shouldn't involve you."

It wouldn't be the first time a bully threatened me. I wanted to argue but Mary's gentle eyes full of worry eased my rising anger.

"If Sarah needs help, she should go to a teacher or an assistant. I don't want to see you get hurt defending her."

I let out a deep breath. "Fine."

•●•

Mrs. Bean greeted me with her usual scowl when I came to class. She gave me a five-page assignment along with my graded homework. But my mind was still stuck on Sarah. I couldn't stop thinking about the ghost to care about the bad grade scrawled on my paper.

"Mayu?"

I turned to Aiden at our desk. "Huh?"

"I called your name five times," he whispered. "What's wrong?"

"Nothing," I said, "I'm fine."

"Usually when people say they're fine, they don't mean it."

"I had a bad morning." I whispered back.

"No talking in class, Mayu!" Mrs. Bean lectured from the board.

Rolling my eyes, I lowered my head and continued jotting nonsense in my notebook. A moment later, Aiden passed his notebook to me with a letter written in it.

*Do you want to talk about it after class?*

*Not sure yet.*

He wrote something again. *You know where to find me if you want to talk.*

"No skipping class," I murmured.

Aiden snorted, "I make no promises."

I made up my mind to talk to Mr. Turner after class. Not just about the ghost, but the dream I had, which was still fresh in my mind. Mr. Turner stood at the board, jotting down equations when I approached him.

"Something amiss?" he asked.

As he raised his arm to write, I noticed the bandage wrapped from his elbow to his wrist and thought about what happened in the infirmary. As much as I wanted to tell him about the ghost, I mentioned quietly that he was in my dream.

"I get that a lot," he remarked.

"No, you were fighting someone," I whispered, keeping my voice low and stern. "And then... you attacked them, but I felt it, like you were attacking me."

Mr. Turner stopped writing. An uneasy look settled on his face. He capped the marker and turned to Mrs. Bean.

"I need to step out of class for a moment," he told her.

"What for?" Mrs. Bean groaned, looking up from her desk. She noticed me and groaned again. "Oh. Make it quick."

We went to the hallway after the late bell and stepped away from the classroom door. Mr. Turner towered over me; his pale skin and golden eyes matched his stony stare in my dream. I swallowed back, fighting down the panic in my throat and told him about my dreams, all of them. Including what I saw in the infirmary.

When I finished, I saw a flicker of shock course through his face.

"This all happened after you crossed worlds?" he finally asked.

I nodded, shakily. "Why can I see you in my dreams? Who were you and Ethan fighting?"

After a brief pause, Mr. Turner let out a breath through his nose. "You're aware that there are mystics outside of this school?"

187

"Yes."

"Not all of them are benevolent. Some seek to harm others. And it looks like one has tried to communicate with you by linking your thought with theirs."

My stomach sank. "Chitose told me it was an Etherian. What does it want with me?"

"Remember, you crossed into another world and survived unscathed. One could imagine the creatures out there that would seek that ability."

The floor spun beneath my feet. Before I could ask, the door swung open and Mrs. Bean poked her head out, glowering at us.

"Are you done yet? The late bell rang half an hour ago, and I need my assistant."

"In a moment," Mr. Turner replied. He hoisted himself off the locker, leaned in and whispered to me, "We'll talk about this later."

Mr. Turner returned to algebra, closing the door behind him. Left alone, I wandered through the hall, wishing he could have told me more about who he was fighting.

• ● •

The gym room was divided by a line of tape across the floor, so students could play dodgeball on one side, and volleyball on the other. I joined a small team in dodgeball, wanting to take my mind off the day.

The game started off exciting. I dodged one ball and jumped back as another zipped by my ear. I caught a few balls of my own, but something felt... off. It wasn't as intense as I remembered. By the end of the second round, the other players were slowing down, exhausted.

Aside from me, Damien was the only one on the other team that never broke a sweat. He could snatch a ball midair, hurl it back at my team, and still have the energy to dodge them. It seemed like we were the only ones having fun.

But I wanted something different. I wanted to challenge myself. See, no one had tried to catch Damien's throws, including me. He threw the balls the way cannons shot their ammo. Everyone avoided him, but I wanted to see if I could catch it.

I stepped forward, readying myself. My eyes narrowed to Damien as if to tell him, *go ahead and throw it. Don't you dare hold back.*

Damien grinned. He had a ball in his hand, pulled his arm back and in one swing, it flew. I didn't have time to catch my breath. I dropped to the ground as the wind ripped over me.

I remembered swerving from Damien's throws, my body darted from the ball as it hissed past me at great speed. The impact broke the silence in the gym, and that's when I noticed the stares. My classmates' eyes were on us. They were on me. I dove to the floor as a rush of red flew past me and exploded in a deafening pop.

"Are you okay!" Mary cried.

She was by my side with Becky-Tran and Ms. Bloom.

"Did that hit you?" Becky-Tran asked.

Unable to answer, I slowly turned to the wall behind me. Several cracks branched from a dent and beneath it lay the deflated dodgeball that could have hit me.

"Damien, what's wrong with you!" Mr. Trouse shouted, storming across the gym. "We were telling you to stop. Why didn't you listen!?"

*Was he? I didn't hear him.* I thought.

"It's not his fault!" I jumped to my feet, holding my head as a dizzying wave came over me.

But Mr. Trouse turned his sharp glare to me. "That was your last warning. Until the end of class, you're both benched."

"What?!" Damien and I shrieked.

"You two want detention then?" he threatened.

Damien's eyes blazed, and he whipped away the same time I did. I stomped to the bleachers, keeping my head down to avoid any curious eyes.

"Bad day, huh?" Lutea guessed. She was sketching something I couldn't make out. My cheek rested on the table, my glasses laid folded on top of my artwork. I wasn't in the mood to draw.

"What's gotten your head on the table?"

Like a broken record, I told her about my day, starting with my sleepwalking, seeing the ghost in class and what Mr. Turner told me, then finally gym.

"No wonder you're so tired," Lutea said, keeping her voice low. "Why didn't you text me about this?"

"I don't know," I grumbled. "I had too much on my mind. I didn't think about it."

"You need a break. Come to the meeting to wind down. We can tell Miss Naiad about the dream."

"You always say that…" I mumbled, heat pulsing through my chest. "You said Chitose could help, and she didn't. What can Miss Naiad do? What am I supposed to do about the fact that something's after me because I crossed worlds, or Sarah has a—"

"Stop it," Lutea commanded. She snapped the sketchbook closed, bringing my attention to her.

"We don't know why this is happening to you, but overwhelming yourself will only stress you out more. For now, focus on something else. We can help you during the meeting."

"Easier said than done." I closed my eyes and tried to think about seeing Elizabeth again and going back to her warm and cozy house. But even that might not happen.

At the sound of the bell, I left the art room and headed downstairs. Mary didn't wait for me, but I imagined she went to the theatre club. I must have been lost in thought, or spaced out again because the next thing I knew, I was standing at the edge of a different set of stairs, one leading to the main doors instead of the library.

Worried, I checked my watch, and my brow arched. It was two thirty-five. I was wandering aimlessly for five minutes.

"Maybe I do need a break," I muttered to myself.

I perked up to the sound of approaching footsteps, and turned around as Sarah skirted passed me. She hurried downstairs but I forced myself to stay where I was.

*She's not supposed to be my problem.* There were assistants everywhere. One of them was bound to help her. But then I remembered that the assistants were at the meeting, as I should've been.

More footsteps bounded behind me and I tensed up as Victoria darted past me. Two girls I hadn't seen before were right behind her. She didn't even notice me. What's the hurry—

At that moment, a horrible realization crossed my mind. Following the girls' path, I pulled out my phone and called Lutea.

"Mayu, are you okay?" she asked.

"I just saw Sarah going downstairs and one of the girls who bullied her walked past me, heading in her direction. I think she needs help!"

"Which way did they go?"

190

The hallway on the first floor was full of loud clamor, and Victoria disappeared amongst the dwindling crowd. But then, I heard a faint scream before it was cut short. I rushed to the sound, stopping in front of the girl's bathroom.

I rushed inside, and found Sarah's backpack on the floor, ripped open and her notebooks scattered. Around the corner, Victoria had yanked a fistful of Sarah's hair, pulling her up and struck her across the face. The other girls cheered Victoria on, holding up their phones, recording her.

"Hey!" I shouted.

Victoria and her friends whipped around at the sound of my voice. She looked stunned, but once she realized it was me, her confidence returned.

"You again? Are you stalking us, you creep? Why do you got be so nosy!"

"Cause she's a loser," her friend replied. Anger flickered in my heart. "They bug us 'cause they got nothin' better to do."

I growled, "I'd rather be a loser than garbage like you!"

Victoria puffed her chest. "Say that to my face!"

"I just did."

As the two girls goaded her to beat me up, Victoria charged after me, bawling her fists. She threw wide swings at me but compared to Damien's throws, she was slow, and her movements were sloppy. I spotted an open palm rushing toward me and whipped out of its way, a sharp breeze passing by.

Suddenly, someone shoved me from behind. I lost my balance and tumbled on the floor. Triumphant howls exploded off the walls. Victoria threw a high five at her friend, then shot a nasty glare at me.

"That's what you get, freak!"

Her words hit like a gut punch, reeling me into an unwanted memory. I saw Rosalina laughing at my pain. Bethany and Nara mocked my cries, and their hurtful words rang in my ears. *This can't be happening.* My fists tightened. *Why* is this happening again?

A low hum filled my head and static pinched the air.

Screams tore off the walls, including my own, as something wrenched me off the floor. My back slammed into the ceiling and the impact knocked my glasses off. Below me, the stall doors flew open, the mirrors shattered into pieces, and water burst out of the toilets and sinks.

191

A terrified rose from Victoria. She was stuck on the ceiling, screaming for help. Her eyes darted around as if trying to make out what was going on. My eyes fell back on the floor where Sarah stood beneath us.

"Sarah!" I struggled to breathe through the pressure against my chest. Sarah didn't respond. She craned back with a wicked grin across her face.

Tears dripped from my eyes. "S-Sarah?"

"Sarah's not here anymore," she answered, coldly. "She doesn't want to talk to you." Her eyes rolled to the bathroom, and she mused. "Looks like those girls are gone... some friends they were."

"Why," Victoria whimpered. "Why are you doing this?"

The ghost looked up.

"Didn't you start this?" she snarled. "You were the one throwing things at Sarah. You pulled her hair, cornered her here and attacked her!"

"It was just a joke!" Victoria blubbered. "C'mon, I didn't even pull that hard!"

"A joke!" I snapped, shock and disgust almost wiped away my fear. "You cried when you were pushed in class. Why was it a joke when you did it to Sarah!"

"Does it matter? That all happened in the past!"

The ghost's eyes narrowed.

The bathroom door burst open with a loud bang. The ghost turned as Lutea stumbled inside. Her appearance must have broken the ghost's concentration because I felt the pressure lift off my chest. I shrieked, grabbing Lutea's attention.

"What the—" Lutea gasped. Her eyes quickly returned to the ghost. "Sarah, are you doing this?"

"That's not Sarah!" I shouted. "That ghost is controlling her!"

Lutea lowered her voice and asked, calmly. "Can I speak to Sarah?"

"No," the ghost said. "She doesn't want to listen to anyone. Certainly not assistants. For all your super senses and powers, you only come when certain people need help."

"We try to help everyone," Lutea implored. "I know what happened to Sarah. Mayu told me. She called me because she knew Sarah needed help! Whatever it is you're planning, it won't fix the problem."

The ghost burst into laughter. "What will then? Let me guess, *I should tell a teacher.*' Or '*I should ignore them, they'll stop eventually*'?" Her voice hardened. "Easy to say when you're not the one treated like garbage! It's easy when you have the power to make them stop!"

"You have the power too. But using Sarah to hurt people isn't the answer."

"I'm *protecting* Sarah!" The ghost roared. "I'm the only one who cares about her!"

"I'm here right now because I care about her too! I can help Sarah, but you have to let them go."

A tense silence fell between the two.

"You want them so badly. You can have them."

The pressure from my chest dispersed. Victoria and I screamed as the floor rushed towards us. I shut my eyes, bracing for impact but nothing happened. I took a hesitant peek and found myself hovering inches above the floor. Victoria was curled up midair, and Lutea had frozen in place, as though she had broken into a sprint and time stopped before she could take another step. In an instant, we jerked back from Sarah. I only had seconds to register the approaching wall.

Blinding pain shattered across my arm and back, sharp aches rippled through me. I held my shoulder, crying. Victoria was groveling, moaning 'help me.' She screamed as she was pulled across the floor by an invisible force.

"Don't do this!" Lutea shouted. She dislodged herself from the dented wall and charged after the ghost.

The ghost swung her arm, and Lutea flew back into the sinks, exploding into a deafening crash. I shielded myself as cold water and ceramic shards sprayed in my direction. Lutea was on her back, surrounded by the shattered sinks and broken pipes.

My head swiveled to Victoria's cries. Her arms shielded her head. She sobbed apologies after apologies to the ghost. Her response was a sharp kick to Victoria's stomach. She choked and gagged, and pleaded weakly for the ghost to stop, and she replied with a small, playful chuckle.

Victoria managed to grovel a few feet before she was pulled back again, like a puppet on strings.

Realizing the ghost had her back facing me, I came up with a plan. A fierce pain cut through my arm when I pushed myself up. Using my good arm, I snatched my phone and, with all my strength, hurled it at the ghost.

It smacked the back of Sarah's head and Victoria dropped to the floor. The ghost turned, momentarily in a daze, unable to notice me until I collided with her.

We crashed onto the floor and the water splashed beneath us. I fought through my panicked mind to remember a trick Hannah taught me. I wrapped my arms and legs around Sarah's limbs, locking her in place.

"Sarah, can you hear me!"

"She doesn't want to hear you!" The ghost screamed, bucking up to break out of my grip.

I persisted. "Sarah, you have to stop this! This won't fix what happened!"

"What will, then?" the ghost shouted. "It's the only way these people learn! You know it's the truth! You hate her as much we do!"

"She's a jerk, but she doesn't deserve this! Sarah, you don't deserve this! I know all you want is to be heard. We all do. That's why I'm here. I don't care what Victoria or Mary said... I wouldn't mind if we talked again, Sarah. So, please come back!"

As the last words left me, Sarah's body stiffened. The ghost let out a pained howl and with a shocking surge of strength, she picked herself up. She lunged back and before I could react, pain exploded across my body. My arms weakened and I dropped to the floor.

I looked at Sarah as her legs buckled and her knees crumbled to the floor. Voices surged all around me and the cries of a ghost and a girl shook the walls.

*This has happened before.* I woke up against the locker. A sharp pain throbbed at the back of my head. An assistant came to help me, but instead of Ethan's face, I was looking at Lutea.

"Easy there. You took a hard blow to the head," she said.

"Lutea..." I choked up. She pulled me into her arms and my eyes welled up. "I thought... I w-was going to..."

"You're safe now," she promised. "I'm sorry..."

I let go of Lutea and asked, "Where's Sarah?"

"Being taken care of elsewhere," said Miss Naiad, kneeling in front of Victoria. "Her and that ghost."

Victoria's face was covered in scratches and her arm swelled with sickly yellow bruises. But Miss Naiad didn't care. She held a phone to Victoria's face, and I could hear Sarah's scream coming through it.

"Marie..." Lutea warned.

"Is this your idea of fun?" Miss Naiad sneered.

Victoria burst into tears and closed her eyes.

194

"Insult me all you want in your head. I've been called worse by better. I'll leave you alone if you tell me why girls like you find enjoyment in this. Or why is it a crime when you're the one covered in bruises."

"We were only playing around," Victoria wailed. "I didn't know she could do this. Why is she allowed to come here if she could hurt others like that!"

"A fascinating question you should ask yourself. Once you've come to your senses." With that, Miss Naiad snapped her fingers. Victoria's eyes rolled back, and her head slumped over her shoulders.

"What did you do?" I asked.

"Better she remembers being thrown into a door than this fiasco," said Miss Naiad. She stood up and patted down her knitted dress, then turned to the bathroom. "Now, what we can do to fix this."

• ● •

When Victoria woke up, bruised and slightly dazed, Miss Naiad took her to the office before a couple of teachers arrived. They stayed after school and heard muffled screams coming from the bathroom, which was already repaired, thanks to Miss Naiad's magic.

Lutea told them she broke up a fight in the bathroom. One of the teachers noticed me and asked if I was involved, but Lutea stammered out that I was curious student who also heard the scream.

I appreciated Lutea for not telling them the truth. I wasn't sure if I could answer any questions. My arm was sore, but I didn't have any injuries that needed to be healed, and I certainly didn't want my memories messed with. But seeing the bathroom, repaired or not, made me sick, so I left.

Pain jolted through my arm as I pushed through the main doors. The bus hadn't arrived, so I sank into the steps. I was shaking and close to crying when the door opened behind me.

"Th-Thought I'd find you out here," Lutea said, softly. "I didn't know you were leaving."

I could barely process the emotions flooding my mind. I wiped the tears from my eyes and stared at the road ahead.

"You almost left these behind." She sat beside me with my glasses in her hand.

I thanked her and put my glasses on. "What's going to happen to Sarah?"

I waited for an answer, but none came. Lutea was staring at the road. Her eyes were nearly closed, almost in trance.

"Lutea?"

She snapped out of it. "S-Sorry, sh-she threw me against that wall pr-pret-ty hard." Lutea brushed back her bangs, revealing thin cracks branching across the enchanted marks.

Worry surged in my voice. "Do you need help? Should I look for Miss Naiad?"

"Don't worry. I-It happens. Tora will repair me as soon as I'm home."

My heart sank. "I'm... I'm so sorry you got hurt."

"Don't be. You di—did the right thing."

Hard to tell if I did. I wrapped my arms around myself, my knees tucked under my chin. "This wouldn't have happened if Victoria had left her alone."

"From the looks of it, Sar-ah would have lost con-trol eventually. Besides, don't you think Victoria has suffered enough?"

I shrugged and looked away.

"'She's a jerk, b-but she doesn't deserve this.'" She repeated. "Weren't those your words?"

I remembered Victoria's terrified expression, nothing like the smug, and arrogant bully from class. And I thought about what the ghost told me: *You hate her as much as we do.*

Lutea sighed, "I take it, you don't wa—ant to talk ab—out the dreams?"

I almost scoffed. After everything, I completely forgotten about it. Honestly, I didn't want to think about anything mystic for a while.

I heard the bus rumble down the street as it drew near the school. It came to a stop and opened its door. Before I left, Lutea told me to text her as soon as I was home. I gave her a small nod, then climbed aboard the bus.

# Friends

**The scent of wet mildew had settled on my clothes** by the time I made it home. I dropped my backpack near my bed, then went to the bathroom and changed out of my uniform when something slipped out of my pocket and hit the floor.

It was my phone, clean and dry, and I had a message from Lutea asking if I had made it home. I was confused at first. I never picked up my phone after I threw it, so how did it get here? Then again, if Miss Naiad could repair the damaged bathroom, she could have made my phone reappear in my pocket.

'I'm home,' I texted back and set the phone on my desk to start the bath.

The hot water burned as I sank into the tub and scrubbed my hair and face to wash the day away. Reaching for the soap, I realized my arm wasn't broken from being hurled into the wall. At the time, the pain was unbearable. However, aside from my neck aching and a stiff shoulder, I was completely fine.

Maybe Miss Naiad had healed me, too.

With my bath finished, I toweled myself down, then changed into a pair of shorts and a dry shirt before heading downstairs. I sat in front of the opened screen, crossing my legs and letting the afternoon warmth roll into the living room. My mind wasn't in it, but I tried to finish my homework to distract me from today. But all I heard were screams. They echoed in my head until a thud from a passing truck made me jump, shattering my concentration.

"What's the point..." I whispered and slammed the book closed. Mrs. Bean's would fail me whether I finished it or not.

The house phone rang, and I checked my watch, seeing that it was already five. Rubbing my eyes, I got to my feet and quickly picked up the phone.

"Hello?"

"Hi, I'm sorry, I didn't call sooner. I was talking to Mom about the sleepover," said Elizabeth.

"No, it's alright." After the day I had, I was relieved to hear her voice. "How's your mom doing?"

"Peachy as she would say," she replied with a petite giggle. "She says she'll pick up around four next Friday, so make sure you're home before that."

"Sure." That didn't sound as convincing as I hoped, and Elizabeth immediately noticed.

"Mayu, are you okay?"

I sniffled. "I had a rough day."

"Do you want to talk about it?"

I deeply inhaled, then breathed out, clearing my cluttered thoughts. "There was a fight at school today...and I got caught in it."

Her breath rose. "What happened? Did you get hurt?"

"I'm alright. I tried to help a classmate, but things got out of control." I scrambled for the right words. "Elizabeth... I miss you. There's so much I want to tell you..."

"What's wrong?"

"I don't know anymore..." I blinked, letting the tears flow.

"I'm right here."

"I... want to know if everything... is normal on your end."

Elizabeth paused. "It's hard to adjust, especially since I only know two people. I have to ask Suzanne for help, and I probably sound like a broken record to her. I keep wondering what you're doing. How has school been treating you?"

"It sucks!" I cried. "My math teacher hates me. My medications cause my seizures more than they treat them. I'm sleepwalking now. Ichirou wants to cancel the sleepover and when I try to help someone... I get dragged into a fight."

Elizabeth was silent. "That sounds like a lot. I'm so sorry you're going through all of this. Have you told anyone about this, yet?"

I wiped my eyes with my shirt. "Ichirou and Hannah know about everything except for the fight. He said the best I could do is switch out of class next month to get away from my teacher."

"That's a good thing. Next month is in two weeks," Elizabeth's voice lifted. "You won't have to deal with the teacher forever. And not a lot of people are willing to stand up for others so easily. Your friend or classmate may have appreciated it, all things considered."

I sniffled. "What would you have done if a classmate was being picked on? Would you help them?"

"Of course. I helped you a lot, didn't I?"

"Yeah."

"September will be over before you know it. I promise when you're home with me and mom, you can take your mind off school for a bit."

"But Ichirou wanted us to reschedule it. He told me this morning."

"He must have changed his mind," she said, sounding perplexed. "Mom spoke to him an hour ago. She didn't mention a reschedule. But if we don't have a sleepover, we could still spend the day together. If we do, and you sleepwalk, I'll make sure you don't leave the house."

I snickered a bit. "Promise?"

"Promise."

I spent most of my afternoon and evening reading on the couch when the headlights beamed through the sliding door. I got up, drew the curtains aside as Hannah and Ichirou parked in front of the apartment.

The exhaustion was clear on Hannah's face. Her eyes were red and puffy, like she was crying on her way home. She wrenched herself out of the car, slammed the door shut and stomped to the trunk. Ichirou got out of his car and hurried to her. He asked her if she wanted to talk. She shook her head, but when Ichirou stepped closer, she leaned her head against his chest. Ichirou stroked her back and comforted her as she sobbed. It seemed like we were all having a bad day.

I wanted to hug her too, or at least say something but no words came to mind, so I waited until they were ready to come inside. When she calmed down, Hannah opened the trunk of her car and hauled out a pizza box so wide, she had to carry it inside the apartment with both arms. She gave me a soft "hi," dropped the pizza box on the table, then went upstairs.

Ichirou stepped inside carrying a similar box.

Closing the door, I turned to Ichirou. "Hontōni son'nani warui kotodesu deshita ka?"

"Taihen..." he muttered.

"At least we have pizza for a week," I said, trying to be positive.

A low metallic groan, then a rush of hissing water from the bathroom meant Hannah was taking a shower. Ichirou turned on the TV and let me pick a movie and I made a plate of pizza for both of us. There's no better cure for a bad day than good food, bad movies and good company.

"Should I make a plate for Hannah?" I asked.

Ichirou stared at the pizza with chagrin. "She'll probably want something different. I'll make her plate."

Later, Hannah curled up beside my brother on the couch, wearing a pair of shorts and one of his green shirts. The movie I picked was an action flick we'd seen months ago, not too new but old enough that we didn't mind small talk or leaving the couch for more pizza. I think it was around the third trip, I sat down with four slices on my plate before I noticed Ichirou staring at me.

"What?" I muffled, mouthful of pizza.

"Did you eat anything...at all?" he asked.

"A little at school." I swallowed, then ate one slice after another and washed it down with a glass of water.

"You might want to slow down. Or chew."

"Let her eat," Hannah moaned. "School lunches taste like crap anyway."

"Are you going to eat something, Hannah?" I asked.

She squinted at the pizza and grimaced. "I'm fine with water."

During the movie's calmer scene, I told Ichirou and Hannah about my day but didn't mention the fight. Talking to Elizabeth relieved my thoughts, and I didn't want them to worry about me. They had enough to deal with, especially Hannah. She had to make three sheets of pizza by herself, only for the customer to cancel their order at the last moment. The manager got mad and yelled at her, blaming her for 'taking too long with the order.'

"...and he made you take the sheets?" Ichirou questioned.

"He was going to throw it away. That would be something else he'd yell at me about." Hannah gulped down a glass of water. "Maybe in a few weeks, I can let this dumb job go, open up art commissions and find a new job."

"I'll miss the discounts," I said, sweetly.

Hannah grinned. "First paycheck I get, I'm buying us dinner, better discount pizza."

Aside from her terrible day, Hannah mentioned one good thing. A friend invited her to a party, and she asked Ichirou if he wanted to come. It was on the same weekend as the sleepover.

"Promise you won't get too drunk," Ichirou teased.

"Please," Hannah laughed. "I'm the queen of holding my drink!"

At eleven, the movie ended, and Ichirou was dozing off on the couch, resting his head against his wrist until Hannah woke him up. She was going to put away the remaining pizza in the fridge but I, along with a drowsy Ichirou, offered to do it instead.

"Go get some rest," I insisted.

"What she said," Ichirou yawned. "You can sleep in my room."

Smiling, Hannah hugged me, kissed Ichirou then went upstairs. I was getting ready to clean up when I noticed Ichirou was nodding off again.

"You had a long day too?" I asked.

"You can say that."

Ichirou worked at an upscale restaurant as a waiter, a host and sometimes a cook. I'd never been to his job and once asked what the customers were like. He replied, "For every Isa I serve, there are five Mrs. Evans." Other than that, what happened on good days or bad days was a mystery to me. He never came home with a "work story" like Hannah and he preferred to sit at the table before heading to the showers and collapsing in bed.

Tired as he was, I had to know if I could go to the sleepover.

"Ichirou?" His weary eyes trailed back to me. "Elizabeth told me you spoke to Ms. Hudson today."

"She called earlier." He sat up and stretched his arms. "Isa knows what's going on. She says you can see Elizabeth, but on one condition."

I gulped. "What?"

"Your sleepwalking," he started. "You said you heard your watch in your dream, right?"

"Yeah. Why?"

"I called Sanders, and he suggested you spend a night in the hospital to monitor your sleep."

"Again?" I moaned.

He smirked. "I figured you'd say that. Sanders told me sleepwalking could be hereditary, though you hadn't experienced this until now. He said you might be anxious about something, which you have been for a week."

Weird, I was so wrapped up in the mystic side of school, I never stopped to think that my sleepwalking might have been from my racing thoughts.

"How do I treat it?"

"You need to relax," he bluntly stated, his voice firm and a little loud. "Remember, take deep breaths, like I taught you."

"What should I do if I sleepwalk again? Should I wake myself up?"

"If that can stop you, you'll need something louder than your watch."

"I don't have anything that loud..."

"I do." Ichirou reached into his pocket and pulled out a black and blue watch. It was analog and digital with the date at the corner, the time in the center and little seconds spinning rapidly beside it. It looked a little worn and too familiar to be brand new.

"Isn't this yours?"

"It's yours if you switch with me."

I stared back at my brother. "No offense, but pink doesn't look good on you."

"No more than it does on you."

Ichirou unclipped the medical band from my watch before I took it off. While holding my wrist, he adjusted his watch to fit me and showed me how to set the time and the alarm. He clipped the epilepsy band onto the strap, and it felt like a textbook had wrapped itself around me.

"It's heavier than it looks," I said. I already missed my pink watch, which was now strapped to Ichirou's wrist.

"It's made of metal. You'll get used to the weight."

"Are you sure this will work?"

"If you can hear your watch in your dream, this one is bound to wake you up. If not, it's loud enough to wake me and Hannah up. If the alarm shuts off, it means it woke you up. If Hannah or I hear it for about... ten seconds or more, we'll check on you."

"You're okay with this?" I said, guilt-ridden at the thought of them losing sleep.

Ichirou shrugged. "I figured you'd rather spend the weekend at Elizabeth's than another night at the hospital."

My eyes watered, and I threw my arms around him, holding him tight. Telling him "Thank you" wasn't enough.

"One more thing." He let me go and pointed to the pizza boxes. "I'm not putting that away by myself."

The bathroom lights pulsed with the loud, rapid beeps blaring in my ears. Cold water flooded up to my knees, and the ghost's cries morphed into a deep, monstrous laughter.

I shot up in a cold sweat and pressed whatever button was on my watch until the alarm snapped off. The room was silent, except for my heart thudding against my chest. I laid in bed and tried to sleep, but once I did, I was trapped in the bathroom again.

At school, news about the fight spread like wildfire. All eyes were on me the instant I came to class, as though they knew a secret about me that I didn't.

*Of course*, I thought. *I was the only one who stood up for Sarah and against Victoria.*

I tucked my head between my shoulders and hurried to my seat. Mr. Baryon stood in front of the board to talk about the situation, but it felt like the kind of stern lecture parents gave their kids.

"How come no one stopped Victoria? Or told her enough was enough," he scolded. "How come only one person cared enough to help a classmate?"

I shrank in my chair.

A girl, one of Victoria's friends grumbled out, "… shouldn't have been so sensitive."

I tensed up. My thoughts flew back to the bathroom again. To Victoria's horrible words and her cries.

Mr. Baryon huffed at the girl, crossing his arms over his chest. "So, someone should pull your hair then, cause it's all a 'joke,' right?"

Nobody responded.

Mr. Baryon shook his head and passed the assignments around. Mary assured me I did my best to help. I knew she wanted to comfort me, but as class droned on, my eyes flickered to the empty seat.

She's only suspended. She'll be back. Hopefully, things will be better by then.

Aiden must have noticed my frustration, because after class, we met at the library and slipped through the corridor. Being away from the noisy hall and ringing bells somewhat cleared my thoughts. I told Aiden about Sarah and everything that happened in the bathroom.

"No wonder you're stressed," he finally said. "Wherever Sarah is, I hope she's getting the help she needs."

"Me too." I leaned against the wall and closed my eyes. I wanted the day to end.

"I can imagine it's a lot to take in now, but things will get better. You have to take it one day at a time, one step at a time. Give yourself little goals. Like, you're going to read two pages today. You're going to copy Aiden's notes today. Or you're going to the meeting for an hour. Something simple."

My eyes fell to the sprites twirling off the branches.

"Do you think I should've spoken to her earlier? If I spoke to Sarah sooner, maybe she wouldn't feel so alone? Or called Lutea much earlier?"

"Dwelling on it, won't change anything. Look at it this way, Victoria won't mess with her anymore and honestly, being out of school is best for Sarah. Mystic kids are lucky to only get suspended. Sometimes we're expelled. Sometimes we're forced to move elsewhere. And sometimes the whole school collapses."

I shrugged, half-heartedly. I was too tired, too burned out to tell him, 'thank you.' When lunch ended, we exchanged numbers before going to class.

•●•

The week went by without incidents in the news or in my mind. I hadn't dreamed about the voice, and I woke up every midnight in my bed and not standing elsewhere in the apartment. There were moments when I wanted to turn off the alarm, but I was worried the voice would come back, so I didn't.

Finally, Friday arrived, and I woke up with no odd dreams or voices calling out to me. I grinned happily, wondering if the mystic world was giving me a break.

Thoughts of the sleepover filled my head. Elizabeth and I had talked about it, but I couldn't believe it was happening! Anytime my mind assumed the worst-case scenario, like the sleepover being canceled, I buried those thoughts in the back of my mind under my classwork or talked to Mary about what we were doing after school.

"Are you coming with me today?" Mary asked with hope in her voice.

I chewed my lower lip. I had tried to find a balance between tutoring and drama club. "I have to get homework done, then I'm going to see Elizabeth."

"Did you still need a ride?" she asked.

"If you can, I appreciate it!"

"Sure..." she returned to her book, hiding her expression behind the pages.

Fridays were particularly bad days in Mrs. Bean's class. She'd give us thirty pages of work and wanted it all completed by Monday. I remembered her saying we had the entire weekend to work on them, as if she expected us to spend our Saturdays and Sundays doing only homework.

The class was especially busy since our graded tests were being passed back. My shoulders tensed up when Mrs. Bean handed Aiden his paper first, then glared daggers at me as she placed my homework face down on my desk and walked away.

"Scared?" Aiden asked.

"A little," I whispered.

"You faced a ghost, and a piece of paper scares you?"

"When it's graded by Mrs. Bean, yes."

"She's been sneering at you and giving you poor grades for a month. What's the worst she can put on the paper?"

He had a point. I flipped the sheet and my heart stopped. There was a bright red, perfectly cursive 'A' at the corner of my paper, and check marks placed neatly beside my answers. I had to blink twice to make sure I wasn't dreaming.

"Nice job!" Aiden praised, patting my shoulder. "I knew you could do it."

"She gave me an 'A,'" I squeaked.

"Looks like there's a note at the bottom."

Beneath my answers was a letter written in neat and formal handwriting in black ink, unlike Mrs. Bean's handwriting.

> *Great job! I'm glad to know that my tutoring paid off.*
> *Come to me if you need any more help with class.*
> -C. Turner

I didn't think my smile could get any wider. Mrs. Bean glared at me, knowing my graded test was on my desk for her to see the A on it. When class ended, I went to the board and thanked Mr. Turner.

"Mrs. Bean often fussed about not having time to grade tests, so I graded them," he said.

"I'm starting to wish you were the teacher instead."

"Sometimes I wish the same. In a couple of weeks, the school will give you a chance to switch classes. Are you interested in doing so?"

"I already planned on it."

"There's another algebra teacher, same floor, different room. His name is a bit hard to pronounce, but he is a good teacher."

"That's good to hear. I'm going to miss you and Aiden, though."

"You can always see us after school. Which reminds me, am I to see you during tutoring?"

"Yeah, I'd like to get this finished." I showed him the math homework, plus the 'extra credit' Mrs. Bean had passed around. It was supposed to be for students who didn't pass the test, but she gave it to everybody.

"Very well, we can work on it," he said as he leaned in and whispered. "Until you can leave class, do me a favor. Prove her wrong, Mayu."

The way he said my name, so smooth like a cello, sent my heart into flutters. I skipped out of class and spent the rest of the day weightless, like I could fly.

I did my homework during lunch, and Mr. Turner checked it at the meeting. He signed it and I was off to the school's main doors. I said goodbye to the club members, and they wished me a good weekend.

*It's going to be a great weekend*, I thought.

I waited at the main door at three thirty on the dot. I peeked outside to see a few cars parked in front of the school, but none resembled Mr. Brown's black luxury car. Anxious, I stepped inside and called Mary. My heart raced when her phone went to voicemail, so I called again. After the third call, she picked up.

"Hello?"

"Mary, I'm at the door now. Where are you?"

"What do you mean?" she said, baffled. "I'm not at school. I'm with Katie."

My heart dropped. "You said we'd meet at the front doors at three-thirty today."

"Oh! Was it today? I thought you meant next Friday."

"We were talking about it this morning."

"It slipped my mind. I'm sorry. You should have texted me earlier."

My insides tensed. "I didn't think I needed to. I thought you knew."

"Well, I can't turn back. Why don't you call Elizabeth, have her pick you up?"

"I'll try..."

"I'm sorry. Hope you have a good weekend." Mary hung up before I could say another word.

I pushed the doors open and sat on the steps. "Deep breaths, deep breaths," I prompted, my leg thumped in place as a flurry of emotions stirred in me. "Deep breaths..."

I called Elizabeth's house. My palms were sweaty, my shaky fingers slowly pressed each number, and I waited for someone to answer. Anxiety spiked through me when the ringing cut to the voicemail. Ms. Hudson wasn't home. Was she on her way to the complex? Or were they already there, waiting? I called Ms. Hudson's cellphone, grateful that she owned one, but that hope drained away when it went to voicemail, too.

I got up and peered at the edge of the street, then checked the time. Shouldn't the bus be here? I paced in front of the school, asking myself, if she would pick up this time? What should I do? My head snapped back as the door opened and Ethan poked his head out.

"What are you doing here?" I asked, shocked.

"Lutea was trying to talk to you, but you left in a hurry," he said.

"What for?"

"Hell, if I know. What I want to know is why you look like you're about to cry."

"I'm not crying."

"Uh-huh, and my arm is perfectly fine," he waved, his arm still wrapped in a brace. Lutea stepped outside, followed by Chitose.

She asked if I was alright and before I could answer, Ethan blurted, "she was crying."

I glared at Ethan. "Not crying."

I fumbled about the sleep-over and how Mary, who was supposed to take me home, left without me.

"So, you're going to sit here and cry about it?" Chitose asked, flatly. "Where do you live?"

"Union Circle." I answered.

"The college complex? That's within walking distance."

"You expect me to walk all the way there?"

Chitose's face tilted, and her eyes flashed brilliant gold. "You've got two legs and a heartbeat. What's stopping you?"

I stared at the pavement ahead, remembering the day I got kicked off the bus, surrounded by unfamiliar houses. "I... I don't want to walk alone," I said in a small voice.

"Who says you're going alone?" Lutea hopped to her feet. "Club is over and you're not too far."

Did I hear her right? "You're going to walk with me? Are you allowed to do that?"

"We're off the job and there's nothing wrong with helping a friend, right?"

A fuzzy feeling bloomed inside me when she said "friend." I checked the time and saw it was almost four. I wiped the tears away and cleaned my glasses before I slung my backpack over my shoulder. Ethan was already on his feet, talking about how he needed to "stretch his legs" while Chitose drifted behind him.

"Guys..." I called out when they were several feet away. "You're going the wrong way."

• ● •

It was Chitose's idea to follow the bus signs and look for familiar landmarks that I'd seen on my way home.

"Which stop do you usually get off at?" she asked.

We made our way down the street. My head swiveled from the passing house to the school as it slowly vanished behind the trees.

"Um... sixth stop," I said. "I remember passing a gas station. Then a convenient store, and—and a library."

"Sixth stop, gas station, convenience store and library," Lutea recited. "That shouldn't be too hard to spot."

"Unless we get pixie-led," Ethan said, eying suspiciously at one of the trees.

The first bus stop was easy to find. It was in front of a mint green house where dozens of wind chimes swayed musically in the breeze. Red capped gnomes were scattered across the front lawn. Their glossy black eyes followed us, and I saw one of the gnomes blink at me.

The next sign stood at the edge of the street, adjacent to a pink house with flowerpots perched on its stone steps. Black cats gathered on rocking chairs and scattered when we walked by. I was sure if Elizabeth saw it, it would be her ideal house.

At the next stop, I jumped back from the dogs barking behind their gated yard. Ethan walked past them, and the dogs shrank away with their tails between their legs. Unphased by their reaction, Ethan asked if anyone would like to race him to the next stop. Excitement shot through me, and I immediately volunteered with a smile across my face.

"It's a losing bet," Chitose warned.

"Sounds like a challenge." I crossed my arms, pride swelling in my chest. "You're talking to the fastest track runner in Lawrence Junior High."

"That explains how you outran the centaurs," said Lutea.

"Because you jumped in front of them," said Chitose.

She had a skeptical look on her face that I knew from previous track meets. Runners and coaches from different schools would look at me and think a small, frail looking girl couldn't possibly win a sprint. That was until I heard the "go" signal and they'd learn how I got the nickname, "Little Bullet."

"If I race with Ethan and win, would you believe me, then?" I asked.

Chitose said nothing.

Ethan patted my head. "You lose, you're buying the snacks."

He bolted down the pavement at lightning speed, casting a gust of wind against me.

"Hey!" I staggered to a running start and raced past Ethan to the bus stop. I cheered triumphantly and jumped in the air. I turned around and saw Ethan slowing down, clutching his bandaged arm.

"Are you alright?"

Ethan smiled weakly, "Still alive…"

Chitose and Lutea helped him readjust his sling. I caught a glimpse of a scar across his neck and remembered the deep cuts and pool of blood.

"You should do this more often!" Ethan exhaled, rolling his neck. "Fresh air, extra space. Way better than a crowded bus if you ask me."

"Flying is better," Chitose whispered.

"You can fly?" I asked.

"It's as easy as walking."

Chitose turned to face me. With a mischievous grin, her body lifted weightlessly off the ground. My jaw dropped with shock as she arched over the street, landing gently on the sidewalk.

I ran to Chitose, looking around to see if anyone noticed us. But there was no one in sight.

"How did you do that?!" I gasped.

"All Ethereal beings can fly," she said like it was common knowledge. "Though to be honest, I prefer fleeting."

"What's fleeting?"

Chitose's unblinking eyes met mine, and an eerie grin crawled across her face.

"I can show you," she whispered, "You might make it to your house on time."

Ethan butted in, cutting off the shivering presence that flowed out of Chitose. "I wouldn't do that if I were you. Not unless you want to have nightmares for a month."

Chitose's lips puckered. "Always want to ruin the fun for me, don'cha?"

"After last time?" He exclaimed. "I still wake up in a cold sweat!"

"I know," She grinned.

"When was the last time you fleeted?" I asked.

"About two weeks ago. We wouldn't have fleeted under normal circumstances, but it was an emergency."

*An emergency*, I thought. Could it have been on the day Ethan was in the infirmary?

"About that," I said. "What happened the night Ethan was hurt?"

"Ethan got hurt. That comes with the job."

"Job?"

"School isn't the only place where mystic activities happen," said Ethan. "We make sure it doesn't get out of control or put humans in danger."

"But it got out of control... didn't it?"

"It happens from time to time."

"By the way," said Lutea. "Have you had any dreams about them?"

"They stopped a couple weeks ago," I paused. "Does it mean they're gone?"

"Cedric hurt one of them pretty badly and the nights have been mostly quiet since," said Ethan.

"They're not coming back?" I asked with hope.

"Nope," Chitose said. "Also, there's the convenience store."

I looked ahead and there was a small building the size of a garage at the corner of the street. I giggled at the simplicity of its name, "Corner Store" on the sign above the door.

"Anyone want a snack while we're passing?" Ethan asked.

"We can't keep Elizabeth waiting," I reminded.

"No worries, I can rush in, grab a few snacks and catch up with you."

Lutea shrugged and Chitose asked for a dark chocolate bar.

"Well, lemonade sounds pretty nice right about now," I said.

Ethan gave us a thumbs up, then jogged into the Corner Store.

I turned to Lutea. "Can golems eat?"

Her eyes lit up. "Yup! As a matter of fact, my favorite meals are rock candy, rocky road and stone soup!"

"She's messing with you," Chitose said. "She can't feel hunger."

"Lucky," I grumbled.

"Is hunger a bad feeling?" Lutea sked.

Chitose and I blurted, "It really is."

"Imagine an emptiness tugging inside of you," Chitose started. "Then that feeling twists into an aching pull the less you eat. If you don't eat, the acids in your stomach will break you down for resources, devouring you from the inside."

Lutea's expression melted into horror.

I interjected, "But it all goes aways when you eat. Especially when it's your favorite flavor or meal!" I turned to Chitose. "Do you have a favorite food?"

She placed her finger on her lips. "I prefer to eat dreams and nightmares. They have a sensational taste that food can't compare with."

"What do nightmares taste like?"

"Varies from person to person. It's hard to describe."

Ethan caught up with us, carrying a paper bag stuffed with bottled drinks, a handful of stringy beef jerky, chocolate bars and packs of cookies.

"I forgot to ask you what kind of chocolate you like, so I bought all of them."

We continued to the next street shadowed by a cluster of trees. The sound of trickling water piqued my ears and drew me to a set of railings on the sidewalk. I leaned over to the stream coursing beneath—

"This is a bridge!" I exclaimed.

Ethan said behind me. "You hadn't noticed? Don't you take this route to go home?"

"Only on the bus. It would go by so fast, I wouldn't have noticed a bridge."

"More reasons to walk then." Ethan peeled the wrapper off the chocolate bar when leaves and accords showered him.

"Again!" Ethan barked at the trees. "Can't we have our snacks to ourselves!"

More acorns and leaves rained on us.

"What's going on?" I asked.

"Offer them one or they'll throw more than just acorns," Lutea warned.

Rolling his eyes, Ethan broke off a piece of his chocolate bar. He held it over his head, and it vanished.

My eyes widened, "What was that!"

I followed Ethan's gaze, straining my eyes between the leaves until he placed his hand on my head, tiling it to the side. They scurried too quickly across the branches for me to see them. All I could make out were their rough, bark like skin, dressed in moss.

Excited, I snapped off a piece of my chocolate bar, ready to raise my hand like Ethan did when Lutea quickly put my arm down.

"I wouldn't do that," She said, panic rose in her voice. "You give the canotila one, and they'll follow you, expecting more."

I quickly plopped the piece of chocolate in my mouth. Small, faint moans could be heard from the trees. "What are canotila?"

"Tree spirits," Lutea explained. "Harmless for the most part. Though the ones in human areas have grown a sweet tooth over the years."

"Figured they got a taste of the candy people throw on the ground," Chitose added. "Though they get very nasty if you harm their trees."

"Yeah, who knew trees could hold grudges like crows," Ethan grumbled.

"I wouldn't," I mused, walking past another tree. More canotila gathered on the branches, eying at the chocolate bar in my hand. They were just as demanding as Tuna.

I ate the chocolate, much to the tree spirit's annoyance.

"Elizabeth and I would read a ton of books about nature spirits and mythical creatures. I've never heard about a canotila."

Ethan dusted the leaves out of his hair. "They're often confused for other mystics due to their nature, like dryads, fairies and goblins. But even those are a little exaggerated in media, if not embellished."

"So, what parts are true? Or fake, for that matter?"

Lutea held her chin and pondered for a moment. "What do you want to know?"

*Everything*, I thought. My mind swelled with millions of questions, and I finally knew the people who could confirm it.

"Is Mr. Turner a vampire?" I blurted.

Ethan, Lutea and Chitose stared in shock.

"Right off the bat, huh." Ethan murmured. "How long have you been thinking about this?"

"I've seen enough movies to tell," I smiled. Being pale, extremely attractive and having cold skin was a giveaway.

"Fair," said Lutea, a cheeky grin rose in her face. "But how much do you know about vampires? What makes you certain he is one? Clearly the sun doesn't bother him. Did you ever see if he had fangs?"

"He could be an elf for all you know," Chitose added.

I paused and thought about it. There were movies where vampires were weakened by sunlight, instead of burning into ash. In other movies, vampires exploded into fire or sparkled in the daylight. I remembered a few movies where vampires could change into bat-like monsters. Could Mr. Tuner do that?

Ethan started to laugh. "I think you broke her brain." He patted my head a few times, halting my racing thoughts. "Calm down, I can see the steam coming out of your ears."

"Got a simpler question?" Chitose asked.

Hesitant, I asked if werewolves only changed under a full moon.

"I can change forms anytime," Ethan explained. "It doesn't have to be under a full moon."

"Where did the myths about the full moon come from? I learned you can see ghosts and monsters during those nights, too."

They groaned.

"This again..." Chitose rolled her eyes. "If you lived in a time where flickering torches and dim lamps were your only lights, you would assume you could only see us during one of the brighter nights. Truth be told, we have always been here."

At first, I didn't understand what she meant, but then the thought settled in. Not knowing what lurked in the dark was scary to ponder but realizing that it might have been there the entire time sent a special kind of shiver up my spine.

My thoughts were interrupted by Ethan rustling through the paper bag for one of the beef jerky.

"Personally, my family and I favor new moon nights. It made hide-and-seek more fun that way." He peeled off the wrapper and bit down the meat. His face puckered up as if something was wrong with the taste, but he continued to eat the jerky.

"So, why stay a secret if stories about Mystics aren't entirely true?" I asked. "Wouldn't it be easier to correct us?"

"We do," Chitose said grimly. "But it's not like we had a clean history with humans to begin with. Many still see us as monsters out to harm them, and some mystics don't make it easy for us to dispute that. You dealt with one not too long ago."

My heart sank. I couldn't forget it if I wanted to. "But I don't think all of you are bad."

Lutea sighed. "We appreciate that, but there's always going to be those who aren't afraid of us, and some who are."

I wanted to say something, but no words formed. Next thing I knew, Ethan had his hand on my shoulder.

"Look at it this way, after centuries of being hunted, we've learned to put up a fight or go down fighting. Remember, we fought monsters, and they ran away from us."

"Right," I said, though hope tangled with the dread in my chest. There was a lot to think about.

It wasn't long until the concrete street gave way to the familiar brick roads leading to the complex.

"Thank you for walking with me."

"It's no problem," Lutea said.

"How are you getting back?"

"Not fleeting, that's for sure." Ethan squinted at Chitose. Her head turned away, but I saw her cheeks pinching.

"The same way we came here," said Lutea. "We can walk back to the school, no problem."

Right as I was about to cross the street, I stopped and turned back to Lutea. "Didn't you want to talk to me about something?"

Lutea looked like she had to think about it, then she waved her hand. "Don't worry about it. You enjoy your weekend."

"You too," I said, though a part of me was curious, I figured she would tell me next week. I ran to the complex and spotted a wine-red Subaru parked in front of my apartment. My heart skipped a beat and a smile spread across my face as I saw her standing in front of the sliding door.

"Elizabeth!"

# Reunion

**I hurried to Elizabeth**, tears rolling down my cheeks, excited yet in disbelief that she was there. I worried I was hallucinating or something, then she embraced me. I dropped the bag of sweets and threw my arms around her, burying my head against her shoulder.

"Come on, you know what happens when one of us cries." Elizabeth's voice was breaking.

"Yeah," I chuckled, tearfully. "Both of us end up crying."

We spun around the yard, laughing until we fell on the grass, still laughing.

"Careful you two!" Ms. Hudson cried. She was as graceful as when she visited me at the hospital. I missed her so much I teared up when she helped me to my feet and pulled me into a warm hug.

"Now, now," she whispered, her hand stroking my head. "Young girls shouldn't cry so easily." She used her sleeve to wipe my eyes, and I felt like a toddler sobbing in front of her mother.

"I know," I whimpered. "I'm sorry I'm late."

Elizabeth said, "We knew you were going to be a little late. But I thought Mary was dropping you off."

"She left without me, so I walked instead."

Elizabeth's eyes widened. "You walked by yourself?!"

"No, I had friends walk with me," I told her before she panicked. I pulled out one of the giant chocolate bars and an extra bottle of lemonade. "This is for you."

Elizabeth gawked. "If we knew she left you behind, we would have picked you up from the school!"

"I called the house and Ms. Hudson twice, but nobody answered."

"Well..." Elizabeth's cheeks turned pink. "We were in such a hurry that Mom forgot to take her phone with her."

"You shouldn't have rushed me out of the house like that." Ms. Hudson chided.

Now it was my turn to stare in shock. Trying to hurry Ms. Hudson was like hurrying a bear out of her den.

"You rushed your mom!" I exclaimed.

Ms. Hudson grinned, "You should have seen her when we got here. Elizabeth fussed that we were late and nearly burst into tears when I forgot my phone."

"I wasn't crying!" Elizabeth protested, redness blossomed in her cheeks.

"You're lying," her mother sang.

I gave her an assuring smile. "It's okay, I cried too before walking here."

I took off my backpack and fished for the keys buried under my school supplies and gym clothes. They were starting to smell bad, so I took them out of my locker.

"Want to come inside?" I asked. "I need to grab my clothes, that's all."

Elizabeth turned to Ms. Hudson who was getting in her car.

"You can go, but don't take too long. We have a lot to do today."

"We won't," Elizabeth and I replied.

The excitement was too much. My shaking hands couldn't fit the keys properly into the lock and I dropped them by accident. After my third try, I unlocked the door, and we rushed inside.

"Your house is pretty!" Elizabeth spun around, taking in the living room and awed at the artwork on the walls.

"You think so?"

"Everything is so close and homey."

At first, I wondered why my small apartment would interest her, then I remembered that she'd never seen the inside of my home until now. All our visits and sleepovers were at her house, and I'd always wait by the door whenever Ms. Hudson picked me up.

I led Elizabeth upstairs, pointing her to the bathroom and showing her my bedroom like a tour guide. The size of my room amazed her, but I didn't think it was a big deal. Elizabeth's room was twice as big, but I let her marvel at it.

"How was school?" I asked.

I emptied my backpack and set the books on my desk and my clothes in the laundry basket.

"It went by fast." Elizabeth said. She sat on my bed, commenting on how soft it was. If you consider worn down soft. "I finally hit a high note in the choir club after weeks of practicing. I thought I'd never get it right."

As I refilled the backpack with clothes for the sleepover, I noticed something strange about our school related conversations.

"You always talked about choir. How come I don't hear about your classes?"

Elizabeth mashed her lips together and she twirled one of her braids. "I didn't want to bore you with droning lectures and long assignments."

"What!" I gasped, faking shock. "Class is boring! Impossible!"

She burst into laughter. "It is when you have to translate a Latin book, then write an essay about it!" she let out a groan as she flopped back on my bed.

"No Latin this weekend, got it," I noted.

I went to the bathroom to change out my school clothes for casual wear. With everything packed up, all that was left was my charger. I reached for it and spotted an envelope on the nightstand. The handwriting on it belonged to Ichirou.

*Here's fifty dollars. Have fun at the sleepover.*

I slipped the envelope into the side pocket of my backpack. Before we left the apartment, I made a detour to the refrigerator for a bag of sandwich meat.

"Is that for Tuna?" Elizabeth asked.

"Mm-hm, she'll meow for hours if no one feeds her." I set the meat on the porch and locked the screen door.

"I might have seen Tuna. She was meowing at the door when we got here. But she ran away as soon as she saw me."

"That sounds like Tuna. Don't worry, she didn't recognize you, yet. She'll change her mind once you give her a good meal."

"I'll remember to bring a snack for her next time."

Elizabeth opened the car door, letting me slide in before she sat beside me. I took in the fresh pine-scented air and thought back to the days we spent riding in the car together.

I got a present for you," Elizabeth told me. "It should be in the front seat."

Ms. Hudson reached for something in the glove compartment and passed it to Elizabeth. She gave me a small white box with a blue ribbon tied around it.

"It's… my way of saying sorry for this summer."

I untied the ribbon, lifted the lid, and my heart stopped. Inside was a shiny red camera. It had a silver lens and a black wrist strap hanging from the side. I used to have a camera like it. Ichirou had given it to me for my twelfth birthday and told me to "Capture the moment."

I took lots of pictures of him, the Hudson's one Christmas, a picture of my parents during those rare moments where no one was arguing. Mom praised me for having a good eye for photography. It made me excited and proud of myself.

Then, during a track meet, I left the camera on the bleachers while visiting a different school. I left it in my bag, then went to get it for the last picture but my camera was gone. My coach, Elizabeth, and a couple of members spent hours helping me look for it. Whether it slipped through the bleachers between games, or someone stole it, the camera, and those pictures, were gone forever.

I wiped the tears away and promised Elizabeth that the camera would never leave my sight. I turned it on and explored the settings. I pushed a silver button on the side, and a burst of light went off.

"Oh, that's where the shutter is."

Ms. Hudson started the car and slowly pulled away from the complex. I rolled down the window, letting the wind whip through my hair as the car drove down the road, passing my school, which I pointed out to Elizabeth. I couldn't believe I was finally leaving with her!

"We're going to one of my favorite places today, and for tomorrow, you can pick where we can go," said Elizabeth excitedly. "Do you have a place in mind?"

"Sekizenkan bath house!" I blurted and we giggled. "I'd like to go to the aquarium, if that's alright."

Elizabeth mused. "I had a feeling you were going to say that."

We crossed freeways and long stretches of land, passing cars and trucks. Elizabeth talked nonstop about where we were going, a place called Twilight Plaza. I suggested it must be a place where everything opens around evening. Elizabeth laughed at the idea but promised it was completely different.

"It has the name because it gives off this ambience of eternal twilight, but not in a bad way, more like a good place to relax after a long day."

The car left the highway, passing a couple of streets until it entered a wide street, smooth and flat with no cracks or potholes.

Trees sprouted near the sidewalk, and festive lights decorated the lamp posts. The buildings packed together looked new, yet old at the same time, with window display shops, niche cafes and food stands at every corner.

As soon as Ms. Hudson found a place to park, Elizabeth and I hurried to the plaza. She pulled me away from a spurt of water that harmonized with the music playing from hidden speakers. The first place we checked out was the largest bookstore I'd ever seen. The building curved like a can and towered over all the surrounding shops.

I turned to Elizabeth and squeaked. "Are you sure this is a bookstore?"

She snickered, hiding her smile behind her hands. "See for yourself."

Elizabeth opened the door, and the aroma of freshly brewed coffee drew me inside. A hanging chandelier glittered above a maze of shoulder high bookshelves. Displays held popular books, bestsellers or author events for all to see. The scent and murmurs of voices drifted from a coffeehouse inside of the bookstore! Customers sat in cushioned chairs by the window, thumbing through pages, sipping from mugs or reading in peace. I blinked, tears pricked the corners of my eyes.

This was paradise!

Ms. Hudson told us to have fun on her way to the coffeehouse. Smiling ear to ear, I followed Elizabeth through the shelves, taking pictures of anything and everything that caught my attention.

I slowed down near a wall of notebooks and journals, each with their own intricate designs and colors. Rubbing my eyes, I thought about getting one for Elizabeth. She had an entire shelf in her bedroom dedicated to the notebooks, but Ms. Hudson told her one day not to get any more notebooks until she finished the ones she had.

"Mayu, are you allergic to something?" Elizabeth asked.

I sniffled again, and my nose wrinkled at the bitter coffee flowing through the bookstore.

"No, the scent is really strong here."

"Is it?" Elizabeth perked up and sniffed the air. "It doesn't smell that bad to me. If it's bothering you, we can leave the store."

My voice quickened. "No, we don't have to! I think I'm not used to the scent." I sighed. "It's been a while since I've gone to a café. I guess I'm not used to the smell of coffee."

The assistant's lounge was as close to a café it could get.

"We're right next to the coffeehouse and it's a busy hour..." Elizabeth trailed off. She pursed her lips, then her eyes sparked, and she perked up. "Do you want to go upstairs to get away from the scent?"

I blinked, partially because my eyes burned, and her words left me stunned. "Upstairs?"

Elizabeth motioned me from the wall of journals to an escalator rolling up to another floor. We got on and I turned to watch the shelves shrink as we were carried to the upper level. Something red caught my attention and I almost screamed in excitement.

*Witch Hazel* posters plastered the second floor. Cat plushies lined the walls with copies of the books beside them. I found packets of stickers, bookmarks, journals, and calico plushies with bright green eyes and a baby blue collar, like my cat.

*What are the odds?*

Among the accessories, I picked up one of the charms hanging off a wall. It was one of the characters from the book, a black cat emerging from a crystal ball.

"Do you want this? It looks just like Tuna." Elizabeth held up one of the charms, a calico cat, playfully curling around the crystal ball.

"We can have a matching set," I added, showing her the black cat.

We carried the charms with us, then explored more of the upper level. I split off to grab a journal for Elizabeth, one with pink petals scattered across a black cover. After that, I returned to the upper floor and found Elizabeth between one of the aisles. She was so focused on reading a novel that she didn't notice me when I pulled out my camera. I zoomed in and snapped the picture at the right time.

Elizabeth jumped at the light and turned to me. "What are you doing?"

"Taking your picture." I showed her the photo.

"That one is a lot better than the first picture of me," she said.

I grinned, "You mean, like this?" I flipped past the pictures and showed Elizabeth her own shocked expression in the car.

Her cheeks flared. "That's a terrible picture of me!"

"It's not!" I teased. "It will be cherished forever and ever!"

Elizabeth's face burned up after that.

We took a break at one of the tables not too far from the coffeehouse. I showed Elizabeth pictures of different parts of the store: an old man in a chair, reading a newspaper, a woman sitting at a lone table, the busy cashiers, the chandelier, and the coffeehouse from afar. Though I didn't get a picture of Ms. Hudson.

"I forgot how great you are with a camera," said Elizabeth. "So, do you like the bookstore?"

"I love it! How did you find this place?"

"Suzanne wanted to see a movie here and we showed up a few hours early, so we walked around the plaza and found the bookstore."

"You went to the movies?" Suddenly, the floating sensation I'd had all day was gone. I didn't mean to ask, but the question blurted out before I could stop myself. "Is that why you canceled on me?"

Her shoulders stiffened as shock washed over her face. "I wanted to spend time with you. And I promised myself I'd take you here after we left."

Elizabeth paused. "I-I understand if you're upset..."

"It's okay. I'm happy I got to spend the weekend with you. I hope we can do this again."

"We just might," she said with a small smile. "Next semester, I plan on coming home every weekend and break so we can spend more time together."

"I like the sound of that plan."

We agreed to find Ms. Hudson at the coffeehouse when a thought occurred to me on the way.

"Want to see if I can take a picture of your mom?" I asked Elizabeth.

Her brows settled over her eyes. "That's a bad idea," she warned. "Mom has eyes on the back of her head."

I pursed my lips, "Let's find out."

We snuck around the shelves, making our way to the café without being seen. Ms. Hudson was sitting at a lone table, reading a magazine. It was the perfect shot. I turned on the camera, zoomed in, and waited for the right moment.

"Don't even think about it," Ms. Hudson demanded.

She remained in her seat, her eyes on the magazine. We emerged, sheepishly from behind the shelf. Elizabeth gave me that knowing, 'I told you so' look.

"How did you know we were here?" I asked.

"I'm a mother. I know everything." Ms. Hudson said. "I think you have had a little too much fun with the camera." She set the mug down and opened her palm in front of me. I knew what that meant from past incidents.

Still, I begged. "I'm sorry I tried to take your picture. I won't do it again, I promise!"

"It's not that," she said, calmly. "Mayu, you shouldn't take pictures of strangers without their permission. I could hear the shutter and see the flashes go off from here."

"I'll delete the pictures! And apologize to the people and..."

"Mayu..." she said my name in that motherly tone that could make anyone lose an argument with her. In a heavy sigh, I gave her the camera. "Do you two have everything?"

"Yes, Mom," Elizabeth said, glumly.

Ms. Hudson closed the magazine and rose from her chair. She checked our items at the register while Elizabeth and I stood behind her like scared puppies.

"She does have eyes in the back of her head," I whispered.

"Told you so..." Elizabeth whispered back.

"Mayu, Elizabeth," Ms. Hudson said. "Smile."

We looked up in time to see the camera flash in our faces.

Ms. Hudson returned the camera after we left the bookstore, and I promised her I wouldn't take pictures of strangers. I didn't need to anyway because Elizabeth was too busy rushing me to a stylish clothing store. The mannequins wore tightly fitted jeans and puffy pastel sweaters, turtleneck shirts and pleated skirts. Handmade clothes lined up the walls and at the back was a 'last chance' section for summer wear. I could never picture myself in fancy clothes, but a midnight blue dress with white embroidery caught my attention. It was my size and the only one left.

"Do you want it?" Elizabeth asked.

"I do..." I saw the price and my heart sank. I guess "last chance" didn't mean it was cheap.

"Don't worry about the cost," Ms. Hudson promised. "Remember, it's your day."

Relieved, I stepped into one of the dressing rooms. My heart raced as I put the dress on and when I emerged, Elizabeth's face widened with shock.

My cheeks burned. "What?"

"You look—

"Beautiful," Ms. Hudson finished.

*Do I?* I turned to one of the mirrors and froze at the girl staring back at me. She was me, wearing something that wasn't a school uniform or my usual clothes. The dress wasn't too fancy, but it wasn't plain. The color matched my eyes, helping it stand out, and it flowed when I twirled in place. I hardly wore dresses and it felt nice to be pretty for once and to look like an actual girl. To know that I could be pretty like Elizabeth and Ms. Hudson.

My eyes fell onto my clothes folded at the corner of the dressing room.

"Are you going to change back?" Ms. Hudson asked.

I turned her, tugging at the ends of the dress. "Would it be alright if I wear this for the rest of the day?"

Ms. Hudson answered with a rare, glowing smile. "Honey, of course you can."

We shopped for a pair of shoes to wear with the dress, then we headed to the next store. A relaxing, floral aroma wafted off the body wash and lotions crowding its shelves. Elizabeth led the way, darting from one aisle then sprinting to the next.

"You should try this one. It's called *Pretty in Peach.*" Elizabeth uncapped the bottle, and the sharp, tangy scent knocked me back, but it melted to a sweetness that was hard to resist. She gave me hair conditioner and lotion with a matching scent.

"If you use these together, your hair will be soft and smell sweet for a month!"

"Will it help my hair grow?"

"Definitely! It won't damage your ends either. Mom can style your hair if you're interested! If she can braid my hair, she can do something with yours."

I smiled, imagining my scruffy short hair as long as Elizabeth's. "That would be nice..."

By the time we stopped for a break, it felt like we were carrying the whole store in our bags. Elizabeth had to have at least ten pairs of lotions and bodywash.

"Are you sure your mom will let us get this much?"

"I think so. She hasn't said anything about it for a while."

"Wait," I said, looking around. "Where is your mom?"

We gathered our bags, feeling like we were hauling textbooks, and searched for Ms. Hudson. Out of a hunch, I looked for a set of stairs, and we found one leading to a floor full of scented candles. Ms. Hudson was at the register with a bag as big as her head, stuffed to the top with candles. It made me feel better about all the bottles we got, knowing that Ms. Hudson was as much of a shopper.

We dropped our bags off in the car, then returned to the plaza for dinner. Ms. Hudson took us to one of the restaurants and found a seat in a red, velvet booth with amber lamps illuminating the table.

Ms. Hudson told me I could order whatever I wanted, and I almost regretted ordering the Friday special. The waiters carted in a fat, towering burger drenched in cheese and bacon, seasoned fries spilling out of the bowl and grilled steak sizzling off a steamy iron plate. I was determined to finish it all. If I could stomach cafeteria food and discount pizza, I could handle this.

"Do you ever eat at school?" Elizabeth asked, watching me scarf down my burger and fries. She had a few crab cakes and scallop soup, and Ms. Hudson a plate of pasta and a glass of wine.

"School's lunches are horrible," I said, muffled.

"Don't talk with your mouthful," Ms. Hudson scolded.

"Sorry." I gulped down a glass of water. "Fights always happen in the cafeteria, so it's hard to eat when people next to you are tackling each other."

"I thought the assistants made sure fights didn't happen," said Elizabeth.

"There aren't any during lunch periods," I explained, something I'd noticed throughout the weeks.

"Ichirou and Hannah aren't letting you eat discount pizza again, are they?" Ms. Hudson asked.

"Sort of..." I looked away, nervously. "But they're so busy with school and work that they don't cook as much. Ichirou can only cook when he has time off."

"And you don't cook on your own because of the seizures?"

"I wish that was the case," I groaned. "Last year, I tried to make a milkshake for Ichirou and his friends, but we didn't have chocolate chips at the time. I used these weird chocolate bars I found in the kitchen that turned out to be laxatives."

Elizabeth snorted, nearly spitting out her water trying not to laugh. Ms. Hudson could only stare, her mouth opened in shock. Her voice faltered, "He did not..."

My face sank into my hands. "Ichirou hasn't trusted me to cook on my own since. He thinks I might poison someone by accident."

"Can't say I blame her." Ms. Hudson took a sip of her wine and shook her head. "I should teach you and Elizabeth to cook. Growing girls shouldn't eat pizza all the time... or poison their families."

"Noted."

I was still hungry after eating dinner, so we ordered desserts. I had strawberry ice cream on top of cheesecake, and I wanted to share it with Elizabeth. She ate little of it.

Curious, I asked, "What are your lunches like?"

She replied, picking the cheesecake with her fork. "Since I live in the dorms, we have a three-meal schedule. Breakfast, lunch, and dinner. Sometimes desserts, but they go away so quickly, you have to eat your desserts and dinner at the same time. Overall, the food is always fresh."

"Private schools seem to have all the good stuff."

"Not always. I have to wake up as early as five in the morning to get a better breakfast. The same for dinner too, it's at five thirty. Show up late, and the food is gone."

"I bet you're always there on time."

"Not all the time," Elizabeth moaned. "I missed dinner and had to eat during After Meals."

"What's After Meals?"

"It's like breakfast and lunch for night classes. I was lucky that Suzanne had a friend to let me inside so I could eat."

"Your school has night classes!" I nearly choked on my cheesecake.

Elizabeth rubbed my back and Ms. Hudson passed me a glass of water.

The motion of the car and the warm evening air made it challenging to keep my dinner down. Elizabeth looked a little sick too, so Ms. Hudson bought us water bottles and rolled the windows down on the drive home. Luckily, we didn't throw up, but we were stuffed from the meal and tired after hours of walking. Elizabeth and I rested in the car and slept during the ride.

"We're almost home, girls." Ms. Hudson announced.

I woke up, slightly drowsy to a cool gust of wind against my face. A familiar scent of sprouting leaves, pine trees and musty bark made me realize where we were.

Coming to view was the Hudson's home, a Tudor-style house, close enough to the woods to hear critters in the branches and distant crashing waves. Pine trees surrounded the home, its needles spotted the pointed black roof and lush ivy vines climbed up the pale walls.

My heart raced as Ms. Hudson pulled up on the segmented driveway. With our bags in our arms, Elizabeth and I hiked up the porch steps to the arched door. Elizabeth set the bags down, unlocked the door. My eyes fluttered as the cool air embraced us, carrying hints of clove and woodland leaves.

It was middle school all over again. The lamps hanging off the walls cast a warm glow across the hardwood floor. Polished shelves walled around the couches in the living room and potted plants sat at every corner or windowsills.

Hoisting my bag over my shoulder, Elizabeth and I rushed up the spiral staircase to her bedroom. True to her liking, the walls were pastel pink, and the cat themed blankets and pillows decorated her large bed. Elizabeth had her own shelf full of books she'd read and journals. She took some of her books to her dorm so we could use the extra space to store our body wash and lotions.

"Don't forget to do your laundry," Ms. Hudson called from downstairs.

"I won't!" she shouted back.

Elizabeth darted to the side of her bed and hauled a white mesh bag of dark clothes out of her room.

"Do you need help?"

Elizabeth insisted. "I can carry them. Relax for now, make yourself at home. We've been on our feet all day."

"Shout if you need anything," I said, settling on the bed.

"Aye aye!" she yelled, hauling the bag out of her room.

I sorted through my bag, setting the bodywash and lotions on the shelves. I picked Pretty in Peach to use when, suddenly, my ears twitched to faint steps on the wood. I whipped around with a startled gasp and caught Ms. Hudson standing in the room. Her hand held over the opened door as if she was going to knock before I turned.

"Didn't think you'd hear me," she said, lowly. Ms. Hudson nudged her glasses up the bridge of her nose then met my eyes. "Your brother called me to check on you. He said you weren't answering your phone."

"He called?!" I patted my pockets, and realized I was still wearing the midnight blue dress. My head swiveled to my backpack and shopping bags, and I found my original clothes. I rummaged through the pockets for the phone, but the battery had died. No wonder I hadn't heard anything from him all day.

I turned back to Ms. Hudson. "I'm sorry…"

"Not to worry," she assured. "Before I was rushed out of the house, he mentioned you'd been sleepwalking?"

I bit the inside of my cheek, hesitant to meet Ms. Hudson's gaze. "I did—I was, but I have it under control. I don't sleepwalk anymore, I swear."

Ms. Hudson smirked, "I've seen you do stranger things. If I can handle your seizures, sleepwalking shouldn't be a problem. You have nothing to worry about while you're here."

I exhaled in relief. "Um, Ms. Hudson, I have a question."

"I may have an answer."

"Elizabeth told me she went to the movies with Suzanne."

"Ah, her," she chuckled softly. "I swear that man feeds her nothing but sugar and coffee."

"How did Elizabeth meet her?"

"They've met before," she said. "Her father and I were colleagues, and we used to drop our daughters off at the same daycare. We haven't stayed in touch for years, so it was a surprise when we ran into each other this summer."

"They were friends for that long? Elizabeth's never mentioned Suzanne before."

"To be fair, Elizabeth was four years old when they met. Sue certainly remembered her."

We heard footsteps bounding upstairs and Elizabeth returned.

"I started the laundry, Mom…" Elizabeth panted and looked at us. "Is everything alright?"

Ms. Hudson turned to her. "Why don't you take a bath first? Let Mayu settle down a bit."

Elizabeth glanced warily at me before giving a soft "okay," and left for the bathroom.

As Ms. Hudson turned to leave, she said over her shoulder. "I wouldn't worry about it if I were you."

An hour after Elizabeth finished her bath, it was my turn. There were three bathrooms in the house, but my personal favorite was the one on the second floor. It had a shower with its own cubicle, an extra powder room that always smelled like roses, and sitting in front of the window with an ocean view, a tub deep enough to submerge myself under.

Once the bathtub was full, I sank into the water, melting away in the peach scented bubbles. The tranquility was cut by Ms. Hudson's voice coming through the wall. Elizabeth was talking to her, but her voice was so soft I couldn't make out what she was saying. They weren't yelling, but Ms. Hudson's hardened tone worried me. After I finished my bath, I helped Elizabeth set up for bed and asked what she and her mom were talking about.

She started, toying with her hair. "You see…There's… someone at school. I always see him in choir practice with one of my roommates."

"Him?" I repeated. "I thought St. Laurel's was an all-girl's school."

Elizabeth's ears turned pink. "It is… but…h-he only visits after school."

"Isn't St. Laurel strict with visitors?"

The pink blush traveled to her cheeks. She knotted her braid. "Yeah. But the rules aren't as strict after school hours."

I stared at her skeptically. "Does Ms. Hudson know?"

She sat next to me in bed, her face was the color of roses. "Mom wants me to focus on school. B-But he helps me study sometimes."

I broke into a smile. "Is that what the talk was about? You met a boy?"

"Never mind." She waved it off and climbed into bed. "It's hard to talk about it."

"How come? I met a boy at school too," I squinted at Elizabeth, adding a teasing edge to my voice. "What's your boyfriend's name?"

"He's not my boyfriend!" She protested. Her face practically matched her entire room. "We should get some sleep. We're still going to the aquarium tomorrow."

"Sure… We can talk about this guy tomorrow."

"Drop it."

She turned off the lights and went to sleep.

My smile faded as questions rose in my mind about Elizabeth. She went to St. Laurel's all-girls private school but somehow met a boy in choir. As weird as it was to know a boy could sneak into that school, it was strange that Elizabeth wanted to spend time with him. She had always avoided boys in Lawrence, even when they were interested in her and would rather hide her face behind a book. So, what made this one different? How come she's never mentioned him to me in our calls?

It was two in the morning, according to the glow in the dark numbers on my watch. The alarm woke me up and I lazily pushed the buttons until it shut off. I laid back in bed, and pulled the blanket over my ears when I felt an empty space beside me.

"Elizabeth?" I sat up. A dim light stretched from beneath the door. It opened and Elizabeth walked inside, holding her shoulder.

"Mayu? Did you hear an alarm?"

"It was my watch, sorry about that," I said, sitting back. And I realized she must have been up before the alarm went off. "Is everything alright?"

"I had to use the bathroom." Elizabeth crawled back into bed and looked at my new-old watch. "What happened to your pink one? Did it break?"

"No, I switched watches with Ichirou."

"You did mention you were sleepwalking. Is that what the watch is for?"

Elizabeth flicked a switch on her nightstand and the cat shaped lamp lit most of the bed. While resetting the alarm, I told her about my dreams, the voice in my head and sleepwalking. I left out the mystic part of it.

"I thought you always heard voices during a seizure."

"That's what I thought, at first. But this one always came back."

Worry settled on her face. "Did you hear it just now?"

"I haven't heard it in a week, and I've been waking up in my bed. It might be gone now. I hope its gone now..."

"That's still concerning," she yawned. "I can't imagine you wandering out of the house. What if you ended up at the beach?"

"I'd sleep swim?" I joked.

"You can't sleep swim." Elizabeth quirked.

"Fish can sleep swim."

"You're not a fish."

The following morning, Ms. Hudson had started cooking by the time we were in the kitchen. It was a hearty breakfast of sunny side eggs slumped over bacon and soft pancakes and sliced strawberries. She didn't want us hungry at the aquarium and she promised to make us dinner later.

I took my time with breakfast, savoring every bite while we talked about the trip to the aquarium. I promised Ms. Hudson I would only take pictures of the animals and no one else.

I wouldn't have to worry about that because the aquarium wasn't so busy. We were the first in line to get admission tickets quickly, but we had to wait a little longer to get the tickets that would let us feed the stingrays and dine at the connected restaurant next door. I wondered what kind of food a restaurant in an aquarium served. Then I quickly stopped myself from thinking the worst and ruining my trip and my appetite.

The aquarium was beautiful. The blue glow of the water drew us to a tunnel where spotted sharks and manta rays glided over us, sea turtles swam with a school of fish and a giant fish the size of a car tire slowed to watch me take its picture. I couldn't believe different animals could live in the same tank.

Elizabeth pointed to the massive yellow moray eels resting in the sand below, then we hurried to the tank full of lionfish. Finally, on our way to see the stingrays, we traveled through a tunnel bathed in a soothing shade of violet. The tour guide at the end of the tunnel said, "Don't look down, look up." Sure enough, the violet light came from a tank above us, home to dozens of jellyfish bobbing idly by.

I took pictures of Elizabeth with a school of colorful fish behind her. Ms. Hudson helped take a good picture of us standing in front of a big tank swarming with the stingrays before feeding them.

One of the caretakers gave us instructions on what to do. "Grip the frozen meat tight in a fist, tucking your thumbs in so the nail won't scratch the stingray's mouth. Lower your arm in the water, loosen your grip and let the stingray suck it."

I went over the instructions in my head as Elizabeth stared worriedly at the stingrays. I didn't know what she was afraid of, touching the water or being touched by stingrays. Her face turned sickly white when she saw the bucket of frozen, chopped up fish brought to us. I volunteered to go first.

The fish guts in my hand seemed colder than the water. The currents were gentle and warm against my skin. The spotted stingrays drifted closer to me, and their smooth, cool bodies tickled my wrist. My grip loosened and a current sucked the food out of my hand. I couldn't stop laughing after I took my hand out of the tank.

"What's it like?" Elizabeth asked.

"It's so weird!" I exclaimed. "Like putting your hand in front of a vacuum. You've got to try it!"

"What if I drop it?"

"Don't worry about it," the guide assured. "The stingray can easily pick it up if you drop it."

Still looking nervous, she tried. The guide gave Elizabeth a small piece, she stuck her hand in the tank, but not one stingray glided near her.

"Maybe they don't like me," she murmured.

"You're too anxious," said Ms. Hudson. "Relax and lower your arm."

"Any lower and I might swim with them—"

A stingray brushed against her hand. Elizabeth shrieked and dropped the food into the water. It floated leisurely until another stingray soared over it, sucking the meal in its mouth.

I stifled my laugh. "At least he got it."

Later, around noon, we settled in the restaurant for lunch. Much to my relief, they had almost every meal except for fish. Elizabeth must not have liked the experience with the stingrays. She looked quite sick, probably from touching frozen fish guts, and didn't eat or drink. She sat and kept rolling her shoulders and I asked if her back hurt.

"I'm alright, we can keep exploring after lunch," she said.

We stopped at a gift shop. I was going through the pictures in my camera when I realized that I hadn't taken a picture of Ms. Hudson. I mean, I tried to take her picture near the octopus's tank, but she was quick to cover her face. She also ducked behind a tank of sea stars, hid her face with her purse, and twice, she used a rack at the gift store to avoid my camera.

"Aw, Mom, can we take one picture of you?" Elizabeth begged when we were outside the aquarium.

Ms. Hudson sat on a bench near the exit doors. "Is a photo of me that important?"

"Of course, it is!" Elizabeth cried.

"It's to capture the moment!" I added.

Ms. Hudson groaned. "Can't you take a picture of each other?"

"We already have," Elizabeth said. "But we don't have a picture of you."

"Girls," Ms. Hudson moaned.

Then I had an idea. "If you won't let me take a picture. You'll have to race us!"

She looked at me with a raised eyebrow. "Excuse me?"

"She's right," Elizabeth agreed. "Have your picture taken, or race with us. From here to the car."

Ms. Hudson peered at the entrance door like she was picturing herself running in heels. I tried to picture it too, but it didn't look right. Not that I was going to admit to that.

231

"Fine then," She relented. "On one condition... we'll take it together."

At hearing that, my excitement grew, though I wondered how the three of us would fit in the picture. I didn't want to ask someone if they could take it for us. Elizabeth had an idea. She and I sat on either side of her mother, then Ms. Hudson held the camera over us.

"Ready?" Ms. Hudson asked.

"Ready," I said, looking at the camera.

"Ready," said Elizabeth.

Ms. Hudson's finger hovered over the shutter, and said, "Smile!"

• ●  •

That evening, Elizabeth and I had dinner at home. As we ate, I noticed Elizabeth wasn't eating as much. Her plate was full, but she had only eaten small slices and portions.

"If you're not going to eat, I'll finish it for you!" I teased.

"I'm not that hungry," she said, and offered her plate to me.

"Elizabeth, you don't leave the table until you've finished," Ms. Hudson said, sitting across from us. Elizabeth ate her dinner in small bites.

That night, I fell asleep easily, but around midnight, a thud jolted me awake. I relaxed when I remembered Ms. Hudson liked to sit on her bedroom balcony. I never knew what she did so late in the night, but I imagined it was reading and sipping wine.

As a crescent moon's light swept into the window, I rolled to my side, facing Elizabeth, who was still asleep, her back towards me. The last thing I remembered before the drowsiness took over was a scar on Elizabeth's back.

Sunday morning rolled in as the sun rose over the quiet neighborhood. I couldn't believe how fast the weekend had gone and I was a little mad. Of all the long and boring weekends I had, the one I wanted to last forever ended faster than it began.

As the sunlight crept into Elizabeth's room, so did the reality of going back to school—back to the mystic world. I had been having so much fun that I didn't want to tell Elizabeth about it and ruin our time together. Between breakfast, spending time playing board games, watching a movie, then helping her pack up, I debated on how I should tell her the truth.

"The earlier I'm at my dorm, the sooner I can start studying for tomorrow," Elizabeth said, pacing. "Now where did I put that brush..."

I was helping Elizabeth look around her room. I couldn't talk to her about the assistants, not while she had her mind on something else.

"I'm surprised you're not in any honor classes."

"There aren't any. Every class is advanced in—found it!" she pulled her pink brush from under her bed.

"Elizabeth? I want to tell you something..."

"One moment." Elizabeth checked her suitcase for the tenth time and paced around the room, rubbing her back. "I know I'm forgetting something."

"Maybe you need to sit down," I suggested.

Elizabeth took a deep breath and sat on the chair. "I'm just," she paused. "I can't believe you're going home so soon."

"I know." I leaned against the bed, my eyes trailed to the ceiling. "I wish I could stay a week again."

"Me too. I almost forgot how fun this was."

"Why did you want to stay in the dorm?"

"I didn't want to," she said. "I wanted to commute, but Mom wanted me to stay on campus." She continued to rub her shoulder.

"What's wrong with your back?"

"I—I've been picking up a lot of heavy stuff. Not to mention that we carried a lot on Friday. It's finally catching up with me." She looked up with wide eyes. "My uniform!"

"What?"

"That's what I'm forgetting," she exclaimed. "My uniform is still in the dryer."

"I'll get it for you," I jumped to my feet.

"Are you sure? I can get it myself."

"Don't worry about it. I know where the dryer is. Unless your washer and dryer aren't in the basement anymore."

"Last I checked, they're in the attic," she joked. "They're still in the basement."

I snickered. "Besides, I want to know what your uniform looks like."

I left the room as Elizabeth rested on her bed. We woke up early to do a lot of activities, then packed up until early evening. She's a little tired.

The Hudson's basement didn't look like one. Part of it was a wine cellar for Ms. Hudson's business, "Mycenaean Fine Wines."

Redwood racks made up an entire wall, full of bottled wine and port glasses from all over the world and a marble table at the center. The washing machine and dryer were tucked in an extra room next to the marble bar. I opened the dryer and black and green blazers and skirts spilled into the basket.

My heart stopped as dread crept into me. The skirts matched the ones Min wore. I looked down, trying to tell myself it was a coincidence. It couldn't be possible. A lump welled in my throat when I lifted one of the blazers and saw a small, familiar emblem stitched in the corner.

# Unravel

**The seal of Erehwon was as clear to me as the emblem** on the letter I'd received almost a month ago. My heart pounded as questions raced through my head. If Elizabeth has an emblem on her school uniform, it could only mean a few things. I needed answers, *now*.

I grabbed the laundry basket and charged up the stairs, taking a breath in the living room. I shouted Elizabeth's name, but the only response was an uneasy silence. Ms. Hudson left to run an errand half an hour ago. I bounded toward the second floor and called out to Elizabeth. Painful moans coming from her room prompted me to hurry, then something heavy hit the floor.

"Elizabeth!"

I dropped the basket and sprinted to her room. I threw the door open, my eyes darted from wall to wall, until they fell on the floor where Elizabeth laid. She was sickly pale and covered in sweat and blood oozed from a pair of lumps swelling on her back.

I rushed to her side and dropped to my knees, hesitant to touch her back.

"What happened to you?" I stammered out. My head turned from Elizabeth to my phone plugged into the wall. Should I stop the bleeding first or call Ms. Hudson?

Elizabeth looked at me, tears welling in her eyes. She lurched forward, and her trembling voice tore into a scream. Black spikes burst from her back, stretching out like arms dragging themselves out of her. My voice hitched as the limbs split apart and sheets of skin coated in blood spilled over Elizabeth's body. A wet, coppery smell slammed into me, hurtling my thoughts into a red fog as Elizabeth's screams rang in my ears.

Someone grabbed my shoulder and shocked all the senses out of me. I swung my arm only for Ms. Hudson to catch it mid-air, her hand clamped around my wrist.

"Shh, shh, it's okay. I'm here. I'm here…"

I blinked. My frozen body crumbled in her arms, and I sobbed. Warmth and relief washed over me until I remembered Elizabeth. I spun back to my friend, whose hand reached out. Her cries, weak and feeble.

"M-mom…"

Ms. Hudson told me to wait outside, but I didn't leave and watched her place Elizabeth's arms over her shoulder. Elizabeth winced and groaned with every movement and the limbs dragged across the floor, smearing blood onto the carpet. She staggered toward her bed as Ms. Hudson whispered, "It's going okay. You're going to be okay."

When she acknowledged her daughter's extra limbs, she carefully lifted them and moved them close to the bed. She turned to me, motioning me to follow her.

In the kitchen, I sat at the table and Ms. Hudson bought a wet cloth for me from the sink. She wiped my face, and I froze at the blood smeared on the cloth when she pulled it away.

"Looks like none of it got into your hair," she whispered.

Ms. Hudson spun to the sink and opened the window, letting in a rush of air that smelled of ocean water and fresh leaves. I remembered the scent from Saturday morning. Elizabeth had been sitting next to me, and we made plans for the day while Ms. Hudson made breakfast for us.

It should've been a normal evening. Elizabeth and I were supposed to give each other hugs and promise to visit the following weekend. I shouldn't be sitting in the kitchen alone while Ms. Hudson washed blood off my face. Tears flooded my eyes as I broke down, hoping the nightmare would end, but when I saw my own shaking hands, it finally settled in that everything I saw was real.

A white teacup clinked on the table's surface. A folded handkerchief rested next to it. I looked up, meeting Ms. Hudson's sharp brown eyes. She sat across from me, still wearing her worn, yet collected, face. Her hands folded together next to a full glass of red wine. She didn't bother to ask if I was alright. Nothing was alright, and we both knew it.

"Elizabeth didn't want you to see her like that," she began, breathing deeply. "She wanted to wait until she had better control to tell you the truth about us."

I stared at her as her words sunk in. Ms. Hudson's expression hardly changed. She glued her eyes to me, as if she wanted me to say something.

"What were those ...things?"

She answered, firmly. "Those were her wings."

"Her wings?" I repeated, my voice cracked in disbelief. Those things that burst out of Elizabeth's back were wings?

"Why does she have wings?"

"She was born with them. Just like me." Ms. Hudson drew another deep breath. "We may look like humans, enough to pass as one, but I'm afraid that's where the similarities end."

Clutching my skirt under the table, I wanted to say I didn't believe it. I didn't want to believe it.

Finally, I asked, "What...are you?"

Ms. Hudson's firm gaze softened. "We're a succubus. It's not something I like to bring up, and obviously, it's not something Elizabeth is proud of."

A memory came rushing back to when I first heard the name. Elizabeth had a lot of books on mythology, but one of the tales that she always read about was a succubus, a creature that seduced men to drain their energy. At the time, it seemed weird of her to read about it the most. But she told me it was out of curiosity.

"You can't be!" I shrieked. "They're not... real..."

Ms. Hudson stared at me. "Mayu, we both know that isn't the truth. You've always been aware of our side of the world, but you'd deny it or blame your seizures for making you see and hear the things that were plainly in front of you."

"But all the time we've spent together, she's never turned into that. I've never seen you turn into that!"

Ms. Hudson pinched the stem of the glass and sipped the wine. "I have had centuries to control what I look like in front of others. Elizabeth only had three years. I did what I could to teach her how to control her appearance so she could have a 'normal' life."

"Couldn't she change back to a human?"

"There's nothing to change back into. Elizabeth has always been a succubus. The only thing that can help her is if she feeds."

"Feed on what..."

Her eyes flickered. "Do you really want me to say it?"

I thought back to the myth, but I couldn't imagine Elizabeth or Ms. Hudson feeding off others.

Ms. Hudson grimaced, "For what it's worth, Elizabeth doesn't like the idea either."

"Can't she live off regular food?"

"She can, but it can't give us the strength we need to maintain our appearance. And if we don't feed for long, we change against our will."

"So, every time... she canceled on me..."

"It was because of what you saw."

It was all hard to take in. I felt weak and heavy at the same time. "April. At the last track meet, she told me she was sick..."

Ms. Hudson's eyes lowered to the table. "I woke up to her screaming that morning and by the time I was rushed to her room, her wings had ripped their way out of her. It took a whole day for them to retract, and she was too exhausted to move. Elizabeth insisted that being nervous about the last track meet triggered her to change so suddenly. But when she was pushed into the locker, she almost changed right then and there."

"She was fighting to keep control."

Ms. Hudson continued, drawing a long, slow breath. "I decided she could no longer be around humans until she could control herself. The school I enrolled her in doesn't have a lot of succubi who can teach her, but she's not around humans that can cause her to change like that."

I wiped my cheeks again before I could speak. All those times she'd canceled on me, and all those times I thought she was upset with me. She had been going through one painful transformation after another.

"I wish she would have told me."

"And what would you have done?"

"What do you mean?"

"You both have a peculiar habit of averting your eyes from the truth. Do you remember the first time your brother and I met?"

"I remember."

It was open house in November. Elizabeth and I were in the sixth grade. We were so worried that Ms. Hudson wouldn't like Ichirou. She terrified the teachers, and neither of the parents wanted to talk to her. But Ichirou spoke to her first, and they became such close friends, he called her Isa instead of Isabella or Ms. Hudson. I never knew what they spoke about, but since Ms.

Hudson had brought it up, maybe there was more to their talk than I thought.

"Ichirou and I had a rather interesting conversation, but a few things stuck out to me about you." Ms. Hudson said. "He told me you had a difficult time when you lived with your parents. Why is that?"

Though I hated thinking about my past, I wanted to answer her honestly.

"'Difficult' is putting it lightly," I began, shouldering my embarrassment. "My seizures used to be... much worse. I used to lash out at people during my blackouts. I bit and scratched them like I was some sort of animal. No medication worked on me no matter how strong the prescriptions were. It wasn't until I moved in with Ichirou when I started to calm down."

I raised my chin and braced for Ms. Hudson's reaction. A lot of people wouldn't believe that I used to be a crazy kid. Yet she remained silent and composed.

"Can't say that I'm surprised," she finally said. "You were always the active one getting into odd situations with Elizabeth, like sneaking out of school." I caught the small smirk on Ms. Hudson's face before it faded. She leaned forward and her fingers laced together. "Tell me, do you recall any unusual injuries from your childhood?"

My brows furrowed. "What does this have to do with—"

"I'm getting to that."

I slumped in my chair and thought back to any injuries I got that were unusual.

"In first grade, I chased a striped chipmunk up a tree during recess and almost caught it. But the branch broke, and I fell. I woke up with a swelling pain in the back of my head and my teacher and classmates surrounded me."

"What happened?"

"My teacher told me I hit my head on the ground. My eyes were open, I wasn't moving, and blood pooled from the back of my head. They called a paramedic and my parents, but all I had was a scratch that was quickly stitched up. Mom said it was a miracle that I survived."

"What did you think it was?"

I shrugged. "Luck? People can survive a two-story fall, right?"

"Not without lasting injuries." Ms. Hudson closed her eyes for a few seconds, then she looked at me again. "Earlier, I told you I've seen you do strange things, but your seizures weren't one of them. I've been to plenty of yours and Elizabeth's track meets to notice."

"Notice what?"

"No matter how badly you scraped your knees falling over hurdles or bruised yourself slipping down the bleachers. You always got back up without a scratch. You never thought that was odd?"

"Everyone joked that I had thicker skin," I said.

Then, I remembered. The crippling pain on my shoulder when I was hurled into the bathroom wall, and the ceramic shards cutting into me. The sharp stings from running through Erewhon's forest and Rosalina's fists against my face, but I never had a scratch on me.

"You can heal much faster than a human should." Ms. Hudson's words cut into me. My gaze met hers, hoping to find a clue that she was joking, except her expression remained serious. "You can heal fast and see the mystical world because you're not human either."

We were both silent. Her words echoed in my mind and no matter how much I wanted to argue, she was right. A part of me had always known something wasn't right about me and I, as Ms. Hudson had put it, had looked the other way. It was bad enough that having epilepsy made me an outcast, I didn't need another reason to stand out.

A phone ringing interrupted the silence. Ms. Hudson stood up and answered the call. Whoever she was talking to, must have asked for Elizabeth.

Ms. Hudson replied, "She can't make it to campus tonight. Maybe tomorrow."

She hung up and we heard noises shuffling upstairs.

"She must be awake by now." Ms. Hudson lifted one of the clean white towels and soaked it under the faucet. "I need to check on her."

"I'll come with you," I said quickly.

She turned to me. "Do you want to? After what you've seen?"

"I just... I want to talk to her. If that's possible."

• ● •

The wings draped over Elizabeth and covered most of her bed. I felt nauseous looking at them, and the sour smell of open flesh wounds wasn't helping.

Ms. Hudson spoke to Elizabeth in a sweet, soothing voice. "Does it still hurt?"

"A little." She noticed me, and quickly faced the window, looking out into the night.

Elizabeth winced when Ms. Hudson lifted one of the wings.

Her voice softened, "No wonder this change was painful. Your wings are twisted again."

"I'm sorry..." Elizabeth's voice muffled through the pillow. "I was in a hurry."

"Rushing the retraction makes the change painful. They'll fold and sink on their own. But we need to stretch them out first."

I didn't like the sound of that. Neither did Elizabeth. She moaned, "Do I have to, Mom?"

"Trust me, growing them out is painful, but twisted wings are worse." Ms. Hudson turned to me. "Mayu, can you hold her hand?"

Nodding, I drew my attention away from the wings and knelt in front of Elizabeth. She glanced at me but said nothing when I wrapped my hand around her's.

Ms. Hudson lifted one of the wings by its bony side, and the sheets of flesh spilled onto the floor. Vibrant red veins pulsed in the wings. Elizabeth yelped, clutching a pillow with one hand, and squeezing mine with the other.

"Breathe, baby girl," Ms. Hudson consoled. "In through your nose, exhale through your mouth."

It was hard to tell if it worked or not. Every touch made Elizabeth flinch and yelp. She squeezed my hand so hard that it turned white. Ms. Hudson slowly stretched the wings over the bed, causing Elizabeth's grip to tighten around my hand. She opened her teary eyes, only to squeeze them shut again.

I didn't realize how long the wings were until they spilled past the bed frame. Ms. Hudson repeated the same process on the other wing and, when it was finally over, Elizabeth let out a deep breath. The blood circulated in my hand again as her grip loosened.

"That should be it. Rest and wait until they sink back in." Ms. Hudson carefully dabbed the towel against Elizabeth's wings. Then she picked up her glasses that had fallen off, cleaned it with her shirt then set it on the nightstand. "Mayu, can you wait with her?"

"I will." I said.

Ms. Hudson closed the door behind her, leaving me alone with Elizabeth.

"You don't have to hold my hand anymore."

"I'm sorry." I said, letting go. "How are you feeling?"

241

"My back hurts."

Looking at her trying to smile, I joked back. "You have thicker skin than I do. I probably would've fainted."

"First time it happened, I threw up and fainted."

"What came first, throwing up or fainting?"

"I don't remember anymore," she frowned. "I wish you hadn't seen this...."

I paused, unable to bring myself to say, 'It's okay.' "Your mom explained it to me."

"Mom told you the truth about us better than I ever could."

"I'm still processing it." I leaned against the bed and wondered if Elizabeth knew if I wasn't a human either. "Have you always known you were... a succubus?"

"No, but I always had a feeling we weren't... normal." Elizabeth stared at the window. I wasn't sure if she was focusing on the ocean or her own reflection.

"When I was four years old, I woke up to a sound in the kitchen. Mom used to work at a diner, so I thought she was coming home. I went to see her and saw something like Mom... with bat-like wings stretching out of their back and horns coming out of their head. Everything was a blur after that. I woke up to Mom, tucking me into bed. No horns or wings. She wore her diner's dress and sang a lullaby to me." Elizabeth blushed. "All those years, I thought what I saw in the kitchen was a bad dream."

"What changed?"

She looked down and shifted in bed as much as she could, but the pain made it hard for her to move. "I was eleven and going to a different school. There was a boy in my class that I liked. Zachary Grey." She sighed dreamily. "One day, he told me he liked me and asked to go out with me."

I gasped, "You had a boyfriend?"

Elizabeth chuckled weakly. "Yeah. We'd sit together in class, and he'd hold my hand in the hallway and give me a present from his parent's candy shop..." Her smile faded. "On Valentine's Day, Zachary wanted to kiss me, so we snuck away from the kids during recess. I had never kissed a boy before and I wanted to know if it was like a kiss in fairy tales, like magic..."

She choked out at the end of her sentence.

"He collapsed in front of me. He was pale, and he stopped breathing. I screamed for help and Zachary was taken to the hospital. My teacher asked me what happened, but I—I was too scared to say something, so they sent me home.

The next few days, I got sick. I threw up everything that I ate. My whole body hurt so much, I thought I was going to die. Then the wings came out of my back. Mom stayed with me, and she finally told me the truth. What she was. What I was.

It took a month before my wings settled in. When I went back to school, I thought things would go back to normal, but it didn't." she sniffled. "Every boy I touched...would suddenly feel dizzy or collapse. I couldn't shake hands with my teacher or tap a boy on the shoulder."

"And Zachary..."

"He recovered but while I was away, he spread awful rumors about me. The girls bullied me so much that Mom transferred me to our middle school. At first, everyone was nice to me, but I kept my distance from them. I tried to deal with being alone, but I couldn't take it until you approached me. Do you remember?"

I started to tear up. "How could I forget? You were my first friend, too."

It was March when I saw her sitting by herself in the cafeteria. Her tray was full, but she wasn't touching it. I always saw her at the back of class, reading or writing but she never spoke to anyone. I'd sit in the front of class, but on a dull day, my eyes wandered back to the quiet girl ignored by the rest of the world. That day in the cafeteria, I decided to sit next to her.

"I wanted to go to high school with you," Elizabeth whimpered. "I tried going to St. Laurel's as a compromise. I thought if I went to a school with only girls, I wouldn't change so often. But after what happened with Rosalina, Mom made me transfer to a different school. One where people knew what I was and could help me control myself."

Just when I needed another moment to register everything, her voice broke. "Mayu... I'm glad we met. And I'm so sorry, I'm so sorry I lied to you." Elizabeth teared up. "But if you don't want to be friends anymore..."

My eyes watered. "Why would I stop being friends with you over wings?" I chuckled lightly. "I met a girl in school with wings on the side of her head!"

Elizabeth's eyes widened, and she mouthed, "what" under her breath.

"I have a lot to tell you about my school. But I'll always be your friend. Wings or no wings, you're still the same Elizabeth I met. You're still her now."

Elizabeth choked up and broke into sobs. All I could do was comfort her. I stroked her hair, which brought a smile to her until my hand bumped against something solid on her head.

"Ow!"

"I'm sorry, but what are those..." I answered my own question when I brushed her hair aside, seeing something small and bone white curving out of her scalp. "You have horns?"

Elizabeth blushed. "Are you going be okay with that?"

"One thing at a time." I glanced at her wings. I could picture her with more feathered wings like a bird or a butterfly like Min's. "They're going to take time getting used to."

"They're ugly, I know. Mom's wings are much prettier than mine."

"Can you fly?"

"Sort of."

"What's it like?"

"Horrible," Elizabeth broke into a small laugh. "Mom tried to help me, but I can't seem to get it right. If I have to jump off the balcony again..."

"Have you tried the long jump?" I suggested. "You're launching yourself off the ground anyway."

Elizabeth held her chin. "It might work if our roof had a runway."

We sat in silence. I rested my head on my knees when Elizabeth asked, "How did you meet a girl with wings? What kind of school are you going to?"

"It's Carter High School," I replied. "And the assistants are from Erehwon too."

Her face brightened

"Lutea is a golem, Ethan is a werewolf, and I think Mr. Turner's a vampire, but I'll have to ask him. The boy I'm friends with can see the fae at the school courtyard and I know a witch named Miss Naiad—like the water spirits. Weird, right?"

"I know her!" Elizabeth bolted up and jerked to a stop before her arms buckled and she collapsed in bed.

"I'm alright!" She winced. "I shouldn't have gotten up so fast."

Dark blood trickled down her back. Elizabeth, still flustered, held her head and closed her eyes. I reached for one of the towels, but they were too bloodied to be of any use.

"I'll be right back!" I said, trying not to panic.

I hurried out of the room and closed the door when Ms. Hudson said a soft, "Thank you." I spun around to see her leaning against the wall, arms crossed over her chest.

"For what?" I realized it as soon as I asked. "Were you listening to us the whole time?"

"Most of it."

I walked with Ms. Hudson to the bathroom.

She continued. "Thank you for talking to her. I think Elizabeth was more afraid of losing you as a friend."

"She doesn't have to worry. I meant what I said."

"I know."

In the bathroom there was a small closet full of folded towels. I pulled out at least four washcloths, hoping it was enough for Elizabeth.

"Before I came upstairs, I spoke to Ichirou," Ms. Hudson said, grabbing my attention. "He and Hannah came back from a party, so he'll pick you up in ten minutes."

"You're not taking me home?"

"Someone has to stay with Elizabeth."

My heart ached at the idea of Elizabeth being left alone in her condition. "Are her changes always this painful?"

"First times are never pleasant, and Elizabeth's change is still recent. It'll take time and practice for her to adjust." Her expression softened. She almost looked... tired.

"Ms. Hudson?"

"I might have gone too far by telling you weren't human. You were still processing everything with Elizabeth."

She was right.

"Why tell me?"

"You're still young, which means sooner or later, you'll undergo a change too."

My insides knotted. "Wait, what!" I choked out.

"Your eyes were a dead giveaway. They're much brighter than I remembered. Your sense of smell and hearing has sharpened so much, you heard me come into the room Friday night when I didn't make a sound."

I clutched the towels and scampered to the mirror. My eyes, deep, sky blue, had a bright, almost electric color ringing around them. How come I hadn't noticed it?

My chest started to heave. "What am I changing into?"

Ms. Hudson, noticing my panic, rested her hands on my shoulders. "I don't know what you're turning into," she spoke softly to calm my racing thoughts. "Unlike us, your change is slow and subtle. But I thought you were better off learning about it now than finding out when it was too late."

I buried my head in her chest, feeling the world crash into my shoulders.

It felt like I was drifting to Elizabeth's room. Half in her house, cradling the basket of damp towels as my legs carried me to the door. The other half was lost in everything: Elizabeth's change, Ms. Hudson's talk and what she finally told me.

I stopped in front of Elizabeth's door and called out to her to let her know I was back. My voice didn't sound right to me. It felt like I was reading a script or something. I shook my head and nudged the door open.

"Elizabeth, I'm going home soon, okay?"

She was fast asleep. I wanted to wake her up, but knowing what she had gone through, I figured she needed the rest. The wings no longer stretched over the bed, and they were slowly easing their way inside her back. I sank to my knees, set the basket beside me, and toweled the blood off her back, careful not to touch her wings. I pulled back, then looked at Elizabeth once more. I wanted to keep the true image of Elizabeth, not as the girl who screamed in agony, but as my best friend.

•　●　•

Ichirou arrived at the house minutes later. He helped me carry the bags to the trunk of his car and spoke to Ms. Hudson. It was mostly casual talk, like how they had been and what they had been up to. I heard them mention more sleepovers for the holidays. It would have been exciting to hear if this were any other night.

With the last bag in the trunk, I settled in the car and my stomach clenched at a spoiling stench rolling off the backseat.

I gagged. "Did something die back here?"

"Her Highness did," Ichirou groaned. "Hannah drank too much and puked all over the car. I thought I got it all out."

"Not all of it." I rolled down the window and breathed in the pine scented air.

"How'd the sleepover go?"

"It... was great. We went to a bookstore and an aquarium."

"You don't sound happy about it. Did you two have a fight? Is that why Isa wanted me to pick you up?"

"No," I said.

"Is Elizabeth okay?"

"She's in bed. Sleeping."

"At nine-thirty?" he questioned.

"Long day."

The car stopped at the red light. "Isa and I talked about you staying for the holidays. Excited about that?"

"I—I am. I was happy to see Elizabeth and we had a lot of fun." I dug through my backpack and showed Ichirou the camera. "She got me this!"

"It looks like your first one."

"I know. I took a lot of pictures. Want to see?"

"When I'm not driving, Runt."

It was a half hour drive home. Union Circle was dark with only a few lights shining through the windows when we arrived. Ichirou parked outside our apartment, then he helped me carry my bags to the door. I unlocked the screen and slid it open. My body jumped as a whirling alarm blasted into my ears.

"Turn it off!" Hannah howled.

Ichirou opened a strange white box near the door. He pushed a few buttons, and the alarm snapped to silence.

"Why did you get a house alarm?" I asked, rubbing my ears.

"Between the vandalisms and you sleepwalking, I couldn't take any more risks." Ichirou answered. "The code to turn it off is taped to the fridge. Please memorize it."

I stepped inside the apartment. It now felt so small and cramped compared to Elizabeth's home. "Have there been any more accidents?"

"Nah!" Hannah moaned. She was on the couch with watery eyes and a carefree smile. "Hiya Mayu! Welcome home!"

"Hi, Hannah. Uh... how're you feeling?"

"I feel great!" she slurred. "But don't tell Ichi, though... he's mad at me."

"I'm not mad!" Ichirou called from the kitchen.

"Yesser-are!" Hannah shot up from the couch. "I won' drink like tha...pinky promise, babe!"

"Pinky promise." Ichirou came back with a bottle of water and sat in front of Hannah. She almost said something to Ichirou but when she looked at me, her watery eyes gained a little focus.

"Mayu, what's wrong?" she asked sincerely. "You look so... different."

My chest tightened. "Different? How?"

247

Hannah scanned me from head to toe with what little concentration she had left. "Hey, where d'ya go las'night..."

"I was at Elizabeth's house."

"Really?" Her head tilted, and she fought a hiccup. "Coulda... coulda sworn you—" Her eyes got big, and she leaped off the couch. She nearly flattened Ichirou, dashing to the kitchen where a deep, guttural moan, followed by her retching, echoed through the apartment.

Ichirou peered into the kitchen. "Need any help?"

"No..." she groaned. She stumbled back to the living room and slumped on the couch.

"Hannah?" I said, leaning toward her. "Are you—"

"Shhh." Hannah pushed her finger against her lips and closed her eyes. I knew I shouldn't take Hannah's words to heart when she was drunk. On one hand, she could be precise, but on the other, she could slur between good advice and random words.

At eleven, I showered, dressed in pajamas, and went to my room. I laid in bed but didn't go to sleep. My thoughts whirled with everything that had happened. Elizabeth was in Erehwon. She was a succubus, and so was her mother, and I had no idea what I was anymore.

# Spiral

**Elizabeth's screams tore off the blood-stained walls.** Her back jerked and twisted as the wings tore themselves out of her. I raced after her, screaming her name, but my movements were slow, and my voice wedged in my throat.

Just as I reached Elizabeth, the wings had engulfed her like a cocoon. Her smothered screams haunted me, and her hands bulged weakly through the flesh. Crying out to her, I clawed at the wings like a frantic animal, desperate to help my friend. Finally, the skin broke and warm blood spilled all over the floor, covering it in a deep red. A heavy, metallic air fell over me, but I continued to dig through the mound of flesh and blood until my hands raked across cold concrete.

The walls dissolved into darkness and dozens of eyes stared at me, glowing like flickering starlight. I scrambled back and raced down the corridor. The floor was ice on my bare feet. Cold air seized my lungs and froze my scream into my throat. A deafening roar bounded behind me, rolling up my back and exploded in the air. I crumbled on the ground and the roar split into different voices of family and friends.

"You always want to be with those assistants!"

"What drew you to Elizabeth in the first place?"

"Why are you always sitting away from them?"

"You look different."

"Why does it matter if we're not human?" someone chortled, their voice ghastly and deep. "You seem to get along with us so well!"

My hands slammed into my ears, and I screamed for this to stop.

"Mayu, wake up!"

My eyes snapped open. Ichirou was in front of me. His wide, worrying eyes were on me, and his hands clutched my shoulders.

"I got you sis," he panted. "It's going to be okay."

It was real. My panicked gasps. The concrete on my feet and the broken streetlight hanging above us. Trembling, I looked up at Ichirou one more time, my voice was weak and shaky.

"*Aniki...*"

I fell into his arms. Everything felt too real to be another dream. His hand caressing my head, his heart beating in my ear and his voice assuring me I was going to be alright.

"What happened?"

Ichirou pulled away and held my cheeks. "You were sleepwalking again, and you left the apartment. You almost walked out of the complex."

I looked around, my eyes adjusted to the darkness, and I recognized the bus shelter in front of the complex. But something wasn't right. It was too quiet, and the only light came from the moon, partially obscured by passing clouds. Finally, I noticed the broken streetlight over us, and the shards of glass littered around us.

"Here," said Ichirou, taking off his sandals. "I'll be fine."

I put them on and took small steps away from the glass. I wrapped my hands around Ichirou's and we headed back to the apartment, which felt so far away from me in the dark.

"Good thing the alarm wasn't a complete waste," Ichirou whispered, letting out a nervous chuckle. "How are you feeling?"

Too scared to answer, I clung to him as though he might disappear. At the apartment, Hannah was at the sliding door, pointing a flashlight at us.

"Is everyone okay?" she called out.

"She's fine now. Mayu walked out of the house in her sleep."

"How did she get out? I thought you locked the door."

"She must have unlocked it."

I was walking behind Ichirou when a chill brushed against my back, raising bumps on my shoulders.

"Hey, what's wrong?"

I looked up at my brother and managed to speak up. "What am I?"

It took him a moment to say something. "You're my little sister."

He let me in the apartment first and Hannah closed the door and locked it. The flashlight barely lit the living room, but I preferred that to the dark. Ichirou went to one of the light switches and flipped it, yet nothing turned on.

"What happened to the power?" he muttered.

Hannah flipped a different switch. "I think the power went out."

Ichirou turned to the kitchen and drew a flashlight from one of the drawers. With a click, a beaming light flooded the living room, hurting my eyes.

"It doesn't look like anything's on," he said.

Surrounded by shadows, I clung to myself, and a question rose in my mind.

"Did I do this?"

"What are you talking about?" Ichirou asked.

"The power... did I do this?"

He gave me a strange look. "Runt, you couldn't have caused a blackout. I think a fuse blew."

Hannah let me stay in her room again while she and Ichirou checked the apartment. With everything locked, Hannah hauled the air mattress and pump from the closet and inflated it. I felt safer tucked between the plush toys and hearing the low hum of the pump.

"Are you sure you're alright?" Hannah whispered. "We can see a doctor tomorrow about this."

I thought back to the nightmare. I could still feel the cold lingering around me. "Maybe I can turn the watch on. I didn't have an accident last week."

"If it helps, but I still think you should see someone."

I pulled the blanket to my shoulder and turned to Hannah. "Do you remember what you said earlier?"

"What do you mean?"

"When you were on the couch. You said I changed."

"Did I say that?" she asked, puzzled. "All I remember was hugging the toilet, puking my guts out then I woke up at home."

"Oh... Nevermind."

I rolled over on my back and closed my eyes. My mind drifted between waking up in darkness, shifting in bed, then sinking into a dreamless sleep.

•●•

A tapping on the door woke me up around seven in the morning, according to my watch. The room was quiet. Hannah must have woken up earlier to start the day. I would have done the same when I heard a conversation outside. I got close to the window and listened to Ichirou talking to one of our neighbors. They asked my brother if there was any power. I flicked a light switch, and the room remained dimly lit by the sunrise peeking through the blinds.

It wasn't our apartment; the entire complex had no power.

I dressed for school and asked Ichirou to take me, despite how tired I felt. The nightmare was fresh in my mind, staying home with no power would have made me more uneasy. I hoped the assistants could somehow help me.

The instant I came to school, I was hit with a flood of noises, stomping shoes, humming static and shouts that made me jump. A man's voice surged through static before a rattling bell tore into my ears. I shrieked, covering my ears and I sank to the floor.

"Can you hear me?"

My skin crawled at those words, but the voice who asked didn't echo in my head. Ethan was kneeling in front of me. His brow narrowed in a worried look.

"It's okay, focus on me," he said, slow and firm. "Take a deep breath."

Though I wasn't sure what he was talking about. I kept my eyes on him.

Deep breaths, I closed my eyes and inhaled, feeling my shoulders relax. The wave of noises quieted to low whispers and murmur. Another deep breath, and my thudding heart steadied to a tempo.

When my eyes adjusted to the lights, I stared up at Ethan. "Where am I?"

"You're in front of Ms. Penn's room," he answered. "I won't ask, you don't look so good."

"I don't feel so good," I confessed. My legs were weak and tired, my arms ached. At least I knew it was a seizure. "Ethan, I don't feel...right..."

"I can walk with you to the infirmary."

He helped me to my feet, and we walked to the infirmary. I kept my ears covered and I stared at the floor to avoid the buzzing light.

Mystic Rising

"Have you noticed anything different about yourself lately?" Ethan asked, gently.

"A lot," My voice was low. "Reflexes are sharper. My senses are sharper. Why?"

"I'm going to be honest with you. Your seizures are real, but your senses and reflexes all point to one conclusion... you may be more like us than everyone here."

"I know," I said. "Remember my friend, Elizabeth?"

"Yeah?"

"Well... I learned she's a mystic, like you. Her mom already told me I wasn't human either."

He breathed sharply. "At least you have some idea of what's going on."

We stopped at the infirmary. Ethan nudged the door open, and I expected blood and bandages strewn across the floor, but it was a clean room with neatly made beds instead. A window across from me showed the grey clouds bubbling over the school parking lot and trees swaying in the strong wind.

"Did you hit your head again?" Caritas asked. She was holding a clipboard, idling by a cabinet full of medical supplies.

"A little." My nose wrinkled at a woodsy scent coming from the purple flowers on Caritas's desk. "Is that... lavender?"

"It's a lovely scent. I use it to keep my patients calm. You know how hectic some days can be. Now, what brings you here?"

Ethan and I glanced at each other. "You want to tell her, or should I?"

I lowered my head, and my hands knotted the bottom of my shirt.

"I had a seizure," I began and with Ethan's help, I told Caritas about my senses.

She had me sit on a bed and asked me a routine of questions and I answered them as best as I could. I mentioned I wasn't human, and Ethan explained how the noises in school overwhelmed me.

"Is there a way to treat my senses?" I finally asked.

Caritas frowned. "The best we can do is give students ear plugs to dull the noises. If you want to stay here, I have reusable sleeping masks to block the light." She checked my eyes, inspected my ears, and stuck a thermometer in my mouth, then waited until it beeped, then she pulled it out and inspected the numbers on it. "Your temperature is a little above average, so try to rest a bit here. We can do a checkup if you like."

She didn't have to tell me twice.

Ethan had to return to class, but promised he'd let Lutea know what was going on. I must have been exhausted because the instant I laid in bed, I dozed off to the distant talking and the first few raindrops pelting the window.

I woke up to the school bell ringing and found myself in the infirmary. I sat up, rubbed my eyes and realized I wasn't wearing my glasses. I didn't remember taking them off. When I jerked to the side, I found them resting on a stand beside the bed with a letter tucked beneath it.

*Meet me at the Lounge when you wake up.*

-Lutea

I slipped out of bed, shaking off the lingering dizziness and after a quick checkup, Caritas handed me a written hall pass, letting me go. The lounge door was open and the moment I stepped inside, a powerful scent knocked me back. It smelled like grilled hamburgers and hot fries, which was exactly what was on the tables. Lutea and Chitose were watching Ethan devour a burger in two bites.

"What's going on...?" I asked.

"Ethan ordered five bags with five burgers." Lutea explained. "He's already on his fourth bag."

I blinked. "How are you not sick?"

"That's what we said," Chitose commented.

Ethan finished his burger. He nudged a bag close to me. "Take one!"

Looking at a hamburger the size of my palm and the cups of crisp golden fries peppered in seasoning, my stomach twisted in hunger. I could see why Ethan was inhaling his meal and if he was offering me one, who was I to say no?

"What's the special occasion?" I helped myself to a burger and nibbled on fries.

"Nothing. That's how he normally eats." Lutea patted the balled up- burger wraps to the side. "Did you sleep well?"

"I slept better than I did last night," I answered.

"Ethan told me what happened this morning. Apparently, you can hear the entire school now."

"Right," I said, somberly.

"Did you see your friend this weekend?"

254

"Yeah. It was the best weekend I've had in months. But then...I found out they weren't human."

I continued. "Her mom, Ms. Hudson, told me something I didn't realize until last night. At first, I thought my senses were an effect of crossing me into Erehwon. But I always had those abilities because I was never human to begin with.... And now I'm wondering if you knew too."

Lutea was quiet for a moment, making me nervous. "We've had our suspicions. For the past few weeks, I searched for information about the last person who crossed worlds."

"What for?"

"Not every day does one cross into Erehwon unprotected and live to ask how. I wanted to see if you were the only one who accomplished that." Lutea adjusted herself in her chair. "After all, there have been fables about people spending a day or two in a forest, then coming home to see a hundred years had passed. And the internet is full of stories about wandering in and out of reality."

My eyes widened. "So, I'm not alone!"

Lutea hesitated. "Yes and no." My brow knotted. "Have you heard of the urban legend in school about a girl who vanished mid-October?"

My heart leaped. "Ellie Wright, the girl with the haunted locker. She crossed worlds?!"

"We think so," Lutea replied. "Her disappearance was unusual, and the search was so infamous, living relatives made websites, hoping to find her. Some of her diary had been posted and it turns out, Ellie could see the Mystics. She was ostracized for it and we think she tried to cross through worlds to get away from her peers." she leaned back in her chair, her arms folded over her chest. "If you're familiar with the story, you know how it ended."

"The school heard a scream, and no one has found her."

"We think the border between worlds, what you fell through... might have killed her."

"That's awful!"

"A similar case happened before that. Another girl, though there's not much on record about her but safe to assume she met the same fate. They weren't the first ones either..."

"What?"

"Humans have always gone on expeditions in search of the mystical worlds. When some powerful people wanted to find us, they tried to make their own gates. They were unstable, and every aircraft and vessel they sent vanished, but they didn't stop until they came close to breaching Erewhon."

"Did they make it through?" I asked.

"They caught Galumine's attention before they could enter our world," said Lutea. "She sent the vessels back, found the gates they used and destroyed it to prevent any more people from vanishing or invading Erewhon."

After Lutea finished, the table fell eerily quiet.

"That's why you're such a unique case. People have crossed worlds, but no human has successfully breached ours like you did. And I realized that...you were more like us than them."

I breathed in, processing everything I heard. "When were you going to tell me?"

"I wanted to tell you last week, but you were worried about heading home. I didn't think it was a good time."

My heart hammered. The air hummed as anger stirred in my chest. I didn't know who I was mad at. Everyone for not telling me the truth or myself for never realizing it.

"The whole time, everybody knew?" My voice hardened. "What else don't I know!"

As I shouted, whips of light split the air and scattered into pieces. Assistants jerked back and some sprang out of their chairs. Chitose dove under the table to dodge the crackling light arching over her. Ethan's face twisted into a snarl and Lutea was on the floor, scorch marks patched around her jacket. For a long moment, all of us were silent.

A warm numbness overtook me, and my thoughts swayed. The flashes of light lingered in my eyes. "Did I do this?"

Ethan's expression relaxed and Lutea lifted her head over the table.

"Since when could you do that?" She inched closer, then asked softly, "How long has this been happening?"

"I don't know," I stuttered. My thoughts raced to the blackout at the complex. The flickering lights and the static in my ears. "What's going on?"

"Remember this morning," said Ethan. "Your seizure, the fever and this?" He motioned to the air and scorched tables. "You might have undergone a change."

"But it's completely normal," Lutea added quickly. "Lots of us have went through one at some point."

The other assistants nodded in agreement.

I swallowed hard, and the hairs on my neck bristled. "What am I changing into?"

"We don't know, yet." Lutea righted a toppled chair and sat in front of me.

"You might be a hybrid," said Ethan. "Half human. Half Mystic. They usually go through changes late in life. It's like going through puberty twice."

"That's even worse!" I exclaimed. The lights above danced wildly at my words.

"Mayu," Ethan warned. "You need to stay calm."

I bit my lip, stifling down the rising panic in my throat. "How?" I whispered. "I don't even know how I'm doing this."

"Deep breaths," Lutea instructed. She pulled the chair closer to me. "Focus on me. Take deep breaths. In and out."

"Deep breaths," I murmured. I inhaled slowly then exhaled.

"Good, keep your eyes on me," Lutea spoke in a soothing tone. "Tell me about the sleep over. What did you do with Elizabeth?"

I tried to forget about the wings and the blood, and instead told them about Twilight Plaza, the bookstore, the bath shop and the restaurant. Lutea reminded me to slow my speech as I was talking too fast. I searched for more details in my memories, like the stingray's skin against my hand. Ms. Hudson cooking, and the movie Elizabeth and I watched. Gradually, the static lessened.

I felt like my mind had finally cleared, and the worrying thoughts vanished. "What should I do?"

"You can't go to class today, not until you get this under control," Lutea said. "If you need time off school, and you feel safer at home, you can go."

I lowered my head and confessed quietly, "I want to go home."

"Is there anyone who can pick you up?"

I shrugged. "Ichirou and Hannah are at work. I can let them know." A deep sigh left me. "C-Could I stay here for now?"

She gave me a gentle smile. "You can stay. You're safe here."

I thanked her, and when I felt ready, I left Lutea at the table. I slumped on the couch, exhausted, and texted Ichirou. I told him I wasn't feeling well and wanted to leave early. He replied that I had to wait until after school, which wasn't so bad. I helped myself to the beverages and snacks and practiced my breathing to calm myself.

I don't know how long I was in the lounge before I checked my phone. There was a new message in my inbox, but it wasn't from Ichirou or Hannah.

*"I'll pick you up after school. Elizabeth and I will be waiting outside."*

-Ms. Hudson.

# Shadow

**As soon as school ended, I hurried to the main doors**, stopping at the steps the instant I saw her. Elizabeth stood in front of her mother's car, holding down a maroon beret as a strong breeze rippled her pink, knitted dress. She waved at me, but her bright smile melted.

"Is something wrong?" Elizabeth asked, tilting her head to the side. My heart pounded as the memory of the nightmare resurfaced.

"You're here," I said in a small, hesitant voice.

"Sure am. I couldn't go to school yet," she whispered. "They retracted this morning."

"It took that long?" I said, concerned and a bit surprised. "Does it still hurt—"

Before Elizabeth could answer, a familiar voice called out to me. I turned to Mary skipping down the steps, followed by the blonde girl from the theater club. I guessed she must have been Katie.

"You were in school today?" Mary asked.

"I was," I replied.

"Where were you? I thought you were upset after Friday. I tried to text you."

I don't remember seeing her message in my phone. Still, I felt bad for not letting her know I was alright.

"Sorry, I wasn't feeling well, so I stayed in the..." My voice trailed off as Mary's attention shifted to Elizabeth.

I gave them a quick introduction. "Mary, this is my friend Elizabeth, Elizabeth, meet Mary!"

Elizabeth gasped, "You're Marietta! Nice to meet you, Mayu has told me so much about you." She held her hand out.

"It's Mary," she corrected and ignored Elizabeth's gesture. "I heard you were going to St. Laurel's Academy. Are you visiting today?"

"Elizabeth's taking me to her home. A blackout happened at my apartment, and the power hadn't returned, yet," I answered.

Mary's brows furrowed. "I'm sorry to hear that. I was wondering if you'd be interested in going to a café tonight with me and Kate. To make up for last week."

As fun as it would have been to sit at a cozy, warm cafe with the four of us, there was too much on my mind for me to join her.

"We could go next Friday, if that's alright."

"Sure," Mary turned to her friend. "Are you ready to go?"

"So, ready!" Katie moaned, holding her arms. "It's freezing out here!"

After saying goodbye, Mary and Kate went to Mr. Brown's car parked behind Ms. Hudson's. I joined Elizabeth in the car and shivered at the pine scent heat flowing through vent. Elizabeth sat gingerly next to me, sucking in the air through her teeth when her back touched the seat.

"Take it easy," I said, cautiously.

"It's okay. It only hurts a little. Aren't you cold, by the way?" Elizabeth tugged the sleeve of my jacket. I was wearing my usual uniform, a white blouse, pleated skirt and leggings.

I shook my head, relaxing in the seat. "Guess the cold doesn't bother me. You look cozy yourself."

"Well..." Her cheeks reddened and she pulled off her beret, revealing the stubby horns, though I could have sworn they were smaller.

"They grow with each change. I haven't restyled my hair yet to hide them, so I wore the beret...then remembered the dress I bought at Twilight Plaza and..."

I smirked, "Were you looking for a reason to dress up again?" She could have easily worn a hoodie and a pair of jeans to pick me up.

"She was," Ms. Hudson confirmed.

"I can do both!" Elizabeth pouted. She put the beret on, and I reassured her we were messing with her.

As we pulled away from the school, I asked Elizabeth how her day went, and with excitement lighting her face, she told me she finished *Witch Hazel* while her wings retracted. Her voice raised a few pitches when she begged for me to catch up with her. I laughed, promising I would.

Elizabeth was incredible.

Her painful transformation was fresh in my memory, yet she could talk about her day like nothing happened. Then I realized that she had endured her change for three years, so this wasn't new to her. I was the only one who found it strange.

The car stopped at a red light and Mr. Brown's car slowed down beside us. Katie was in the back seat with Mary who burst into loud laughter that could be heard through the window. I couldn't remember the last time Mary was happy with me. She usually sat in the passenger seat, talking to her dad, almost forgetting I was there.

"How are you feeling?" Ms. Hudson said, taking my attention away from the window. "Ichirou told me you had a rough morning. Sleepwalking again, a mild seizure and you said you were sick?"

Elizabeth frowned, "I thought your sleepwalking stopped."

"I thought so too, until I woke up in front of the complex," I said. "And the sickness... it's not what I told Ichirou."

Ms. Hudson's eyes narrowed.

I told them about my change. Ms. Hudson didn't seem surprised, and Elizabeth gave me a sympathetic gaze.

"I'm sorry you had to go through with that," Elizabeth said. "First changes are never pretty."

"It's... It's alright," I murmured. Then I mentioned discovering my powers in the lounge.

"You can do that now? Since when!"

"Now," I said, but in a jolt, I remembered the wisps of light curling out of my phone and the flash that sent Melanippe flying. And before... back in Lawrence Middle School when Rosalina flew into the locker.

My mouth started to dry up. "I think I've always had this power. When I fell into Erehwon, I—"

Color drained from Elizabeth's face. "*You* fell into Erehwon!" she erupted.

I peeked at the rear-view mirror and saw a flicker of panic had broken though Ms. Hudson's calm demeanor.

"You heard about that too, huh." I said.

"Everyone heard!" Ms. Hudson exclaimed. "I was at home pacing for hours as soon as I got the alarm."

"I was in the middle of choir when it happened," Elizabeth said. "It sounded like a tornado siren was going off. Everyone was sent to their dorms, and we didn't get a safety announcement until midnight."

"I didn't know I caused that much panic." I said, softly.

The car stopped at a red light and Ms. Hudson leaned back in the seat. She rubbed the bridges of her nose and drew a deep breath.

"Who else knows?"

"Every assistant at school."

Elizabeth gasped, "Does Mary know?"

I shook my head. "She was with me when we snuck into the library, but she couldn't see the doorway because of a spell."

"How did you cross over in the first place?" she asked.

"Nobody knows, yet," I muttered. It felt strange knowing I had such an impact on an entire world.

We finally arrived at the house, and it was clear that we needed to process everything. I hung my jacket, left my shoes at the door and we sat at the kitchen table.

Curtains danced over the sink as the salty sea air rolled through the window. From the dark clouds bubbling over the waves, I didn't have to be a genius to know a storm was brewing. Ms. Hudson closed the window and an amber glow bloomed from the lantern above the table.

She set a glass kettle on the table with a dried flower bulb inside. Honey gold tea swirled at the bottom and rose quickly to the top. The flower unfurled and blossomed at the bottom. I used to think this was an expensive kettle, but looking closely at the markings engraved on it, made me wonder if it was using magic.

I spoke first, hoping to ease the tension in the air. "You told me you knew Miss Naiad. Have you met her?"

A smile broke through Elizabeth's worrying expression. "You won't believe this. But Miss Naiad is my literature teacher!"

My eyes widened. "Seriously!"

"Seriously!" Elizabeth burst with excitement. "She mentioned working a second job after class. I never would have guessed she ran a club at your school."

"What kind of school do you go to? Can you learn magic?"

"You can, but it's an advanced course and the teachers like Miss Naiad are strict about it." Her eyes met mine. "I can't believe you crossed worlds! All by yourself!"

I shrugged, half-heartedly. "Like I said, it was an accident. Now the big question is, what am I. The assistants say I might be a hybrid."

"Most likely the case," Ms. Hudson said, placing two porcelain cups in front of us. "They're so common nowadays, you'll pass by hybrids more than a full blood mystic."

Ms. Hudson poured the tea into the cups and sweet floral billowed with the steam. "Was there any information about your biological parents? Files, photos or records that were kept?"

I blew at the tea before I answered. "It was a closed adoption. Mom and Dad said they never met them and I don't remember what they looked like."

Ms. Hudson hummed. "In my experience, mystic and human parents wouldn't give up their child unless they had a reason to. Was there anything that could lead you to them?"

"Let me check…"

I shuffled out of my seat and went to the phone hanging off the wall. I called Ichirou and when he answered, an explosion of clamor and ambient music poured through the speaker.

"Hey, is Mayu with you?" he asked. Someone in the background shouted his name and he yelled back, "Wait a minute!" he must have moved someplace quieter, because his voice was much louder. "Sorry, work is chaotic today."

"I thought you called off," I said.

"Oh, hey Runt. I did, but a customer reserved the restaurant for a birthday party. Everyone was called in and no one's happy about it."

"When will you be home?"

He answered grudgingly, "Well, our cook just quit, so not until midnight. Hannah will be off work in a few hours, so sit tight with Liz and Isa. I gotta go—"

"Wait! I have a question. Do you have any papers about my adoption. Anything about me or my parents?"

"I only have a copy of the adoption certificate and my custodial certificate. If there are records, Mom and Dad has them. Why do you—hold on," his voice pulled away and he shouted, "I'm on my way!" He quickly returned, "Ask me when we get home."

The call ended before I could say, "Bye." I hoped his shift wouldn't last until midnight.

"What did Ichirou say?" Elizabeth asked. "And what did I just hear from his end?"

"Another crazy night." I gave Ms. Hudson her phone. "Ichirou says our parents may have the records."

"Is that a problem?"

"They don't like to talk about my adoption." And it would've been weird to call my parents out of nowhere. They'd swarm me with question after question about school and home and avoid the adoption topic entirely.

Elizabeth took a sip of her tea, and I followed her lead. Hearing the chaos of the restaurant almost stressed me out.

"So much for that..." she moaned.

"Not quite," said Ms. Hudson said. "We can't find your parents. But we might find out what you are in my study."

Elizabeth's brightened up. "Can we go there?"

"As long as you don't leave a mess behind, alright?"

"We won't," Elizabeth and I said, though her response had more excitement to it.

I'd never been to Ms. Hudson's private study nor to the third floor where it resided. Elizabeth told me Ms. Hudson kept the books that she'd collected over the years there, and some were so old, they were out of print. Elizabeth had to ask for permission to read them, but she couldn't leave the room with them. I never would have imagined myself seeing the study for myself until now...

We crossed the dimly lit hall and stopped in front of the door at the end. My heart fluttered when Elizabeth nudged it opened, and the scent of a million pages flooded the air. Books lined the walls in different sizes, neatly packed in bookcases, and a lone mahogany desk sat in the middle of the room with two small couches facing a table. Everything shined with cleanliness.

On the desk, sat a leatherback journal, an empty mug and an ink bottle and fountain pen. Those were things I imagined Ms. Hudson using, more so than the slim black monitor and keyboard she had. A golden easel rested beside the keyboard, but it was the branch that made my head tilt. It arched over the desktop, clutching a glass in the shape of a teardrop.

"That's a DimLit," Elizabeth's voice was right beside me. "It gathers sunlight from the outside and glows whenever the room gets dark. Wanna see?"

"Sure."

Smiling, Elizabeth skipped to the window. The sky beaming through the window was steely grey as storm clouds hung over the house. Elizabeth pulled the curtains and the study room got dark. An amber glow blossomed from the desk and cast our shadows against the books around us.

"DimLit," I whispered. It finally hit me; the teardrop glass decorating the clubroom shelves, how the light glowed without a switch on the walls or a cord across the floor. Then I thought about the hanging lights in the kitchen, the ones in the walls.

I gasped, "They're all over the house!"

"DimLit is a common tool Mystics use. We have them in our dorms too. Mom says it helps cut the electric bill."

She pulled a book from the shelves and set it on the desk. The faded title on the cover read, *"Legendary Beasts and Monsters Throughout History."* Dozens of colored tags were poking out of the dull, yellow pages, Elizabeth's handy work, no doubt. She always put color coded tabs on any chapter or sentence that caught her interest.

"You read all of this?" I asked.

"I read them a long time ago," Elizabeth said, setting two large books on the desk, causing it to shake. "Sometimes, I'd copy what I read into my journals since Mom doesn't want the books to leave her study."

"No wonder you can read so fast. How long did it take you to finish them?"

"Depends on how invested I am. Sometimes a day. Sometimes a week if I'm not too busy. *Witch Hazel* took me the longest to read because I was getting used to school and living in the dorm."

"That's the same with me… minus the dorm."

My eyes trailed to the shelves, taking in the different covers and titles. Ms. Hudson had every subject and genre; cooking, finance, history, science and art.  Some of the titles were in different languages, but I only recognized English, Japanese and French. Ichirou had taken a language course a couple of years ago and for his final project, he had recorded me asking him something in Japanese and he answered my questions in French. We had a lot of fun, and he got extra credit for it.

"I didn't know your mom reads French."

Elizabeth raised her head from a book she was reading.

"She used to live in Europe long before I was born." She leaned against the bookcase with a reminiscing gaze. "When I was little, she'd sing 'a la Claire Fontaine,' to help me sleep."

My head tilted to the name. Elizabeth set the book on the desk and straightened her back. "It goes like this."

She closed her eyes, and a soft, ethereal voice flowed from her lips. The weeks of choir practice truly showed as she rose smoothly to a high octave, something she used to struggle with. Although Elizabeth didn't speak French, the language rolled with such elegance, as if she were a native speaker.

Memories of the lullaby flooded back to me as a gentle hum Ms. Hudson would sing every morning. You could always tell she was in a good mood when you woke up to the tune carried throughout the house.

"I forgot how beautiful your voice is."

Elizabeth blushed. "You should listen to mom. I'm convinced she used to be an opera singer. Did your mother sing to you?"

"Mom worked a lot, but on nights when I couldn't sleep, she'd tell me stories. The only time she'd sing was when she was gardening. She said music helped the flowers grow."

"You rarely talk about your parents, and I've only seen them once during graduation. What are they like?"

"Mom is..." I paused to find the right words to describe her. "Firm, but gentle at times. She's a journalist photographer. She takes pictures of nature and publishes them in magazines and articles. Dad used to be a paramedic until he got injured and retired early. He may seem mean at first, but he liked telling jokes and would sing karaoke on weekends. He wasn't the best at it, but he enjoyed it."

Elizabeth let out a soft laughter. "Did you sing karaoke with him?"

"I'm not so good at it either. We stopped karaoke after Ichirou... moved out." I trailed off and Elizabeth didn't pry.

I pushed the memory down and skimmed the shelves. A book, titled *Mystics and Human Interactions Over Time* caught my attention. I gently pulled the book off the shelf and brought it to the desk. The first paragraph was interesting, describing how mystics had existed before humans and, for a time, many were revered as gods.

"Mayu, I've been meaning to ask you something," Elizabeth said. "Do you remember anything before you were adopted?"

I looked up, my back leaned against the shelf as I thought back to my earliest memories.

"It was... sad. Grey walls, cement flooring, cold air with a strange smell to it, like metallic water. The happiest moment was after I was adopted. I was holding my parents' hands, feeling the warm sun against my skin for the first time in my life."

Next thing I knew, Elizabeth was beside me with a saddened look on her face. "I'm so sorry that happened to you."

I shrugged. "It was a long time ago. I don't think about it a lot." In fact, I try not to think about it at all. Yet, every now and then, the details will surface in my dreams.

I read through Mystics and Human Interactions Over Time until I stumbled across a chapter titled "History of Mystic Hybrids."

"I found something!" I set the book on the desk, we pushed our glasses up the bridges of our nose and read the passage together.

*"Not to be mistaken for mystics with human traits, these hybrids are directly the result of a human and mystic producing a half-breed offspring. Half human children date back to the earliest known hybrid, King Gilgamesh and Cú Chulainn, both revered as fantastic heroes or feared as horrific abominations for their unpredictable nature and unique powers that exceeded both their parents. This section contains entries of every half human hybrid found across the world over the centuries—from vampire slaying Dhampir to mighty Nephilim."*

"Sounds like a good start," I said.

Elizabeth came up with the plan. Amazing as the book was, it didn't hurt to check elsewhere for updated details. If a hybrid caught our interest in the book, I would look them up online. If the description matched me, Elizabeth labeled their names in the book with color coded tags. We had green for 'I'm definitely this hybrid,' pink for 'It's possible' and blue meaning there were enough similarities to be considered 'green.'

With the plan in motion, Elizabeth logged onto the computer, and I sat at the desk, ready to type the name. We skipped the passage about dhampir since it was clear I wasn't a half vampire but stopped at the cambion. They were hybrids born from a human mother and an incubus, the male version of a succubus.

I stared at Elizabeth. "You're not a cambion, are you?"

"Cambions can't grow wings like we do. They can be born with small horns or none."

"Were you born with horns?"

"Mine grew the same day my wings emerged. Mom says its normal."

We continued to read. One article described cambions to be sickly, weak and sometimes underweight at birth, but grew into healthy beings with a succubus or incubus like beauty. The most famous cambion was the wizard, Merlin.

"It's possible you could be one," Elizabeth suggested. "Cambions are a lot more common than you'd think. Without the horns you wouldn't tell one from a human. Some have spent their whole lives never knowing they were hybrids."

I scratched my head. "Do you consider epilepsy as... sickly? And can they have powers?"

"Merlin did," Elizabeth pointed out and stuck a pink tag on the cambion chapter.

Seal children became a possibility the more we read about it. They were hybrids of selkie mothers and human fathers. Like mermaids, their lower halves were seal-like except they could shed that off for human legs and wear the fur as pelts. The seal children often had dark hair, eyes like the sea and were natural born swimmers. Those traits sounded like me, down to being a good swimmer, despite never taking lessons. Except there was no passage about seal children controlling electricity. Still, Elizabeth placed a blue tag on it. The next hybrid we read about was a zmeu.

"What's a zmeu?" I asked.

"They're half human," Elizabeth paused. "Half dragon!"

She turned to a page in the book, showing me a picture of a scaled human with dragon- like claws and wings spanning from their back.

"I don't want to know how that's possible."

"There are legends throughout the world about dragons shapeshifting into humans and falling for women and men. Have you noticed how every monster slaying story had a prince or a knight from a faraway land defeating dragons with ease?"

I nodded.

"Those were the dragons in disguise," she snickered. "If you read a story written by one, it's often a tale of forbidden love with the dragon, dramatically faking their deaths so they can elope with their lovers. It's an inside joke."

"Wait, what?" The thought of dragons writing a book made my head spin.

"Anyway, zmeu children are usually the result and they're found all over the world. The earliest sighting of a zmeu was in Romania."

Still stuck on the "heroes were dragons all along," idea, I looked up zmeu online. Much to Elizabeth's amusement, the first article I clicked on talked about dragon-slaying fairytales.

"They start off looking like humans," I said, reading. "But slowly gain traits of a dragon, like hardened scales, brute strength, and a fierce temper..." I instantly thought about Damien Black and his strength, scales, and the fire behind his eyes made way more sense.

"Not me, but it sounds like one of my classmates in gym."

"How about this?"

Elizabeth showed me an illustration of an elegant Asian woman dressed in layers of robes. Furry, cat like ears poked from her head and she wore a look of confidence while the man in the illustration bowed before her.

"A hanyou?" I said, reading the title next to the picture. The kanji characters next to them translated to "Half" and "Demon."

"They're hybrids born from a human and a yōkai," I murmured.

Elizabeth continued, "They can pass off as humans and most have a variety of mystic abilities and can use magic. Maybe your powers are your hanyou traits awakening."

"Found something?" Ms. Hudson called. She stood at the door carrying the platter with the glass kettle on it.

"We think Mayu might be a cambion, a selkie child or a hanyou." Elizabeth told her.

"I can see that," she mused, setting the platter on the table. "Though, you can't look at hybrids alone. You must consider that not all of them have been documented yet."

I stuttered, "...We hadn't thought about that."

Elizabeth sighed, "Guess we have to start over."

"Not necessarily," said Ms. Hudson.

We joined her at the couch. She suggested I make a list about myself first, then research the mystics who might have those traits.

"I have sharp reflexes, heal fast and can control electricity, apparently," I started.

"There is another trait you've forgotten," Ms. Hudson added. "You can cross through worlds. That should narrow down your search."

Elizabeth returned to the desk and brought an old maroon book over. It had no author or title on it, but there were sticky tabs hanging out from the old pages. "I can think of hundreds of mystics who can heal and use electricity, but it's not common to have ones that can do all of that, and cross worlds."

The book listed legendary mystics by type: creation and rebirth, elements, light, darkness and finally, destruction and chaos.

Mystic Rising

On one of the pages, beautiful woman, clad in armor descended from the clouds, with bronze wings stretching from their backs.

"A Valkyrie can create lightning storms and cross between worlds. And some have settled down with humans, so a hybrid must exist." Elizabeth flipped through the pages until something caught my eye.

"Hold on, what's that?" I placed my hand on the page, stopping at an image that sent shivers down my spine. A mass of twisting darkness loomed over a desolated ancient city.

"Old Horns..." I muttered. My throat tightened as if I said something forbidden. "Living Shadow and... The Manic King. Malus. What is this?"

Ms. Hudson leaned close, and her face went ashen white.

"It's a really obscure creature," Elizabeth began. "Supposedly, it was around the age of the primordial beings that predated humans or mystics."

"Are they around?" I asked, my eyes fixated on the image.

Elizabeth raced to the desk, taking the book with her. She typed the first name, Old Horns and hundreds of articles appeared. "There are legends surrounding shadow-like beings that follow their victims into their dreams. Whether feared or worshiped, they influenced people by drawing out their worst impulses. Mayu, why do you want to know about it?"

My legs weakened. "I've seen this before. When I fell into Erehwon, I was in a dark place. There was something... around me." With a jolt, I realized what Elizabeth said. 'It follows people in its dreams...' "My sleepwalking..."

"What?"

"Every time I went to sleep, I felt something watching me, chasing after me. Next thing I know, I'm sleepwalking!"

"Mayu, you can't be sure," Ms. Hudson cut in.

"I know what I saw!"

"There are a lot of possibilities." Ms. Hudson shut the book. "Let's not focus on this one thing."

"Don't you believe me!" I yelled. "I've been seeing this in my head for weeks!"

"And how could *you* stop it?" Ms. Hudson snapped, scarlet flashed in her eyes.

The room fell silent.

"Go downstairs," she said, calmly. "Take a few books if you need to. We'll put this aside for another time."

I didn't listen. I was out of the room and down the first flight of steps when Elizabeth called my name.

I stopped and turned. "What."

Elizabeth stepped back. "Mayu. I'm sorry."

"Why did she make us stop? I know what I saw. I know what I've been seeing."

"But didn't you want to find out what you are?"

"I did, but this is important! It's already made me leave the house once! Now when I have a chance to know about it, suddenly your mom wants to stop me." I scoffed. "She didn't stop when she told me I wasn't a human!"

Elizabeth flinched. "Mom was worried about you, that's all."

"I'm tired of people worrying about me! I don't want any more worries! I want help! I want answers!"

The hall was silent and so was Elizabeth. She had a hurt look on her face. Then she wiped her eyes.

"When you fell through, what did it look like?"

"It didn't have eyes, but I knew it looked at me. Ever since I crossed over, I've had this feeling that something is watching me."

Elizabeth grabbed my arm and pulled me to her bedroom. Although they had cleaned up the blood, traces of the scent lingered in the air. Elizabeth rushed to her bookshelf and grabbed handfuls of journals.

"What are you doing?" I asked.

"I'm not stopping because Mom says so. When I get back to school, I'll look for more information about the Malus. You can keep reading."

"We can't go back to the study," I reminded. "How can I read them?"

She gave me three black cat-themed journals that must have had hundreds of pages filled with her handwriting. "I told you, I read everything a long time ago. And I always took notes."

Ms. Hudson arrived to the living room in time for me to stuff the journal in my backpack and zip it up.

"Ichirou called and said the power came back on at the apartment," she said. "He'll be on his way home shortly."

"Alright," I said, my voice was a pitch higher than normal. I put my backpack on, and the weight of the journals pulled on my shoulders.

The rainfall drowned the awkward silence in the car. Elizabeth and I tried to talk about what to do tomorrow to relieve the tension, but we both knew Ms. Hudson was suspicious. We pulled up at Union Circle and Ms. Hudson called Ichirou.

"Sorry, I just got out the restaurant," he said, his voice reverberating through the speakers. "Things calmed down and I finally talked my boss to let me leave early. I should be home in thirty minutes."

"That's fine," Ms. Hudson said sternly.

"Uh oh," Ichirou chuckled. "I know that murderous tone anywhere. What idiot got under your skin this time, Isa?"

"Nobody," she answered while my ears grew hot. "We can wait in the car until you and Hannah arrive."

"I don't want to keep you and Elizabeth out too long. You've done enough picking Mayu up today. Hannah's job is much closer to the apartment. She'll be home soon."

Ms. Hudson's eyes narrowed through the rear-view mirror. "Call me as soon as you get home. Drive safe."

"You too, and I'll see you later, Runt," he said.

"I'll see you later." I replied, avoiding Ms. Hudson's glare from the rear-view mirror. Ichirou hung up and the beating rain continued to drown out the awkward silence. For a moment, I thought Ms. Hudson would keep me locked in the car until I spilled the truth.

"Elizabeth needs to be ready to go back to school tomorrow," she said, unlocking the doors. "Stay downstairs and keep the lights on until Ichirou and Hannah come home."

"I will."

I gave her and Elizabeth one last goodbye and left the car. I unlocked the screen door, and the alarm blasted in my ears. *Great, at least that was still working.* I punched in the code, and the alarm went off with a high pitch squeak. As I turned to lock the screen door, Ms. Hudson had driven out of the complex.

The apartment felt emptier in the dark. I flicked the lights on, dropped the backpack on the couch, and called Hannah. She didn't answer, so I called her job, and someone answered on the first ring.

"Thank you for calling Percy's Pizza," Hannah spoke in her cheery professional voice. "Will your order be pick up—"

"It's me," I interrupted. "How's work?"

"Hate it here," she groaned. "Are you doing okay at home? I heard the power came back."

I whipped back to a flash of light, and thunder tore through the skies. My voice trembled when I said to Hannah, "I wish you and Ichirou were home."

"You and me both. The power has been going in and out here, but my boss won't close early—" A man barked Hannah's name, demanding to know who she was speaking to. "Hang in there, Mayu. We'll be home soon."

Hannah hung up, and I set the phone on the base. I turned the TV on, and the noise added to the rain outside. I stopped at a nature documentary and sat on the couch to read Elizabeth's notes. I skimmed through a paragraph, lulled by the narrator drone about the depths of the sea.

I jolted up as thunder erupted outside. My heart raced, my breath caught in my throat as I realized I almost went to sleep. I couldn't let the Malus control me again. I had to stay awake. I hurried to the kitchen, opened the fridge and rummaged through leftovers for a pack of canned lattes. Hannah bought them a month ago to help her stay awake.

I popped the can open and took a few sips. The latte was cold, and the sharp bitterness woke me up. I finished the can and took a second one with me to the couch.

I hopped on the couch, opened the journal and my eyes flew across the pages and stopped at the Malus. Its origins were unknown. Its earliest sighting was unknown, yet its path of destruction haunted the kingdoms that watched others fall under its shadow. It fueled the strongest emotions in anyone, (happiness, fear, anger, etc.) pushing them to the brink of madness. Villages rose to empires, driven by a strong desire for conquest, then fell to ruins by that same force that spurred paranoia. Most mystics weren't immediately affected but long exposure could turn benevolent creature into a rabid beast, devoid of its sentience. Supposedly, there was a mystic of starlight, described as having "eyes embedded in its wings" that could cleanse the land of the malevolent shadow(?)"

The question mark in parentheses was Elizabeth's way of saying there wasn't enough information about it. Still, I flipped through the pages to find this mystic with star eyes on its wings. I could check the laptop for more information.

A sharp noise snapped against the glass and my head jerked to the screen door. Sheets of rainwater slammed into the street and battered the apartment, like angry fists pounding on the walls. Worry knotted in my stomach, and I crawled off the couch to call

Ichirou and Hannah again. It rained so hard, I couldn't see the street outside the complex.

The phone kept ringing when I called them. I paced around the couch, begging in my mind for them to pick up, fearing that something bad could have happened on their way home. I hung up, dialed Ichirou's number and then a light beamed through the screen door. Relieved, I whipped around and hurried to open the door. The light grew brighter, and the rumbling engine drew closer, its monstrous roar tore through the walls.

I jerked up with a gasp to a loud, violent thud in my ears. Bright light stung my eyes, and a noisy clamor reverberated around me. A hand on my shoulder made me jump and I whipped around to a girl in a school uniform. My mind reeled, but before we spoke up, shrieks leapt from the other kids as another thud shook the bus.

My heart dropped to my stomach.

*This is a dream. This is an embarrassing dream where I'm heading to school and I'm in my underwear.* I looked down to the same blouse and skirt enveloped in my oversized jacket. My phone buzzed in my pocket, and I answered.

"H-Hello?"

"Mayu, are you at school?" Hannah asked.

"No, I don't think so. Not yet." My words tumbled out of mouth. I gripped my kneecaps, to make sure everything was real. "Hannah, where are you?"

"I'm at home. What's happening?"

"When did you get home last night?"

"An hour after you called me," she answered. "Why?"

"But I called you again last night and you didn't pick up."

"I didn't get a call from you. When I came home, you were asleep on the couch. I woke you up, but you must have been so tired, you didn't say anything, and you went straight to your room."

"When did I leave the house today?"

"Around seven-fifteen. What's going on?"

Fear slammed into my chest. "I never went to bed last night. The last thing I remembered was sitting on the couch and I woke up on the bus!"

"Oh no..." Her voice trembled. "I asked if you needed a ride to school, but you walked out of the apartment without saying anything!"

The bus stopped in front of the school, and I struggled to get out of the seat. Everyone left except me.

"Where's Ichirou?"

"He's sleeping right now. But I can pick you up—"

I shrieked, "No! Don't pick me up yet!"

"Mayu, this is serious. You went to school in your sleep!"

"I know, but I have to go."

"This is more important than class!"

"I'll talk to you later."

"Don't you dare hang up on—" I hit the red end button and her voice cut out. I tucked the phone back into my pocket, I turned to the school, hoping someone there had an answer.

# Pandemonium

**I made my way up the busy stairs**, to the assistant's lounge. The door was open but before I could rush inside, an assistant, a tawny girl with dreadlocks, stopped me on their way out.

"Whoa there!" she said, holding her hands up. "I'm sorry, but students aren't allowed inside."

"Is Mr. Turner here?" I blurted, anxiously. "Or Lutea, or Ethan?"

"Ethan and Cedric are here but—" The assistant was interrupted when Mr. Turner called out to her.

"You can let her in."

Her brow furrowed and she stepped aside to let me in. Mr. Turner was sitting at one of the tables with Ethan, grading papers using a fountain pen when he looked up at me.

"Is something wrong?" he asked. "Usually, students don't rush in here unless it's an emergency."

"I know what's making me sleepwalk!" I cried, startling them. "What do you know about the Malus?"

Rubbing his ear, Ethan shifted his gaze to Mr. Turner.

"I've heard of them," Mr. Turner answered, setting the pen beside the graded papers. "Allusive and ethereal. Cannot be seen nor touched but can have a strong influence on humans. I never heard of one causing their victims to sleepwalk."

"How did you hear about the Malus?" Ethan asked.

"I was looking in a book," I told him. "There was a picture of it, and it looked like the thing I saw when I fell into Erehwon. It's been following me in my dreams since then!"

The commotion in the lounge got a little quiet and some of the assistants turned their attention to me. But then, the bell rang and almost like they didn't want to hear more, most of the assistants hurried out of the room. A few kept their eyes on me on their way out.

Mr. Turner swept the papers into a neat stack and straightened the edges. "Tora and Marie won't be at school until the late afternoon. Are you willing to wait until then?"

"I think I can," I said.

"This sounds like something Chitose should look into as well," he said. "Did you text Lutea? She might know more about the Malus."

"I rushed straight here. I didn't think to do that." I grabbed my phone and sent Lutea a message: 'Need to talk to you now. I'm in the lounge. It's an emergency.'

"You can stay here until this is resolved." Mr. Turner stood up and handed me ten pages of math work stapled together. "Something to keep your mind busy."

With the school quieting and the assistants leaving, it was me and my unanswered questions in the lounge. I took Mr. Turner's seat and set the homework aside. I couldn't focus on math with the Malus on my mind. I wanted to read more about it, but Elizabeth's notebooks were at home.

Now the Malus frustrated me. The least it could've done was take my backpack with me. My phone buzzed and I quickly opened the inbox to see if Lutea replied. But the message wasn't from her. It was from Aiden.

'Hey, are you okay? I don't mean to bother you, but I haven't heard from you lately.'

I replied, 'I'm in the assistant's lounge. Everything is a little hectic on my end.'

A moment later, Aiden texted back, 'Want me to stop by? Do you want to talk about it?'

I pondered this, sent a reply but the screen suddenly went black.

"What the—" I muttered under my breath and pushed the power button. The screen lit up, then shut off again. The battery had died. I guess I never got to charge my phone while I was sleepwalking.

"Great..."

I shoved the phone in my pocket, then turned to the math papers. There was a cup of pencils on the desk, and I took one and worked on the first page. Surprisingly, math momentarily took my mind off everything that was happening. I had finished the first page and moved to the second when the scrape of a chair sliding on the floor broke my focus.

I spun around, wondering who was here, since all the assistants had gone to class. There was a girl opening one of the cabinets. Her tied up, mousy brown hair draped her back, passing over the wrinkled blouse. She wore a wrinkled white blouse and a dark pleated skirt that reached her ankles.

My brow arched. "Sarah?"

She whipped around with a shriek. A small cup fell out of her hand, and it burst when it hit the floor, spreading chocolate pudding everywhere.

"M-Mayu?" she squeaked. "What are you doing here?"

"I was going to ask you the same thing. I thought you were suspended."

"I still am," she said in a small voice.

A roll of paper towels sat on the counter, and I tore off a few sheets and wiped the pudding off the floor. Sarah kneeled beside me and helped. Her cheeks had a peachy glow and the dark, half-moon circles under her eyes had faded, like she had finally got some sleep.

"Miss Naiad told me I could stay here until my suspension was over," Sarah explained. "I've been coming here after what happened in the bathroom."

"Were you in the lounge yesterday?"

Sarah nodded, "I was in the far corner..."

"But I stayed there all day, and I didn't notice you."

She shrugged. "Nobody ever does."

With the floor cleaned up, and the towels tossed in the trash bins, Sarah grabbed two more cups from the cupboard, and I joined her at a different table. There was an open journal filled with big, messy handwriting. I read a few lines, and it reminded me of a verse.

"You write poetry?"

Sarah quickly closed the journal. "It's for me...It's supposed to keep me grounded."

"I didn't mean to pry," I said with an understanding nod. "I'm glad to see you're alright."

"You were worried about me?"

"I did throw a phone at your head and tackle you."

Her brows knitted together, she frowned and held her chin. "No wonder my head was hurting so much..."

"You don't remember?"

"I usually don't. It comes to me in bits and pieces, like a dream."

"What happened to the ghost?" I asked.

My skin bristled as a cold breeze skittered up my neck, and a hollow voice rose in my ears.

"I'm still here..."

"Stop it!" Sarah commanded.

I flinched and the icy presence melted away. My mouth fell agape.

"Sorry," Sarah murmured, her cheeks started to turn red. "I'm not used to this. Chitose has been teaching me how to control her."

A thousand questions whirled in my mind. "I can't believe she's still with you after what happened."

Sarah went silent. I wondered if I said something too personal, but she spoke again.

"Th-They were going to exorcize her...but I wanted her to stay. I wanted her to protect me, like she always would."

"Would?" I repeated.

Sarah stroked her arms, and her voice trembled. "She saved me. When I needed her, she took over so she could protect me."

"Wouldn't you get blamed for hurting others?"

Sarah bit her lip and her grip tightened. Her face fell to the table, eyes obscured by her hair.

Reflexively, I reached to hold her shoulder but stopped myself. I could feel the ghost's presence shrouding her.

"Mary said you had a mental breakdown on the first week of school. She told me to stay away from you because of that. What happened?"

Sarah lifted her head. Her voice was barely audible. "Ghosts can read emotions. They can see people for who or what they are. She was uneasy about the assistants and warned me to stay away from them. In class, Victoria was already talking about how weird I looked. Mary seemed bothered by me, but we never spoke to each other. I wanted to ignore them. Ignore her too, but... she was in my head. We got into an argument, and I didn't realize I was speaking aloud until I shouted at her to leave me alone."

"So, you didn't have a breakdown. It was a misunderstanding."

"Would anyone believe me if I told them I was arguing with a ghost? Besides, everyone left me alone after that. Except for you."

"It's kind of hard to ignore you when you sit in front of me," I mustered a half smile before it faded. "If you told everyone to leave you alone, why was Victoria picking on you?"

"Because she could," Sarah said, dark and distant. "Who would want to help 'Crazy Sarah'? No matter how much I avoided her or ignored her or told her to leave me alone. She thought it was funny to follow me. To get her friends to mess with the 'freak.' To call me slow and stupid every day." Her voice hitched and broke into sobs.

"I just wanted it all to stop."

As she wiped her face with her shirt, I gently placed my hand on her back. The cold presence faded.

"I know, believe me, I know."

Sarah looked at me, tears in her eyes.

I turned my watch over, showing Sarah the medical band.

"I have epilepsy. When I was in the sixth grade, I had convulsive seizure during class and went to the hospital. When I came back, everything changed. My classmates stared at me from afar, expecting me to have another violent seizure, and my teachers treated me like I was made of fragile glass. To make matters worse, there was a girl who started a rumor that I faked my condition for attention, and everyone believed her."

"How did you deal with it?"

"I couldn't at first. I kept to myself, focused on studying and reading. Pretending I was in the world of books than in class. But then, I met someone. Another quiet girl like me. She didn't bother me, and she didn't believe the lies. She told me something I'll never forget."

"What did she say?"

"'They don't have what you have to live with. So, how would they know what it's like.'" I stared at the medical band and sighed. "The teasing and rumors didn't stop but having someone see the real me, and still be my friend helped me through those years. And...I realized bullies aren't creative people."

Sarah blinked.

"You can only be called 'Crazy' and 'Freak' for so long. After a while, their faces and their voices sound the same. It's like they copy each other's homework, y'know? They call us weird, but at least we can think for ourselves."

Sarah sniffled, "Right."

My little smile returned. "I'm sorry for what you had to go through. You didn't deserve that."

"Why are you apologizing? At least you wanted to help me, and she attacked you."

"What do you say we start over?" I offered my hand to Sarah. "Hi, I'm Mayu Hinamori."

Sarah hesitated at first, then shook my hand. "Nice to meet you. I'm Sarah Blaine." She said and for the first time since I met her, I saw life glimmer in her dull, dark eyes.

"You want to hear a joke?" I asked.

"Sure."

"I was looking for vegetables this morning. My search turnip'd fruitless."

Sarah raised her eyebrow and after a few seconds of pondering, she snorted into laughter. I could hear the ghost exasperate at my joke.

●

Chitose first arrived around noon in wisps of smoke in the middle of the lounge. Then Ethan opened the door and held it open for Lutea and the other assistants. Sometimes, it was easy to forget they were Mystics until their disguises unraveled. The one who had stopped me that morning removed her glasses, revealing sharp green eyes, and her dreadlocks hissed and curled on top of her head. Another assistant brushed back their curly red hair, revealing a pair of stubby goatlike horns. And an assistant's platinum blonde hair and striking blue eyes rippled into a dark shadowy figure that whooshed straight to one of the tables.

Somehow, Sarah and I felt like the odd ones out.

"Ethan already told me what happened," said Lutea, sitting across from me. "I tried to text you to see if you wanted to talk earlier."

"My phone's dead," I said.

"Oh, I'm sure there's a charger somewhere," she said. "So, what's this about the Malus?"

Lutea, Ethan, Sarah and Chitose listened as I told them about the presence in my dreams, my sleepwalking, and how I woke up on the bus on the way to school.

"Did you know this existed? Or what it was?" I asked Lutea.

She answered in a hesitant crack. "Mayu, there are worlds that we don't know about, let alone what lives in them. Everyone has heard of the Malus, but none of us here has faced it before. We only knew what it could do."

"So, anyone can be influenced by it?" Sarah asked, curiously.

"Depends on how close you are to it and how long you've been exposed to it," said Chitose. Her gold eyes flickered at me. "If you

281

did come across it when you passed through worlds, you wouldn't have come out as sane as you did."

"I've been feeling a lot of strong emotions lately," I pointed out.

"You've been stressed, for understandable reasons," Lutea corrected. "We're talking about being driven to insanity. The kind that has you laughing mad in a padded room."

"Perhaps it doesn't want to drive Mayu insane," Chitose said. "She was under its control long enough to leave her apartment. It could have taken her anywhere, but instead, it brought her to school."

My heart stopped.

"...Maybe it wants to learn?" Sarah muttered.

"No..." I remembered something Chitose said not too long ago. "It wants something from here."

Our conversation was interrupted by loud shrieks rolling down the hallway. Assistants tensed up as their focus darted to the door. A hand slapped against the door's window and a girl's face emerged, whitened with fear.

Ethan was already at the door but as soon as he opened it, the girl and ten other students stampeded inside. The assistants tried to calm the situation while a few raced out of the lounge.

Static crackled from the PA system, which I had never noticed was above the door until now. A man's voice came through, and someone mentioned it sounded like the principal. He tried to sound formal, but his voice shook.

"This is not a drill," he stressed. "I repeat, this is not a drill. We are going into lockdown, this is a—" the loudspeaker snapped off, and the lights sputtered out, enclosing the school in darkness.

Lutea and Chitose ordered the students, Sarah and I included, to hide under the tables. My arms wrapped around my shaking knees, my heart knocking in my ears. Sarah had curled into a ball and the trembling girl choked down her sobs. Chitose and Ethan stood near the door, their backs pressed against the walls and their eyes locked on the window.

As tension loomed in the heavy air, I thought back to the stories Ichirou and Hannah would tell me about the lockdowns. Ichirou called them an annoyance since they were mostly drills or false alarms. The worst one happened when a brawl broke out during a pep rally, but there were terrifying stories. Not urban legends about haunted lockers, but scary ones, like when a stranger broke into the school with a weapon, or when a couple of boys threatened any girl they saw, telling them they'd die if they screamed or ran away.

I tried to tell myself that if Ichirou and Hannah could survive lockdowns as crazy as that, then I could too. But the tightening pain in my chest warned me that something in the school was just as dangerous as an armed person.

Heavy footsteps thundered against the floor outside. Inside, Lutea, Chitose, Ethan and Teier stood by the door with their backs against the wall as the footsteps faded. A moment later, Lutea approached our table, making as little sound as possible.

"How's everyone doing?"

"Could be better," I whispered shakily. "What's going on?"

"There's something here..."

We turned to Sarah.

"There's... something here..." she repeated, clutching her shoulders. "We must leave... No!" she growled. "I'm not staying!"

Knowing what or who she was talking to, I reached for Sarah's wrist. She jerked up, hitting her head against the table, and the thud startled the students around us.

The blow snapped Sarah back in control. "Sorry," she said, rubbing her head.

"Sarah, what do you mean?" Lutea asked, warily. "Does she know what's here?"

"She doesn't know what it is," she stuttered. "It's all over the school, moving..."

"I can check," said Chitose.

"Be careful out there," Ethan told her.

"I know."

The girl with us and the other students shrieked when smoke swirled around Chitose, and she vanished. As Lutea and I tried to calm her down, the girl whipped her head side to side, expecting us to vanish, too.

"It's okay. We won't hurt you," Ethan promised. He moved closer to us and Lutea took his place by the wall. "She's going to check and see what's going on. She'll be back."

Fear took over the girl, and she fired out questions with tears in her wide eyes. "Who was that?"

Ethan said to her, "She's, my friend. She's going to help us."

"What's your name?" I asked the girl.

I knew it wasn't a good time for introductions, but I understood what she was going through. She needed a distraction to cope with what she saw.

Surprisingly, she answered in a trembling voice. "It's Julia. Julia Lovelace."

"Could you tell us what happened?"

Julia breathed through her nose. "I...I was at lunch. It was windy outside, so we sat away from the windows... Then they shattered all at once! Everyone ran away from the glass and then the tables—" she choked up.

Ethan rubbed Julia's back. "What happened to the tables?"

"They moved! They moved on their own and flew all over the cafeteria. Everyone ran away and I—" she gasped. "Where's Anona?"

I tensed up, remembering the girl with antlers from the club meeting.

"She was with me. I thought she was with me," Julia shot a teary glance at Ethan. "Where is she? Is she here?"

He frowned. "Everything happened too fast. If you have her number, don't call her. Send her a text to let her know you're safe. After the lockdown, I'll look for her."

Juliae whimpered and buried her head in Ethan's chest, muffling her sobs.

A moment later, a cold presence rose behind me. Sarah and I turned to the shadow forming on the wall, taking the shape of a human body. Fear shot through me, and I backed away, watching the darkness form into Chitose.

"How bad is it?" Ethan asked.

"The cafeteria is destroyed," she said. "Other assistants on the floor are guarding the classroom, but the glass hurt a lot of students. We need to seal the school."

"Seal the school," I whispered. "What does that mean?"

Lutea answered with a stern look on her face. "It means you and everyone else need to leave the school. Let us do our jobs and handle this."

That wasn't something I could brush off, but the way Lutea said, "do our jobs" made me realize how different I was from her. What could I have done? I barely knew how to use my powers. At least the assistants knew what they were, and they could face any threat. I felt like I was a part of their group, but at that moment, I was only a student that they needed to protect.

We waited for an eternity for the principal's voice to come back on the speaker, for the power to turn back on, but none of that happened. Sirens drew near and footsteps raced across the floor. Someone knocked against our door, frightening us. A flashlight beamed through the windows and a man from outside announced himself as a security guard.

"Badge number?" Lutea shouted.

The officer gave her his number. "How many are there?"

"Eighteen."

"The school's being evacuated. You need to leave immediately and head straight to the main doors! Do you understand?"

"Loud and clear!" Ethan called.

The security guard moved on to knock on other doors and delivered the same message to the other classes.

Moments later, a commotion stirred outside, letting us know the students were being evacuated. Everyone crawled from the tables and gathered at the door. My small group was the last out of the lounge to shuffle into the passing hallway.

The tension in the air was palpable. Despite daylight peering through the windows, parts of the school remained shrouded in shadows. I wrapped my arms around my chest for comfort and stayed close to Lutea. She craned forward, narrowing her eyes to see what was ahead of us. Sarah caught up to me on my left. Her worrying eyes scanned the walls, as if searching for something only she could see. Julia walked in front of me, curling her arms around Ethan's arm, like a small child.

We rounded the corner as teachers, security guards, and other assistants herded students to the stairs, sharp gasps rose among the whispers, then dwindled to whimpering sobs. I pushed forward on trembling legs, wondering what was in the school and what happened to the cafeteria.

Another gasp caught my ear as it broke through the noise and a whimper crept closer to me. I clenched my hands, heart hammering as I glanced over my shoulder. The whimpering had stopped, and my breath stopped. Then a piercing scream tore from my throat.

# Luminate

**I could still hear it chasing after me.** The wet splat of its hands skittering across the floor. The horrific scream hurtling down the corridor. Its ear-splitting scream hurled from its mouth. I rounded the corner but at the worst possible time, my feet slipped, and my shoulder crashed into the linoleum floor.

I scrambled on all fours, catching a glance at the creature. Its sunken white eyes caught my gaze. Its pale skin stretched taut over its bones as it bent back. It lunged so fast, I barely had time to react. Icy hands pinned me to the floor. And a foul breath spilled out of its mouth. I screamed and thrashed beneath the creature, when the surge of heat rose and bolts of lightning scattered between us.

The creature reeled back. Scorch marks ran across its skin and its cries rose into a guttural roar. I scrambled to my feet, chest heaving in panic, and bolted down the hall until I crashed into another body.

My mind exploded with fear, and I jumped back, screaming. As did Aiden when he lurched, his red headphones dangled around his neck.

Questions flew across my mind. But our attention was drawn to the creature's ghastly cries.

"Is that a—" he started but I interrupted him.

"We have to run!" I screamed, tugging his arm.

He staggered for a few feet but ran back to the creature. I was about to protest when I saw it. A red glow pulsing through Aiden's arms. He threw his hands at the charging creature and the walls lit up with a brilliant flash of light.

A painful howl erupted from the creature as it crumbled on the floor, only to be doused by another burst of light. With a strangled cry, it rolled on its belly and scurried down the hall. Its body plunged into the darkness and silence engulfed the frantic steps.

We waited with bated breath before Aiden finally turned to me. A glowing ball of light hovered over his hand, casting our shadows against the lockers.

He mustered a weak smile. "Just in the nick of time, huh?"

My jaw went slack. "What did—how are you doing that?"

"I never told you?"

"No!" My voice rang off the walls. "How did you find me?"

"I heard a scream and ran to it. I'm glad I came when I did."

I paused to catch my breath and realized we were the only ones in the hallway. "What happened to everyone else?"

"I saw them heading downstairs when I heard you. They're probably outside."

"But I was with Sarah and Lutea!"

"Maybe they ran ahead... In any case, we should go before the wendigo comes back."

Shock coursed through me. "That was a wendigo!" I exclaimed. But the more I thought about it, the creature did resemble the man-eating monsters. Still, it was unnerving to know I had faced one in real life.

"Yeah, I've heard a lot about them but never thought I'd see one up close. We should really go, though."

Aiden and I headed to the stairs. I listened for the wendigo, but it never emerged. It still didn't stop me from holding Aiden's hand.

"You never answered my question," I said, ignoring the butterflies in my stomach. "Since when could you control light?"

"Since I was five," he replied. "It took me years to get the hang of my powers, but I had lots of practice messing with the lights in class."

"If you don't mind me asking, are you a mystic?"

"I'm human."

"Last time I checked, humans couldn't control light."

He grinned. "Last time I checked, humans couldn't turn into plasma balls. How did you do that?"

"Not sure. I'm still trying to figure that out."

We continued walking in the darkness, and having Aiden around made it more bearable. His hand wrapped around mine like a blanket on a cold night. His voice made my stomach flutter, and I inched close to him. But it didn't last long. I stopped myself and stared ahead and felt the butterflies melt into lead.

"What's wrong?"

"We should have found the stairs by now..."

My hand slipped from his. I glanced back and as far as I could see, there were nothing but rows of lockers, stretching farther than our school should.

Aiden's eyes whipped back to the hallway. The color drained from his face as he realized it, too. He sucked in a breath, threw his arm out and the light shot through the darkness, leaving a brightened path behind. We watched it shrink to a fading speck.

"How is this possible?!" he cried.

"I don't know!"

I sped down the hallway with Aiden. There were faint whispers in the distance and bounding footsteps. Yet all we saw were endless lockers and empty classrooms behind closed doors.

"This... This can't be right," Aiden said, under his breath. He cupped his mouth and shouted, "Hello! Anyone here!"

His voice traveled down a hall where I felt a strong breeze pulling us toward the dark. We stared ahead, then glanced at each other.

"Do you think that'll lead us outside?"

"Where else would the breeze come from?" I asked.

A ball of light formed over Aiden's hand, and we headed down the path. The railings caught my attention, and I instantly knew they belonged to the stairs leading to the library.

"These look like the only stairs here," Aiden said, furrowing his brow. "Why is that?"

"I'm not sure, but maybe this can get us out of here. I think I hear something."

I let go of Aiden and hurried to the stairs, drawn by the breeze and voices coming from the first floor. I peered over the railing, and hope drained into the black pit below. The stairs trailed further down than they should have. My yelps sank into the darkness as though something below was breathing in more than the wind. Deep down, something ancient was watching us.

"Mayu!"

A boy's urgent cries brought my attention back to the light. His name, Aiden, flickered back in my thoughts. The fog in my mind cleared, and the numbing, fleeting sensation crumbled into fear.

"What's wrong?" he asked, his voice sinking into the pit. "What's down there?"

288

Backing away from the steps, a gust of wind rushed up from the depths, carrying a deep, haunting moan with it. I tore my eyes from the pit and yanked Aiden by his arm, prompting him to run.

As we ran down the hall, I spotted a classroom with its door open. We hurried inside, locked ourselves in, and found a supply closet in the back of the room to hide in. It was dark and cramped, but better than being in the hall.

I wasn't sure how long we were in the closet. It felt like an hour had passed, but the time on my watch was the same as when I left the lounge at eleven-forty. A few moments later, Aiden pulled out his phone, but it didn't have a signal and my phone was dead.

Another light formed between Aiden's hands, and it grew as he pulled them apart.

"Is this bright enough?" he asked.

We were already sitting shoulder to shoulder, but feeling the darkness swell, I inched closer. "Can you make it brighter?"

Nodding, Aiden parted his hands, making the light grow. Seeing his arms tremble, I held his hand, and the shaking light steadied.

"You're really good at that," I remarked.

"I should be," he said, softly. "My little sister, Natia, is scared of the dark. She always wants me by her side at night. Sometimes I'll read her stories, other times, I'll study while she sleeps."

"She's lucky to have you as a brother."

Aiden was quiet at first, then he sniffled. "Mayu," he whimpered. "Mayu, what's going on here?"

"I don't know." My hands clenched. "Lutea said they were going to seal the school. Maybe that's why we're trapped here."

"But why us?" he emphasized.

"I don't know, but I'm sure they're looking for us."

The voices in the hallway grew louder, but between the wendigo and the presence at the stairs, neither of us were eager to leave the room.

"What are you thinking about?"

I looked at him quizzically. "How did you—"

"Remember, I sit next to you all the time."

"Oh, right," I huffed, my eyes settled on the light. "Have you heard the story about the girl who disappeared?"

He nodded. "I heard her ghost lives in the locker. I never saw her, but I always got an eerie feeling walking past it."

"Can't say I blame you. She also knew about the mystics, but she died when she tried to cross into another world."

"...You think we're in another world?"

"I don't know what this place is. But when I heard the wendigo and its screams. It made me wonder if that was the same scream everyone heard that day, or was it her last scream?"

"We have to find a way out of here," I continued. "There has to be a way out and if the others know we're missing, they'll look for us."

"So will the wendigo and god know what else is in this school with us!"

"The same one that ran away from us. With your powers and mine, I think we stand a chance. We won't become another ghost story."

He exhaled, "Alright, let's do this." Aiden got up first and helped me to my feet. "You got my back?"

"Always."

We eased our way to the classroom door. Aiden slowly turned the knob and nudged it open, giving us enough space to leave. With our backs against the lockers, we rounded the corner to the sound of voices. As they became clearer, I recognized one of them being Miss Naiad.

We stayed quiet and made it down the hall when we noticed something that wasn't there before, the cafeteria door.

Aiden and I stopped and stared at it for a moment.

"Has that always been there?" he asked.

"I don't know," I replied, then realized something. "Do you think we're back? Back in our world?"

"Only one way to find out. But if this opens to another dark pit, I'm going back to the broom closet."

"I'll be right behind you."

We pulled the doors, and my eyes fell to the glass shards littered across the floor. The wall sized window had completely shattered. The chairs were overturned, and the tables had holes punched through them.

"I heard about the windows breaking in class," Aiden muttered. "But this is way worse than I thought."

My voice shrank. "What happened here?"

"And where's Miss Naiad?"

"I'm right here," her voice joined us.

With a startled gasp, I whipped around but Miss Naiad wasn't there.

"Who were you talking to?" Lutea asked. My eyes darted around, but we were still alone.

"Lutea!" I called out. My heart leaped when she called back. I could hear the panic in her voice.

"Mayu? Is that you? Where are you!"

"I'm in the cafeteria."

"I don't see you! Can you see us?"

"No, we can hear you," said Aiden. "A-Are we dead?"

"You're not dead," Miss Naiad answered. "You're in the Ethereal Plane, a space between the living world and the afterlife. How did you get there?"

"We're not sure," I replied. "Can you get us out?"

"I can," she said, calmly. "But I will have to create a breach first."

"What's a breach?"

"It's a temporary doorway between worlds."

"How long will that take?" Aiden asked.

"It shouldn't take too long to make. Relax and stay where you are."

The surrounding air changed, and the wall to my left rippled like a mirage. Lutea's voice came more clearly through the ripple. Relieved, I stepped toward it, wanting to get out of this world so badly until Aiden tackled me to the floor. A chair flew over our heads and exploded with a deafening crash.

I screamed in shock, "What was that?!"

Aiden's face was full of fear. "It came from the tables."

My eyes veered from the walls to the wreckage. Something emerged from the broken pieces. Small, light blue creatures, as tall as pencils with green wings stared at us through beady eyes.

I tilted my head to the side. "Are those... fairies?"

Aiden faltered, "Worse... they're pixies! We need to run! *Now!*"

We bolted for the breach and the pixies burst into a frenzy. They swarmed around the ripple, so we charged through the door and dove into the dark, endless hallway.

Aiden swung his arm, releasing a blinding flash of light, disrupting the swarm.

"Now would be a good time to turn back into a plasma ball!" He yelled.

"I would if I knew how!" I yelled back.

We skirted around the corner, but my feet were lifted off the floor. Sharp stings pierced my arms as the pixies dug their claws into me. I screamed and thrashed to break free, and another burst of light blinded the pixies. They let me go and I shrieked as I fell and cried out in pain when I hit the floor.

I craned my head to see Aiden running towards me. But the pixies got to him. They lifted him up and dragged him into the dark, his terrified scream was cut off by a sudden crash followed by a frightening silence.

At that moment, all my senses awoke. My heart hammered in my chest, a scream rose in my throat, and pangs jolted through my body. Finally, in one agonized cry, a flurry of electric light tore the empty world apart.

# On Edge

**I lurched up in someone's arms**, pain ached through my body and my limbs felt weak and heavy.

"Easy now, you're okay," Lutea murmured.

I had enough strength to look up at her holding me before she set me against the locker.

I panicked. "The pixies! We got to—"

"It's alright, the pixies are dead," she said, and I froze. "I don't know what happened to them, but they were dead when we found you."

"Found me?" I repeated, confused. "How did you get here?"

"Oh, no you're not in the Ethereal Plane anymore. You're back on the other side. Don't know how that happened either."

Lutea handed me my glasses. I put them on, and the first thing I saw were the pixies on the floor. I jerked back, my head ached but as my eyes adjusted, I noticed they weren't moving. Scorch marks covered their ice blue bodies like wood over an open fire.

"They're dead," I exhaled in relief. "Where's Aiden?"

Despite Lutea's protest, I pushed myself up and looked for him. Across the dead pixies, I found Ethan on his knees, his hand on Aiden's shoulder as he turned him on his back.

My heart raced, the drumming in my ears was almost deafening.

Aiden wasn't moving, his shirt was singed, his face was eerily pale, and a bruised, sickly lump welled up in his right arm.

"Cedric!" Ethan roared. Immediately Mr. Turner appeared at the corner of my eye, rushing down the hallway. The next words Ethan shouted made my heart stop. "He's not breathing!"

I cried out, scrambling to Aiden but Lutea had locked her arms around me, stopping me. I squirmed in her arms and wailed for her to let me go. But Lutea's stony grip tightened.

"Mayu, don't get too close!" she warned.

My knees buckled and I crumbled to the floor in tears. Mr. Turner gave Aiden chest compressions, locking his hands over his chest and repeatedly pushing it down repeatedly.

*Wake up*, I pleaded.

He pinched Aiden's nose closed and put his mouth over his. Nothing. He continued pushing down on Aiden's chest and repeated the process.

*Please, wake up!*

Aiden's hand twitched and he jerked to life. His eyes opened and he hurled out a volley of dry, ragged coughs.

Mr. Turner said to Aiden with a slight tremble in his voice. "Welcome back. Nearly lost you for a moment."

Lutea let me go and I stumbled next to Aiden. His glossy, bloodshot eyes met mine.

"I think my arm's broken," he rasped.

I burst into tears again. "It is broken!"

Ethan carefully helped Aiden sit up. His face tightened when he cradled his swollen arm, then jumped back at the pixies but we told him they were dead.

"This looks bad," Ethan mumbled, steadying Aiden's arm. "Cedric, can you reset the bone?"

Mr. Turner squinted at the bruises. "Not here. It can be done at the infirmary. But it needs to be steadied first."

An idea crossed my mind. "He can use my jacket!" I offered, taking it off.

Mr. Turner had no argument with that. He wrapped it around Aiden's arm and shoulder, turning it into a makeshift sling.

"This is the best we can do until we can get you to the infirmary," he said, tightening the jacket.

Aiden flinched in pain.

"Does she need help as well?" Mr. Turner called out to someone. I wondered if he was talking about me, but our eyes didn't meet. I turned around and Chitose stood up, carrying Sarah on her back.

"Sarah's exhausted, but overall fine," she replied.

*Where did she come from?* I pondered this but I wasn't sure if I should ask now.

"Want me to carry her?" Lutea offered.

Chitose shook her head. "She's light. I'll meet you at the infirmary."

Her eyes flashed white, and they vanished in a cloud of swirling shadows.

"Can both of you walk on your own?" Lutea asked.

It didn't look like Aiden could, but he managed to push himself up. Together, we headed downstairs, away from the dead pixies.

Aiden's arm slipped out of the jacket-sling when the knot came undone. The pain was so much, he had to stop at the steps on the first floor. Lutea held Aiden's arm, moving it closer to his chest and Mr. Turner re-tied the sleeves. All I could do was talk to Aiden, reassuring him we were close to the infirmary.

"Chitose should have fleeted you too," I said. It was already painful for him to go down the stairs.

"Not while he's awake," said Ethan. "Trust me, you don't want the nightmares that come with it."

"I'll take nightmares over this," Aiden grunted through the pain. "I guess going to the hospital is out of the question."

Mr. Turner assured him. "If it eases your mind, Caritas and I used to be field doctors. If anyone knows how to treat a broken bone under high stress, it's us."

"And Miss Naiad sealed the school after the evacuation to keep the pixies in," said Lutea. "Until they're dealt with, we're trapped in here with them."

My eyes widened. "But they're dead, aren't they?"

"Not all of them."

I faltered as the horror set in Aiden's face. "There's more?"

"We'll explain everything as soon as we get out of here while it's still quiet."

Aiden hoisted himself to his feet, and as we continued down the hall, my ears twitched to small wings buzzing from afar.

Noises emerged from the infirmary, growing louder the closer we approached it. Lutea opened the door, and a sharp scent of blood slammed into me. Assistants were laying in beds and sheets placed on the floor. Caritas darted between beds, bringing medical supplies to the wounded assistants. Helping her were the only assistants who were wounded but could still walk around.

The sight of it was like a medic in a war.

"What... happened?" I asked.

"The pixies," Lutea answered. Ethan set Aiden on one of the empty beds. "The cafeteria wasn't the only place they attacked. It happened everywhere, and damn near everyone were hurt."

"And trying to fight off a swarm only caused more damage." Ethan nodded to the wounded.

I moved to the side to the sound of footsteps and Caritas raced to Aiden's bed.

"What do we have?" she asked.

"Fractured right arm." Mr. Turner told her. "It needs to be set."

Dizziness rolled over me as I knew what they had to do. Once, during a track meet, a runner from a different team landed badly on a hurdle and snapped their ankle. The paramedics had to reset the bone before taking them to the hospital. I couldn't stomach it then, and I couldn't stomach it when Mr. Turner and Caritas had to do the same for Aiden.

Aiden at first tried to hold the pain in with quick breaths, then he winced and groaned when Caritas lifted his arm. Mr. Turner's hands closed around it, and Aiden cried out as the bone crunched under his skin. Caritas wrapped the broken arm in gauze, then a cast, while Mr. Turner kept it level. When it was over, Aiden slumped on the bed, sweat beaded his face.

"There you go. The worst of it is over," Caritas said, soothingly.

Mr. Turner left to treat the others and I took his place, sitting next to Aiden. Caritas told us to shout if we needed anything then hurried to another bed.

"Oh, what a day," Miss Naiad's voice rose behind us. "Never expected a pixie infestation to happen here."

She wound around the desk and, with a flick of her wrist, one of the stools slid to her and she sat before me and Aiden.

"How are you scholars holding up?"

"I'm alive, that's a start," Aiden replied.

"Yeah, could be better," I said.

Miss Naiad snorted, "Understatement of the year. So, how did you end up in the Ethereal Plane? Fell through another door?"

I told her what happened in the hallway where I was walking with Lutea one moment, then the next, hearing the wendigo's cries.

"Did anyone else hear it?" I asked.

"Everyone was crying to some extent," Ethan said, leaning against the wall. "If I heard it, I'd assumed it came from the students."

"Same here," Lutea said. "I didn't realize you were missing until after we heard a scream."

"What scream?" I asked.

"A loud one that traveled down the hall. No one knew who screamed or where it was coming from. But it made everyone panic and run in different directions. That's what triggered the pixies to swarm in a frenzy."

I covered my mouth in shock. "They heard me…"

"That's what led me to finding her," said Aiden. "Everyone was running, and I charged toward the scream. I saw Mayu use her powers and she ran into me before I knew what was going on."

"So, neither of you know how you ended up on the other side," said Lutea.

"They may not have caused it," Miss Naiad spoke up. "You could cross into the Ethereal Plane by accident if someone opened a breach or if a creature of fae, like the pixies took them."

Lutea and I realized that at once. "A pixie could have taken Mayu, and the wendigo happened to be there."

"More than likely, however, it sounds like Aiden might have jumped into a breach, so for all we know, both are a possibility."

Out of curiosity, I asked Miss Naiad, "Is a wendigo a creature of fae?"

"It's no more mortal than you are. It can't hurt you as long as you're on this side of the world, though."

I was relieved but worry settled in Lutea's face. "Who's to say it can't cross over the same way Mayu and Aiden did?"

"Possible," Miss Naiad said. "Though, the Ethereal Plane is vast and hunting it down would be like finding a flea on a mammoth. We'll burn that bridge when we get there."

"Wait, so how did we get back?" Aiden asked. "Did we run through a breach? Did the pixies drag us back?"

"Turns out, neither!" Miss Naiad piped up. "She dragged you back."

She pointed to one of the beds where Sarah was resting.

"Ghosts are ethereal beings. And if that one was strong enough to pin two people on the ceiling and fling a golem across a bathroom, then she could open a breach to tear you two out."

My jaw dropped. "She saved us?"

"I'd be shocked if we didn't have our hands full with the pixies."

"How bad are they?"

"You've seen what they've done. But that's not the worst of it. Unlike us, they can travel freely through the Ethereal Plane and this world seamlessly, which makes it hard to contain them."

"You can't banish them from the school?" Ethan suggested.

"I can. But that would release the swarm into the neighborhood. I need Tora's help to make a gateway."

Lutea checked her phone.

"He's on his way," she said. "He says if you're going to banish the pixies, we'll need at least one door open. Everything has to be closed."

"There are a lot of doors to close," said Ethan. "It wouldn't be much of a problem, but half of the assistants are down."

"So, have the remainder split into pairs to cover each floor." Miss Naiad turned around. Her voice projected across the infirmary. "Oi, anyone who can still move, listen up!"

The few uninjured assistants circled around Miss Naiad, and she explained the plan. She and Tora would use a banishment spell and send the pixies away. But to be sure they were all gone, all the doors and windows in the school had to be closed except for the back exit doors.

"What about the cafeteria?" an assistant asked.

"Keep the doors closed," Miss Naiad told them. "The same for any classroom with a broken window. Make sure the pixies have only one way out."

"And if we spot a pixie?" Lutea spoke up.

"If it doesn't attack, don't engage. But defend yourself, nevertheless. Have your partner watch your back."

Ethan cleared his throat. "Chitose and I can work on the first floor."

"I can help," I offered.

Miss Naiad's sharp gaze flickered in my direction. "You got lucky when Sarah pulled you out of that realm the first time. Don't push it."

"Mayu can come with me," Lutea said. "She survived the worst when they attacked."

I would've felt proud if Miss Naiad weren't glaring daggers at me. "And if you get pulled back into the Ethereal Plane?"

"I have a plan," Lutea promised. "We need to go to the lounge to get some bait and supplies."

I didn't have time to ask Lutea what her plan was as the assistants were divided into groups. Mr. Turner stayed in the office with Caritas to help the wounded. Miss Naiad opened the school's back doors. Ethan, Chitose, and a few assistants closed the door on the first floor.

Lutea and I went with a small group to the second floor, armed with spare flashlights from the infirmary. Torn papers dangled off the wall, lockers were dented, and some of the windows on the classroom doors had shattered. I peeked inside the room and my stomach sank. Glass littered the floor, and the desks were upturned. I hate to imagine being in a classroom when it happened. How scared the students and teacher must have been.

"We can't leave this one open," Lutea said, closing the door.

I pulled away and checked the other room. Aiming the flashlight inside, I froze when I recognized the closet where Aiden and I hid in. It was so small, yet that was where we felt the safest.

"See anything?" Lutea called softly.

"No." I stepped back and noticed something glittering at the corner of my eye.

"What is this?" I swept my light across the floor, and the beam sparkled on piles of white powder. "Weren't there dead pixies here?"

"They turned into pixie dust," said Lutea, closing another door. "Usually harmless, but it can either grow into fungi or more pixies."

I gulped, "How long does it take for that to happen?"

"In a building like this? You're more likely to have black mold instead of pixies. We may have to deep clean the school after this."

We arrived at the assistant's lounge. With the power out, she didn't need to use her ID to open the door. The lounge looked bigger and more unnerving in the dark. A nearby clock ticked off each second. After being stuck in the Ethereal Plane, it was nice to hear the faintest sounds from the real world.

"What kind of bait do we need?" I asked.

"Sugar," Lutea told me, opening the cabinets. "Violent as they are, no pixie can resist sweets. When we were in the cafeteria, we noticed all the food was gone."

"They ate all of that food?" I grimaced, thinking about the school's plain and tasteless meals. "Any chance the indigestion could stop them?"

"If only." Lutea hauled out an armful of spices and two paper bags of sugar. "We should also look for extra bandages. They should be in the cabinet near you."

I turned around and opened a cabinet, but it was completely barren. "Lutea..."

She turned to me and noticed the empty cabinet. "Chitose might have fleeted here earlier for the supplies. That's alright."

We grabbed two tote bags and gathered the rest of the sugar, sweets and spices from the counters and cupboards.

"Mayu, I need to ask you something."

I turned to Lutea. "Yeah?"

"It's about the dead pixies we found."

"What about them?"

"Did you kill them?"

I hesitated. "I don't know how I did it. I saw Aiden hurt and lost control over myself."

"It's okay, you were going through a lot. What matters is that you were able to defend yourself. If you can't use that power at will, yet, you can use this for now." Lutea took out two black skillets and handed one to me.

"Gah!" My hand dropped to the floor when I tried to lift the skillet. "What's this made of? Iron?"

"Pure, cold iron. Old fashioned but perfect fae repellent." Lutea held her skillet and twirled it around as though she was adjusting to a new sword. "If a pixie comes after you, hit it. Hard."

I would have given myself some practice swings but a rustling, followed by a metal clatter drew us to the cupboard. A small pixie crept from the shadows. It looked at us, and its small eyes narrowed to slits as it screeched.

Pixies burst from the corners of the wall, trying to get us. I gripped the skillet and swung with all my might, knocking a few out of the air. They nipped at Lutea's face and raked their claws on her, but they only gained broken teeth and battered arms. Lutea swung her skillet like a tennis racket and the pixies tumbled to the floor.

We raced out of the lounge when something knocked me against the locker. The skillet dropped from my hand, and I reached for it only to watch it slide away as the pixies dragged me back. Lutea ripped one of the bags of sugar open and hurled it past me. The pixies' heads turned, and they dropped me on the floor. I remember getting up right as Lutea rushed to pull me to my feet. We took off as the pixies tore the bag to shreds.

"Now what!" I shouted.

"Mayu, how tall are you?" Lutea asked.

I answered, though confused by the weird question. "I'm five feet tall, why?"

Lutea stopped. Her hand was on my shoulder and the next thing I knew, she shoved me inside one of the lockers. My legs were tangled, and my arms pressed against my chest.

"Don't move! Don't get out until I say so. I'm going to keep the pixies distracted!"

I called her name again as her footsteps raced across the floor. I jumped, hitting my head against the locker when the pixies hovered in front of it like wasps. They touched the surface, and jerked back whipped with loud, ear-ringing screeches. Suddenly, the pixies flew back as a howling wind funneled through the hall. Hanging papers were ripped from the walls and the locker doors swung open, filling the roaring air with loud, thunderous bangs.

Then, as fast as it came, the wind settled, and the noises faded. For a moment, I waited anxiously in silence before two voices emerged.

"Took you long enough, Tora!" Lutea said, frustrated. "Where have you been?"

A man's deep voice grounded out words that were in another language. Lutea replied sharply in the same tongue.

Then the man, whose name I guess was Tora, called out to her, "Where are you going?"

"Mayu's in here," she said, and stopped in front of me. I could make out the cracks across her face. "Still breathing in there?"

"Kind of losing feeling in my legs," I grunted.

"Give me a second," Lutea tinkered with the locker and pulled the door open.

I stumbled out and took in big gulps of air. My legs were weak and shaky at first before I regained my balance.

"I thought I was going to suffocate in there!" I exclaimed.

"Sorry. It was the only way to keep the pixies away from you. At least it worked."

"Where did they go?"

"Somewhere upstairs," Tora's deep rippling voice rolled up my spine. I turned around and stared up at him and my heart dropped in fear. He was taller than Mr. Turner, almost eight feet tall, with a wide, angular face. Fangs protruded from his lower jaw, pointing to his narrow brown eyes. Runic sigils covered his arms and wound its way to his neck, disappearing beneath dark dreadlocks tied to the back with a few strands hanging off his shoulders.

He snorted, "You shoved your friend in a locker? Aren't bullies supposed to do that?"

"I had no choice," Lutea told him. "Steel was the next best thing to keep them away."

He shrugged and let out a soft grunt. I shrank behind the man, frightened by everything about him. His boots thumped like cannons with each step.

"Never thought I'd see pixies come to a school, of all places." He mumbled.

"How come?" I asked, my voice sounding tiny and soft.

"Steel and iron are common in human-made structure. It's dangerous for the fae."

My brow furrowed. "What about the ones in the courtyard?"

"Those are sprites," Lutea corrected. "They're spirits of the plants and flowers. Iron doesn't affect them the way it does for the fae."

"As long as they're taken care of," Tora added. "What kind of damage have the pixies caused."

"They knocked out the power, ate the school's lunches and hurt a lot of kids, you name it."

"I heard they took someone into the Ethereal Plane."

"We're not sure, yet. But it looks like they might be targeting Mayu," Lutea motioned to me.

My heart thudded at her words. Tora stopped walking. His thick brow settled over me.

"Wh-Why me?" I stuttered.

"Good question," he agreed. "They usually don't snatch hybrid children."

"Could be because she killed some of them," Lutea said. "Do you have anything that can protect her?"

"I might," Tora replied. "Short Stuff, come here."

I squeaked. "I'm not that short—"

"Hold still."

I blinked at first, thinking Tora had the same light as Aiden, when a shimmering light coursed through his tattoos, from his elbow to his outstretched hand. He tapped my forehead, and a shiver raced down my spine and spread through my arms and legs. A strange mark pulsed in the back of my hands and quickly faded before I could get a good look at it.

"Whoa," I whispered, clutching my hands. The tingling sensation rolled off me. "What happened?"

"Binding rune for protection," said Tora. "It makes you invisible to fae, including the pixies."

I glanced at my arms and legs and frowned. "I don't look invisible. Are you sure it's working?"

Tora scoffed, "If you do not trust my work, you are more than welcome to hide in another locker."

⁘

Miss Naiad joined Tora in the hallway leading to the exit doors. Lutea and I hid at the stairs, watching them tear open the bags of sugar and dumped it on a pile in the floor. I couldn't hear what they were saying, but the light banter and small laughter I heard between them gave me the impression they were more like old friends than colleagues.

Not that I doubted Tora's skill in magic, but I was wary about sitting out in the open. I would have asked to hide in the infirmary until they came. Tora and Miss Naiad stepped back when the high-pitched screeches rolled from every corner of the school. A cloud of pixies swarmed the sugar. They piled over each other, greedily shoving handfuls of it in their mouths.

I jerked up and fear raced through me when a pixie caught my gaze. But I guess the sugar was more important than me and it joined the swarm in the feeding.

"It's working," Lutea whispered, her arm wrapped over my trembling shoulder. "They can't see you."

Tora and Miss Naiad weren't fazed by the frenzy. They held their arms and streams of light swirled from their hands, radiating a multitude of colors.

They chanted and the color changing light wove around the backdoor. The frames turned into roots and an image rippled open to a deep forest. I could smell ancient bark and hear waters rushing in unseen rivers and waterfalls.

A strong, warm wind hurled the pixies toward the doorway. As the last pixie shot through, the forest rippled back to the school's parking lot. The light faded away, and the door molded back to its original form. All that remained in the hallway were shredded remains of the bag of sugar.

"Phew!" Miss Naiad heaved, catching her breath. "I see you still got it, old man!"

She clapped Tora's shoulder and grinned.

"Who are you calling old?" He hoisted himself up, holding his hands against his knees.

I peered over the corner. "Are the pixies gone?"

"Most of them," said Miss Naiad. "There is one more thing we need to do."

●

With most of the danger out of the school, naturally, the next step was going to be clean up. Lutea and I, along with the other assistants, checked the classrooms for stray pixies and set the turned over desks and chairs back in their original spots. If they were broken, we let Tora, Miss Naiad or an assistant who practiced magic fix them.

The only thing they couldn't fix was the cafeteria's window. The tables were repaired, but Lutea told me fixing a window so large in seconds would raise suspicion to the public.

"But seeing tables fly around isn't?" I remarked.

Lutea smirked.

I should have known Miss Naiad already took care of that issue. The instant she saw the cafeteria (moments before Aiden and I barged in), she had already cast a massive spell over the school called Revision. It doesn't erase your memories entirely but alters it so anyone who saw the attack would remember it differently or forget minor details.

"Will this affect us too?" I asked.

"If you didn't witness it, it won't tamper with your memories," she explained.

We headed upstairs, where I watched everything repair itself, as if the world was put on rewind. Shredded papers mend themselves. Dented lockers molded back into shape, and broken glass flew to the empty doors, sticking together like a puzzle and reforming into windows, wiped clean of every crack.

"I can't believe they did all this damage."

"That's what happen when you force a fae into a place like this."

I stopped on the third-floor steps and turned around. Cracks splintered across Lutea's arms, up her neck, and reaching the tip of her brow.

I frowned. "Are you sure Miss Naiad or Tora can't fix you?"

Lutea glanced at her hands, tightening them into fists, then relaxing. "I can after we're done here."

I nodded. "What did you mean when you said they were forced?"

"Remember what Tora said. They wouldn't fly in here on their own because of the iron. Something drew them here, or forced them inside, causing them to panic," her voice lowered but I caught the words under her breath. "And around the time most of us were on break too…"

Panick spiked through me. Not because of what Lutea said. A prickling sensation rolled through me, and without thinking, I sprang back as something white with wings shot past me. It smashed into Lutea's face, and her body tumbled down the stairs and erupted in an explosive crash.

# 22

# Reconcile

**I found Lutea at the bottom of the stairs**. She was on her back, cracks broke across her face, her vacant eyes stared up at the ceiling, and her arm was broken into pieces. The pixie that struck her was dead in the corner of the floor.

It was Tora's booming voice that startled me out of my daze. "What happened!" he roared, but I couldn't answer. A hand shook my shoulder, yet I couldn't move. I stood there, staring at my friend. But she stayed motionless on the floor. I could hear her last words, the crash and silence.

Tora's hand reached pasted me and turned Lutea's head to the side. My stomach turned at the engravings on her forehead, cracked and chipped away.

"She's not dead." His words echoed in my head. It slowly brought my attention to him. Tora pointed at the engravings.

"Has she ever shown you these?" he asked.

I stayed silent.

"The markings keep a golem active. If they're removed, it deactivates them. It does not mean they are gone forever."

The words were caught in my throat. "She—she's going to be alright?"

"Yes. However, I cannot repair her here."

I glanced over my shoulders to the sound of footsteps. Miss Naiad slowed down behind us. Her worried expression turned to shock when she saw Lutea.

"Can you take her back to the infirmary?" Tora asked her.

Miss Naiad nodded and gently pulled me away from Lutea. I didn't' move.

"I can't," I said, weakly. "I can't..."

"Please," Miss Naiad said, gently. "Let him help her."

She pulled me close to her, letting my head rest against her chest and I broke down.

"She's going to be fine," Miss Naiad murmured. "She'll be fine..."

I cried until my eyes were puffy and my head ached. When I could no longer cry and my sobs dried up, Miss Naiad finally let me go. My head ached behind my puffy eyes. I held Miss Naiad's hand, and we made our way back to the infirmary.

On the way, I found one of the pixies slumped against the wall, and its head pulled toward the floor. My insides tensed up, but when it didn't move at our steps, I quickly realized it was dead. Seeing the vicious creature lie peacefully ignited a burning hatred in me. I charged at the pixie, but Miss Naiad's hand tightened around my arm, jerking me back before I could kick it.

"Taking your anger out on a corpse won't fix this," she said.

'*I know,*' I wanted to tell her. I hated them too much to care. If it weren't for them, Aiden and Lutea would have been safe. No one would have gotten hurt. The one that hurt Lutea meant to hurt me.

'*Why did I have to jump out of the way?*' I berated, '*Why didn't I warn Lutea before it attacked her. Why did—*'

"Mayu," Miss Naiad spoke up, interrupting my thoughts. "None of this was your fault. Don't have that weighing in your mind."

I choked on my words and didn't know what else to think about.

"Don't think for now," she told me. "You've been through enough. Let us handle the rest."

I had no argument against that.

In the infirmary, I slouched on the bed next to Aiden's. I couldn't bring myself to talk to him when he asked what was wrong. I wanted to tell him everything and yet, the words wouldn't form. All I could do was shake my head and look away. I checked the time on my watch and almost burst into tears. Between the lockdown, the wendigo and the pixies, it felt like a day had gone by. It had only been three hours.

For the remainder of the afternoon, Caritas, and Mr. Turner helped with the wounded assistants and Miss Naiad left to complete the repairs and clean up.

Sarah woke up around three thirty, scared and confused until Caritas and Aiden told her she was in the infirmary. When she calmed down, Aiden was the first to ask her what happened.

Sarah told us the ghost warned her about the wendigo and told her to run when she heard me scream. She left the school, but after she realized I wasn't with her, Sarah went against the ghost's wishes and returned to the school before it was sealed. By the time she found us, the ghost opened the breach and all she remembered were seeing the pixies struck by "strings of lightning."

"You can thank her for that," Aiden said, pointing at me.

I didn't know what impressed me the most: Sarah's relentlessness or commanding the ghost.

Within an hour, the assistants left the infirmary, patched up and more than ready to go home. Voices faded and the clamor quieted into small talk around the room. Miss Naiad came to us with a purse around her shoulder and offered to give Sarah, Aiden and me a ride home. The three of us exchanged concerned looks. When a witch offered to give us a ride, I had a hard time imagining her carrying us on a broomstick.

We left through the back door and followed Miss Naiad around the building to a station wagon with a beige roof and brown doors parked beneath a tree.

"Is this her car?" Aiden whispered.

"I don't know," I whispered back.

Sarah shrugged.

I thought Miss Naiad may have disguised the car so it could blend in until she unlocked the door to the driver's seat.

She glanced at us. "Are you getting in?"

The car doors flew open.

We shuffled awkwardly into the beige, velvet seats. There were candy wrappers spilling out of the overstuffed cup holders and a giant blue sweater on the backseat. The bold black letters read, "SOCCER MOM" with a soccer ball in place of the o's."

"Soccer Mom?" I said, quietly.

"Maybe she likes soccer?" Sarah whispered.

"Her? No way," Aiden whispered back.

The sweater yanked itself out of my hands, folded itself and landed neatly on the passenger seat. Miss Naiad's icy blue and burning gold eyes stared at us through the rearview mirror.

"Got a problem with soccer moms?" She asked.

"No ma'am!" I said and rambled about the time I used to play soccer when I was younger.

"Really?" she mused. "To be honest, I don't get the game. Anyone with a limb can kick a ball, but my boys love it. If you ask me, it would be more fun if they used their magic in the game."

"Wouldn't that be cheating?" Aiden squeaked.

"That depends on how much of a sore loser you are." She switched the ignition on, and the car rumbled to life.

Miss Naiad drove down a street behind the school. I saw colorful houses and lawns decorated with gnomes and flamingos. Then we slowed down in front of a house at the end of the street. Stone steps sloped precariously to the ground. Fresh paint coated the wall, but the elements had beaten the roof without care.

"This is my house," Sarah said, softly.

"You live here?" I asked, almost in disbelief.

"My dad's in the middle of flipping it. He's a carpenter." Sarah pulled her backpack up from the floor and crawled out of the car and I followed her.

"Thank you for helping me and Aiden," I said. "I don't know what we would have done without you."

"No problem." Her cheeks pinched. "Thank you for talking to me."

"We can talk more during class if you like."

She nodded, affirmatively, and turned to the house. She hurried up the porch as the front door creaked open. I couldn't see who was there, but the moment Sarah walked inside, the door closed. Miss Naiad pulled away from the lone house in the shade, but I never took my eyes off of it until we left the street.

We drove through another neighborhood that had little to no trees blocking the sunlight. Aiden stared through the window, like he was lost in thought. His injured arm rested in a sling while he toyed with his headphone wires.

"How's your arm?" I asked, cutting through the silence.

Aiden looked down, not realizing what he was doing. "It doesn't hurt anymore," he said. "I wonder how long I have to keep this on."

"Six weeks." Miss Naiad said. "Sorry, healing craft has been heavily restricted for field use, otherwise I would have mended the bones myself."

"It's no big deal, I can go six weeks with one arm."

The car pulled up into a driveway next to a sky-blue bungalow. A woman on the porch, who might have been in her twenties, jumped to her feet. She almost resembled Aiden, having the same tan skin and long wavy brown hair that reached her back. The moment she saw Aiden, her curious eyes flashed with anger.

"Oh... no..." Aiden groaned.

"Aikeni!" she bellowed, stomping toward the car. Her next words exploded into another language that I wasn't familiar with. Frustrated, Aiden replied to her in the same tongue. They spoke so fast, I couldn't catch a phrase or a single word. The woman finished in a huff, until her eyes fell on Aiden's cast. "What happened to your arm!"

Aiden and I stood outside for air and leaned against the car. Miss Naiad told Kaiah, Aiden's older sister, what happened, and she accepted the pixie attack a lot better than I imagined. Anytime Miss Naiad mentioned something Aiden did, like saving my life, Kaiah twisted in his direction, shouting, "Aikeni!" like he was in trouble.

"Aikeni?" I muttered, turning to Aiden.

"It's my name in our language." He moaned again and rubbed his reddening cheeks. "Sorry you have to hear her like this."

"It's okay. She reminds me of someone else I know. She'd probably do the same."

Kaiah finished her conversation with Miss Naiad then faced me. I flinched, thinking she would blow up like a volcano. But as she scanned me, her attitude softened.

"You're Mayu, right?"

"Yes, ma'am," I said and bowed slightly to Kaiah. "I'm so sorry for what happened to Aiden. Please don't be mad at him."

"Don't worry about it," Kaiah said, waving her hand. "Not the first time my brother threw himself into danger, like the idiot he is."

"Love you too, sis," Aiden grumbled.

"Anytime bro," Kaiah pinched his cheek. Aiden batted her hand away. "At least he tried to help you. Though, I don't blame him for going above and beyond. You're even cuter in person."

I stammered a weak, "Pardon?"

"Kaiah..." Aiden warned.

Kaiah continued, "Do you how frustrating it was listening to Aiden talk about you? He would ask me tips about girls and—"

Aiden sprung up and shoved Kaiah away. "Times up. Stop talking. Go inside. Now!"

"What?" Kaiah said, coyly. "It's true, you asked if there was a nice spot for you two—"

"Shut up, shut up, shut up!" he yelped, pushing Kaiah away. Their argument continued until they were inside the house. Miss Naiad and I returned to the car, and I was more than ready to go home after today.

"Teenagers," Miss Naiad snorted. "Such peculiar creatures, if you ask me. You think you've figured them out, then they do the craziest things imaginable."

I kept my attention on the passing road, listening to the usual 'teen' lecture I'd heard so much in the past. Miss Naiad went on about how she got a call to the library and "found a certain succubus with glasses lurking in the restricted section."

My blood ran cold. I looked up and met Miss Naiad's piercing, mismatched eyes in the mirror.

"I finally got your attention."

"Is Elizabeth okay! What happened to her?"

"She should be in her dorm by now, provided she doesn't sneak out again." Miss Naiad said. "Did you know she was going to sneak into the library?"

"No! She never mentioned that, I swear!"

"I see," she paused and turned the corner on a different road. "The penalty for a student breaking into a restricted area is immediate expulsion. Elizabeth is an excellent student who has never gotten in trouble until now. So, tell me why she risked it to read about the Malus?"

"I know what's causing me to sleepwalk!" I told Miss Naiad about the Malus and how Elizabeth and I discovered a book about it in Ms. Hudson's study.

After a long moment of silence, Miss Naiad finally said, "Mayu, I say this with the utmost honesty. Stay away from the Malus. This is beyond something you and Elizabeth can handle."

"How could I when it takes me over every time I sleep? I slept walked into school today because of that Malus!"

The car turned a corner, and I recognized the apartment complex.

"I will reach out to Galumine about this."

"And how long is that going to take?" I snapped. "I can't wait another day or night, or the next time I close my eyes."

Miss Naiad was silent. Her voice softened, "Can you wait a few moments?"

"For what?"

"For someone to come help you with this. It may not be Galumine, but you won't have to wait another day, or night or the next time you close your eyes."

I wanted to sigh in relief, yet I couldn't shake off the feeling I had crossed a line with Miss Naiad.

I nodded weakly, "Yes, I think I can wait."

"As of today, you're leaving this alone. You saw what the pixies did, you know how dangerous mystics can be. You two are not prepared for what's to come."

I slumped into the seat. Miss Naiad drove into Union Circle and slowed down near my apartment. I was finally home after everything that'd happened.

When I got home, I plugged my phone into the charger. The instant it turned on, my notifications exploded with messages and missed calls from Ichirou and Hannah. I wanted to text them a paragraph of apologies and a believable explanation. In the end, I called Ichirou from the house phone, and he immediately answered.

"You better have a damn good reason why you haven't picked up the phone." Ichirou wasn't yelling, but his voice was stern and sharp, which was worse.

"I'm sorry..." I said, softly.

"I don't want an apology. I want an explanation. Where have you been?"

"I was at school and my phone died."

The phone beeped, telling me that someone was calling from the other line. It was an unfamiliar number, so I ignored it.

"Where in school? And how did you get home?"

The phone beeped again.

"I was at the lounge, then at the infirmary. I got a ride from Miss Naiad."

"*Who* is Miss Naiad?"

"One of the assistants."

I waited for him to ask, "what happened?" Then he said in a sharp sigh, "Look, we're on our way back home and then we are going to talk about this."

"Alright," I murmured, and he hung up.

Moments later, Elizabeth called me, and I'll admit, I was happy to hear from her.

"I heard you were trying to sneak into a restricted library," I started.

"I was trying to find a decent book about the Malus," she told me. "But it was only accessible to upper-level teachers and students with certain permits."

"Did Suzanne have a permit?"

"She wasn't involved in it. I had help from another friend, and we snuck inside." Her voice rose excitedly. "It was incredible! An entire museum and its own library dedicated to old books, ancient scrolls, and relics from... everywhere and different times."

I could hear the smile in her voice. "Were you able to find anything about the Malus?"

"I did but as soon as I opened the book, the words vanished from the pages and the covers fused with my hands."

"What!"

"I should have known the school had placed spells on the artifacts. Miss Naiad released the spell on me and sent me to my dorm. My hands are alright now. They still feel like dry old paper, though."

"I can't believe you snuck into a library... to help me." Guilt gnawed at my chest. "I didn't mean to get you into all of this trouble."

"It's fine. Anyway, are you alright? I heard pixies attacked your school today." She explained before I could ask. "Suzanne is friends with one of the assistants. It's gotten everyone worried over here."

"Erehwon is another world. Why are they worried?" I stared at the screen door, anticipating Ichirou's return.

"Mom asked the same thing." Elizabeth's voice got closer to the phone. "News of your 'arrival' is still on everyone's minds. They're thinking the 'anomaly' is going to draw the attacks here. I don't know who started the rumor, but it has the teachers feeling uneasy."

"They don't have to worry about me causing any more trouble. Elizabeth, I think we should stop trying to solve this."

"If it's about what happened in the library, don't worry about it. I'll find another way."

"You don't need to get into any more trouble. And its clear Miss Naiad and your mom are terrified of it. What chance do we have at beating it?"

"Maybe not beat it, but keep it at bay," Elizabeth said. "Come on, I don't want you to give up. You've done so many incredible things!"

"Did I?"

"You crossed worlds and came out unharmed. You're the one who knocked a centaur off their hooves and lived to talk about it! You're an urban legend over here."

"Why is it when you say it like that, it sounds amazing?"

"Because it is. In two months, all I did was sing in a choir, and eat with night students."

"Hey, I'd rather eat late than get chased by another monster," I joked, then I thought about how normal her life sounded. "Elizabeth, how do you do it? How can you handle a world of mystics and magic?"

"It's not easy, but not impossible to get used to. Mayu, if I can handle it, so can you!"

"I don't know..."

"Then what about you? Don't you want to find out what you are?"

Sure, I wanted to know what I was, but anytime I got myself involved with magic and monsters, it always ended with me or my friends getting hurt. There was a pause before Elizabeth spoke up again. "Mom's calling the other line."

"Good luck. Hey, Elizabeth?"

"Yeah?"

"If you're in another world, how can we still use the phone?"

"No idea," she said. "Hopefully, I'll call you tomorrow."

"Hopefully," I repeated.

And Elizabeth hung up.

I stared at the screen door, growing more anxious. I thought about them lecturing me and probably giving me a strict curfew. The house phone rang again, and it was the same unfamiliar number. Curious, I answered.

"H-Hello?" I tried to say, formally.

"Finally, you picked up!" Chitose groaned.

My brow wrinkled. "How did you get my number?"

"You wrote it on the club's invitation," she answered. "I'm at the complex. May I come in?"

"Where?" I opened the patio screen and took a few steps outside.

"Look up."

My eyes traced up to the clouds drifting in the pale blue sky, and Chitose hovering upside down over the complex.

"Hi!" Her voice through the phone matched her calling out to me as she waved. "I'll be inside shortly."

I slipped back inside the apartment. "Should I leave the door open? Hello? Chitose—"

I yanked the phone back as an ear-piercing static tore through the phone, then it cut to silence. A swirling gust of wind rose behind me. I whirled around until my eyes caught a dark mass oozing from the ceiling. Chitose peeled out of the darkness and floated gingerly to the floor.

If it were any other situation, I would have run screaming out of the apartment.

"How come no one saw you?"

314

"Cloaking," she said. "I don't have to let people see me if I don't want to."

Ignoring the bumps rising on my shoulders, I quickly accepted it and was glad no one saw her. "What are you doing here?"

"Miss Naiad asked me to check on your dreams, though I already intended to do that." Chitose wandered around the living room. "Is anyone else here?"

"Ichirou and Hannah should be on their way—" I realized what would happen if they came home and saw Chitose. "Could you make yourself invisible to them when they arrive?"

"Sure. Is there a place we can talk privately in?"

I led Chitose to my bedroom and warned her it was a little messy. It didn't stop her from peeking curiously inside my closet.

"How are you supposed to help me with my dreams? I thought you eat nightmares."

"I have to look through a dream to eat nightmares," Chitose explained.

"So... you're going to eat whatever's making me sleepwalk?"

"Ew, no. I'm—" Chitose and I flinched when the alarm went off again, followed by the screen door opening and closing.

"Mayu!" Hannah shrieked.

The alarm immediately snapped off and footsteps bounded upstairs. Before I could tell Chitose to hide, Hannah stormed into my room.

"You got some nerve!" She yanked me into a tight hug, shoving my face into her chest. "Hanging up on me and scaring me to death!"

"Can't breathe!" I gasped, "Hannah! I can't breathe!"

"You're lucky I'm not strangling you! I swear if you hang up on me again, I will break into that school and drag you out myself! You got that!"

I squeaked a nervous "yes" and Hannah finally let me go. Chitose stood motionless in the corner of my room.

"What are you looking at? Is someone here?" Hannah asked, following my gaze, but it looked like all she saw was my dresser.

"N—No." I said quickly.

That didn't stop Hannah from checking under my bed and opening my closet, all while Chitose's eyes followed her movements.

"When you're done killing each other, there's burgers downstairs," Ichirou said, standing by my door.

"I needed to see her." Hannah closed my closet door and left my room, but Ichirou stayed and kept his eyes on me.

"Ichirou," I started. "I—"

"Anything you want to tell me, personally?" he said, firmly.

I swallowed nervously. "A-Are you mad at me?"

"Let me think about it," he answered before leaving.

"A little tip on understanding people," Chitose spoke. "Never ask an angry person if they're angry."

•  ●  •

Ichirou, Hannah and I sat at the table, an awkward silence hung in the air. I wanted to say something to them—apologize or ask how their day was going, but my words stayed wedged in my throat.

After another tense moment of silence, Ichirou spoke first.

"So, I thought the point of giving you a phone was so we could contact you at any time. The last thing I expected you to do was hang up on Hannah and turn your phone off."

"I didn't turn it off!" I interrupted. "My phone died in school. I didn't get the chance to charge it until I was home."

Ichirou paused. "Alright, if it died, then why didn't you call us another way? Or called us sooner?"

I chewed the bottom of my lip. I didn't know what to tell them. I didn't know where to start. It was like speaking to Elizabeth on the phone again. All the stories and events tried to surface through me, wanting to be heard loud and clear.

"Runt, I get it. You don't want to tell us because you don't think we'd believe you. Right?"

I stared suspiciously at Ichirou.

"This may come as a shock to you, but we used to be teenagers, too. I've kept secrets before. But it never got to a point where it put my life in danger."

"I'm not in danger."

"Sleepwalking out of the house to Who-Knows-Where qualifies as 'dangerous.' Now, I get that your phone died, but where did you go after you hung up on Hannah?"

"I was in school!" I almost yelled. "Why don't you believe me?"

"Because someone from the school office called me, and asked if you were absent because you never showed up to your classes. So, where did you go?"

My stomach sank. My head hung low as I told them the truth. "I went to the assistant's lounge.

"Why?"

"I slept walked to school. I didn't think I could focus with that in mind. Mr. Turner told me I could stay in the lounge. I didn't know I was supposed to let someone in the office know."

Hannah interjected, "Mayu, you should have went to the office in the first place. This is serious, you could have gotten hurt. If you weren't in class, what were you doing in this lounge?"

"And are students supposed to be at an assistants lounge?" Ichirou added.

"They can be," I grumbled. I wracked my head for an explanation, but I decided to tell the truth.

"I wanted to clear my head and see if I could get help. But then the lockdown happened, and everyone panicked in the hallway. I got separated from Lutea and the other assistants." My words rippled as tears welled in my eyes. "...Aiden was hurt trying to help me, then Lutea... she was hurt too."

"Are they alright?"

"Aiden got a broken arm. And Lutea..." I choked up. It hurt remembering the details.

Hannah's hand caressed my back. "Why didn't you tell us?"

"I didn't think you would believe me. I didn't know where to start."

Ichirou said, gently, "Honestly, I'd prefer if you told us something crazy rather than keep it bottled up."

"Y-You won't be mad at me?"

"Runt, I was upset and worried about you. You scared us half to death. We were circling around the streets, looking for you."

"I'm sorry..."

"Look, let's put this behind us. I'm glad you're safe. But next time, if something is bothering you, please talk to us. And take your charger with you."

I sniffled, feeling the tension lift from our shoulders. "Okay."

After dinner and small talk, I went straight to my room. There, Chitose was lying on the floor. Her eyes were closed, and her hands rested behind her head. She looked like she was taking a nap. I

317

thought about bringing her a small dinner plate but remembered that she didn't eat regular food.

"Glad to hear everything went well," she said. "I would have phased down there if they didn't believe you."

I closed the door.

"That would have scared them, and you'd give yourself away as a Mystic."

"But they would have believed you if you told them the whole story." Chitose sat up, and her steely blue eyes locked on me.

"I thought it wasn't safe for Mystics to reveal themselves, yet. Weren't there people who still saw you as monsters?"

"But you're one too."

My chest tightened at her words.

"I can tell that your family cares about you, and I doubt they'll be afraid of you."

"They won't but..."

"So why keep it a secret?"

I slumped on the bed, leaned back and sighed deeply. "Ichirou and Hannah act like nothing bothers them, but they're always stressed out about something. Paying rent, going to school and work... looking after me. If I told them about the Mystic world and they believed me, they'd want to help me."

"Is that a bad thing?"

"What could they do about me changing? There's no medication that can treat it or MRIs to explain why it's happening. They can't do anything about it, which will only stress them out more. So, what's the point in telling them?"

Chitose answered when the door suddenly knocked.

"Runt, are you alright?" Ichirou called out.

"I'm fine!" I replied. Knowing Chitose was cloaked, I opened the door wide enough to meet Ichirou's curious stare.

"Were you on the phone?"

"N-No?"

"Who were are you talking to?"

"Myself," I answered. "You said you'd rather hear crazy, right?"

"Crazy, yes. But I could've sworn I heard someone in here."

"I didn't hear anything," I said, nervously. "Ichirou, would it be alright if I go to bed early?"

"I won't stop you, but are you sure you're feeling well?"

"Perfectly fine."

Ichirou lingered. "Hannah and I are going to lock the doors. Try to stay in bed this time, Runt. Maybe turn on your watch too."

"Not a runt."

"Sure thing, dwarf!"

I closed the door and listened to Ichirou's footsteps travel downstairs and fade to silence.

I heaved, pressing my back against the door. "That was close. Chitose, I thought no one can hear you when you're cloaked."

"What do you mean?" she asked, her head cocked to the side. "They're not supposed to."

•●•

That night, I changed into my nightwear and sat on my bed to discuss the plan with Chitose. We had to whisper since Hannah and Ichirou could have been awake. I had forgotten what Aiden told me about humans being able to see and hear the mystic world, but for now, I wanted to focus more on my sleepwalking.

"What's going to happen to me?" I asked.

Chitose sat crossed legged in me. "I will put you to sleep and look through your dreams to find whatever's controlling you."

"What happens when you find it?"

"I won't know yet. But I will do what I can to draw it out of you. If I find it."

"Will I wake up from it?"

"No, you won't," she said. "Once you're under my spell, nothing will wake you up until I release you. So, no pinching. No throwing water at you. No true love's kiss. And yes," she heaved. "I've been asked about that many times."

I smirked, but the thought of being trapped in a deep sleep sounded like a nightmare itself. "If you chase it out, and it somehow comes back, what then?"

Chitose shifted. "If it makes you feel safe, I can create a Dream Link between us."

"Dream Link?" I repeated.

She nodded. "We will be connected through your dreams. I'll know when you sleep, and your dreams will come to me as though they were my own. If you're sleepwalking, I can wake you up before you leave your bed."

I looked at Chitose, warily. "If you could do that, then why did you wait this long to tell me?"

Her expression softened and her gold eyes melted to a hazel brown. "Keep in mind, I'm still an ethereal being inside of a human

319

vessel. I can create a link with you, but if something happens to me like a severe injury or death," Chitose placed her hand on her chest. "I will immediately merge into you, and you'll become my new vessel. Given what's been going on, I doubt you want something else controlling you."

A hard lump welled in my throat. "There's no way around it?"

"This is the best I can do for you. I won't force a link on you if it makes you uncomfortable."

I thought it over, letting her words sink in so I fully understood what was happening. I considered turning on the alarm, but who's to say the Malus could make me sleep through it.

"You promise you'll wake me up?"

Chitose chuckled, softly. "If I didn't keep my word for every person who asked that, then half a city would be in the coma ward."

"Alright..." I said and let out a deep breath. "Let's do this."

"Make sure you're comfortable," she reminded.

I nearly forgot. I tucked myself under the blankets and my head sank against the pillow. I had to resist the urge to bring my calico plush close to me.

Chitose's eyes flickered at the plush on my nightstand. "I won't stop you."

I pulled my calico and held it close to my chest. My cheeks burned up. "So, what happens next? Do you chant something? Do I close my eyes?"

"No need."

Chitose's eyes flashed a brilliant white and a heaviness settled over my eyes. Everything went dark and my worrying thoughts drifted away.

# Change

**I woke up, eyes squinting at the sunlight** peeking through the blinds. I rolled to the side and reached lazily for my glasses. Half-dazed, my mind clung to the dream I had about a winter night. I patted my nightstand and felt a piece of folded paper sitting under my glasses. I lifted my head and picked up the note. Seeing Chitose's name written on it, I unfolded it and read the letter.

*"Nothing was there. But I made the link anyway. Sleep well."*

A smile creased my face, relieved that it was finally over. I glanced at the time on my watch and my tired eyes shot wide open. It was already eight o'clock, and my alarm hadn't gone off! I put my glasses on, leaped out of bed and scrambled to put on my school clothes. I snatched my backpack and phone and rushed downstairs, wondering why no one woke me up when I almost crashed into Ichirou.

"Whoa! What's the hurry, Runt?" he yelped. He was wearing a green apron over his sweater and a pair of jogging pants. "Why are you dressed up?"

"What do you mean?" I asked.

"You're in uniform. Why?"

"School?" I blinked, as though he were speaking in a different language. "Why didn't anyone wake me up? Who turned off my alarm?"

"I did," Ichirou said, heading to the kitchen. "It was going off, but you didn't wake up."

"That didn't worry you?"

"Runt, sometimes I sleep through my alarms, too. And I have six."

I stared at Ichirou, eyes furrowing. "What about school?"

"Carter's closed!" Hannah called from the couch. She was typing on her laptop while a show was playing on the TV. "It's been on the news since this morning."

Hannah explained what I should have known. The incident in the cafeteria left the school closed and as far as anyone knew, strong winds hurtling stones caused the windows to shatter. I'd heard of winds pushing cars and launching rocks at buildings, so that story sounded more believable than pixies attacking the school. No one knew when Carter would reopen, but Ichirou told me someone would call to let him know. It was a matter of waiting.

"Then why are you two here? Don't you have school too?" I asked.

"Holiday," Ichirou and Hannah replied, then returned to their routine as if it was another lazy day.

Aiden texted me; first to tell me about school being closed, then he asked how I was doing. I told him I was doing well, all things considered, then asked what he was doing on his day off.

'Chores,' he replied. 'You'd think my parents would give me a break since my arm's broken. They said I had another one.'

I snorted and replied, 'You'll pull through. You always do.'

I wished I had Sarah's number, or a way to contact her, and I wondered how she and the ghost were doing. I tried to talk to Mary, but she would say simple things like "ok" when I told her something, and "nothing" when I asked what she was doing. Eventually, I stopped texting her.

As my morning drifted into noon, I helped with the chores around the apartment, finished up any homework I had and spent the evening reading Witch Hazel in the living room. The algebra was complicated, and the chores exhausted me, but it was the closest to a normal day I had in a while, so I didn't complain about it.

Before I knew it, a week had gone by and I adjusted to the routine sleeping in, tidying up the apartment and talking to my friends, mainly Aiden and Elizabeth. Then, on Sunday night, the house phone rang and when I picked it up, I heard this robotic answering machine tell me that John Carter High School would reopen on Monday.

I wasn't thrilled about coming back to school, and neither were the students. A heavy tension hung in the air, and rumors about the incident flooded the hallway.

Miss Naiad's revision spell worked because I overheard students talking about seeing things thrown at the windows before it broke, and the tables being knocked over when everyone fled the cafeteria—just like what I heard on the news. The more I heard these stories in passing, the more it bothered me, knowing that it was a spell altering their memories.

Whether it was pixies or the wind, it was clear everyone was anxious, as if waiting for the next disaster to strike, including me. My head darted to paper fluttering on the wall. I rounded the corner with bated breath, and sighed in relief to see a regular hallway, and my body seized up to the sound of a girl sniffling behind me.

I pushed those thoughts down and hurried to class. I wanted to talk to Ethan, who looked just as tense as I felt. We jumped at the sound of static coming from the PA, then the principal's voice came through the speaker.

"This is not an emergency," he stated. "This is a statement regarding last week's incident..."

First, he thanked the teachers and assistants who helped during lockdown, and then his tone changed from gratitude to seething about the *other* incident. While Aiden and I were in the Ethereal Plane and the assistants were dealing with the pixies, stores and cars were vandalized by a small group of students from Carter—those released shortly after evacuation. The police had only caught a few, but the school was now under investigation to see if there was a link to us and the arsons and break-ins a month ago.

After that, I could only mouth the words, 'Are you serious?'

"As of now, there will be new rules!" he boomed.

Students could only head from one classroom to another, no detours, no bathroom breaks, or trips to the library. Teachers could only write passes for the assistants, and they couldn't stay out for long—five minutes at most. To punish us more, he announced that all after-school clubs were closed for the time being, and no one could see the guidance counselor to change classes.

"Why are we being punished for what others did?" I asked Ethan during class. "Why do they think we caused those attacks. You knew who did it."

"We do. Humans don't," he emphasized in a hushed tone. "They never caught the ones who did it, let alone identified them. To them, the case was never solved."

"There's nothing you can do about it?"

Ethan shook his head. "Usually, we let it die down over time, but thanks to a few wanna-be criminals, the police believe they have a lead."

I frowned, distraught about it all.

Ethan sighed, "These things happen, Mayu. Give it a month, things will be back to normal."

"Why do I get the feeling you might have jinxed us?"

He snorted softly and smirked, "Welcome to our world."

With her suspension ending a week ago, Sarah returned to class, though it seemed like I was the only one happy to see her back. Victoria sat at a different table away from us, and I caught her friends glowering at Sarah like she was the bully.

"How was your week?" I asked, wanting to start a conversation.

"Mostly boring," Sarah replied. "I watched TV and slept throughout the day" Her attention shifted to the empty seat beside me. "...what happened to Mary?"

"She might have taken the extra day off. She's done it before." I glanced at the textbook, my hand tapped anxiously on the pages as I remembered the messages Mary never responded to. I hope she was alright.

"Miss Naiad told me she changed her memories," Sarah said.

I looked up. Sarah cast a cautious glance at Victoria's table.

"She doesn't know what really happened."

"Only the part with the ceiling," I said. "But she's not going to bother you anymore. Apparently getting beaten up by the person you bullied sours your reputation."

"I appreciate it." Her eyes returned to her journal.

I ruffled my hair and kneaded the pen absentmindedly.

"Sarah," I called. "Would you like to have my phone number? All week I was wondering what you were up to, and I'd like to hang out outside of school one day."

"Oh," she sounded shocked. Her cheeks reddened. "I'd like to but can't use phones. It's something to do with ghosts interfering with electricity. You'll only hear static on my end."

"Can you text?"

Her shoulders relaxed and she smiled, softly. "I prefer that over talking."

The rest of the day was a constant shift between tense and relaxed. Upon seeing the steps, I froze, remembering Lutea's cracked, lifeless body on the stairs. I spun around and took another route to class, even if it would have made me late. Math came and went with no issue and there was not much to do in Gym besides volleyball. Dodgeball was banned and Mary wasn't there. I texted her during lunch and started to get worried when I checked my phone after Gym, and she never replied. My heart thundered with worry, but I told myself she was fine.

I stopped in front of the art room, fighting back the tears when I saw Lutea's empty chair. Teier was substituting for her. Everyone in class knew she was hurt during the lockdown. Teier told them she fell down the stairs and broke her leg. My stomach churned at the memory.

Teier assured us she would be back and suggested we make a get-well card for her. My classmates pitched in, drawing pictures, writing wishes for her recovery and signing the card. Teier was nice, and he got along with everybody, but art class wasn't the same without her.

Mary came to class the next day, but she acted like she never saw my messages. When I asked, she told me she was "busy at home" and didn't have time to look at her phone. She didn't talk about what she did and wasn't in the mood to talk in class.

Sighing, I spoke to Sarah and Mary's eyes stayed on the book in her hand. I continued writing and talking to Sarah until a stinging pain throbbed behind my eyes.

"Are you alright?" Sarah asked.

"I think so." I took off my glasses and rubbed my temples. My vision cleared and blurred. No aura crept around me, and my thoughts didn't fade. "I'll be right back."

I went to Mr. Baryon and asked if I could use the bathroom. The new rules were still in place, the principal made sure to remind us over the PA. But the classroom wasn't too far from the bathroom. Mr. Baryon wrote a hall pass for me and I sped into the girl's bathroom, holding my breath long enough to wash my hands. I turned the faucet off, when an icy breath brushed against my ears. "*She's mad at you.*"

I gasped, whipping around to see no one. The ghost's voice returned, creeping around me like mist. "*I'd watch my back with Mary if I were you. Sarah thought you deserved to know.*"

"What makes you say that?" I asked but the chills had vanished. The bell rang, signaling the end of class and with no time to find Mary or talk to Sarah I hurried to algebra.

That day, we had to turn in our binders to be graded for the semester. There was a bin on Mrs. Bean's desk, half full of binders, and I added mine to the pile. I ignored Mrs. Bean's glare and took my seat. As I sat next to Aiden, I noticed star and heart shaped stickers decorating his cast, and the words "Get well soon," scribbled around them.

"Your sister?" I guessed.

He grinned. "Natia got a little carried away with her sticker." Aiden lifted his arm, showing more stickers covering his cast. "They glow in the dark too."

"It's cute."

The awkward silence was interrupted when Mrs. Bean asked Mr. Turner to bring her printing paper from the lounge. In a reluctant voice, he reminded her about the new rules. I heard what sounded like a pen scratching across a piece of paper, then I glanced over my shoulder to see Mr. Turner leave the room. I knew she wanted to get rid of him because she never needed printing paper for class.

"So, are we not going to talk about this?" Aiden whispered.

I turned to him, static buzzed in my ears.

"About what?"

"I heard what happened to Lutea. I'm sorry."

"It wasn't your fault."

"It wasn't yours either."

"That pixie tried to attack me, but it got her instead. All of them were after me and she got hurt, like you."

"I've had worse. Have you spoken to someone?"

"Aiden, I just want to have normal day for once."

"Hard to do that, don't you think?"

I opened my book, ready to do next month's assignment and my big blue binder slammed on top of my notebook. I jumped, letting out a startled yelp.

Mrs. Bean's hovered over my desk with her beady eyes locked on me.

"This isn't some social group for you to talk," she sneered. "I want to see you finish the work in your binder. It's an important part of your grade."

"I did every assignment," I said in protest. I finished all of them during the week-long break.

Her nose wrinkled. "Check again. You missed assignments from when you were absent. Twice."

"I already did those!"

"I don't want to hear it. Finish them all or fail." Mrs. Bean straightened her back and returned to her desk. But before she could sit, the buzzing light flickered off.

"Again!" She groaned. "What is wrong with these lights?"

The pressure in my head lessened and I sighed in relief. "Thanks," I muttered to Aiden.

He raised his brow and whispered. "That wasn't me."

Mrs. Bean pulled up the blinds and sunlight poured into the room, stinging my eyes. Mrs. Bean simply barked at us to continue our work. She grumbled under her breath, "...shouldn't take a man this long to bring paper..."

I guess the gym teachers wanted to try something new. A badminton court occupied a small area in the gym, next to the volleyball net. I wasn't bad at it, and I saw Mary at the court, talking to one of the juniors. She was smiling and seemed happy around them. I jogged to the team and asked if I could join. Mary's expression melted into a strange grimace.

"I'm sorry, there aren't any more rackets," she said. "You can join next time."

*Next time*, I thought. *Not the next game?*

"Can I join one of the teams?"

"Sorry, we're trying to keep the numbers even."

I stood beside the net and watched Mary play with the other members. After a couple rounds, I drifted to the volleyball section and played with Becky-Tran and Damien. My ears twitched when I heard Mary's laughter leap from the badminton net.

*She's mad at you.* Those words stuck to me so much that after the bell rang, I decided to talk to Mary. I wanted to hear it from her and not from a ghost. I hurried out of gym and found her in the hallway with her friend, Katie.

Katie peered over her shoulder, and her eyes thinned into a nasty scowl. "Don't look now, but your stalker is back."

I stopped dead in my tracks. *Stalker?*

Mary heaved. "I don't feel like talking to her."

Shock coursed through my legs. Is she talking about me? I wanted to run over to Mary, ask her what she meant. Why did Katie call me a stalker? But would following them make it worse? I turned and ran in the other direction.

• ● •

Friday, the principal announced the last day to change classes, and I made sure I was one of the first students to meet my guidance counselor. I sat in a closet space of an office in front of a tired woman with a red scrunchy tangled in her bushy black hair. Her name was hardly readable on the worn-out plaque at the edge of her desk.

"What classes would you like to switch from?" she asked dully.

"Mrs. Bean's." I started. I felt my phone buzz in my pocket. I took a quick glance and saw it was Aiden asking where I was.

"Something important?" the guidance counselor said.

"No ma'am." I closed the phone and tucked it in my pocket.

"And whose class would you like to switch to?"

I forgot the other teacher's name. Then I remembered what Mr. Turner had told me about him. "He has a name that's hard to pronounce."

My phone buzzed once more.

Pursing her lips, the guidance counselor typed the name. The clattering keyboards were interrupted by my phone buzzing again. I wheezed out a soft apology and checked the phone, seeing Aiden's name on the screen again. I looked back at the guidance counselor, who continued her typing.

"I'm sorry, but his class is already full," she finally said.

My stomach dropped. "What does that mean?"

"Exactly what I said. He has too many students in his class as it is. I can't let you in."

My phone buzzed again, and this time, I yanked it out of my pocket and stuffed it in my backpack.

"Maybe you should turn that off," she insisted.

"Isn't there some way to fit me in? Or another math teacher?"

"The only one open teaches pre-calculus. Why do you want to transfer out of Mrs. Bean's class?"

"She's horrible! She put me in the back of class so I couldn't see the board. She yells at me every time I talk—"

She interrupted me. "Are you allowed to speak in her class?"

"No, but she never yells at the kids who do. She fails me all the time, even my answers are right."

"Mm-hm," she nodded. "Have you been seeing a tutor?"

"Yes!" I tried not to raise my voice. "Mr. Turner—Mrs. Bean's assistant. He helps me with my homework, and she still gives me low grades."

"Did she ever tell you why?"

"She always says it's because I wasn't specific on my work, or I missed a day in class."

"Why did you miss a day?"

"Does that matter?" I snapped.

"Yes, it does," she said, her tone sharpened. "I see she marked a week off due to a medical emergency, but it looks like you missed three more days." She took her attention away from the computer. "Mayu, is it possible she's hard on everybody? Most kids I meet say she's a hard worker but not biased."

I knew Mrs. Bean was no "good teacher." Especially when mystics couldn't stand her.

"I just... I don't want to be there anymore."

"Listen, I know you don't want to hear this, but not all teachers you meet will be nice. Some people try to avoid hardships and find an easy way out of life, but that's not how the world works. There are college professors like her who are hard on students are you going to quit every time a teacher does something you don't like?"

My track coach was nicer than Mrs. Bean, and she made me do ten laps around the field for being late. Every word out of Mrs. Bean's mouth was something mean. Everything she did was out of spite.

"You have her class this afternoon. Does she know you're here?"

I didn't want to go, yet. I wanted to stay and convince her to let me switch. Or ask her why the other algebra class was too full. In the end, all I could say was nothing to the counselor as I looked up at her.

"I think you need to go there now."

Nothing felt real anymore. I was going to be stuck with Mrs. Bean, getting nothing but bad grades and mean stares all year. I told myself, It's only for a year. That I wouldn't have her forever. Except the three months I endured in her class so far felt like a year already.

Mrs. Bean was at the door when she noticed me and stopped me before I could enter her room.

"You're over ten minutes late," she glowered.

I didn't want to say, "I'm sorry" but my apology slipped out like a bad habit.

Her lips smacked. "You're like your brother. He thought he could show up and leave when he felt like it, too. I bet he told you he used to do that."

"Ichirou doesn't talk about you."

"I don't care what your brother has to say about me." She closed the door behind her, and her voice hardened. "I don't know what's going on between you and Cedric but he's my assistant, not yours. Aiden is my student, not your servant."

"Aiden's a friend," I grumbled out. "And Mr. Turner's a student assi—"

"I don't want to hear it," she cut me off, sharply. "I am the teacher. I'm your superior. I'm above you and you're just a student. Even if you go to the principal or administration, they'll believe me before they hear you out. So, don't act like the world revolves around you." She pulled the door open. "And don't think you can cry to Cedric. He's not in class today."

Every fiber of me screamed to walk away, but I didn't. I will never understand why I did it. I stepped inside, wiping my tears and saw the desks rearranged in the room. Instead of two desks close together, they were spread apart and reassigned to different students. We were only a row apart, but it felt like Aiden was miles away.

After school, I walked down the sidewalk, passing the other students, lost in thought. I wasn't like them. I wasn't one of them. I wasn't human, but I wasn't like the assistants either. What did they call me?

*An anomaly*

Even among the mystics, I was still the weird one. Who was I to think that I could fit in with them when they didn't want me? Elizabeth and her school only knew about me because of an accident. I was only important because I had to be watched. So, I wouldn't cause any more problems.

I stopped walking to clean the tears off my glasses. I knew I shouldn't have thoughts like that. I should have thought of the good that happened. I met Lutea, whom I considered my friend. She had been kind enough to tell me about a world I was afraid of.

She also got hurt because of me.

A familiar mew drew me to the complex. Tuna was at the sliding door, meowing and pawing hungrily on the screen.

I sniffled and approached her. "Long time no see, Tuna," I called, gently.

She spun around, her fur bristled and her back arched in the air. I stopped, my brow came together with worry. I looked around for a stray dog or Ichirou, but it was just me. I moved closer, and she puffed up and hissed at me.

"What's wrong?"

I stepped closer and Tuna hissed. Her growls were loud and harsh.

"Tuna, it's me. What's wrong with you?"

I held my hand, and, in a blink of an eye, Tuna lunged at me. Pain pricked my hand and teeth broke through the skin. I shrieked and Tuna darted off into the bushes. I staggered to my feet and ran for the door. It opened as Hannah stepped out, and I crashed into her, sobbing at the pain.

"She's never done this to me."

I knew cats had sharp claws and teeth, but I never thought a little bite could hurt so much. I never thought my sweet little cat would hurt me.

"Cats don't attack for no reason. Maybe she's sick or saw something that frightened her." Hannah said. She pulled a medical kit and a bottle of peroxide from the bathroom medicine cabinet.

"This might sting a bit." Hannah dabbed the cotton on my hand. The peroxide, cold at first, burned into the open wound.

"Ow!"

"I told you it was going to sting." Hannah pulled the cotton ball away. "You know we have to tell Ichirou about this? We don't want you getting hurt again."

I sulked at my band aid on my hand, thinking about my day.

"Looks like you've had a rough day before the cat," Hannah said.

"Kind of..."

She mustered a small smile. "Good thing I stayed home for an interview, then. Makes quitting that job more worth it."

She stuck the band aid over the scratches, but my gaze lingered.

"Hannah is—was your manager always mean to you?"

"Not always. Though it seemed like he came to work every day with a chip on his shoulder." Hannah leaned against the tub, shoulders relaxed. "Bad customers I can handle. They leave you alone once they get their food; it's different when your boss is there all day, looking for reasons to yell at you."

"Why? Why is everyone so mean to each other?"

Her features softened and gave a resigned sigh. "There are people who believe they're more important, superior or better than others and expect the world to cater to them. Sometimes the world does, and they lash out when it doesn't. If they think they have something over you—power, money, popularity—they'll hurt you for not bending to their whim."

"So... people are like Mrs. Bean."

"Wanna talk about it elsewhere?"

I nodded slightly. We went to Hannah's room, and I sat on her bed. She went to the kitchen and brought me a glass of water. Between sips, I told her what happened with the guidance counselor and Mrs. Bean.

Hannah scoffed under her breath. "She hadn't changed one bit. Her or that guidance counselor."

"I don't get it. Why does she hate me so much?" I asked and I realized something.

Mrs. Bean was mean to me when she learned I was Ichirou's sister. She assumed Ichirou did my homework or tried to find some way to smear my brother's name. Then it was what she said about him today.

"Hannah," I continued, looking up at her. "Why does she hate Ichirou? He only told me she was a difficult teacher, but there's more to it. Isn't it?"

Hannah sat back in her chair, tucking her knee beneath her chin. "It's not something Ichirou likes to bring up or remember."

"More like he doesn't want to remember high school at all."

"Can't say I blame him. Ichirou was a quiet kid. Never bothered anyone and just wanted to be left alone. But the other kids would pick on him, no matter how much he tried to avoid them. They broke his glasses, ripped his sketchbook apart, and beat him up when he fought back. Then he'd come home to parents who'd yell at him, like it was his fault."

Mystic Rising

I squirmed in place. The memories bubbled back to me of Ichirou coming home with bruises on his face and blood trickling down his nose. Our parents would argue with him about getting into fights again. I never liked hearing them shout, so I would hide in my room and try to block it out.

"What does Mrs. Bean have to do with it?"

"She made it worse. Despite the beating and bullying, your brother became one of the smartest students at school, outshining Mrs. Bean's so-called 'star students.' That's how he got her attention.

She claimed praising Ichirou for his grades discouraged the other classmates, so she took it upon herself to fail him for the smallest reasons, from writing his answers on a separate page, to writing in pen instead of a pencil. When he couldn't take it, Ichirou and I snuck into the library and did our work according to her syllabus, thinking we could turn it in when we felt like going back."

"The librarian didn't mind?"

"Nah. The old man understood our situation. If we were quiet, he didn't care. But one day, Mrs. Bean saw us in the library. Next thing we knew it, the former principal banned students from going to the library unless we were with a class. Ichirou had no choice but to go back to Mrs. Bean. He showed her the finished work, proving he wasn't 'skipping to be lazy' but she failed him and made him redo all the assignments."

"How's that fair?"

"'Life isn't fair,'" Hannah grumbled nasally, sounding almost like Mrs. Bean. "Words she'd loved to say. Life is hard enough as it is, but she had to make a point of how 'nothing ever goes your way.'"

Hannah let out a deep breath. "Months later, we had to take an important pre-college exam where the higher you scored, the more eligible you'd be for those high-profile universities. Mrs. Bean bragged about how her favorite students were going to Ivy League schools, or something. But Ichirou got the highest score the school had in years. It was supposed to be something to celebrate until Mrs. Bean reported him for cheating and with no evidence to prove it, Ichirou's test score changed to a zero."

"Are you serious?!" I spat, shocked and angered.

"And the worst part? If you cheat, it's on record and you won't be able to enroll in any college. Between the fights, his parents and his health...he broke down in front of me."

"Ichirou never told me."

333

Hannah rolled her shoulders. "I know. It was me and my parents who knew. We went with him to the department of education to clear things up, and Ichirou was able to retake the exam. He scored lower than the first time. Passable, but no Ivy League would enroll him."

"And nothing happened to Mrs. Bean," I guessed.

"She treated the whole incident like it was no big deal, called it 'karma' or something. She never knew he retook the exam, so when he came to class, I'll never forget what she said to him: 'You always act like you're better than everyone. Maybe now, you'll know what it's like to fail.'"

My eyes widened.

"She said that so confidently, and you know what, she deserved what came next. Ichirou blew up at Mrs. Bean. He called her everything he could think of, including *a miserable bitch who hates anyone smarter than her.* He stormed out before Mrs. Bean could get a word in. I followed him to the hall and that was when he fainted."

"His lungs collapsed."

"All of that stress for months finally took its toll on him. After he recovered, the first thing he did was change classes. I'll always remember how angry Mrs. Bean looked when he returned to school. She'd glare at Ichirou from afar, but he never engaged with her. Not once did he ever look back at Carter until now."

I sat back to take in the entire story. "If Ichirou didn't like that school, why did he enroll me there?"

Hannah looked at me, sympathetically. "We heard people from college say Carter changed for the better when they hired assistants. He had hope you wouldn't have to go through the same mess we went through."

●

Hannah let me stay in her room to rest. I wasn't in the mood to talk to Elizabeth or answer Aiden's texts yet. My mind replayed the day Ichirou's lungs collapsed. I was crying by his bed, scared that I was going to lose my only brother. I cried when we were home, and our parents argued with him for yelling at a teacher. I cried for him not to leave when he stormed out of the house and never came back.

Sometime later, Ichirou came home from work. Hannah must have told him about Tuna scratching me because the instant he walked through the door, he wanted to check on my hand.

"See, this is why I don't like cats," he mumbled.

He asked if I could take off one of the bandages to see how bad the scratches were. As I did, I stared at the grey strands mixed with his hair and the dark circles under his eyes.

"Runt, what's wrong?"

I wiped away the tears. "Why didn't you tell me about Mrs. Bean?"

"What do you mean?"

"I told her what happened," Hannah said. "Everything she did."

I looked at Ichirou and I saw the regret in his eyes. "I didn't think she was still at the school. And when you told me you had her, I assumed she would have moved on by now."

"Apparently she hadn't," I muttered.

I asked myself why I never showed him my graded work, the ones where Mrs. Bean scrawled over the paper. My mind was so wrapped up in the mystic side of my school, it was hard to pay attention to the 'normal' side.

"I'm going to have a talk with her," he said.

"You're going to cuss her out again?" Hannah asked.

"I can't make promises. But first, the cat." He held my hand, looking at the cut. "Where is it? Where did she scratch you?"

"On my hand." I looked down, and my gut twisted. The deep scratch on my hand healed on its own, leaving no scar to prove it was there.

Hannah looked; her eyes narrowed. "That's weird. It was there a few hours ago!"

Ichirou guessed, "Maybe the cat didn't scratch hard enough. It could have been a skin tear."

"Yeah, that must be it," I said, still staring at my healed hand and wrist. "It was just a scratch..."

That evening, I had finished showering and toweled off when I noticed my hair was longer than usual, reaching past my shoulders.

I guess it was time to get another haircut, I thought.

I wrapped myself up, then checked my reflection, wiping the steam off the mirror. My eyes slowly widened as I took in every detail of my face, seeing myself almost clearly like I was wearing my glasses.

But they were in my bedroom.

I changed into my night wear and hurried to my room. I put my glasses on and jerked back when the lens distorted my vision. I took them off and my eyesight cleared up. It didn't last long as the edges of the shelves blurred and the small words in my notebook turned fuzzy.

I set my glasses on my nightstand. Tuna growled at me the way the dogs growled at Lutea and Chitose. She avoided Elizabeth just like the stingrays did. My cat was afraid of me because she couldn't recognize me. Because I was changing.

My mind went in circles. Should I tell Ichirou and Hannah about the mystics or call Ms. Hudson for advice. She said my change was subtle, but what was I changing into. No answer or suggestions came. I pushed the thought down, hoping I could sleep on it. But then a small voice, my voice chimed mockingly in my ears. *'how long are you going to keep up with this act?'*

# Guidance

*It's going to be okay*, I thought, going to school Monday morning. My change was normal. It happens to hybrids. I won't sprout extra limbs or turn into a beast in the middle of class. If I did, Ethan was there to help. The assistants could help. As long as I stayed calm, I could control my powers. So, it's going to be okay. Ichirou called the school before we left the apartment. He was going to talk to Mrs. Bean, the principal, and Mr. Turner. Maybe I could finally change classes. So, it's going to be okay.

Sarah and I were in class, talking about our weekend when Mary caught my line of sight. She sat at a different table in class, treating me as if I didn't exist. I decided I was going to talk to her in person, since she never answered my calls or texts anyway. At the sound of the bell, I hastily slid my notebook in my backpack, my eyes fixed on Mary as she hurried out of class.

"Don't do it," Sarah warned. Her eyes darkened with an eerie focus. Her voice was low and stern, making my skin crawl. "She's not going to listen to you."

Chills trace down my spine. "I have to know what's going on with her."

I threw my backpack over my shoulders and stepped into the hallway. I passed through the students and found Mary before she reached the second floor.

"Mary!" I called. She flinched, then marched forward. I caught up with her and asked, "Mary, what's going on?"

"You tell me," she snapped, stomping ahead.

Her sharp voice weakened my pace, but I hurried to her side, trying to meet her eyes.

"Where did that come from?"

She didn't answer.

"What happened? You've been ignoring me for a week, pretending I'm not here."

"Oh, am I supposed to feel sorry when it happens to you?"

I was speechless at first. "When have I ignored you?"

"All the time!" Mary shouted, whirling back. A few students turned their heads to us. "You always choose them over me. If it's not Lutea, Damien, or that club meeting, it's your preppy rich friend who doesn't go to this school!"

"What?" I shrieked, heat flared in my chest. "I've always helped you and went to Theatre Club with you. Ever since Friday when you left me at school, you haven't even tried to talk to me."

"Because I only matter to you when you don't have anyone else!" she burst. My chest lurched and static cut through my ears. "You can't cherry pick who you want to hang out with, and pretend others don't exist. That's not what friends do!"

My legs shook and the words wedged themselves in my throat. "I'm not—I didn't mean to..."

Mary tore her glassy eyes away and wiped her face with her sleeve. "I don't want to hear it. I can't deal with you anymore..."

She pushed through the crowd of onlookers. As the late bell rang, I forced myself to move. I had to move away from the students staring at me. Away from the whispers snaking into my ears. I rushed to the stairs and the sight of Lutea's body on the ground returned, her eyes staring up at the ceiling.

"Stop it, stop it, stop it," I hissed, holding my head.

I circled back and took another route as students hurried into their classrooms. My mind was in a daze.

"It's going to be okay," I whispered, taking my glasses off to wipe the tears away. "...It's going to be okay..."

I put my glasses back on and my first clear vision was the library back doors. I reeled back and headed for the stairs, pushing down the urge to turn back. Before I knew it, Mrs. Bean was at the door, glaring at me.

A hard lump welled in my throat.

"Got a call this morning," she seethed. "Have a meeting scheduled with your brother this evening."

"Okay," I said, not seeing why she was pointing out the obvious. I walked ahead, but Mrs. Bean stepped in front of the door, blocking my way.

She crossed her arms. "What did you tell him?"

"Everything."

"So, only what you want him to hear."

I clenched my fists. "What's your problem with me, anyway?"

Mrs. Bean jerked back, her hand splayed across her chest.

"Excuse you? I don't like the tone you're taking with me. I don't have a problem. You're the one who doesn't turn in any work, you skip my classes, you show up late and disrupt my students. I swear it must be a family thing to act so entitled!"

My heart pounded. "I always turn in my work. Look through my binder. You'll see I did every stupid paper you throw at me!"

"Is that what you told your brother, I'm 'throwing' things now?" Mrs. Bean mocked. "You didn't turn in your binder, so you're lying to cover it?"

"What are you talking about?"

I peered over her shoulder. My binder laid my desk, looking flatter than I remember. A trash can by Mrs. Bean's desk was stuffed with balled-up papers. My handwriting was too small to see it, but I recognized Mr. Turner's signature on one of the crumpled papers.

She couldn't have...

Mrs. Bean followed my gaze, then stepped in front of my line of sight. "It was already empty. Don't start making up lies now!"

"You're the one that's lying!" I shouted. My pulse raced and darkness crept into the corner of my eyes. "How can you call me entitled when you fail me for the smallest reasons and throwing away my work? How is that fair!?"

"Guess no one ever told you: Life isn't fair." Mrs. Bean turned her back on me, like Mary had, as if nothing mattered.

I balled my fists and the next words erupted down the hallway. "Who are you to decide that, you miserable *bitch*!"

Mrs. Bean became rigid, and her small black eyes rolled to me. "What did you say to me?" she seethed.

But I didn't care. I was sick of seeing her face, hearing her voice, and the way she treated me.

"I've done nothing to you, so why do you hate me? Because Ichirou's my brother? What did he ever do to you? What have I done to deserve this? I don't even know you!" I inhaled sharply and wiped away the tears. My voice cracked. "You don't know a damn thing about me..."

I stormed off and Mrs. Bean barked threats of suspending me or expelling me from school. I made it down the hall when she shouted at the top of her lungs that I had failed her class for the entire year, and never allowed back. For once, I agreed with her. Anywhere was better than being with her.

I took sharp breaths going downstairs, rubbing my shoulders for comfort. I wished desperately for someone to stand by me, for a comforting voice to tell me, "It's going to be alright." But when I thought of my friends, I remembered Aiden's broken arm. Lutea on the floor. Then Mary's words came back to me. *'You only want friends when it matters to you...'*

I was in front of the library's back doors again, and this time, I didn't turn away. I gripped the handle and pulled it open. All I could think about was Erehwon. Its labyrinth of trees, clear rushing water and deep blue sky. Free from prying eyes and gossip in the air. No Mary. No Mrs. Bean. There was a shred of hope that I might see Elizabeth again. I needed to talk to her, to tell her everything.

I reached the corner and raced down the old, dusty aisle, and stopped. There was no Min or a desk, and no mystical door waiting for me. My legs gave out and I sank onto the floor, as if my body were injected with lead.

I begged in tears for the door to appear. For the other world to take me away. Amid the watery vision, thin whips of light rose out of my tightening hands, tearing black lines onto the walls. My throat closed, fire coursed through me and in one anguished cry, the light tore the walls apart.

· ● ·

The ground moved through the dull grey halls. A shining light drifted between my eyes and pulled back as strangers in white leaned toward me. I fought to scream, but my throat was weak. I tried to move and get up, but my limbs stayed on the mattress beneath me. The strangers faded away and familiar faces appeared before me. Dr. Sanders, Ichirou and Hannah. I thought I may have seen Elizabeth and my parents, too.

Voices came and went. I only remembered what Dr. Sanders and Ichirou talked about; my sleepwalking, dazing off, and losing track of time. The clearer their words were, the more they sank into my thoughts. "Pulled out of school on medical leave."

· ● ·

The day I came home from the hospital, Ichirou explained what happened to me. The librarian found me on the floor, having another grand mal seizure after the power in the school went out again. It was suspected the lights going out suddenly caused my seizures.

The librarian called the ambulance, and I was in the hospital for two nights, which shocked me more because it felt like I was going in and out for a few hours. Some things I saw and heard turned out to be real, like our parents and Elizabeth visiting me, Dr. Sanders talking to Ichirou.

"It's going to be for a couple of weeks," Ichirou said when I asked about my medical leave. He told me my absence wouldn't affect my grades, and he spoke with Mrs. Bean. I think he was trying to cheer me up, telling me changes were happening in the school. So, until I could go back, I should relax.

For the next two mornings, I passed the time reading and watching TV, grateful that I didn't have to spend my break at the hospital. Aiden and Sarah would text me when they could, and I spoke to Elizabeth in the afternoon. Though it felt nice to talk to my friends, my heart ached at seeing Mary's old messages. It took a few days to work up the courage and prep talk from Hannah before I finally deleted Mary's number.

On a lazy Thursday morning, I lazed in bed, with the window open, breathing in the crisp air of late autumn. My mind drifted to a dream of sounds, chirping birds, brushing leaves, talking from a TV, then loud tapping against the sliding door.

It must have been the neighbor again. I pulled the blanket over my ears and tried to sleep. I awoke to footsteps bounding upstairs, then my bedroom door swung open.

"Didn't know you were sleeping," said Ichirou.

I groaned and pushed myself up. "I was..."

"I guess you weren't expecting company, then."

I stared at him, and my brows knitted together. "What?"

"One of your friends stopped by to see you. She said her name's Lutea."

Lost for words, I fumbled out of bed and snatched my glasses off the nightstand, my legs were tangled in the blanket

"Careful!" Ichirou warned.

He was ahead of me, but I hurried past him on our way downstairs. It was like stepping into a dream. As I turned the corner, I saw Hannah first at the door, talking to Lutea—her voice full of life and her eyes lit up when she noticed me. I tackled her in an embrace, the stoney impact finally convinced me she was alive and well.

"Missed me that much, huh?" Lutea whispered, hugging me back.

"You have no idea." I pulled away and a faded white line hidden behind her bangs caught my attention.

"Don't knock her over!" Hannah teased. "She doesn't need to see the doctor twice!"

"Huh?"

"Remember," Lutea said. "I twisted my ankle and hit my head falling down the stairs."

At first, I was confused but quickly realized it was a made-up story to cover the pixie attack.

"Right!" I said, playing along. "How are you feeling?"

"As you can see, I'm walking again and my head's all patched up, too!" She stepped back and spread her arms. "I heard you were taking time off school. Are you doing well?"

"I am now. Was my seizure that bad?"

"Not everyday someone at school gets carted into an ambulance and, from what I heard, you've got a reputation for yelling at a particular teacher..."

Hannah scoffed, "She had it coming!"

"Trust me if she hadn't done it, I would," Ichirou said, ruffling my hair. "Are you staying here for the day?"

"No," Lutea replied. "I'm running errands with my dad, and we happened to pass by the area. Since we're out of school for the time being, would it be okay if Mayu came along?"

I spun around to Ichirou. "Can I go?" I begged. "Please? I'll have my phone with me! I'll take the charger too!"

Ichirou turned to Hannah.

"She's on medical leave, not grounded." Hannah pointed out. "But first, I'd like to exchange numbers."

"I have no problem with that," said Lutea.

"And be home by five and make sure you'll call us, right?" Ichirou added.

"I will!" I beamed.

I raced to my room to change clothes, then swiped my phone and charger from the nightstand. I was in such a hurry to leave I almost left Lutea behind! On our way out, I shuddered from the breeze and zipped up my jacket. As I did, my eyes wandered to the scar crossed over Lutea's markings.

"How is your head doing?" I asked, lowering my voice.

"Not too bad," she whispered. "I'm still being repaired, so I won't be back in school until next year. I can't believe a pixie of all things took me down."

"What did you expect?"

"Something a little more dignified than that."

I chewed the bottom on my lip and asked, "Did it hurt?"

Lutea said with a smirk, "I can't feel pain, remember?"

She stopped in front of a wide, green jeep parked outside of the complex. The thick black wheels came up to my shoulder. With the window open, I got a good look at Lutea's "dad" in the driver's seat.

"Ready to go?" Tora's striking eyes beamed at me. Figures, a massive man (or an orc) would have a bigger car.

"Is she coming too?"

"Her brother said it was okay." Lutea opened the door and I climbed into a soft beige seat. The car slumped down a little when Lutea hoisted herself inside, sitting next to me.

"What have you been up since stay?" she asked.

"Not much," I answered. "My doctor didn't want me to do anything that would stress me out, so I'm giving school and mystic life a break."

"Such a trivial way to speak about us," Tora said in a deep, booming voice. "Especially since you're a hybrid."

"Sorry..." I squeaked.

"To be fair," Lutea chimed in. "You went through a lot. At the very least, you earned some time to wind down, right?"

I chewed my lower lip. "You're not mad at me?"

"What for?"

"It was my fault you were hit by the pixie."

Lutea scratched her head. "You'd prefer it hit you, instead?"

"No, I..." I paused to take a breath. "I always feels like I made things worse by being around. You get hit by arrows, thrown into a wall, struck by a pixie. Maybe... if I was out of the way, I won't mess things up for you."

Lutea chuckled warmly, "We're not perfect. We mess up and make mistakes all the time—once, I used to work at a summer camp and played baseball with some eight-year-olds. I didn't see the ball in time, and it smashed into my face."

I stared at her stunned.

"I tried to laugh it off and told the kids I had terribly dry skin. Though I was scared I blew my cover."

"Did you?"

"I don't think so. The next day they gave me a ton of lotion and face cream, and they were more careful with passing the ball to each other.

Point is, mistakes happen," she continued. "All that matters is learning from it to better yourself. Tora learned to use stronger material when he fixed me."

Tora grunted.

"Thanks…" I leaned back and watched the houses pass by as the Jeep merged into the highway. "… how far is your house, Lutea?"

"*Our* house," Tora corrected, sounding more relaxed. "As for distance, you rather take the long way, or the shortcut?"

"Shortcut," I said, nervously. I didn't miss the small, crooked grin on Tora's face.

The engine revved, and my back hit the seat when the Jeep sped down the road. In a single, startling jolt, cars and trucks tore into clusters of green and orange leaves. The gliding Jeep bumped up and down on an uneven path tucked between vast stretches of green fields, dotted with lazing cows and galloping horses.

My voice cracked with excitement. "How did you do that?"

"Drifting!" Lutea cackled. "Much easier to make than gates!"

The Jeep slowed in front of the only house around for miles, shrouded by trees. It was a cozy white ranch holding up a massive black roof and smoke trailing out of its chimney. I stepped out and took in the rich, leafy air. The wind rustled through the trees and water trickled nearby.

Lutea leaped out of the Jeep, making it bounce up. "Hope you don't mind the place. It still needs a tune up for the season."

"I like it here." I said. Before I forgot, I pulled out my phone to text Ichirou. I hit send, though an hourglass appeared next to the message. I checked the phone for a signal, and it only had one bar.

"Connections are pretty spotty…"

"The signal is stronger in the house." Lutea nodded to the front door.

She hiked up the steps and the wood groaned under her feet. I followed and noticed black scorches and claw marks raked across the porch. The damage trailed off to a mound of rigid scales piled resting on the far side of the porch.

I leaned in to take a closer look and with my feet on the creaking wood, a pair of dark, shiny eyes flicked open. The mound shifted and unfurled. Two scaly arms stretched out and its claws scraped against the porch. A long head crowned with two curved horns rose, and it's mouth peeled back to reveal rows of sharpened teeth.

Mystic Rising

It was a dragon.

My breath hitched. I crept back and a low snarl rippled from its throat as its back arched toward the ceiling. My mind jolted to Tuna, who had done the same thing before she attacked me.

"Don't run," Lutea whispered, stepping in between me and the dragon. "Wren doesn't know who you are. Running will trigger her to chase you."

I gulped.

Lutea jerked forward, startling the dragon before she tackled it. I jumped back, my hand covering my mouth in shock as Lutea stroked the dragon's neck. Its claws clasped my friend's shoulders, but it didn't scratch her. Wren's snarls broke into yelps and soft chitters, and Lutea grunts of struggle lightened into laughter.

"Good girl, who's a good lil' girl!" She purred. Wren licked Lutea's face with a long pink tongue. Her hand brushed Wren's head and their chitter melted into a low thrum, reminding me of...

*Wait, is it...* My thoughts jumbled. *Can dragons purr?*

Wren flopped to the side with a mighty thud, shaking the floor and rattling the window. I thought she would fall through the porch, but she rolled on her back, looking more like a playful kitten.

"You can pet her. She won't bite." Lutea promised.

"Are you sure?" I asked, trying to hide the fear in my voice.

"Trust me, if I'm not in danger, Wren won't harm you."

I stepped cautiously toward Wren, squinting and looking away when I reached for her head. Fear spiked through me when her rough tongue flicked across my wrist. She rubbed her head against my hand, beckoning like a cat for more pats. Her scales were coarse, yet warm to the touch like a plate of stone baked under the sun.

"See? That wasn't so hard," Lutea said.

"Yeah," I stammered, "Not too hard."

Wren stopped purring. Her head dropped to the floor and a harsh, strained gurgle wrenched from her jaw. I'd been around Tuna enough to know what happened when an animal started to "hiccup." The scales on Wren's neck flexed and tightened, and bright flurries of embers splattered from her mouth. I jerked back as the flames added a new black spot on the porch with a sharp smell of burnt fish.

"Got too excited, huh," said Lutea with a light chuckle.

She patted Wren and the dragon cooed at her. "Mayu, would you like to meet Mizuchi?"

"Mizuchi?" I repeated the name, then turned a narrow glare at Lutea. "You have a dragon named 'Water Dragon'?"

"He picked out the name, not us."

We walked off the porch and Wren slithered between us, keeping her small eyes on me. Right around the house was a massive pond glittering beneath the sunlight. A little way from it was a shed and surrounding trees roaring in the breeze.

Lutea lifted an upturned bucket off the ground and a few toads leaped out and scampered into the tall grass. She turned to a metal tank tucked behind the house, the size of a car with a tube protruding at the bottom that poured water out into the soil. The path of water drew me to a garden full of sprouting plants and lush vegetables.

"You grow your own food?" I asked. "I thought you didn't eat."

"Tora eats. A lot. And so do the dragons," Lutea grunted, pushing the tank lid open. Inside were clusters of fat, silvery fish as big as dinner plates. I had never seen fish that large except at the aquarium.

"Occasionally we have friends come over, and what kind of host would we be to not have something to dine on."

Lutea dunked the bucket inside, scooping up four fish flopping and she pulled the lid closed.

"Come on." She motioned ahead and we headed to the pond.

"Watch your step. It gets wet over here," Lutea warned before I planted my feet in the deep muddy ground. Looking around, the only dragons I saw were dragonflies skimming off the water's still surface and heard frogs croaking within the grass.

"Where's Mizuchi?" I asked.

"You might want to take a few steps back."

Lutea plunged her hand into the bucket and yanked out one of the fish. It flopped in her hand, splashing water at us, but Lutea kept her grip on it. In one swing, she hurled the fish over the pond and the air boomed as the water burst like a geyser.

Thick, curved antlers sprouted amidst a mane of white fur. A long head coated in smooth scales leaned toward us. Its sharp eyes seemed to follow me. Every nerve and fiber of my being screamed for me to run, but I froze, caught in the dragon's gaze.

I heard a hollow voice warbling from its throat: *'your name...speak it.'* The dragon easily towered over a two-story house and when my eyes flickered to the pond, my stomach fell at the sight of its body coiled beneath the surface.

"Tell him who you are," Lutea said, nudging the bucket close to me. "He's waiting for you."

I planted my trembling hands firmly on my sides and looked up at the dragon.

"My name is Mayu Hinamori," I called, shakily. "N-Nice to meet you, Mr. Mizuchi!"

I bowed to the dragon.

Seemingly satisfied, Mizuchi lulled back, and the words rumbled from him. '*As it is well, Mayu Hinamori...*'

"Now give him a fish," Lutea prompted.

I swallowed my fear, took a deep breath, and dipped my hand in the bucket. I flinched at the icy water and almost shrieked as cold bodies brushed past my fingertips.

"Do you need any help?"

"I...I think I can do it." I reached into the bucket again. The fish gathered around my hand. Something soft nibbled at my fingers, and when it swam near my palms, I closed it like a trap and yanked the fish out. It flopped frantically out of my grip and hit the ground with a dull splat.

"Sorry..."

Lutea chuckled, "Not everyone gets it right their first time."

I gazed up at Mizuchi. He let out a sharp hiss and dove at me, opening its jaw. I shrieked as my legs gave out, my hands went to cover myself but a swirling rush of air and a fierce roar like crashing waves filled my ears. Blue scales whizzed by and Mizuchi plunged back into the pond, splashing water across the field. It wasn't until the water receded that I noticed the fish I dropped was gone.

"Show off!" Lutea cried. She ducked down, narrowly avoiding a spurt of water jetting out of the pond.

I flopped against the soaked grass, shaking and dumbstruck.

"You live with dragons!" I realized and my voice broke into laughter. "You live with dragons! How did you end up with dragons!"

Lutea held her hand out, and helped me to my feet, but my legs wouldn't stop shaking. "Tora and I were in the Netherlands and heard rumors of an albino bear eating campers' leftovers. Wren was a hatchling at the time, and we couldn't find a nest, so we brought her here."

Before anyone could stop her, Wren knocked over the bucket and gobbled the last fish.

"Mizuchi, on the other hand, fell here from the sky after a bad storm," Lutea pointed to the house. My eyes widened, remembering the dragon's massive size.

"He was in bad shape and Tora, and I spent weeks taking care of him. We didn't know he could talk until a month later. He told us his name and asked if he could stay with us."

"Can Wren talk?"

"Eventually, in about... ten years. She's still a baby."

"Ten years!" I shrieked. "How old is Mizuchi?"

"Too old to laze in a pond all day!" Lutea shouted. She ducked again, avoiding another waterspout.

We sat on the dryer parts of the grass and watched Wren and Mizuchi play. Wren spewed fire across the pond, causing steam to billow into the sky. Mizuchi poked his head out and snorted water at Wren. She would shake the water from her scales, and sprint around the pond. Apparently, dragons could get the zoomies too... that's a scary thought.

"So, what happened before your... incident?" Lutea asked, keeping her eyes on the dragons. "I know you did not have a seizure that bad for no reason."

I stared at the pond, curling my arms around my legs.

"My cat attacked me," I started. "Mrs. Bean was being Mrs. Bean. Mary and I aren't friends anymore...she told me I cherry picked people whenever it was convenient for me."

She winced, "Oh, it was *that* bad."

"... Do you think I cherry pick my friends?"

"Not from my experience." Lutea laid back, resting her head on top of her hands. "From club meetings and art to walking with you, I know you try to spend time with everyone. You usually came to us when you needed help, but we also chose to help you."

"Do you do it because it's your job?"

"Do you see me working now?"

Before I could answer, Tora's thunderous voice broke the silence.

"Lutea, are you going to let me work on you?" He was leaving a shed ten feet away from the pond.

"Sorry, we got a little sidetracked." Lutea propped herself up to her feet, then she helped me up.

"Of course," Tora huffed. "When you're ready, bring Wren over here. The kiln is not going to heat itself."

•  ●  •

The shed was way bigger on the inside. Staircases lined the wall, spiraling around a tree that hung from the ceiling by its roots. Beautiful models of planets hovered in midair, drifting slowly. I headed toward the stairs, eager to see more wonders, but I stopped to the call of a woman's voice.

"Welcome!" she cheered,

I whipped back to Lutea. "Did I hear someone?"

She bit down her smile. "That was Syla."

I looked around curiously at one of the hanging lanterns. A spotted salamander looked at me through the glass, not minding the fact it was engulfed in flames.

For a moment, I was at a loss for words. "Is she a salamander?"

"Of course I'm not!" A voice chanted from the flames. Soon, the other lanterns chirped in the same cheery voice.

"Nice to meet you!"

"Make yourself at home."

"Do you prefer tea or coffee?"

"B-Both?"

We passed through a corridor that opened into what looked like a workshop. The lanterns fixed to the wall greeted us on our way.

"Welcome back, Lutea!"

"Hello, sweet Wren!"

"I hope your repairs are going well."

"Have you been a good girl!" Syla cooed.

As I walked into the workshop, I caught a scent of freshly cut wood coming from a pile of logs near a long table. Blueprints draped the surface and standing behind it were old, worn shelves stuffed with books stacked messily over each other and jars labeled in an unfamiliar language. Inside crystalline bones, furry plants, and dark clumps of metal.

On the other side of the workshop, ceramic bowls and vases sat neatly on the floor next to a long, stone bed with an open fireplace beneath it. It was when I turned to the table where Lutea sat that I noticed someone was missing.

"Where did Tora go—"

A bright orange light drenched the walls and Syla roared at Tora as he passed the lanterns.

"Trim the grass!"

349

"Turn off that kettle!"

"Patch the roof!"

Tora groaned, patting a small fire on his shoulder.

"Is she always like this?" I whispered to Lutea.

"Not unless Tora's behind on chores," she said.

"They will have to wait until you're fully repaired. Can't have you deactivate mid-work again." Tora pulled up one of the chairs and sat in front of Lutea.

"I haven't locked up since yesterday!"

He brushed her hair back and inspected the sealed cracks across the marks. His expression, mostly stoic but unreadable.

I added, nervously. "If its not too much trouble, can I help?"

Tora squinted at me. "You patched roofs before?"

"No, but I'm willing to learn!"

"Roof's not going to fix itself," Lutea muttered.

A low, groan rippled from Tora. His eyes settled on me. "Could you grab the dragon ash from the shelf?"

I blinked. "The dragon's what?"

"White jar above you." Lutea said.

I turned to the shelf. All of them had something white. White scales, white herbs, white shards of crystal, and fluffy white feathers.

"Two jars to your left," Tora added.

I trailed past jars of albino tadpoles and white claws to find a jar as big as my head filled with white sand. I shimmied it off the shelf and set it on the table next to Tora. My eyes caught the design of a body on the blueprint paper.

"Did you make Lutea?"

"No," He answered, drawing a measuring tape across Lutea's arm. "My magic is strong, but best I can do is reactivate her marks"

"In other words, I'm one of a kind!" Lutea proclaimed, puffing her chest up with pride.

"Do you remember who made you?" I asked.

"No. My earliest memory was realizing I had eyes just as I opened them. A couple worked as restorationists in a museum, and they purchased me at an auction. The husband was in the middle of restoring me, so imagine his shock when I spoke to him."

"That would certainly scare someone silly."

"We scared each other," she said, chuckling softly. Her eyes fell wistfully to the blueprints. "They were nice people. They took care of me, as if I was their own child."

My heart throbbed. "How did you meet Tora?"

"Yes," Tora dragged. "How did we meet?"

Lutea smirked. "We were hiking in the mountains. I stepped a little too close to the edge, slipped and fell..."

"Right into my old home where I woke up to a golem on my chest and a hole in my roof. Thirty years and my ribs still ache at the memory."

"I said I was sorry!" Lutea fussed.

"Thirty years!" I choked. "How old are you?"

"Me?" she beamed. "I'm old as dirt!"

Tora grunted, "You *are* the dirt."

With that he stood up, jar and hand and headed to a large stone vat at another table.

He called over his shoulder. "Are you coming?"

I realized he was asking me, and I hurried to his side. The table had been recently cleaned but faint smudges stained the surface. Tora lifted a lid off the vat and the scent of fresh mud rose from inside. It was a mixture of dirt and soft chunks of clay soaking in water.

"Are you familiar with pottery?" Tora asked, uncapping the jar.

My head shrank into my shoulders. "N-Not really."

"Are you willing to learn, as well?"

I nodded.

He reached over my head to a nearby shelf and pulled out a large measuring cup.

"Add the dragon's ash into the batch," he instructed. "Then stir until the water has been mostly absorbed into the clay. Make sure it doesn't dry up. Any questions?"

"Is this clay for fixing Lutea?"

"Not fixing. Remaking her body," he corrected. "At least one durable enough that a pixie can't deactivate her. Ash made from dragon's bones should do the trick."

He gave me the measuring cup, and for the next hour, I was alternating between pouring dragon's ash, dry clay and water into the batch, and stirring it until everything mixed in. I had to take off my jacket and roll up my sleeves when Tora showed me how to mash the clay together with my hands. My opened palm dug through the cold, earthy sludge and mixed it together until my arms cramped up and my fingers went numb.

Opposite from where I was, Tora and Lutea had placed already made pieces inside of the kiln. Tora clicked his tongue and Wren hurried to the kiln. She planted her feet on the floor, her belly lowered and in a single breath, a fierce, bright fire spewed from her mouth and into the kiln.

The intense heat swept across the floor. The clay warmed up as the water started to evaporate, but I pushed myself to continue. Finally, Tora told me to take a break. I sank against the vat, catching my breath. I would have wiped the sweat off my brow, but my hands were caked in clay.

"Here." Tora gave me a damp towel and a cup of fresh water. I wiped my arms clean, then gulped down the water so fast, it was gone before I knew it.

"Wait for it," Tora said and in seconds, the water swirled from the bottom and refilled the cup to the brim.

"Not bad," he muttered, inspecting my progress. With an open palm, Tora dug into the clay, and scooped handfuls of it onto the table. I watched as he flattened and molded it into the shape of bricks.

"How are your arms?" he asked.

"Much better now," I replied. "I think I can make more clay after this."

"You won't for today," he said. "You have something more important to work on."

I raised my brow.

He turned to Lutea at the kiln. "We'll be back!"

"'Kay!" she replied.

"Where are we going?" I asked, worried.

"We're going outside."

A soft grunt and nod to the doorway prompted me to follow Tora. Half of the lanterns screamed at him, but the other half spoke kindly to me down the corridor. On our way to the door, Tora hoisted up one of the wooden crates off the floor and carried it on his shoulder.

Gusts of wind tasseled my hair, tickling the back of my neck. I shivered at the cold and put my jacket on and zipped myself up.

"We need to discuss what you did," Tora stated. We stopped at a grassy clearing, far from the pond and shed. He set the crate in front of me, meeting me at eye level. "Causing a blackout at the school is immensely powerful, especially for someone as young as you."

"What do you mean? I didn't cause a blackout."

"You did." My shoulders stiffened at his hardened voice. My mind returned to the last moments in the library. "You lost control, causing far more destruction than anyone could predict. Do you know what that means?"

I lowered my head as my cheeks burned with shame. "I'm not like other hybrids?"

"Oh, no. I've met children who reduced their school into mere bricks with their mind. But you've proven to be too dangerous to be left alone, unchecked. The lounge. The pixies. Now the blackout."

"Is that why I'm here? So, someone can watch over me again?"

"And to ensure, you can have better control when you return to school."

I looked at Tora. He opened the crate and pulled out the last thing I expected him to own. A flat screen TV which he placed on top of the ground.

"I have seen enough hybrids with powers as strong as yours. I've seen how dangerous it can be when they suppress it. It never ends well."

"I could barely do that," I mumbled.

"You shouldn't have to. You should harness it. Control it, instead of it controlling you. Start on drawing your powers, then focus on a single target."

I stared at my reflection on the black screen. "I don't know how to bring it out."

"Think back to the moments you did."

He moved to the side. I wasn't sure what to do, other than stare at my own face. I thought how angry I must've looked when Mary yelled at me, or every time Mrs. Bean spoke to me. Even after a week, it stung hearing their words.

My brows weighed over my thinning eyes. My heart raced as their voices returned and my agitation ignited into rage. A light sparked from the TV, and it flickered to life. A bright blue screen beamed back at me before I heard loud pops, like fireworks. Static crackled in the air, electric arcs twisted out of the TV as smoke spewed from it.

"Get down!" Tora shouted, throwing himself in front of me. As a loud explosion boomed in the air, I dove into the grass, curled into a ball and covered my head. Glass shards and metal pieces rained across the land, reaching the pond.

Electric arcs snapped across the sky, lighting the land, before a crashing thunder deafened my ears. I heard faint pops from the house followed by a car alarm blaring from the Jeep. I didn't move until the destruction quieted, and the alarm died out. When I did, my weak knees buckled, the ground flipped and I found myself, caught in Tora's arm.

"Are you hurt?" he asked.

I managed to shake my head before a wave of dizziness came over me. Tora gently sat me down and I held my head to steady my swimming vision. As the world steadied, my eyes fell on what was left of the TV—a scorched, crumbled mess of glass and charred wires and wisps of smoke vanishing from its remains.

●

Lutea opened the back door to the house, and I covered my ears at the loud, hissing whistle coming from the kitchen.

"Oh, crap!" she cursed and darted to the stove. She twisted the knob and the whistling wheezed to a stop.

"Knew we were forgetting something," she hissed between her teeth.

"I told you to turn off the stove!" Syla scolded. Her flames motioned flippantly from inside the table lamp.

Lutea checked the fridge, noting about the power being out, then lifted a phone that was on the table. I stayed at the door, but a sickening feeling rolled over mem upon seeing the buttons had sprung out of their sockets and melted to a plastic puddle on the floor. Lutea left the phone on the counter then opened a window over the sink.

"It's singed here too!" she shouted.

The lamp fire fluttered and Tora's voice resonated from the flames.

"I'm not surprised. The electronics here are also burned. Wren is shaken up. She knocked over the pottery and toppled the shelf, but your parts and the kiln are fine. That's all that matters."

"Do you need our help?" Lutea asked.

"No. Stay there for now. Check to see if anything else's burned." The flame snuffed out on its own, leaving the house in silence. The salamander inside of the lamp stayed in place and kept a watchful eye on me.

I looked away, catching a glimpse of the exposed wooden beams over our heads, and wood-made couches sitting adjacent to the table. My gaze lowered to something dark on the floor and my heart sank. Scorched marks snaked across the wood, singing the potted plants.

"I'm so sorry..."

"Has anyone ever told you that you apologize way too much?" said Lutea.

I stopped myself before I could say "sorry" again. "What else should I say?"

"Not an apology. It was bound to happen." She lifted the kettle off the stove and shook it to hear the water splashing inside. "You can sit down, if you like. No need to take your shoes off either."

I slipped my foot back into my shoes, then quietly moved to the table and took a seat. Lutea pulled a mug from one of the cupboards and a canister of herbal tea.

"I didn't know I was... this destructive," I muttered.

"For what it's worth, you weren't always like this." She poured what was left of the water into the mug, then turned to me, stirring the tea. "I don't remember you blowing up our TVs and phones in the lounge. Certainly, gave us a scare, though nobody was harmed. Until the next day when you killed the pixies swarming a hallway. That was quite the range."

"What does this mean?"

"It means something I've always suspected. Your powers are growing stronger over time."

A lump formed in my throat. But when I thought about it, I realized it too. Though that only raised a new fear in me.

"What's going to happen to me if it keeps going? If it goes out of control again?"

"We'll make sure you don't," Lutea promised. She sat at the table across from me and passed me the mug. "It's hot," she warned as I carefully held it. I caught a sweet aroma coming from the steam that calmed my racing thoughts.

"Do you know what kind of hybrid controls electricity, like me?" I asked. "...or mystics?"

She leaned back and the wooden chair creaked under her weight. "While I know hybrids who do, your powers aren't electric based, it's energy."

"Energy? Like what Aiden can do with his light?"

"Similar but as far as I know, Aiden's light is intangible. Both of you can draw your powers from yourself. However, unlike electrical abilities, you don't absorb energy from your surroundings, you overcharge them at a rapid rate, causing them to burn out or shut down. It's powerful, but it can tire you out if you use it excessively."

"How do I keep it under control?"

"You need to strengthen your body, so it can keep up. At least that way, you won't tire yourself out."

I didn't know how Lutea could have so much faith in me. "Do you think I can do this?"

"I know you can. Believe it or not, you're way stronger than you think you are. No matter what puts you down, you always pick yourself up."

"Don't give up!" Syla chimed. Her flames fluttered off the salamander's back. "Don't give up! Don't give up!"

Lutea laughed. "Syla sure thinks so."

"Alright." I drank the tea and looked at Lutea with newfound confidence. "So, what's the next step?"

"You can help me find anything else that got burned. That's a start."

# Bittersweet

**I'd wake up early to do stretches in the living room** before Lutea and Tora picked me up around nine, always on time, too. There were few cars on the road, which made drifting from the highway to the countryside a bit easier. My heart leaped at the sight of horses, big and small galloping or lazing about in the fields. But it couldn't compare to the rush of arriving at the ranch house, being tackled by an excited dragon and greeted by talking flames.

The first thing Tora wanted me to do was run laps around the house. Lutea ran with me and if I stopped, Wren would try to tackle me or Mizuchi would spray me with water, which only happened once, and he missed me by a hair.

After that, we settled for breakfast in the house. The food would take up the entire table; sliced grilled herring and steamed vegetables, frosted sweet rolls, a warm cup of coffee for me, and a liter of mead for Tora. We'd feed the animals next, then start on the chores.

Tora taught me how to patch up a roof, change oil in the car and mold clay into shape. I was labeling the jars and Tora worked at the turntable, using magic to heat the sides, draw out air bubbles and traces of water. I once asked Tora why he never used magic to fix the house.

He simply replied, "Over reliance on magic will leave you slacking in your other abilities."

Speaking of abilities, once we were finished with the chores, we stepped outside to train. Tora had a TV screen ready for me to practice on, so for the next few hours, I would stare at my reflection, thinking about Mary and Mrs. Bean until the TV burst into a flurry of crackling light and charred pieces of glass and wires.

When the smoke cleared up, the pieces crawled back to the spot they exploded from, rebuilding a new screen on its own as if nothing happened.

"Again," Tora called out.

Training ended around four, we had another meal, and I was home by five, though it felt like more time had passed. I cleaned myself up, ate dinner at home and spoke to Elizabeth over the phone about my day.

That was my routine for the next three days, including the weekend. It was tiresome at times, but I overall enjoyed my time at the house. As my senses sharpened, I started to notice the smell the flowers carried over in the wind, see the birds tucked between the branches and hear croaking toads in the distant fields.

Though, it wasn't pleasant at home. Tires screeching down the road tore into my ears, and the rotting garbage from the dumpster churned my stomach. Anytime Ichirou or Hannah cooked, I had to lock myself in my room with the window open so the spices wouldn't sting my eyes or clog my throat.

Lutea, sympathetic about my situation, gave me a pair of earplugs and a sleeping mask to dull my senses, but Tora was against it.

"You need to adapt to the new sensations," he grumbled.

Easier said than done. My hearing was so sharp, I had to keep the phone at arm's length when I told Elizabeth about it.

"You're not alone in that," she said. "A lot of students are sensitive to light and sound, which is why most of them take night classes. It takes time getting used to."

*That made sense*, I thought. Aside from the airplanes roaring through the skies and beaming streetlights, the complex was easier to tolerate at night.

"Do you have super hearing?" I asked.

"No, but I'm more durable compared to humans. Mom says it's because our bodies have to support our wings and horns. A car could slam into me, and, at worst, I'll have a few scratches and a sprained ankle. Can't say the same for the car."

"That sounds oddly specific."

"Mom has a lot of *interesting* stories," she giggled. "So, when are you going back to school?"

I climbed out of bed and checked the sticky note on the back of my door. "I have an appointment next Saturday for a checkup. If everything's alright, I should be back at school the Monday after that."

"But that's near the end of November," Elizabeth said, worried. "You'll probably have three weeks left before the holiday break. You should've taken the rest of the year off."

"I thought the same thing too, but I can't fall behind in class."

"You're on medical leave. Your grades won't change until you come back." Elizabeth fell silent. "You're still worried about the Malus, aren't you?"

The hair on my neck stood on ends. "I don't know what Galumine did to take care of it, but I can't shake the feeling this was handled too easily."

"Maybe to us it seemed difficult. I think you're anxious because you're close to returning to school. From what I heard, there haven't been any incidents since the pixie incident."

"I know…" My eyes wandered to the night sky. "I hope I'm overthinking things."

• ● •

Wednesday morning, Tora left on an errand shortly after breakfast. With the housework done and Lutea's repairs in progress, we started my training early, though that was its own chore. It was hard to focus when gusts of frigid wind blew the anger away. I shivered in my jacket, more worried about getting frost bite than blowing something up.

"Let's take a break!" Lutea called out and I couldn't be happier. At that point, I didn't care about Tora's penalty: blow up a TV or rotate the dragon compost.

I welcomed the heat radiating in the shed and sat at the chair close to the kiln. Lutea gave me a wool blanket that hung from the wall, and I wrapped it tight around my shoulders.

"Is that hot enough for you?" Lutea asked.

My teeth clattered. "I can feel my fingers now. And I'm a little hungry again."

"I can make some stew while we wait for the pieces to finish."

"That sounds great." I mused, thinking of a tantalizing veggie beef stew. Who knew someone with no sense of taste or smell could cook the most amazing meals?

Lutea checked on the kiln, using an iron rod to stoke the fire and nudged the parts inside. She closed the kiln and the thud of the door woke Wren from her nap. She shimmied to the table and her soft scales curled around me. The thrumming purrs and crackling flames almost lulled me to sleep.

Almost.

"Lutea, can I ask you something?" I said, my fingers fidgeted with the wool blanket.

The fire's glow saturated Lutea's face. "You already did but ask away."

"Have you ever been so mad at someone for so long, you get tired of being mad at them?"

"Can't say that I have. Is this about Mrs. Bean and Mary?"

"It is…"

"Why are you still thinking about them?"

"I can only use my powers when I'm angry. But I'm tired of being angry. I'm tired of thinking about them."

Lutea pursed her lips. "You know, I had time to think about it, but I'm not sure if anger is your source of power."

"I'm pretty sure it is."

"I was there when you blew Melanippe away. You weren't angry. You were afraid. Rage may ignite your powers, but I don't think it creates it."

"I never blew anything up while happy."

"Because rage is the easiest emotion to draw out. But what if there was another way to bring out your powers?"

I shrugged. "If there is one, I'd sure like to know."

"Try meditation!" Syla piped up from the table lamp and her voices chanted around the room.

"Yes, meditation!"

"Along with tea!"

"We have relaxing tea back at the house!"

Lutea's eyes lit up. "Sit up for a second. We're going outside."

"Again?" I moaned. I just got comfortable too…

"Syla gave me an idea. Don't worry, you can keep the blanket."

Lutea brought two empty crates outside. I sat on it, curling into my chest and tightened the grip on my blanket, as if the wind had snatched the warmth from it.

"We've been doing this all wrong," Lutea said. "You need to think about your power, not as something destructive, but a part of you. What it looks like and how it feels. Imagine it flowing through you."

I shuddered. "How will meditation help?"

"Think of it as washing away your thoughts, then restarting with a new blank slate."

Lutea sat cross-legged on the crate.

"Is it a good idea for you to sit this close?"

"Guess we'll see. Take a few deep breaths with me."

I crossed my legs, planting my hands on my kneecaps when a thought occurred to me. "Do golems need to breathe?"

"Mayu..."

"Sorry."

I straightened my back and closed my eyes. The prickling air broke my focus and I thought of the warmth in the shed and the flames lapping in the kiln.

"Don't think about the cold so much," Lutea insisted. "Close your eyes and hold your hands together."

"Why?"

"You need a closer area to channel your powers to. Not a TV that's forty feet away."

I shut my eyes, and, despite the cold, I forced myself to focus on shuddering leaves on the creaking branches. I breathed the cold in through my nose and it settled my lungs. Then I exhaled slowly and drew another deep breath. Then another until a new warmth stirred in my stomach. It rolled down my shoulders and grew into fire in my hands. As each breath escaped, a ball of light emerged in front of me, pulsing like a heartbeat in my hands.

A smile spread across my face. "I—I did it!" My voice cracked.

Lutea smiled back, "You did it! Oh, be careful with that!"

My hands parted, and the ball grew. The light didn't sting my eyes like the sun. It was more like the calming waters in the sea with tides washing over my worries. It brought me to the bottom. To voices I was certain I had heard before.

'Cease what you are doing, child!' Mizuchi roared in my head.

A grip on my shoulder jerked me to wakefulness and the light in my arm swallowed up the land. The impact of the ground shocked me into a turning world, where whips of lightning split the trees into splinters and the pond billowed into steam.

Tora's voice bellowed through the chaos. "What did you *DO*?!"

"It got out of control!" Lutea cried.

Before I could speak, a tight, twisting pain in my stomach forced me on my knees. My insides seized up and heat surged up my throat. I doubled down and coughed, hard and heavy until the fire in my throat lurched out of my mouth and red blood splattered on the grass.

361

My heart throbbed in my chest, and my body froze on the spot. But the world shifted, beneath me and the blood-stained grass spun in my vision. Lutea's cries for help and Tora's calls were distant.

"Don't panic, you're going to be alright," she whispered into my ears.

Lutea pulled me back, tearing me away from the blood and practically carried me to the ranch. I saw toppled trees, and some were set ablaze. Water washed through the grass and flooded what looked like deep trenches that were seared into the ground.

Lutea brought me inside of the house and had me sit on the couch. She dabbed a wet cloth against my lips and chin. She stepped back and Tora knelt in front of me. His coarse hand cupped my forehead.

"No blood from the ears or eyes," he muttered. "Can you breathe clearly? Through your nose and out the mouth."

I took a small, shaky breath, tasting a faint copper in my mouth. My voice came out weak and raspy. "I'm sorry..."

"Stop apologizing," he stressed. "You wouldn't do this on purpose. Straining yourself is normal." He settled on the couch in front of me.

"This is supposed to happen—" Dry coughs hurled out of my chest and when my throat cleared, I felt Lutea's hand on my back and a blanket around my shoulders.

"Easy..." Lutea soothed. She gave me a small cup of tea, and I held it close to my chest. "You kind of pushed yourself passed your limit. The more you use your power, the more stress it can put on your body."

"Is that what happened?" Tora asked.

"We tried to find an alternative way for Mayu to draw out her power and, well..." Lutea gestured to the disaster outside.

"I see," Tora rolled back onto the couch, and another language rippled from his mouth. "Rage gives you short bursts of power, but difficult to control. Yet, tapping into its source is somehow more destructive."

"She may need a limiter, if that's the case," said Lutea. I raised my brow, wondering what she meant but she didn't go into detail.

"It'll take time to make, even for a rushed job. For now, stick to what works. No more of... whatever this was."

Ashamed, I lifted my head but all I could say was, "I'm sorry—"

Tora's gold eyes flickered at me. "If I hear one more apology out of you, you're cleaning up the backyard."

I glanced at the destroyed backyard through the window, seeing scorched lines on the grass and splintered trees rocking in the breeze. I took a slow, experimental sip of the tea and the ginger taste washed away the blood in my mouth.

•
●
•

The next day, still shaken from the blood, I wanted to focus more on exercising and helping Tora. He taught me how to chop the damaged trees to be used for firewood and crafting. My woodwork, according to Tora, was "decent," and needs improvement, (no need to exert too much strength in bringing the axe down) however, he wanted me to focus more on my power.

"You cannot avoid using your powers for long," Tora warned.

Later, Lutea and I were in the kitchen, making a soup called Lohikeitto. She seasoned the salmon, and I was rinsing the vegetables in the sink, but my attention was drawn to the shed through the window. I knew the pottery was a portion of the shed, and it was much bigger than it looked inside, but as the days passed, I realized there were other corridors and doorways that reminded me of the clubroom door. Sometimes, I'd catch a scent of pine from thick forests, saltiness and algae of ocean tides, or moss in a humid swamp.

"Mayu, the sink's running," Lutea called.

I looked down and the vegetables were floating in the sink.

"I'm sorry!" I yelped and quickly turned the faucet off, then unplugged the sink to let the water drain.

"No worries." Lutea picked up the carrots and yellow onions, shook off the water droplets and set them on the cutting board. The sound of the knife chopping the onions to pieces filled the air.

"Were you thinking about something? Or did you space out again?"

I figured it wouldn't hurt to pry. "Where does Tora go? I know he isn't always in the shed, and I've seen him go through doors that open to different places."

"That's because he is going to those places." Lutea held down the leek and sliced the stem into small pieces. "He's being called back to Erehwon a lot more than usual."

"What for?"

"He helps stabilize any of the remaining gates, so what happened to you doesn't happen again." Lutea scooped a handful

363

of the onions and dropped it into the pot where the broth simmered.

I sat at the table, wanting to continue the conversation. "How does a gate become unstable?"

"Gateways are like doors. They open and close, but sometimes, they don't close all the way, which is what happened to you when you fell through." She sprinkled in a few spices and flour, then added the potatoes into the pot.

"How do you make gates, anyway? Do you use magic?"

"There's more to it." Lutea lowered the flames and joined me at the table. "Think of it this way. When you punch a hole in a wall of the house, what usually happens?"

"I get in trouble?"

She chuckled, "Besides that. The hole doesn't necessarily lead outside. It opens to the inside of a wall. Its structures, the beams, and other things. For now, let's think of this in-between as the Ethereal Plane."

I nodded understandably.

"Now, if you do the same thing, punch a hole through the wall again, you've made an opening leading outside. Let's say, outside is Erehwon."

"The gates are holes punched through the worlds?"

"That's the simplest way of putting it, but yes. It's how we travel and how we make the clubroom's door. You're entering a different world."

My eyes widened with shock, but it explained why the room was much bigger inside.

"So, what is the Ethereal Plane? Miss Naiad said it was the space between the living world and the afterlife."

"Yes, and no?" Lutea's voice rose at the end, as if she wasn't sure either. Before she continued, she returned to the pot and poured cups of cream and vinegar in it.

"I've never been there myself and neither has Tora. We know that it's a warped reflection of reality where time and space are greatly altered. Unless you're an ethereal being like a spirit or fae, you can't access the Ethereal Plane without a breach."

My heart felt heavy suddenly. What about the Malus? Can it open a breach?"

Lutea paused, her eyes darted to the unlit lantern in front of me before returning to me. "As far as I know, the Malus cannot open its own breach. It must find one, but..." her voice lowered. "I think it's trapped there in more ways than one."

"How?"

Lutea hesitated. "My guess is that it used to be an ethereal being, but it was forced into a vessel that acted as a container. I have a few ideas about who did it, but if it was them, the Malus must have been so dangerous if it had to be cast that far from reality. It can't bring itself into this world unless it had a compatible body..."

*And one happened to cross its sight.* My worried gaze trailed to the sky.

"Scary concept, I know."

I glanced at Lutea. "How do I know what I was thinking about?"

"You're easy to read. And you hadn't talked about the Malus until now. Look at it this way: Tora and Marie have gone great lengths to keep you two apart. That's why they're reinforcing the gates."

"But it's not the only one," I said, darkly. "I read the Malus is a primordial; beings that have been here long before humans and mystics. Are they still around?"

"They're rare to find. And most of them won't cause as much trouble as the Malus."

"Have you seen one?"

"Once." Lutea took the lid off the cauldron and scooped a spoonful of stew into a small bowl. "It was mistaken for a small island, said to vanish every century. Tora and I excavated it ten years ago. We found a lush forest thriving with rare animals and isolated human tribes on its back. Overall, completely harmless."

"Whoa," I mouthed. "As scary as that sound, I kind of want to see that."

"We've been keeping track of it, so if we go there, you can come with us."

She gave me the bowl and after it cooled down, I took a bite. The cream was rich, and the salmon was rightly seasoned and flavorful.

"Good?" Lutea asked.

I gulped down another spoonful. "It's great!"

A cheeky grin crossed her face. "Not bad for a 'monster,' right?"

"I guess not," I took another bite, relishing the soup as it warmed the cold feeling brewing in my stomach.

• ● •

I was in the hospital Saturday morning for my final check-up. My heart and blood pressure were normal and nothing unusual came up in the MRI scan. Before I was discharged, Dr. Sanders had to ask the same round of questions from his clipboard. I answered them honestly, but halfway through, Ichirou got a phone call, and he stepped out of the room to answer it. I looked over at Dr. Sanders.

"Something on your mind?" he glanced up at me from his clipboard.

"Yeah," I said, quietly. "Remember the old lady who took my glasses?"

"Deborah? Yes, though, what brought this up?"

"Did you notice something... strange about her?"

"Stealing people's glasses sure was an indicator," he said, smirking. "Where's this coming from?"

I squirmed on the bed, and my hands twisted the bottom of my shirt. "What would you do if your patients weren't... human?"

His eyes held me for a moment, then a hard sigh blew out of his nose. "Mayu, I've been a doctor for thirty years. At this point, I know one when I see one."

My heart hammered. "D-did you tell..."

"No," he said, setting the clipboard on his lap. "We have an unspoken rule to not disclose information about our nonhuman patients unless they put others in danger. Far as I know, you're no danger."

*Tora would say otherwise.* "Do you know what I am?"

Dr. Sanders gave me confused look. "I thought you were keeping it from me. I wouldn't blame you if you were." He looked at the door and I could faintly hear Ichirou talking to someone.

"He doesn't know yet," I whispered.

"I figured as much." Dr. Sanders turned back to me. "When were you going to tell him?"

"Maybe when I figure out what I am."

"Best of luck, lass," he said. "But keep this in mind. You're 'round him more than I am, and Ichirou is a lot more perceptive than you give him credit for."

· ● ·

Returning to school on Monday was like my first week all over again, yet it wasn't. It was the same castle of glass with the same rowdy students rushing inside. But something felt new about it.

Ms. Penn and Ethan welcomed me back with open arms. I came close to sitting three rows apart from the girls until one of them, Janie Lovelace, called for me to sit next to her. Ethan and Ms. Penn joined us in a big group to discuss the latest assignment. When class ended, I headed to Physical Science and found Sarah at the door. I didn't have to call her name, she turned, and her face brightened as she rushed over to give me a hug.

"I thought you'd never come back!" she wailed.

"I can't stay away from school forever," I joked.

We walked into class, and I was taken aback by the new faces at the tables. Sarah told me a lot of students had switched classes while I was away. We took our seats, and I asked Sarah what else I missed when I felt a pang of anger at the back of my neck. I tilted back and caught Mary's eyes darting into the pages of her book, *Wuthering Heights*.

"Someone sure isn't happy," I murmured.

Sarah shrugged. "She has been more distant since you left. Are you going to..."

I shook my head. There was nothing I wanted to say to Mary and my anger towards her evaporated about twenty TVs ago. At the sound of the bell, Sarah and I met with Aiden, who waited by the lockers.

"Welcome back! Enjoy your stay?" he asked.

"It could have been a little longer," I sighed, teasing a bit. "It feels weird to be back."

"It felt weird not having you here. Are you ready for algebra?"

"No... but I heard things have changed."

"Oh, it did!" He beamed. "You've got to hear what happened to Mrs. Bean!"

Aiden motioned me to follow him up the stairs. I couldn't begin to imagine what class was going to be like after I had yelled at Mrs. Bean. I begged Aiden for an explanation, but he wanted me to wait.

"Wait for what?" I asked.

We entered the room and cheers erupted from the students in class. Someone shouted, "welcome back!" and another asked if I was feeling better? I mewed the quietest "thank you" at them before turning to Aiden.

"What did I miss?" I whispered, noticing the empty seat at the teacher's desk. "Where's Mr. Turner and Mrs. Bean?"

"Mr. Turner is at the main office," he said. "As for Mrs. Bean… You might want to sit down for this."

Aiden and the other students took turns telling me what happened the day after I was taken to the hospital. Mrs. Bean and Mr. Turner were called into the main office by the principal. It was unusual for a teacher and their assistant to leave at the same time, so Aiden, along with a few students snuck out of class.

They saw Mrs. Bean and Mr. Turner in the main office talking to Ichirou. That alone was hard to imagine. When one of the school secretaries asked why students were out of their rooms, Aiden told them how Mrs. Bean bullied me for months.

"The principal threatened to suspend us if we didn't leave the office," Aiden said.

"Obviously, that didn't happen?" I guessed.

"Your brother stood up for us. He asked the principal why he was so eager to get rid of us instead of hearing us out. Mr. Turner not only agreed with Ichirou, but he vouched for you. He kept a record of every time Mrs. Bean yelled at, bullied, and harassed you or the other students.

Mrs. Bean looked like she was going to blow up at him!

She said you had to come forward with evidence that she bullied you. But the next day, the story spread, and the entire office was crowded with kids and the other math teachers!"

I gasped, "Why?"

"Because they were wondering why so many people were in their classes. The ones who transferred were from Mrs. Bean. Three other math teachers came forward, and that was the final straw."

"What happened to Mrs. Bean then?"

"Suspended until next year," Aiden answered slowly, as if he was processing it too. "There's talk that she might resign, but she's not coming back soon." He spoke as if he barely believed it himself, but I saw the hope light up in his eyes.

"Settle down everyone," Mr. Turner called from the door. Everyone scurried to their desks. It looked like no one was sitting in their assigned seats, so I took the chance to sit next to Aiden in front of the board.

Mr. Turner cleared his throat, grabbing everyone's attention as he moved to the front of the room. "First of all, I'd like to welcome our fellow student who took a medical leave of absence. It's nice to have you back."

"Thanks," I squeaked, feeling my cheeks blaze.

"And second," he added. "I had just returned from the main office. Mrs. Bean has yet to update us on whether she will return to Cater's. So, I will be your substitute until further notice."

A student raised her hand. "Are assistants allowed to do that?"

"Are you going to get an assistant, too?" another had asked.

Mr. Turner answered, "I am qualified to substitute. And I'll only need an assistant if I can't handle the class alone. That won't be a problem, will it?"

We shook our heads.

"Good to know." Mr. Turner faced the board, holding the marker. His wrist danced graciously across the surface, leaving behind a trial of equations written with easy to read, perfect calligraphy.

"I like to play a little game. Today, you'll work in groups of four to solve each problem, but here's the catch." Mr. Turner faced us, capping the marker with his palm. "The group who answers correctly will reduce the amount of homework tonight. One problem per page. You have a minute to find your teammate."

I paired up with Aiden, and we joined two other students. We exchanged ideas, broke the problem down and came up with a possible solution. When it came to answering the question, one student from each group shared their answers with Mr. Turner and he wrote them on the board. He told us which answer was correct, then he gave us a new problem that was more challenging.

By the time class ended, everyone left with almost no homework.

Aiden and I were heading out when Mr. Turner called us from the desk. "Mayu, Aiden? Do you have a moment to speak?"

Trading glances Aiden and I approached him.

"Did you enjoy yourselves today?" he asked.

"It was the best," I replied, cheerly. "I'm actually looking forward to class tomorrow."

A small smile radiated his face. He seemed happier teaching us than being an assistant. "I have something for both of you. Our meeting has been relocated in the lounge for the time being."

"Relocated?" I questioned. The joy in my heart started to sink.

"Yes, the library had to be shut down for repairs," Mr. Turner explained. "The meetings were cancelled as a result so we had to move it to the assistants' lounge."

He gave us two invitations with Erehwon's emblem along with ornate decorations around the border and cursive letters.

Mystic Rising

"You can sign it before school ends, and hand it to Min. It will be opened today. And another thing." He lowered his voice and his expression hardened. "Tomorrow, the assistants are going to have another staff meeting elsewhere, meaning we will be away from the school."

"What for?" Aiden asked.

"What happened to the library?" I pressed.

Mr. Turner was going to answer, but he noticed students entering the room. He said under his breath. "The meeting regards the past few incidents and as for the library... Aiden can tell you more."

We were walking to Aiden's class when I asked about the library. "You heard about the blackout? It happened the day you went to the hospital."

My gut sank. "Sounds like it was more than a blackout."

"That's an understatement," Aiden huffed. "Rumor is it was bad wiring in the old lights that sparked into a fire."

"A fire!?"

"Yeah, all the books and the shelves near the back door went up in flames and spread to the computers. Everyone thought it was intentional..."

He started to slow down, falling silent as he put it together. I could only give him a look of remorse when he realized it.

"You caused the fire?"

"No one told me there was a fire. I didn't do it on purpose either. Was anybody hurt?"

"No, you were the only one who went to the hospital. In face the fire happened right after you left. What do you remember?"

"Not much. Certainly not a fire."

The bell sounded and we stopped in front of Aiden's class.

"We can talk later," he said and promised he'd meet with me after art. But I couldn't wait. I went straight the library to see what happened. The doors were locked and a dim light outlined the tables near the window, leaving the rest of the library shrouded in shadows.

"What happened?" I murmured. I gave the handle a small pull when a familiar, keeping voice cried out to me.

"The library's closed!"

I whipped around to see the old librarian, holding a cardboard box. He readjusted his frameless square glasses and broke into light laughter.

"Welcome back! How are you feeling?"

"Good?" I answered, still getting used to people being so nice to me. "Do you know what happened to the library?"

"'Course, I was there when it happened. Almost gave me a heart attack." The librarian put the box down and fished out a ring of keys from his pocket. "The computers were turning on and off and the lights were flickering like crazy. Then it suddenly exploded! Couldn't go through the front, so I ran to the back. Lo-and-behold, I found you on the floor. I shouted for help and pulled you out."

"Thank you," I said. "And I'm sorry for worrying you."

"No need to apologize." The door clicked, but before the librarian stepped inside the darkened room, he turned back to me. "That reminds me, were you with someone that day?"

"No, it was only me. Why?"

"I thought I saw someone with you. The power had gone out by then, and it was too dark to see them. I'd call them your friend, but they took off the moment I saw them."

"I don't remember seeing anyone there."

"Well, I know my eyes aren't the sharpest. Heck, it's a miracle I found you when I did. But I coulda sworn you weren't alone. It was so dark, it looked like a shadow was standing over you."

I tensed up as fear rose in me.

"You take care now." The librarian said, then picked up the box and slipped inside the library.

· ● ·

I couldn't get the librarian's words out of my head and the more I thought about it, the more eager I was to return to the library after school.

"But all of the doors are locked," Aiden reminded, walking beside me. "How did you plan on getting inside?"

"We could sneak in through the English AP room," I said. "It's connected to the courtyard."

"You take English AP too?" Aiden asked.

"I don't. Mary did—" I halted my stepped and veered back to him. "*Too*?"

"And Mary? Do you mean Marietta Brown?"

My jaw dropped. "You know her?"

"Barely," he huffed. "She sits at the front of class, and I sit in the back, but I remember her name. Someone called her Marietta, and she made a big deal about being called Mary instead. Do you know her?"

"We used to be friends," I said, hesitantly. "Have we been passing each other this entire time?"

"I think so. What are the odds."

We arrived in English AP, and like before, it was oddly empty with the door left open. School ended moments ago, yet there wasn't a teacher inside the room.

"He tends to leave early from what I heard." Aiden said and we crept inside before anyone noticed us. My hands trembled when I closed the door. Memories of Mary and I sneaking inside rushed back to me at an instant. I pushed the thought down and focused on the black door connected to the courtyard.

"The sprites aren't awake," Aiden told me. "They're hibernating until spring. They won't open the door or take the weight off it like last time. There is a key around here that we can use."

"Right! Last time they were in the teacher's desk."

"They're always at his desk." Aiden stated.

He opened one of the drawers and shuffled through bins full of phones and envelopes. I pulled another drawer open and checked between stacks of papers and files for the keys.

"Why do you want to see the library?"

"The librarian told me he saw someone there when he tried to help me."

I turned to Aiden, noticing his somber gaze on the papers. I thought about it for a while and worked up the courage to ask him. "Aiden, when I had that seizure, you were in Mrs. Bean's class, weren't you?"

His shoulders stiffened.

"I was," he replied. "And... I heard what you said. I heard everything. I was going to find you, but the fire alarm went off. We were rushed outside, and I was so worried about you. And then I saw you carted off into the ambulance."

"Aiden..."

"I kept thinking about what I could have done to help you. I should have helped you! I wanted to get up and chase after you when you left. I don't blame you if you're mad at me but I truly am sorry."

We stood in silence, avoiding our gazes, waiting for one of us to speak up.

"I'm not mad at you. I never was," I said.

"I would be." Aiden brushed his hand against his hair, almost revealing his blind eye before his bangs swept over it. "I want to help you one way or another."

"You're already helping me. You always were, and I never asked you to. Why?"

Aiden looked away, but I saw the redness forming in his cheeks. "I don't know. I like... talking with you. You're nice, you're smart, pretty—brave and a little unpredictable, but in a good way."

Heat blossomed in my face. "Even though we almost died."

"My family motto is, 'What's life without a few risks?' I'm glad I met you."

"I'm glad I met you too," I repeated. "You're brave and thoughtful too. You're like a knight that doesn't back down, and you're funny, too."

"I hope you mean I'm not funny looking."

"Nope in fact..."

I stood on my tiptoes, surprising Aiden when my hand brushed against his burning face. I tucked his bangs behind his ears and stepped back, smiling. His eyes, rich russet brown and pale like seafoam, sent my heart fluttering.

"I think you look great."

# Descent

**"Found it!"**

I snatched the key from the drawer and unlocked the door. We pushed it open, gritting our teeth through the cold air rushing in.

The courtyard was eerie to say the least. Dead leaves scattered across the cobblestone path and barren vines crept down the gazebo, clinging to the columns like withered veins. My eyes landed on the door tucked between two darkened windows. I peered inside, cupping my hands around the glass, but daylight couldn't break through the darkness inside. Aiden and I pushed the door open, and the first sound I heard were my footsteps hitting the hardwood floor.

The carpet was peeled away, and the shelves were gone, leaving the library a vast, hollow shell. All that remained was the librarian's half circle desk with boxes stacked on it.

"I wonder where the librarian went..." I murmured, taking in the open space.

"Hopefully, not here. This place is creepy." Aiden said.

A ball of light rose in his hand and something on the floor caught my attention. I got a closer look, and my heart throbbed in my chest. Black lines branched wildly across the floor and dark patches dotted the ceiling where the lights used to hang.

"You did this?" Aiden faltered, following my gaze.

"I didn't know." I turned away from the light and followed the scorch line to the back of the library. It ended, well rather, it began in a small corner that wasn't burned.

"This is where I was," I said, softly.

Aiden got closer and my shadow shrank against the wall. "You don't have to answer this," he said. "But why did you come down here?"

I rolled my shoulders. "So much was happening at once. I didn't know what else to do. I thought going here would clear my head."

And I wanted to cross into Erehwon again and leave all my problems behind. After all, I survived the journey the first time. Before that memory resurfaced, I noticed two odd shapes on the floor.

"Can you bring that light over here?"

Aiden brightened the area and his eyes narrowed at the strange shapes.

"Are those shoe prints?" he asked. "Were they from the librarian?"

"Trust me, if he were that close to me, two people would have gone to the hospital. He said someone stood over me, but they looked like a shadow. It stood right here in front of me..."

He gulped. "Where did it come from?"

I stood over the footprints and the instant I faced the wall, an itchy shock crawled down my skin.

"What's wrong?"

My throat tightened. "Lutea told me the clubroom doors are breaches too. And they don't always close the way they should. Sometimes they can get left open."

Shock filled Aiden's face and his head swiveled back to the wall. "Do you think a breach opened that day?"

"No, only the wall was here."

I thought about it, and so did Aiden. "Unless it opened when your powers went out of control. Maybe they reopened the breach..."

I forced myself away from the wall, the footprints, and paced back to the courtyard. The light vanished from his palm as Aiden helped me open the door. I returned the key to the teacher's desk, then we took a break to let our thoughts settle. I leaned against the blackboard and Aiden sank to the floor. Silence buzzed in our ears.

Fidgeting with the headphone wires, Aiden finally spoke up. "We should head to the lounge. Tell an assistant or Miss Naiad about what we found."

"They'll tell us to stay out of it," I said.

"Yeah, but they can at least do something about it. And it doesn't hurt to take your mind off this. Might as well, since they won't be here tomorrow."

My chest clenched at his words. I held my arms and turned to the windows, dreading what was to come.

•●•

I woke up with a startled gasp to flashes of lightning and crashing thunder. Raindrops drummed against my window, somewhat calming my racing heart. If it were another night, I would have pulled the covers over my head and dozed off to the storm. But all I could think about was the last time it stormed at night. The Malus controlled me and made me leave the apartment. It had a hold over me that I couldn't fight off and I shuddered to think what would happen if I didn't wake up on the bus.

As the storm continued, I rolled to the side, wondering if I would ever fall peacefully to the sound of rain. Just as my eyes settled, a figure crossed my vision at the back of my room. I jerked up in bed and the figure froze.

"Take it easy, it's me," Chitose whispered. Her body peeled from the shadows, emitting a scent of burning leaves. Her eyes, gleaming in different colors, met mine.

I sighed in relief as my muscles relaxed. "You almost gave me a heart attack..."

"The way you reacted, I thought I did," she remarked. "You woke up suddenly from a dream. So, I came to check on you."

The flash of lightning and crack of thunder brought our attention outside. I slowly moved away from my window, as if it would cave to the hurtling wind and battering rain.

"If the weather is keeping you up, I can put you to sleep again if you wish."

I didn't respond.

"Mayu..." Chitose drifted close to my bed and sat at the end of it. "What's on your mind?"

I hesitated to explain it at first. Aiden and I had told Miss Naiad what we saw. Aside from a light scolding for sneaking into the library, she assured us that the breaches were closed after my "little outburst," as she put it.

"Are you sure you have to leave for this meeting?" I asked.

"It's more than a school's disciplinary meeting. It concerns both worlds, so we must attend." Chitose paused. "If this is about the Malus, it can't hurt you anymore. If something crossed through worlds that day, we haven't noticed it or anything unusual since your medical leave. You may be overthinking it."

"Am I?" I whispered. "Can it see me or sense me from here?"

"Can you?"

I leaned forward, tucking my knees under my chin. "I think it's been in my head long enough for me to tell… It used to be a pull at the back of my thoughts. But now, it's like a nagging urge that gets stronger." My eyes watered. "It's never going to leave me alone, is it?"

Chitose didn't answer, but her grim silence told me I was right. "If it truly has that strong of a hold on you. Why not stay home? Perhaps transfer schools."

"That's a bit extreme, don't you think?"

"I think you should do whatever makes you feel safe."

It felt too… cowardly to run away, like I had lost, after everything I'd done to keep the Malus away; Ichirou giving me the watch and setting up the house alarm. Chitose watching over me in my dreams, Miss Naiad and Tora strengthening the gates and keeping the breaches closed. We tried everything and all it did was anger the Malus. And if I transferred schools, what would stop it from following me from the other realm? It was stubborn and relentless…

And so was I.

"Mayu?" Chitose called, gently.

Anger boiled in me. I threw the blanket aside and got out of bed, yanked my backpack and crept downstairs. In the kitchen, I slowly pulled one of the drawers open and grabbed two of the flashlights along with a pack of batteries.

"What are you doing?" Chitose's voice floated around me.

"Preparing myself for the worse," I whispered, tucking the flashlights into my backpack. "I won't have time to do this in the morning."

I moved to the cabinet and grabbed a handful of granola bars, and three bottles of water from the fridge. After that, I returned to my room and set the backpack in front of my bed.

"Do you think something will happen?" Chitose asked.

"If it does, I don't want to be caught off guard. If something attacks me, I want to fight back." I reached under my bed and pulled out a shoebox. Inside, tucked between crumpled papers, were a pair of yellow track shoes.

"What are those for?"

School shoes aren't good for running. Not long distance anyway," I explained. "Is there anything I can use to protect myself?"

Chitose pulled back, her eyes shifted from silvery grey to rusted gold. "Iron is a good deterrent against ethereal beings and fae. Though you're lethal yourself."

I thought of anything in the apartment made of iron I could bring to school. There were cast iron skillets in the kitchen, but they were too heavy to carry and buried under pots and pans in the cupboard. Taking them out would make too much noise.

"If it means anything. Cedric isn't going to the meeting. After all, he's still substituting until a teacher can take his place."

"Thank you," I told her. "If you can, please let Galumine, Miss Naiad—anyone knows we might need help tomorrow."

"Promise you won't do anything too reckless."

"I'll try," I said.

With that, Chitose's body vanished in wisps of smoke. A faint and sweet scent lingered in my bedroom. It only dawned on me why her scent was appealing. She smelled of incense.

I crawled into bed and pulled the blanket to my neck. It was three in the morning when I dozed off to the soothing rain and thunder rolling in the distance.

∙ ● ∙

The rain continued the following day, pounding on the roof of Ichirou's car on the way to school. Inside, the heat roaring from the vents muffled the radio, so we barely heard the weatherman's forecast.

"Trying to outrun the rain today?" Ichirou asked.

I stared at him.

"You're wearing your running shoes out here?" He kept his eyes on the road. The windshield wipers squeaked as it swatted the rain away.

"They're water resistant, and my school shoes would get ruined in this weather," I said, which was partially true.

"I thought you had boots for that."

"I couldn't find them on time," I lied.

I wiped the condensation from the window. Water streamed down the side of the road and the trees whipped viciously in the wind.

"Can I ask a favor?" said Ichirou.

"Yes?" I turned back to him.

"I don't care what time it is today, but if you want to come home, call me. I'll be at the school in ten minutes to pick you up."

"Are you sure?"

"I'm not letting you walk out there by yourself or catch the bus in this mess, alright?"

"Alright," I repeated.

A moment later, the lights from the school's windows peered through the swaying trees. The wide-open doors were like gaping maws, drawing in students desperate to get out of the rain.

"Ichirou, please be careful on the road," I said.

"I'll try my best."

I gave Ichirou a longing hug, and reluctantly, left the warm comfort of the car. I bristled at the cold and raced to the school's entrance. My shoes splashed in the puddles, but the water never seeped through, and the soles held a firm grip on the ground.

The thunder rumbled throughout my first class. The rain pummeled the windows so hard, the girls moved to the desks closest to the door. Couldn't say I blamed them. Anxiety jolted through me when the lights flickered until Ms. Penn turned them off. She was worried about my seizures, which I appreciated, even though flickering lights never triggered them.

On my way to physical science, I noticed there weren't a lot of students in the hall and once loud and bustling noises quieted to small talk and nervous chatter. There were only seven kids in class, so Mr. Baryon held off the day's lesson and put on a movie, using a whiteboard I never knew was in the room.

"Everyone seems worried," I whispered to Sarah.

"We all are," she muttered. "Most of us are here because the storm knocked out the power. This might be the only building in this street with working lights."

"Most of us?" I frowned, "How long have you been out without power?"

Sarah held her chin. "She woke me up around three thirty. So, the power could have gone out around that time. I wanted to stay home but my dad didn't want me home alone with no light or heat."

*Technically, she wasn't alone.* "Does your dad know about the ghost?"

Sarah shrank in the chair. "He does, but he tries not to think about it."

I was going to ask what she meant when a bright flash lit the room then a booming crash shook the window. Students gasped and yelped in surprise, then calmed down once the thunder receded into faint rumbles. Moments later, someone at a nearby table asked if anyone had signal in their phones. The other students checked their phones, and I could see the wariness in their eyes. Feeling my stomach knot, I glanced at my phone and saw two small bars at the corner of the screen.

"Maybe the connection is down," I mumbled.

Sarah had a grim look.

After class, Sarah and I were in the hall, joining the other students. The darkened skies and heavy rain made the outside look like grey walls. I couldn't see anything past the street, except the headlights driving down the road.

Every now and then a bar would appear on my phone, then vanish before I could call Ichirou or text him. Aiden called out to me from the crowd and hurried to our side.

"You look distracted," Aiden said.

"The phone's not working," Sarah told him.

"I think the storm's messing with the signal. At this point, two cups and a string would have a better reception."

I sighed, giving up on trying to reach someone. "Guess I'll be catching the bus. Do you two have a ride home—"

A loud ring erupted from someone's phone. Then bells sounded from another phone, then another. Before we knew it, chimes, song lyrics, vibrations and every sound a phone could make filled the hallway. Footsteps slowed down and everyone traded worried glances.

Aiden looked around. "What's going on..."

A strong, pounding thunder shook the school with such force, cracks tore across the floor. I screamed, jumping back and bumping into Aiden. Students shouted at us, but I was focused on the cracks until they vanished with the flickering light. A bunch of students walked around me, Aiden and Sarah, scowling at us for not watching where we were going.

I whirled around to my friends, and their faces whitened with fear. "Tell me I'm seeing things," I said, shakily.

"We saw it too," Sarah said.

The cracks appeared again in another flash, but no one reacted to it, except for us. We hurried to the main doors. I zipped up my jacket and adjusted my backpack on my shoulders when my phone rang. Relieved, thinking Ichirou had called me, I answered it and static tore into my ear. I yanked the phone back, but I heard her voice reaching to me from the other line.

"Mayu? Can you hear me?" Elizabeth's voice bobbed in and of the static. "Are you still at school?"

"Elizabeth? I said, shocked. Aiden and Sarah leaned in to listen. "How are you calling me? What's going on?"

Static garbled her panicked words. "—out of the school!" she cried. "Erehwon—in lockdown—"

The crash was sudden and loud. I lurched back, tumbling on the floor before the wall hit my shoulder. I was laying on my back, groaning at the pain throbbing in my head and back. Beneath me, the floor shifted, and Aiden's strained voice met my ears.

"My ribs would appreciate it if you'd get off of me."

"I'm sorry!" I scampered off him and Aiden rolled to the side, hugging his chest and gasping for air. The phone was still in my hand, but Elizabeth's voice fell silent. Everything was silent.

As I stood up a horrible pit formed in my stomach when I saw the hallway spanning far into the darkness. The phone tumbled out of my trembling hand, and dropped to the floor with a loud, echoing clatter.

"How," Aiden's voice shook. "How are we back here!?"

"I don't know." My chest heaved with fear. Then a soft moan drew my attention to someone on the floor. "Sarah!"

We rushed to her side. Tears trickled down her wide, glassy eyes, and her limbs crossed over her chest, stiffening then going limp.

"What's wrong with her?" Aiden cried.

"I don't know!" I shrieked in panic.

I turned Sarah to her side and her breathing slowed down. Her eyes settled and her neck went slack. For a scary moment, nothing happened. Then, Sarah rose without making a sound. An itchiness crawled down my skin when Sarah's dark eyes landed on us.

Aiden jerked back, but I stayed rooted to the floor, staring back at the being inside her.

"You're not Sarah..." I said.

Her face contorted into a sneer. "What tipped you off, Sherlock?"

"Is that the same ghost who possessed her?" Aiden asked.

I nodded.

The ghost growled. It was weird having Sarah glare at me or speak with hostility in her voice. "You know, it's rude to talk about someone in front of them."

"I thought you weren't supposed to possess Sarah anymore," I said, sternly.

Sarah's brow notched. "Only when she asks, but a nasty blow to the head knocked her out when we fell here."

"How did we get here? Was there a breach or fae?" I glanced around but saw the endless floor and lockers.

"Something else pulled us here." The ghost stood up, stumbling back a bit before catching herself.

"Can you open a breach?" Aiden asked. "Pull us out like you did before."

"What do you think I'm doing?" The ghost planted her hand on the locker and her dark eyes narrowed with focus.

At first, I wasn't sure what she was doing, until I saw locker rippling under her palm, like water. A low, rumbling hum pulsed in the air, and the ripples grew stronger and faster. But then a sharp sound, like crackling static snapped in our ears. We jerked back, crying out in pain as the noise pierced into our heads.

"What was that!?" was all I heard from Aiden. My ears were still ringing.

The ghost waved her arm, cursing under her breath. "She actually did it!" she hissed.

"Did what?" I groaned, holding my head.

"That witch sealed all the breaches!" The ghost clutched her arm and her words dissolved into more cursing.

Aiden exclaimed, "We're trapped here, again?"

"Not for long," I said, steadying my trembling voice. "Remember, we can still be heard from this side of the world. We can call for help and—"

The ghost flashed a cold, menacing glare at me. "Oh sure, scream in this hall and cause another riot. Only this time, the assistants aren't here to stop it, or realize we're stuck here!"

"What about Mr. Turner? He's still here!" I shouted in protest.

"And where is he?"

"Upstairs on the third floor," said Aiden.

"*What* third floor!"

Lightning flew across the hallway, revealing the endless corridor with no stairs in sight.

My words caught in my throat. "Why don't we try going through the main doors instead of a locker."

The ghost said, agitated. "You clearly don't know how this world works."

"It doesn't hurt to try," Aiden said.

382

We made our way down the hallway before stopping in front of the school's main doors. Aiden and I eagerly pushed it opened, the low creak roared down the row of lockers stretching into the darkness in front of us. We closed the door and peeked through its window, seeing the street drenched in rain and water flowing down the pavement. Yet the doors only led to another corridor.

No way to escape and no idea what to do, the three of us sat in front of the door and watched the rain continue for several minutes. Lightning briefly lit the walls, and thunder rattled the windows, breaking the sinking silence that hung over our heads.

A moment later, the ghost sat up against the wall and let out a sharp sigh through her nose. "So, what's the plan?"

"Hide in another closet?" Aiden said, rolling his shoulders. "It felt safer there than out here."

I glanced at the hallway. It occurred to me that there were stairs in this world. The one beside the library. The one with the darkened pit at the bottom.

"I was thinking about something," I said. "If Miss Naiad sealed the breaches in the school, how did we get here."

"Your guess is as good as ours," the ghost replied. "It must have been powerful enough to break through the spell."

"Any chance it might be here?" Aiden asked.

The ghost snorted, "What, you think it's gonna kindly let us go if we ask?"

"Doubt it."

"What if there's a breach that Miss Naiad missed," I suggested. "She's strong, but maybe there's a gap or a blind spot that could be here."

"If there is one, where would we start?"

"The stairs. The one in the middle of the school. They were the only ones that led somewhere."

Aiden stirred in place. "Do you really want to go there?"

The ghost added, "Just because it leads somewhere, doesn't mean it'll lead to something good."

"How about we take a peek?" I said. "If things look bad, we'll run back here and find a closet."

I stood up, straightening my back. I unslung my backpack, unzipped the pockets and pulled out the flashlights. I gave one to Aiden and the other to the ghost.

Her hand tightened around the flashlight. Hostility rose in her voice. "Were you expecting this?"

"I didn't want to be dragged back here anymore than you do. But I'm tired of being caught off guard."

"You planned on fighting monsters with a flashlight?" Aiden said, skeptically.

"So, nothing can sneak up on us," I clarified. "And so, you don't exert yourself."

"Thank you, but I'll manage." He returned the flashlight to me. "You have my back?"

"Always."

The ghost rolled her eyes. "Seriously, get a room," she groaned.

I slipped my backpack on and tugged on the tails, tightening the straps around my shoulders. I turned the flashlight on, and a brilliant white light filled the hallway. We sauntered toward the stairs and stayed close to the lockers, keeping an eye out for anything that might jump at us. Aside from the heavy rain and our shaky breath, everything stayed quiet. It was almost too quiet for my liking.

We peered over the railing, aiming our lights to reveal more staircases spiraling toward a floor several stories down.

Aiden gulped. "At least there's a bottom."

"And yet, you want to go there because of a gut feeling," the ghost quipped. "Has anyone ever told you how weird you are?"

"Says the ghost talking to a human light bulb and a walking plasma ball."

We moved slowly down the steps. Our lights brightened the deeper we traveled until we reached a pristine, linoleum floor, shrouded in darkness.

"There aren't any windows," Aiden noted. His light shined across a row of grey, beat-up lockers.

"Such a brilliant observation," The ghost muttered, sarcastically.

"Guys," I chided, my attention on the lockers.

There was something familiar about them. It reminded me of a photo I saw in Hannah's room. In it, Hannah stood stiffly beside four people, dressed in a buttoned down, black military jacket and navy-blue pants. The lockers behind them were the exact color as the ones in front of me.

"This is my brother's school," I blurted out. "This is what the school looked like when he went here."

"How long ago was that?" the ghost asked.

"Seven years."

I never went to John Carter when Ichirou was a student. I had only seen it in pictures and heard the crazy stories. But to walk down the same floor as they did, passing by the same lockers sparked a little excitement in me. It was like I was following their steps. Hannah told me she would draw hearts on her lockers with a marker, and I scanned the lockers, hoping I'd find it.

"Are you sure it was seven years, and not seven decades?" Aiden called out a few feet away.

His light shone inside a desolate classroom. The chipped walls and plank wood floors were painted in a thin layer of dust. Metal chairs with flat wooden boards for desks sat neatly in a row in front of a crooked chalkboard.

The ghost sneered, "I didn't think I'd see rooms like this again. Thanks for that."

I stepped back and peeked inside of another room. A dim bulb flickered over the checkered floor. The desks laid in disarray—turned over with the chairs knocked to the side, as if the students fled in a hurry and never returned. At the back of the room were eight rusty brown lockers. All but one was closed. I turned the doorknob, but nothing happened.

"How did we end up at the old school?" Aiden asked. "And why do the classrooms look even older?"

"Lutea told me the Ethereal Plane is like a warped version of our world," I said. "Time and space work differently here."

"Does this mean we're traveling back in time?"

"No," the ghost replied, a few doors ahead of us. "This is where the lines between space and time blur. We can be stuck here for days and perhaps a minute may pass on the other side."

Aiden grimaced, "But when Mayu and I were stuck in the Ethereal Plane, we weren't gone that long... were we?"

"Maybe time distorts the deeper we go?" I guessed. "What are the chances of us finding a breach?"

"Limitless," the ghost replied. "But I don't want to spend an eternity finding it."

We continued down the hall for what felt like thirty minutes before coming to a stop at a forked path. On the right, voices drifted down the corridor and to the left, soft currents of air drew us to another set of stairs.

"That air has to come from somewhere," I muttered.

"But voices could mean there's people around," said Aiden.

"Do you recognize them?" the ghost asked.

I listened carefully. "They're moving farther away."

We turned to the corridor on the right, following the whispers and drifting small talk. Aiden and I said hello, and asked if anyone could hear us, but no one answered. The talks continued. There were one-sided conversations, arguments, crying and a faint, blood curdling scream that sent an icy shiver down my spine. I felt Aiden's hand settle on my right shoulder, cold and shaking.

"Something doesn't feel right," I said.

"I think we took a wrong turn," he agreed, passing by me. The cold hand tightened on my shoulder. A panicked shriek wrenched from me as I twisted back, seeing no one behind me.

Aiden and the ghost spun around.

"Are you okay? What happened?" he asked, rapidly. "You look white as a..." his eyes fell on the ghost.

"What," she spoke, nonchalantly.

Before I spoke up, a manic burst of laughter exploded between us. We threw our backs against the wall, my head jerked from side to side, as the laughter bounded down the corridor, its crazed rounds were drowned in stifling silence.

Aiden, keeping his back on the locker, hissed through his teeth. "What was *that*?"

"The dead," the ghost answered. My trembling hands tightened around the flashlight. "This is where lost souls roam when they can't pass on."

"Wh-Where did they come from?" I asked.

"The other side, when they were once alive. Do you still want to go?"

I chewed the bottom of my lips. "Maybe we should take the stairs," I said in a small voice. "I heard little from them."

"For now," she said, warningly.

We pulled away from the lockers and headed for the stairs. Feeling the breeze carried up from the bottom gave us a little comfort, a possibility that there was a breach somewhere below.

The crisp, linoleum steps gave way to creaking wood that stopped at a long narrow hall. What little light there was, came from seeping mist coating the old floorboards. No one knew where it came from, and nobody liked the idea of moving forward. But with so few options, we pressed on.

The floor groaned under our feet, sounding louder than anything in the hall. Mist framed around the box shaped lockers and crawled beneath classroom doors. No one dared to look through the fogged-up windows. Though, in a morbid way, the area reminded me of haunted houses in carnivals. I was going to make a joke about it, to lighten the mood until we saw the dead.

Their bodies were made from the mist around us, drifting in and out of existence with haunting looks of fear, anger and sorrow. I pressed my shoulders against Aiden's and his hand slid into mine. We held on to anything that was alive, warm, and solid.

"They don't seem to notice us," Aiden whispered, probably wanting to make small talk.

"I don't think they know we're here," I whispered back.

"You wouldn't want their attention," said the ghost. The only one who was unfazed. "Sometimes they don't know or can't accept that they're dead. It's too much to handle. So, they relive their human lives, then starting over when they 'die.'"

I frowned, "They're stuck in an endless loop. Will they ever find peace?"

"D'unno," the ghost shrugged. "Lot'a people can't handle death very well. Especially if it was unexpected or painful. To them, this is their peace."

"Are there ghosts who know they're dead?" Aiden asked.

"Oh, you two might want to be careful with those." The ghost's black eyes craned back at us. "They don't take too kindly to the living. Got some unfinished business or they're angry that their time ran out. They'll either attack or possess you, so keep your guard up. Don't let your mind wander too far."

"...And what about you?" I asked, pointing the flashlight at her. "You're not hostile to us."

"You should know, I'm only hostile to anyone who hurts Sarah."

"That's reassuring," Aiden muttered. "While we're on that note, how did you and Sarah... meet?"

The ghost had an unsure expression. "She called out for help. People were hurting her and—" suddenly, the ghost reeled over, groaning in pain, her hand clutching the side of her head.

"'Kay, okay, I won't tell them! Stop shouting!" she demanded.

Aiden and I stared at her.

The ghost straightened her back and rubbed her head.

"Sorry," she said in a deep breath. "It's still a personal story and Sarah doesn't want me to talk about it yet."

"She can hear us?" Aiden asked. "Has she been listening to us?"

"I told you she hit her head earlier. She just woke up." The ghost gently patted her head. "Now, if only she could stop talking so loud."

"Can we talk to her?" I asked.

"Not in this world. I'm not letting my guard down for a second, here."

"Lucky her," Aiden remarked.

We continued down the hall, following the breeze to another set of stairs. A man, dressed in old suspenders and shrouded in mist sat crouched at the corner. Dark liquid seeped from his disheveled hair to his chin. His hands clasped together as he muttered a prayer. As we passed the man, I swore his prayers slow down before we reached the bottom.

Snaking roots covered the ground on the next floor. Barren trees sprouted out of the cracked walls. The air, now stuffy and humid, held a rotting scent that made my stomach recoil.

Aiden gagged, "Now this place smells like death!"

"Where are we?" I gasped between small breaths. The stench was overpowering.

"We're still at the school but at a different time," said the ghost.

She swept the flashlight around and she jumped back, with a terrified scream. Aiden and I pointed our lights at the ghost and nearly screamed. Four grey spiders, the size of oranges, were clutching one of the bare trees. The faces on their abdomens scrunched up in the light and their thin legs skittered up the trunk.

We jerked back and stuck close to each other.

The ghost's voice shook, "Please tell me we're close to a breach."

"F-Follow the air," I mustered. "It's getting stronger, so we must be close."

"Not unless we're walking into a monster's den," Aiden remarked.

A branch snapping nearby jolted the life out of us. Our lights whipped off the ground and trees, then landed on a row of needle-like legs that carried a large centipede into the darkness.

The ghost glowered at Aiden. "How 'bout don't talk about monsters while we're here."

Thankfully, most of the giant insects scurried from us as we hastily pressed on. A few creatures stared at us when we ducked beneath low-hanging branches. Their pale skin gleamed under our lights. Their large heads lulled to the side, as if watching us with wide, clouded eyes.

None of us knew what they were, but they didn't hurt us. They clung to the lifeless trees like the canotila and it made me wonder if this world was their home.

I seized up when a wave of darkness swept over the cavern. The ghost and I whirled back as Aiden collapsed on the ground. His eyes, wide and glossy, darted in every direction. He clutched his neck as if struggling to breathe.

"Aiden!" I cried, racing to him. "What's happening to him!"

The ghost rolled Aiden to his side. Glowing red veins crawled across his face and arms, light flashed in is eyes, and mist erupted out of his body.

A chill ran though me as the praying man's bloody face stared back at me. With a twisted scowl, his misty form drifted back and melted between the trees.

"We need to get him out of here!" the ghost commanded.

We dragged Aiden to his feet and carried him down the path until our shoulders were tired and our legs weakened. When we couldn't push forward, we set Aiden on the ground. He woke up, coughing and vomiting in the corner.

I rubbed his back and whispered shakily. "It's alright, you're going to be okay."

"Can you stand?" asked the ghost.

"He needs to rest!" I argued.

"The longer he rests, the more likely something will take him over again. Do you want that?"

"It's okay," Aiden grunted. He pushed himself up, then sank against the trees. But he slid to the ground and his voice broke.

"You were so far away." Tears rolled down his face. "I tried to call out to you, move, or do something. It felt like... my thoughts were being pushed down and..."

"It can't hurt you anymore," said the ghost.

"I felt what he felt!" Aiden yelped, suddenly. "I saw his memories like they were mine! He worked with the school's founder. He had a family, a home," Aiden choked up. "They're all like this... all of them..."

He looked at me, and I understood what he meant. It didn't escape my notice that the crying spirits were living people like us. I didn't miss how some of them looked to be our age or wore school uniforms like ours.

"You can't help them. Their time has long since passed," the ghost said, sternly.

Aiden stumbled to his feet. "H-how could you say that? Aren't you a spirit like them? Weren't you alive like us?"

She growled. "Every soul has a sad story that binds them here, but it's not our problem to fix. And before you moan, 'he had a life, he had family,' he clearly didn't care about yours when he tried to take your body!"

Aiden stammered. I wanted to argue that the ghost was being harsh, but she was right. We were in no position to help the dead, no matter how much it hurt to hear them cry or see the pain on their faces. We couldn't bring them the peace they needed.

"Their lives are over, and we'll be next if we don't focus on getting out of here."

With that, the ghost turned her flashlight to the tunnel ahead. Aiden reluctantly followed, creating a small, warbling light in his hand. I couldn't stop thinking about the ghost and the rest of the dead.

"Hey," I called out.

The ghost whirled back, beaming the light at my face. "What now?"

"What's your name?"

"What makes you think I have one?"

"You were alive at some point, so you should have a name." I responded, eyes squinting. "And it feels wrong to call you Sarah when you're not her. So, who are you?"

She rolled her eyes and kept walking. I glanced at Aiden, wondering if I hit a touchy subject when the ghost spoke up.

"What did you say?" I asked.

"Leila," she said softly over her shoulder. "My name's Leila."

The beaten path opened to a marsh. Damp grass grazed our kneecaps and pools of still water reflected our lights. We dragged ourselves to the drier parts of the marsh where bare, scraggly trees stood. Moss dressed the trunks and torn strips of cloth clung to their branches. Leila said it might be a good sign. Seeing life in a lifeless realm could mean we were close to a breach.

My legs trembled at the thought of getting out, but it turned to exhaustion when my knees buckled down before I could take the next step. I wasn't sure how long we were walking but the toll it took hit us like an earthquake, knocking us down and fighting for balance until we buckled down near one of the trees.

"That's it!" Aiden heaved like he ran a mile without stopping. "I'm never walking again after this!"

Leila lay sprawled on her back. "You're tellin me. This is the longest Sarah's ever walked! Aren't you tired?"

It didn't take long to realize she was asking me.

"I am, but this is mild compared to track in middle school." I cracked a smile, reminiscing about jogging laps around the runway and at the ranch.

"You're a track runner?" Aiden said, piqued with interest. "No wonder you're so fast."

"So fast, my old school named me Little Bullet." I beamed. "By the way, how are you feeling?"

"That guy's memories are fading but I'm mostly alright. I'm still me. Though I'm a little hungry. Doubt there's anything to eat here."

"Well," Leila mused. "I hear bugs are edible. That centipede back there looked mighty fat and tender."

Aiden wretched. "Not in a million years!"

"No need, I brought snacks and water for everyone," I blurted, stunning my friends.

Leila scoffed. "You brought snacks like this was some hike?"

"We draw our power from ourselves, so we need something to eat to replenish it." I opened my backpack and passed a water bottle and snacks to them.

"You're so weird," Leila said. Nonetheless, she scarfed down the granola bar.

The flashlight dimmed, so I grabbed a pair of batteries next to my phone. My heart sank, remembering Ichirou's words before we parted and Elizabeth's panicked voice.

Aiden said, munching on the granola, "So, I get that the Ethereal Plane is a warped reality, but why does it look like a marsh?"

"Did you honestly think the realm of restless spirits, would look like our school?" Leila asked.

"Well... kind of."

"You're not entirely wrong," I said. "I once read that this area used to be a huge marshland, before people settled here. We're still in school, just thousands of years before it existed."

Aiden snorted, "Great, how long will it be before we run into some dinosaurs."

I snickered, then my eyes flickered to a silent Leila. She was staring intensely into the darkened marsh.

My smile faded. "Leila—"

"Shut up," she hissed.

Aiden snapped back, "Hey, what's your problem—"

"No, seriously, *shut up*. Something's here."

We listened. A body gently brushed between the trees, followed by familiar, hitched sobs and wobbling whimpers. I jumped to my feet and drew the light to the source of the sound.

The wendigo froze, caught in our light like a mange animal. It crouched under the arched roots, its lips peeled back, revealing sharp teeth. A charred black scar ran across its gaunt face and bony limbs.

My heart stopped. "Oh..."

"...shit," Aiden muttered.

We inched back, and as if we stepped on a landmine, the wendigo exploded into a frenzy, charging at us. We bolted for the corridor, leaving the backpack and one of the flashlights behind. Only the trees kept us apart, but it might as well be the wendigo's playground. It wove around the branches, using the trunk to launch itself at us until its body jerked back, launched by Leila's power. It smacked into the trees with a sickening crack, then fell slack on the ground.

We scrambled for an exit, having lost our flashlight. Aiden used his light to brighten the cavern and my eyes darted to the first opening I saw.

"Come on!" I yelled.

We charged forward, but an icy claw clamped down on my ankle. It yanked me into the dark, and I let out a terrified scream. Aiden twisted around and a bright flash of light shone in front of me. The wendigo's screech punctured my ears, but its grip released me, and Leila quickly pulled me to my feet.

She ran with me to one side, separated from Aiden by a cluster of trees. He barely dodged the wendigo, jumping back as it launched itself into one of the trees. It quickly recovered, then skittered around until it faced me and Leila.

It crouched low to the ground, teeth bared and ready to pounce, then another burst of light sent it reeling back. Leila and I veered around the trees and rejoined Aiden. Together, we made it onto dry land and hurried through the tunnel.

With only one flashlight and Aiden's power barely lighting the walls, we weren't sure where we were going. But we focused more on getting away from the wendigo. We ran about twenty feet when Aiden's scream, and the crash of him hitting the ground forced me to turn back. The wendigo pinned him down and the light vanished.

I sprinted after them and threw myself on the wendigo's back. My arms and legs locked around its skeletal body. Its skin was frozen leather and reeked of decaying meat. The wendigo jerked from side to side to shake me off, flailing its arms like it'd been set ablaze. It lurched back. I had no time to react before a painful shock wracked through my body. My arms went numb, and I dropped helplessly to the ground.

The wendigo cocked its head at me and was hurled into the wall by an invisible force. The cavern shook and dust trickled from above. The floor spun beneath me, and the impact almost knocked my glasses off, making my vision blur. The wendigo was swiping its arms like a madman. Leila didn't see the arm in time, and it knocked her into the wall with a thud.

My breath quickened and my heart drummed madly in fear. If I did nothing, my friends wouldn't survive, we wouldn't survive. I pushed myself up, gripping a stone lying on the ground.

"Hey, over here!" I shouted and hurled the stone at the wendigo.

It whipped off the wendigo's head and it snapped in my direction, barring its teeth. And with all my strength, sprinted down the corridor. The wind roared in my ears and the cavern blurred in my vision. The wendigo continued chasing me, but I was far from its reach. I ignored the screams hurled at me and focused on the heat gathering in my hand. My chest tightened, my legs burned, and the wendigo's cries edged closer.

As snaps of electric blue caught the corner of my eye, I dug the soles of my shoes into the ground, keeping me steady as I whirled back. Time had slowed down, and the wendigo's dull, milky eyes widened at the light of my powers. My scream peeled off the walls and strips of heat spiraled around us. At the speed of a heartbeat, the wendigo was there in one pulse, then gone in a flood of searing light.

I collapsed on the ground, clutching the pain squeezing in my chest. My throat lurched at the smoke rising from the wendigo's charred remains. It was dead. I killed it. I killed it with my own power. My hands were shaking, my legs were shaking, I was shaking.

My hitched cries broke into a small, maniacal laughter. "I... I did it!"

I sat up, expecting Aiden or Leila to rush in and call me crazy, but a deafening silence was the only response.

"Aiden...Leila?" I called.

The only light came from the flashlight that I dropped. I quickly picked it up and aimed it at the tunnel, but no one emerged. I knew I ran straight, so why couldn't I see them? Why couldn't I hear them when I called their names? Could they hear me? My hesitant steps turned to a frantic sprint to find my friends.

I cried out for Aiden, Leila, and Sarah until my throat was dry and ragged. Every few feet of light led into another tunnel, and the overgrowing agitation and panic bombarded my mind with questions.

*Why won't they answer me?*

*Were they safe? Hurt?*

*Were they even alive?*

The last thought brought my mind to a screeching halt. No. I can't think like that. Not when they need me. No matter what, I have to find them.

*I will find them.*

With newfound energy, I raced through the corridor. The air was colder, nothing like the swampy humidity of the cavern. There were roots on the ground, as thin as shoelaces, but the further I ran, the thicker they became until I had to slow down to make sure I didn't trip over them.

A faint light brought my attention to a cavern where a draft bristled the hairs on my neck. My shoulders tensed up, but I pressed on with hope that my friends were close by.

Locked on to the light, I was about to call out to Aiden when my voice froze at the colossal roots, knotted and twisted out of the mound that resembled a trunk of a massive tree. Finally, my eyes landed on the center where someone was waiting for me.

# Vim & Vigor

**"Wondered when you were going to show up."** Mary glowered down from the mound of roots, framed by a dim glow from above like a morbid stage light.

I stared at her in stunned silence, trying to make sense of what I was seeing.

"Mary?" I stammered out. "What are you doing down here—how did you get here?"

"I have my ways…" Her cheeks pinched into an eerie smile. "Though it was hard getting here after someone cast a spell over the school. Which assistant did that? Do they know you're here?"

"It was you," I whispered. A lump of panic wedged in my throat. "You opened the breach. You already knew about the assistants."

"I told you, I'm very observant. That's what made me unique. I found out what they were on my first day of school."

Mary danced gracefully across the roots, displaying her flawless, porcelain white arms.

Fear quivered in my voice. "What are you?"

"I'm different. I'm not like other humans," she answered. "I've always had this ability to see the hidden worlds. It came easy for me to sense different beings and see through their disguises."

"Worlds?"

I thought about the shadow the librarian saw and the shoe prints that stood in front of the wall. The size perfectly matched my own, something Mary noticed when we changed clothes in the locker room. She told me she liked it because it added more to our odd similarities.

I said more to myself than Mary, "I guess... we have a lot more in common than—"

Mary cast a seething, wicked glare. "We're nothing alike!" she bellowed.

The ground shook violently, throwing me off balance. I tumbled back, slamming my hands into my ears but every word she hurled rattled me into numbness.

"You don't live with parents who boss you around every day, telling you what to do! You came to school a week late and had seniors fawning over you for simply existing! You even have a preppy rich girl for a best friend! How can you compare to me? How can you understand what I've been through!"

I struggled to protest but Mary continued her rant.

"My whole life, everyone treated me like I was different, because I wasn't one of them! I wasn't born to be a human! My true place was with the assistants, with the supernatural. I was meant to be part of their world, the place where I fit. The place where I can finally shine..."

Mary flashed a menacing look, and my body suddenly went stiff. I couldn't turn my head or command my feet to run.

"...So why did they choose *you*!"

A strong force blasted me off the ground. Sharp pangs wracked across my back and my mind reeled with shock.

"We could've been friends," Mary simmered. "You weren't a loud, babbling gossiper desperate for attention, or a creepy, wanna-be loner. You only cared about taking notes and doing your homework. What did the assistants ever see in you! Why did they pick you!"

"They didn't choose me!" My voice strained. I pulled myself up, trying to meet her eyes. "I only spoke to them. I needed help with class."

"As much as you write!"

Pain hurled into my stomach, forcing me down on shaky knees. I curled into a ball, gagging down the food that surged up my throat.

"I bet you pretended to be stupid to get to them!"

I rolled over, gasping through the pain. The instant I saw the cavern entrance that I had come through, I forced myself to my feet, but my legs rooted themselves to the ground. My back stiffened like a board, and I was thrusted in the air, hanging over the winding roots, like a helpless puppet before their master.

"You don't know how much it hurt seeing you with that invitation," Mary snarled. Her eyes, darkened with hatred, seared into me. "I saw them for who they were first, so why did they pick you! They should have had their eyes on me, not you!"

"Do you even know them?" I grounded out.

Mary looked at me, surprised.

I didn't care if she had me strung up in the air, her rants angered me more than they frightened me.

"For all your obsession with the assistants, did you even try to get to know them? Have you ever spoken to them or asked them to join their meeting!?"

She seemed taken aback at my words. "I was going to. The day we snuck into the library. I wanted to meet the assistants outside school hours. Then you vanished. I saw you disappear before my eyes! I was so scared, then... he called out to me."

I followed her gaze to the mound of roots shaped into the base of the tree. Except, upon a closer look, it resembled more of a cage.

My heart pounded in my ribs. "Malus..."

"He calmed me down and guided me out of the library. Then he came to me in my dreams and warned me the assistants were not to be trusted. He was trapped down here and cried for help, but they ignored him! No one else could hear him except for me."

"You ever wondered why?" I argued in protest. "Even in the Mystic world, it's dangerous when something reaches out to you in your thoughts!"

"And you know this, how?"

"Because it spoke to me in my dreams, too."

"*Liar!*" She bellowed.

A scream ripped from my throat as her power threw me back. The sharp crack of my shoulders hitting the ground snapped me awake. Stars washed through my vision and my insides twisted in pain. My glasses were knocked off, blurring the already distorted world where the ground threw me off my feet.

"He's been by *my* side," Mary seethed. "He's helped me hone my skills that would have gone to waste had I pretended to be a human. Now I can make doorways to their world whenever I want to and control the fae. And you have the nerve to tell me he speaks to you."

A deep tremor shook the roots and small pebbles leaped off the ground. I could hazily trace out Mary's outline in the distance, but it was the large objects orbiting her that my heart sank with dread.

"You think you're not like those other girls. You think you're so special, and entitled to everything," she said, coldly. "But the truth is, you're only human, like the rest of them. Weak, slow, stupid and pathetic."

I bolted faster than I ever had. The ground lurched in waves. Splinters showered over me, and sharp rocks cut through my legs and arms. I saw a rock flying at me, and pain whipped across my face.

Another explosion shocked me awake. I was on my back, head aching and eyes rolling up to one of the arching roots. I shielded my face from the dust piling on top of me, feeling something warm oozing down the side of my face. I pulled my hand back and it was drenched in dark red blood.

*She could have killed me.* Tears blurred my vision and stung the cuts on my face. *She almost killed me!* Memories of our time class and gym swirled through my panicked mind. I thought we reconciled after what happened in dodgeball. I thought she cared about me after I stood up for Sarah. Was she always mad at me? Had she always hated me? Was she really my friend?

The horrible shock crashed into my trembling body as an explosion erupted nearby. My lips mashed together to stifle the cries as I burrowed through the narrow gaps on my belly. These weren't as smooth as the ones above. My jacket only protected my arms from the sharp branches pricking my legs and snagging strands of hair. The pain was blinding but I fought down the urge to make another sound that would give me away.

"None of this had to happen," Mary said, smoothly. "All you had to do was to be by my side, supporting and cheering me on like friends are supposed to. You could've given me the invitation, but you didn't. So, for everything you've done, for ruining my life, you'll get exactly what you deserve!"

Her last words jolted me back into another time and place. In the hallway where I was trembling before Rosalina. Her ear grating cackle bounced off the bathroom walls where Victoria towered over me, her arm raised to hit me. Her slimy, smug grin matched Mrs. Bean's after she told me I was beneath her. She turned away satisfied, like I didn't matter to her. Like I didn't matter to Mary.

*Why was this happening again?*

No matter if I avoided old faces or met new ones, I always end up in the same spot. Crying and cowering from people who beat me down with their fists and harsh words, then they laughed at my pain.

*Has my life been nothing but a joke?*
A hot spark of light leaped from my tightened fist. The cut on my hand vanished. I remembered Lutea's face, full of wonder at how fast I healed. She always admired my determination to learn, and the strength to pick myself up, no matter how hard the chore was or how exhausting my powers had left me. And no matter what those people called me or how much they threatened me, I never backed down.

*So, what was stopping me now?*
The last thing I wanted to think about was dying. But the thought of dying in fear and hiding from Mary pushed me through a wide gap and back to the surface. I didn't need to say a word to get Mary's attention. She spun around and happened to catch me in her gaze.

"I thought you died," she said, planting her hand on her hips. "Are you done running? Are you finally going to admit I was right?"

My fists relaxed and I looked up at her. "Aiden and Sarah were dragged into this world with me and got separated. I don't know where they are or if they're alright. Mary, I don't want to argue with you anymore. I want to find my friends and get out of here."

"So, what you're saying is, you're running away, like a coward?"

Anger clenched my chest. "No, I want to make sure that they're safe."

A loud scoff rung off the walls. "I'm in the theater club, stupid! You're just lying to get out of here, using other people so I'll feel sorry for you. Nice try though, but I think Victoria can act better than you!"

Static hummed in my ears and sparks of light whipped off the ground around me. My blurry vision sharpened to clarity, and I could see the large rocks and chunks of torn roots floating around her.

"Fine," I growled. "Have it your way."

I sprinted at full speed, hurdling over roots and zigzagging around the debris shooting past me. My focus was on Mary, and I forced myself to run faster to close the gap between us. A swirling, electric-blue light erupted in my hand, and, with all my might, I swung my arm. As it struck the ground, whips of searing energy exploded between us. Mary's cries broke into coughs as scorched debris and smoke scattered in different directions.

I staggered back, catching my breath as my vision swayed. Mary picked herself up, still coughing through the smoke. Her hair was tasseled, her shirt covered in dirt and singed at the edges. Though she wasn't harmed, her once pristine face crumpled into fear when she noticed me.

"You have powers?!"

Despite my ragged breathing, I jeered at her. "You wanted to know why I was so close to the assistants, right? It never occurred to you that I was more like them?" A small smirk tugged at my cheeks. "I thought you were the observant one."

Mary let out a frustrated wail, and I was wrenched off the ground again. Suddenly, a wave of blinding light ignited the cavern. Mary cried out and her powers released me. A terrified shriek tore out of me until my fall slowed to a stop. Before my feet touched the ground, a pair of arms swept around my waist, picking me up.

"Sorry to keep you waiting, this place is a labyrinth!" Aiden panted.

Dirt and grime spotted his face, but he was holding on to that reassuring smile. Over his shoulder, Sarah tackled me in a hug. I had so many questions, but I was shaking with relief to see them again.

"What are you doing here?" Mary bellowed.

We turned to her.

Aiden tilted his head, trying to make out her figure from afar. "Marietta? How did—"

"It was her," I interrupted. "Mary opened the Breach that brought us here!"

"She's like us," Sarah whispered, narrowing her eyes. Leila's chilling presence emerged. "This all your fault?!"

"I didn't do anything!" Mary yelled and a powerful force flung us back.

I heard hands clap and a light flashed in Mary's face. I threw myself to my feet and ran towards Aiden. He wasn't blown too far from Leila. Mary, whose vision hadn't recovered, fired roots aimlessly at the cavern, hitting everything except for us. We ducked behind a net of groves far from Mary's attacks.

"What's going on!" Aiden yelped. "When and how did Mary get powers?"

"I don't know yet. All I know is that Mary can open the breach, but she won't let us go!"

Explosions ripped through the air near us. We ducked down and hurried to another corner, far from the hurtling debris.

"Can you open a breach, here?" Aiden asked Leila. "Are you far from the spell to make one?"

"I think so," she replied. "But I can't do much with her chucking this cavern at us."

"So, either we force her to open the breach, or stall her long enough to make our own," I said.

"We'll need her distracted first."

"That I can do," Aiden said. "I'll keep her busy, take her attention off of you."

"Please be careful," I pleaded.

His face whitened; his voice shook yet he held on to that small, reassuring smile. "Don't worry, I got this."

He slipped away from us then emerged to the surface. His voice, sharp and fierce when he shouted Mary's full name, boomed through the cavern. Mary turned in his direction, and a wave of light washed over her. Leila and I climbed out and I charged after Mary before she recovered.

"How are you doing that!" Mary yelled.

She swiped her arm, and chunks of roots and stone tore from the ceiling. The pieces spun around us and crashed into the walls. Fire flowed through my arm and the blast of light slammed into the roots, incinerating it into a cloud of burning ash.

"Of all the people to give power to, why would they choose the class psycho and the loner who sits in the back of the room?"

"Why do you care? You have powers too!" Aiden retorted. He cast a crescent-shaped light, but Mary leaped out of the way.

"That won't work—"

The light burst into rapid flashes, blinding her. The flickering light and changing colors hurt my head. I slowed down and forced my eyes closed. Upon opening them, I caught a glimpse of the roots behind Mary. The shadows cast against the crevices resembled hollow, misshapen eyes held up by a wide, malformed mouth.

"Ya tryin' to give us a seizure?" Leila shouted.

"Sorry!" Aiden cried.

The pulsating lights faded and the face on the mound vanished.

Mary hauled herself up, rubbing her eyes. "See?" she huffed. "You can't control it, so why were you chosen?"

Leila groaned, "Chosen by who?"

"She thinks the assistants gave us our powers," I explained, then shouted at Mary. "Which isn't true! We came to them for help because our powers are difficult to control."

"Yeah, because it's given to irresponsible and unstable people." Mary faced me, and I was lifted off the ground until she jerked back, letting out a cry as she hit the roots behind her.

"Like you're more stable!" Leila yelled, holding her arm out.

A surge of dread rushed through me, weakening my legs, and I collapsed to my knees. Before I could warn Aiden and Leila, Mary laughed. The three of us traded nervous looks. The laughter grew more distorted and louder with every second, shaking the cavern.

"Oh," Mary sang, her voice twisted with the guttural snarl of something else, something deep and hollow that sent shivers down my spine. "You want to see unstable?"

My arm caught one of the branches as the ground shifted and quake beneath my feet. Roots writhed with life, slamming down on the walls and writhing with life. Sarah's scream cut short, and I saw Aiden pinned against the cavern walls. The roots clamped over his hands and wrapped around his neck, choking out his scream.

No matter how much I pleaded for Mary to stop, all I could do was watch Aiden jerk and shudder under his restraints, before streams of light jetted out of him.

It sliced through the roots and battered the cavern with so much force, its walls started to cave in. My back slammed violently into the ground, as roots and debris rained down around me.

I wasn't sure if the ground was still shaking, or I was. Using what little strength I had left, I hauled myself to my feet. I fought through the throbbing pain and ringing in my ears to make out what I was seeing. Nothing looked the same. The roots bulged and snaked out of places. Pieces of it lay scattered around me. I cried out to my friends and a stony silence met my ears.

A faint glint of red drew me to the wall, and my throat seized when I found Aiden, hanging from one of the branches. It snapped and my fear exploded into one big cry as he hit the ground. I ran close and found him... floating. He was unconscious, but mostly unharmed.

"You're welcome..." Leila rasped.

Leila was beneath one of the groves. Her eyes were locked on Aiden, then her outstretched arm dropped, and her head thumped against the ground.

"Leila!" I dragged myself to her. She had cuts on her face, and blood stained her tattered clothes.

"Leila, Sarah, please wake up!" My frantic cries weakened into tearful sobs and choked gasps. "Please, wake up..."

A new voice, cold and ancient broke into a sinister laugh. Gripped in fear, I slowly turned. Mary was on her feet, covered in scratches. Sickly violet and black veins decorated her pale, white skin. Tears, as dark as ink, ran down her cheeks and her lips stretched into an eerie grin.

"Well done!" a guttural voice emerged from her. "Such a riveting performance! Truly, you have proven yourself worthy of becoming my vessel."

Shaking and wracked with pain, I reached for the power within, channeling the heat when a sharp pain pulsed through me. I hunched forward, assaulted by one gut wrenching cough after another. A hot lump rolled out of my mouth and blood splattered on the ground. Blackness crawled from the corners of my eyes.

"Finally reached your limit. Perfect," Malus purred, its voice dug inside my head.

A heavy feeling washed over me. I clenched my eyes and forced through the icy, heavy air that pushed into me.

"Rest your weary mind. No need to feel frightened. You are truly a gifted being, blessed to cross into the garden..." its voice cracked.

A small, faint cry rose from Mary. "You said you wanted me! You chose me!"

In that second, I let out one last scream. Bright bolts of energy speared out of me in waves. The tightness in my chest was so horrifically strained, each pulse in my heart sent a sharpness, like my veins were being ripped apart. I screamed as the white-hot pain of my powers ripped out of me and ignited the world in a blinding light. Finally, after an agonizing eternity, the light sputtered out.

●

Voices resonated all around me; sounding soft and urgent before a deafening, animalistic roar blasted in the air. It continued for several seconds, then a woman's voice emerged, soothing yet overpowering as she spoke in a strange language. Arms cradled me and my head settled on someone's shoulders. A soothing hum wrapped around me and washed away my worries and fears.

Birdsongs and chirping crickets stirred me out of my sleep, and I woke up to glimmers of light peeking through the leaves. I shifted weakly, feeling the cool grass brush against my skin. With what little strength I had, I sat up, struggling to make sense of my surroundings.

"You never cease to surprise me."

I whipped around to see a pair of piercing green eyes on a warm, tan face. I jumped back and tumbled in the grass.

"Ow..." I groaned.

Galumine giggled. She was as beautiful as I remember, tall and graceful, with glowing inscriptions trailing down her cheeks and bare shoulders. Her feathered dress ruffled as she leaned forward and helped me up.

"Easy now, little cub," she spoke in a deep, soothing tone. "I do not wish to see you hurt again."

"Wh-where am I?" I croaked. "What happened to me? Where's—"

"You're in Erehwon once again. But keep your voice low, or you'll wake your friends."

She gestured to the side.

My eyes followed her arm to the colossal ancient tree behind us. Clumps of moss carpeted the twisted trunk and mushrooms sprouted from its arching roots. The branches stretched wildly overhead, blossoming in leaves and small flowers of beautiful colors. A soft, bell-like chime and faint glow drew me to a pair of butterflies, one sparkling green and silvery blue. Their wings were sprinkling powder on Aiden.

My heart leapt and I called out his name before I could stop myself. He stirred but didn't wake. The scratches and injuries had healed, and his torn clothes looked new. Including the headphones.

The blue butterfly floated over the grove, and I found Sarah curled up against the roots. Specs of powder landed on her hair, like fresh snow. She let out soft and deep breaths, her eyes relaxed as though she was having her first, longest sleep-in ages. I pulled away from Sarah and continued around the tree until I slowed to a stop in front of Mary. All traces of the ink-black veins vanished, and her deathly pale face returned to a creamy complexion.

My stomach felt uneasy. When Galumine's hand settled on my shoulder, I stepped back and looked up at her.

"Are they going to be alright?" I whispered.

"They will. Scales from the Marla butterflies can put anyone in a deep, though temporary slumber while it restores all injuries."

I blinked, my mind struggling to remember why that name sounded familiar. "Marla..."

"You've heard that name from one of my assistants, though they changed it to Marlene."

"Min?"

The wings chimed, like Min was saying, "yes" The blue butterfly's wings rang like a small bell.

"Oh... that's her sister then. Mei-Mei." I cupped my hands and Mei-Mei landed gently in the middle. "Thank you so much."

She chimed again and leaped into the air to join her sister.

"Mayu?" Galumine called. She opened her hand and my glasses materialized before me, looking good as new. "Would it be alright if we talk in private. We wouldn't want to disturb those who are resting."

I wanted to stay by their sides, but I had a feeling we wouldn't be gone long. I followed Galumine through a narrow path tucked between the tree trunks.

Sunbeams broke through the canopies. A thousand leaves shuddered overhead, sounding more like waves roaring down a stream, than the wide river that flowed calmly through the forest. After being in the dark, surrounded by spirits and rotting roots in the Ethereal Plane, seeing anything alive was magical.

My gaze wandered to the tiny, winged creatures stitched to the trees, their gem-like eyes watching my movement as Galumine walked ahead.

"We're here," she announced. The narrow path opened to three standing stones, cracked, mossy and tangled in vines, and a fourth fractured into pieces.

"This is one of my favorite spots." Galumine settled on an upturned stone, and I did the same. "It... feels nostalgic to be here. Away from the troubles of the world and secluded so we may speak in privacy."

That was when I noticed the lack of music in the air. The tiny whispers vanished, and I didn't see little eyes peeking at me through the foliage.

"I'd like to apologize foremost."

I turned to Galumine's gentle expression. "Had I known you and your friends were in the Ethereal Plane, I would have acted sooner, and you wouldn't have suffered through the Malus' possession."

"What do you mean? I fought it off!" I insisted.

Galumine sat quietly, folding her hands over her lap.

"You resisted it, that I saw. But the Malus is still a being of old who had control over you from the very beginning."

My brow furrowed.

"Chitose noticed it in your dreams. At first, she believed the Malus was speaking to you through your mind, as it often did. However, upon closer look, we realized what it did. When you fell through the gate and your powers awoken to shield you, the Malus, in an attempt to take your body, it planted a small portion of itself into you."

My vision spun. "It was already inside of me?"

"It hid in the deepest parts of your mind, influencing you in your most vulnerable times. First in your sleep and when you were in a state of distress."

Aiden's words echoed in my thoughts: *Why did you go to the library in the first place?*

I told him it was to get away from my troubles, but deep down, I wasn't sure what drew me there. Why was there a pulling sensation compelling me to go to the library where the breach was? And then, when we were pulled into the Ethereal Plane.

"It was my idea to travel deeper. I thought there was a breach there." I held my head, my mind lost in the horrors we saw, the danger we were in, and the danger that could've happened...

"You had good intentions." Galumine's voice rose in my ear. "The Malus simply steered your thoughts to what it wanted."

I sniffled, wiping the tears from my face. "I never stood a chance, did I?"

"If it's any consolation, the overuse of your power and the toll it took on your body weakened its hold on you. Turns out a being with no living body as a host does not cope well to the waves of mortal pain. It couldn't do much when I expelled it from you and resealed it."

"Thanks," I mumbled, then something occurred to me. "How did you know we were in the Ethereal Plane?"

"Funny enough, I intended to see you myself. But when a breach opened at your school, despite the spell placed on it, I had to lock down Erehwon again, closing all the gates on such short notice, and sending guards to monitor them. As if things couldn't get any more chaotic, your friend Elizabeth sought me out. She begged for me to help you."

My mouth hung in shock, and Galumine laughed.

"I'm guessing this is unusual for her?"

I blushed. "It wouldn't be the first time she's helped me. She's not in trouble again, is she?"

"Elizabeth is certainly not one I would worry about," Galumine said. "I am more concerned about you."

"What do you mean?"

"In four months, you've crossed into Erehwon on your own, restrained a possessed classmate, killed a swarm of pixies, shut

406

down the electricity at your school, and recently confronted an ancient primordial being. Those are no small feats, let alone easy ones."

"I know..." I stared at the ground as my ears warmed.

Though Galumine's voice was gentle and motherly, it felt like I was being scolded.

"I'm not reprimanding you. I need to warn you," she said sternly. "Your actions have acted as a beacon to both the Mystic and human worlds. The Malus was one of many beings drawn to your powers. Some have already encroached your neighborhood."

"Th-those attacks? The voice that spoke to me."

Galumine nodded. "One had tried to communicate with you, unaware of the Malus' presence. It retreated after Cedric's final confrontation, but I can't guarantee they won't come back or that something else won't target you."

I thought back to the voices I'd hear, and the dreams of "them" fighting in the forest.

"Galumine, I need to tell you something." I struggled to get the words out. "I've heard a voice long before I fell into Erehwon. I thought it was a side effect of my seizures, but it always asked if I could hear it. Then it warned me about the assistants being dangerous. It stopped the same night Mr. Turner hurt them. How would they know about me back then?"

"I see..." Galumine looked at me with narrow eyes and fire flickered behind her irises. "Then that is more reason for you to hear my plea. You can stay here in Erehwon. Under my protection, no harm may come to you. Here, you can learn to control your power in safety."

"H-how long would I have to be away?"

"Your power is not one you can master in a short time. I won't force you to stay, but I'd prefer if you remained here for the time being."

It felt like the world was caving in on my shoulders. I didn't know what I wanted to say. We raised our heads toward the chiming bells coming from the leaves above.

"I will let you think on it." Galumine raised her arm to the sunbeams. Soft beads of light gathered on her fingertips and pulsed into the shape of butterflies with luminous blue and soft green wings. Min crawled delicately across Galumine's hand.

"Can you speak to the butterflies?" she asked.

I shook my head. "Min said I wouldn't hear butterflies' voices."

"It takes time to listen. Min and Mei-Mei want to tell us—" a loud scream brought our attention to the grand tree, and the butterflies fluttered away. "...Your friends have woken up."

# Compromise

**I went ahead of Galumine,** rushing down the pathway, to their voices. Just as I crashed through the thicket, I was blinded by a sharp blast of light.

"Can you stop doing that?" Mary screamed.

I rubbed my eyes, and my first clear vision was Aiden and Sarah standing in front of the grand tree. Mary, covering her eyes, had her back against one of the large roots.

"Everyone, it's okay!" I shouted, grabbing their attention.

Sarah spun around. Her long skirt caught her legs, and she fumbled over until I caught her. Her arms wrapped around my waist, and she sobbed on my shoulder.

"I thought you were gone!" she whimpered. "I thought we weren't going to make it!"

My voice cracked a bit. "I thought so too."

Aiden fell to his knees in front of us and we pulled each other into a tearful embrace.

Sarah pulled away and her shock filled her wide eyes. She jerked back as Mary screamed and Aiden leapt to his feet shouting, "what is that!"

My head craned back as Galumine emerged seamlessly from the greenery.

I quickly got up and stood between them. "Don't worry, she won't hurt us. This is Galumine. She created the assistant's program and brought us here."

Aiden made a face and his head tilted to the side. "I think I've seen you before. You were at the meeting, but you didn't have horns, or wings, or glowing tattoos."

Galumine let out a petite laughter. "With this reaction, I think it was a good call to cast an illusion on myself. My appearance can be overwhelming to some. I'm sorry for frightening you."

She bowed her head, introduced herself then explained to us the rescue from the Malus and brought us to Erehwon, the world of Mystics, to recover.

"We're in another world?" Sarah asked, her head swivel between the trees, the glade and the streams flowing around us.

"For the time being," Galumine replied. "I will send you home safely. No harm shall befall you in my realm."

"Then why is *she* here?" Aiden threw a sharp glare at Mary.

She glared back, still hiding behind the groves. "You're the one that blinded me first and I can't use my powers anymore!"

"What do you mean?" I asked.

"I can't *use* my powers! It's gone!"

"Not gone, weakened," Galumine corrected. "Sharing your body with the Malus enhanced your latent abilities. But now it is no longer a part of you, your abilities have returned to its dormant state."

"Are you serious!" Mary bellowed. "So, they get to keep their powers, but I can't!" She pointed an accusatory finger at us.

A brow arched curiously over Galumine's eyes. "Every human has a dormant ability. It will take time and practice, but if you have the patience for it, you can reawaken some of what you could do."

My body tensed, dreading a repeat of the same pain I felt before.

"That's not fair!" Mary exclaimed. "I actually worked for my powers, they didn't! I didn't have assistants hand them to me like they did!"

"Handed?" Aiden asked, shocked. "Who told you that?"

"You know that's the truth!" Mary retorted.

"No one handed us anything," I said, calmly. "Do you think we asked for our powers. You think we *wanted* powers that we can't even control. That ends up hurting us if we try to control it?"

"But you still have them," she argued. "Don't lie, if you were surrounded by people with powers, you'd want to be like them too!"

"My, quite a zealous spirit for one so young," Galumine said with a soft gasp. "However, you are incorrect in your assumption as to what my assistants do. They offer guidance to students and aid those whose abilities have awoken, or had it thrust upon them with no way to control or comprehend it. Only a mystic with ulterior motives would inflict such a harsh burden upon a child.

Which the Malus clearly demonstrated when it shared its power with you."

"He was trying to protect me. He told me the assistants wanted to suppress him because he knew the truth about them! That they cherry picked students to be one of them."

"So, all of this mess is because you weren't picked," I scoffed in exasperation. "Mary, the truth is you could have spoken to the assistants. You could have spoken to us, but you trusted a voice in your head, a face you've never met because it told you what you wanted to hear."

Aiden joined me, sounding just as disgusted. "How could you go through the Ethereal Plane, see what we saw, and still think the assistants can't be trusted?"

"That's because you took the dangerous route," Mary sputtered out. "He cared about me enough to show me the safer parts, wherever the roots were. He showed me shortcuts around the school, so if I were upset or needed help, I could slip through portals around the school."

"Portals?" Sarah repeated.

"There were more breaches," I explained. "Like the one in the library. You were right there with me that day, weren't you?"

Mary's shoulders shrank. "I left the other world and I saw you on the floor. But the fire spread, so I ran. Next thing I knew, a spell sealed all the portals, cutting me away from him. I didn't want to lose the only being who understood me. I practiced for weeks to break through!"

"You've been opening breaches around the school," I said.

Aiden's eyes widened. "I must have jumped into one of the breaches to save you."

Then I remembered something else Mary told me. "You said you could control the fae. Including the pixies?"

Mary squirmed. "They were supposed to come to the courtyard. They didn't listen to me and flew all over the school."

"You caused all of those people to get hurt!"

"But no one died, okay."

"I died!" Aiden exploded.

Mary flinched. "This isn't right, it's four of you against me, and none of you are hearing my side of the story! How I was alone and made fun of for being different!"

Before I could protest, our argument was interrupted by Galumine's deep voice resonating in the air.

"I have heard plenty," she spoke. "Your story, though tragic, is no more different than your peers. But it is clear you never wanted to meet those like you. You never cared for a connection. You wanted to be superior to those you looked down on. To have what you believed they would never gain. To gain what you believed belong to you."

Mary stayed silent.

"You say the Malus cared for you, but that creature only uses humans to sustain itself. It couldn't have full control over Mayu, so it fueled your resentment to get what it wanted, as it has done with many who fell to its sway."

"Y-You're wrong!" Mary cried.

"I apologize for the Malus' deception. But I see you show no remorse for the damage you've caused. And with such apathy toward your kind, I cannot let you go without precaution."

Galumine drifted closer to Mary who backed against the tree, her face whitened with fear.

"I'm not dangerous," she begged. "Okay, I made a few mistakes, but I'm only human! It's in our nature to mess up!"

"*Only human...*" Galumine's voice deepened with a sharpened edge.

The forest fell deathly silent. Galumine's wings ruffled in a dizzying wave, revealing a dozen glassy green eyes embedded in the feathers. My heart slammed in my chest, and I scampered back with Aiden and Sarah, but Mary had nowhere to go. Her back was against the tree trunk and the arching roots caged her in, leaving her at the mercy of Galumine.

Fire gleamed behind her eyes, and the inscriptions beamed like sunrays coursing across her arms. In that moment, I felt something emitting from her, something far more ancient than the Malus.

"If these 'mistakes' are of your human nature," She spoke in three different voices. "Surely, you won't mind if I correct this, in *my* nature."

Galumine raised her arm and Mary dropped to her knees as she cried out in pain. Glowing marks trailed up Mary's wrist and spiraled around her arms. Then it vanished. The light surrounding Galumine vanished, the eyes closed, and the feathers settled.

"What happened to her?" Aiden asked.

"She placed a spell on her," I answered softly.

"It's a seal," Galumine's triple voice melded back into one. "Marietta Brown, I bar you from any ethereal touch. Once you step foot out of Erehwon, no longer shall you enter any realms outside of the one of your origins. No longer can you tear open a breach or create one until you've learned not to discard your kind and treat us as a commodity."

The leaves shivered at her voice, then all fell silent. Mary opened her mouth to speak, but only sobs broke through. She wailed apology after apology, but it was clear Galumine wouldn't change her mind.

I didn't see the sneering princess in the cavern or the girl who yelled at me in the hallway. All I saw was the classmate sitting alone on the bleachers with a book in her hand.

Despite Sarah's shock and Aiden's soft protest, I stepped between Galumine and Mary. I sank to my knees, meeting Mary's eyes.

"She could've changed your memories," I told her. "That's what Miss Naiad did to Victoria after Leila attacked her, then the other students who saw the pixies. You could forget everything and go home... but only if you want to."

Sniffling, and wiping her tears away, Mary's chin jerked from side to side as she shook her head.

"I've seen these markings on another magic user. His name is Tora, and he told me he has it to keep ethereal beings from possessing him." I continued. "This is a protection seal. That means nothing will control you. Or influence your mind. So, when you want to speak to the assistants, you can come to your own conclusions."

I turned back to Galumine. "Right?"

She leaned her head to the side. Sunbeams glinted off her horns and her eyes flickered like flames behind glasswork.

"Do you understand what Mayu is saying?"

Mary flinched and answered in a small voice, "Y-yes, ma'am."

Galumine breathed out and the sound of nature returned to the air; crickets chirped, and bird songs swirled around us. The trees shuddered in relief, as if letting out a breath they were holding for a long time.

"Now that your wounds have healed, I can send you back to your realm, back to school."

We shifted uncomfortably in the grass.

Aiden spoke up, "Is school still open?"

"You'll leave as though mere hours have passed in your world. Marietta, you may want to stand back."

Mary shimmied awkwardly to my side.

Galumine waved her arm and the grand tree rumbled. Birds and insects flitted from the shivering branches and leaves fell delicately like snow. I watched in awe as the twisted trunk creaked and a threshold unfurled at the center. Inside, white mist swirled into a rippling image of the school's main doors.

I whispered to myself, but Galumine heard me. "What are you?"

"I am the keeper of this world." She raised her voice. "This is a one-way path back to your school. You may go first, Marietta."

Mary scurried to the threshold. Her image melted through like paper sinking in water. Aiden and Sarah followed, but before they reached the other side, Aiden turned back to me.

"Are you coming?" he asked.

"In a moment," I said and looked up to Galumine.

"Would you like to remain here?" she asked.

I chewed the inside of my cheek. "About the mystics that have noticed my powers. If I stay here, they'll still target me, right?"

"Most likely."

"Will it be the same when I'm home?"

"Correct."

"And the assistants who watched over the neighborhood; Ethan, Chitose and Mr. Turner. They'd have to fight it off."

"To the best of their abilities. Do you desire protection from them?"

"I was thinking maybe they could use a little help."

Her sharp green eyes grew with surprise.

"Rather than being a beacon, my powers can be a warning. Beware the hybrid who outran centaurs and can vaporize any Mystic, Fae, or otherwise." I sounded more confident than I felt.

A gentle smile chipped through her stoic face. "Very well. Erehwon will be here should you change your mind."

I slipped into my backpack, hearing the flashlights knock against each other inside.

"One more thing," I said, facing Galumine one more time. "Can you let Elizabeth know I'm alright? Or ask her to call me tonight?"

"You have my word."

I jogged back to Aiden and Sarah at the threshold. Together, we stepped forward and bright red lockers swept across the trees. Sunbeams narrowed to daylight pouring through the main doors. Mary sat on the steps. She glanced at us momentarily before facing the doors again.

The lights were off, and the school was empty. The heavy rain had softened to a light drizzle, and sunbeams poked through the clouds. I nudged the main door open and bit my lip at the crisp air outside.

"We're back," I laughed, shakily.

"Finally!" Aiden cheered. "I never thought I'd miss this school!"

I unzipped my backpack and grabbed my phone. The instant the screen flashed on, messages flooded my inbox from Ichirou and Hannah, asking if I was alright and needed a ride.

I texted to both: "Don't worry, I'm fine. I'm waiting at the front door with Aiden and Sarah. Can you pick me up?"

Hannah immediately replied: "I'm in the car with Ichirou. We're on our way now."

"How is everyone getting home?" Aiden asked.

"My brother's picking me up," I said. "What about you?"

"I always walk home," Sarah said, and perked up. "I have an umbrella in my locker, but it's on the second floor."

We turned to the hallway behind us. Reluctance played on Aiden's face before he straightened himself up.

"A hallway shouldn't scare me." Aiden checked both sides of the hallway and when it was clear nobody was around, a ball of light appeared in his hands. "Mayu, are you coming?"

"I got to keep an eye out for Ichirou."

"Alright. Be careful," he said.

I noticed he stared at Mary for a second, then walked away with Sarah before she noticed. An awkward silence fell between us. I listened to the light rain and texted Lutea about training next weekend. Mary's sniffles brought my attention to her. I peered over her shoulder and noticed a leaf cradled in her hands, vibrant green with gold veins traced across it.

I said, gently, "The assistants may seem scary at first. But they're very nice once you get to know them."

Mary looked at me, then we jumped at the sound of musical chimes blaring from a phone. Mary dug the dazzling pink phone from her pocket and answered.

"Hi Dad," she murmured. "Yeah, I see you right now. I'll be out in a moment." She hoisted herself up and without turning to me or saying a word, she opened the door and hurried to her father's car.

"We're back!" Aiden announced, dispersing the light.

Sarah caught up with him, carrying a long, black umbrella and an oversized sweater that reached her kneecaps.

"How'd the trip go?" I asked.

Aiden said, jokingly, "We got the umbrella and didn't run into monsters,"

Sarah quipped, "Aiden jumped at his own shadow upstairs."

"Did not," he grumbled. "Where's Mary? Did she leave?"

I nodded. "I tried to talk to her again, but she said nothing back."

"I'd be surprised if she did." Aiden sat beside me. "Do you think she took your words to heart?"

I leaned forward and stared at the rain. "I guess time will tell."

After a moment of waiting, we got restless and played rock paper scissors to pass the time. I thought I was pretty good until I went up against Sarah. She predicted anything Aiden and I chose and beat us one-on-one. We talked about plans for the weekend when Ichirou called me.

"We're almost at the school," Hannah said, loud and clear, meaning she had the phone in her hand.

"Please tell me you're still there." Ichirou said, windshield squeaking in the background.

I choked up at their voices. Hours had passed, but it felt like days since I spoke to them. "Yeah, I'm here."

"Did something happen?" Hannah asked.

"I'm alright. Could I ask for a favor?"

"Ask away, Runt," said Ichirou.

I chuckled, wiping my eyes and smiled at Sarah and Aiden. "Would it be okay if you gave my friends a ride home, too?"

# Holly

**I woke up early Christmas morning** and, wanting to look my best for my first visitors, I put on a midnight blue sweater embroidered with white snowflakes, black leggings, and a matching skirt. I met Ichirou and Hannah in the kitchen where a song played from the laptop at the table so we had something to listen to while we cooked.

"And where did you learn to make this?" Ichirou raised a brow at the ingredients to make a creamy pork and apple casserole.

"Lutea and her dad taught me."

I offered to make my own meals during training, and Tora and Lutea were more than happy to teach me. Before winter break, Tora gave me some of his homemade cider, a gift for my improvement and not destroying the backyard again, and the apples he grew and enchanted with a spell to keep them fresh for a year.

"You didn't poison anyone, did you?" Ichirou asked.

"Of course not!" It wasn't poison, but I mistook a jar of pixie dust for sugar.

"I hope this is enough for everyone," Hannah said, spraying cooking oil in the pan.

Ichirou snorted. "If it can feed a big eater like Mayu, it should be enough."

And so began the process of me and Ichirou chopping apples and onions while Hannah seared the pork bits in the pan. After much sautéing and mixing, we left the casserole to simmer and cleaned up for the next recipes. Hannah seasoned the hen, and I set the ingredients out for an apple rice cooker cake when Ichirou's phone rang.

It wasn't usual for his job to call him on his day off. Ichirou usually waited until the third ring, but he hurried out of the kitchen and answered before the first ring ended. So, it wasn't his boss or a co-worker. Whoever he was talking to was brief and it must've been urgent because rushed upstairs, continuing the conversation with someone, then headed to the patio door, zipping up his winter jacket.

"Everything alright?" Hannah called.

"Yeah, I'm picking up something. I'll be back." Ichirou stopped at the door and said aloud, "And make not to put laxatives in the cake!"

"It was one time!" I groaned.

Ichirou smiled and went to his car.

"I wondered where he's going," I pondered.

"He got in touch with your parents recently, asking for a favor," Hannah said.

"What kind of favor?"

She shrugged. "No clue. But there have been no arguments, so it might be a good favor."

"They're talking to each other without fighting?"

"Right?" Hannah chuckled. "It's a Christmas miracle."

By noon, dinner was done with most of the meal in the oven. I gathered the scraps of hen, added buttered shrimp, then rolled it in a paper bag small enough to fit my hand. I nudged the screen door open, gritting my teeth as snowflakes pinched my face.

The fresh snow partially covered Tuna's paw prints. She'd still wait at the door for food yet run away when I answered. But that doesn't stop her from snatching the meals I'd leave her.

"Merry Christmas, Tuna." I stuffed the bag under the snow, hoping one day, she would recognize me again.

An hour later, Kaiah stopped by and dropped off Aiden and Sarah. Aiden had a gift for me, but as eager as I was to open it, I had to uphold an old tradition that everyone needs to be in the house before we exchanged gifts and Ichirou hadn't returned from his errand run.

"Hope you don't mind one exception, since I already opened it," Aiden said with an impish grin.

It was a new game he got, a steampunk fantasy that took place in a world with floating islands, and a heroine who could control the wind. Aiden hadn't played it yet, wanting to experience the game with us.

So, we agreed to take turns, with Aiden going first. We were immersed in the heroine's journey, exploring the world with her until the first boss ambushed us. Its attacks were lightning fast and knocked off more than half the heroine's health. Sarah and I shouted strategies on how to beat the boss, but it was too late. The screen faded to black and red letters emerged in the center: "YOU FAINTED. Try Again?"

"My turn," I chuckled.

Aiden passed the controller to me, and the heroine returned to the starting point. I was moments away from entering the boss fight when the phone rang.

Hannah answered it, then she called into the living room. "Mayu, it's for you!"

"Sorry, I have to get this."

Knowing who was on the phone, I passed the controller to Sarah. As I said hello to Elizabeth, Sarah shrieked. The monster in the game had attacked her.

"Goodness!" Elizabeth gasped. "Are you having a party or watching a horror movie?"

"We're playing a game," I replied, hurrying to my room as Aiden and Sarah groaned in defeat. "How's it going on your end? Are your roommates enjoying themselves?"

"Very much! Suzanne's been eager to see you all day!"

At the sound of her name, Sue's cheery voice burst through the phone. "Hi Mayu! When are you coming over? Can you stop by for a visit today?"

I pulled the phone away but could still hear her as if she were in front of me.

"Mayu has company right now," Elizabeth told her. "You'll see her tomorrow."

Sue moaned, "She can't bring them over? Move the party over here? There's so much space here!"

"Maybe some other time," I said, though the idea of Aiden and Sarah meeting Elizabeth and her friends wasn't too bad of an idea. Ichirou's car pulled into the snow-covered lot.

"I got to go. Ichirou's back. We're going to open presents soon!"

"Okay, enjoy the rest of the day," said Elizabeth. "Happy holidays!"

"And have a blessed Yule!" Sue yelled.

With a lighthearted laugh, I ended the call and rushed downstairs. The moment Ichirou was inside, his eyes flickered to the new game on the screen. He and Aiden were talking about the graphics and the sound design before Hannah reminded them that we were waiting to open our presents. Aiden paused the game, and we gathered around the tree.

Hannah fished underneath the tree, shaking off a few ornaments as she pulled out a small red box.

"This one... is for Aiden!" she announced.

I hid my smile when he peeled off the red wrapper. My heart pounded when he held the present in his hand; bright red and shiny to match his headphones.

"You got me a music player?" he asked.

I fumbled on my words. "You pay so much attention to me in class, you can tell when I'm lost in thought. Sometimes, I pay attention to you too, and notice you always have your headphones with you, but I never heard you listen to a song."

Aiden fell silent, but his cheeks still glowed. "Most people leave you alone if they think you can't hear them."

"Do they still work?"

"Somewhat."

Ichirou cleared his throat, drawing our attention to a large pink present, fitted with a white bow at the top. To Sarah, from me and Aiden.

Sarah's eyes lit up. She slowly tore the wrapper and her mouth fell open at the leather notebook, bound with a strap and a heart-shaped lock. A pair of keys came in their own package, along with a pack of pens.

"It's for your poetry," I said. "And Aiden got something for you, too."

Sarah shifted the papers aside and her face lit up at the pair of pink headphones and a matching music player inside.

Aiden said, sheepishly, "I don't know what songs you listened to. I wanted to ask, but Mayu told me it would ruin the surprise."

"It would," I argued.

"They're great." Sarah wiped the tears from her eyes. "I got something for you two."

Her face reddening, Sarah passed us a couple of envelopes. "I don't know how to wrap gifts."

Inside the envelopes were beautiful, yet abstract, drawings of a calico cat sitting by a window and a single star shining in the night.

"Sarah, that's beautiful!" Hannah praised. "An artist and a poet, you're very talented!"

Sarah stuttered. "Actually, my friend Leila drew the pictures. I wrote the poem inside."

"Do you want to share some of your poems with us?" I said. Sarah's cheeks flared and she buried her head in her new journal. I guess that was a no.

The next gift was for me from Aiden. The first thing I noticed after carefully tearing off the wrapper, was the fur poking out of the box. It was a plush cat, like my calico, only a tabby with white fur and black and grey stripes.

"Aiden, this is cute!" I squeezed the toy against my cheeks.

"After you told me what happened to your cat, I thought this would cheer you up. And, like Sarah's gift," he lowered his voice. "...there's more."

I dug eagerly through the shredded paper and found a familiar red book. A tabby cat with piercing green eyes stared at me from inside a jar. The silver, cursive letters at the top read: *Witch Bottle*.

Excitement jolted through me. I wanted to thank him, ask him how he got *Witch Hazel*'s sequel when it wouldn't come out until next spring, but I couldn't form words. I burst into an ecstatic scream and tackled Aiden in a tight hug.

Overall, we had a great party. Aiden, Sarah and I used the laptop to download songs into the music players, then we ate and played games until night came. After Kaiah picked up my friends, I settled on the cough with Ichirou and Hannah. We watched old and new Christmas movies for the rest of the night.

The next morning, I set my backpack on the table, double checking to see if I had everything. I barely slept last night, my mind was anticipating seeing Elizabeth and meeting her roommates.

"Make sure to keep your phone charged, okay?" Hannah reminded me.

"I know," I said.

"Let us know if you need anything," Ichirou added.

"I will."

"Do you have everything you need? Clothes? Books? An extra charger?" Hannah asked, warily.

"Babe," Ichirou grunted, hoisting my backpack over his shoulder. "She's going to Isa's. It's not the first time she's been away from home."

"I know, but two weeks is still long," Hannah groaned, wrapping her arms around me. She ruffled my hair and pecked me on my cheek. "Be on your best behavior!"

"I'll try my best," I laughed and hurried behind Ichirou to his car.

I sank into the passenger seat, melting to the heat pouring through the vents. Ichirou joined me in the driver's seat, and I noticed the beige envelope in his hand.

"Dropping off mail?"

"Nope," he said and handed it to me. "This is for you. Got this from our parents yesterday. I would have given it to you then, but you would have cried like a baby in front of your friends."

"Not a baby."

"But you do cry a lot."

I pouted. My expression changed when I read the date written in the envelope's corner, January 10th, and a name beneath it that I didn't recognize.

"Holly?" I muttered. "Who's Holly?"

"Look inside," Ichirou insisted.

The rumbling car was loud in my ears. I tore open the envelope and carefully pulled out an old photo. A pale little girl, about four years old, stood against a green wall. She wore a white shirt, decorated with tiny different colored handprints. Her short, unkempt hair framed around her face, and her wide blue eyes seemed to capture the light of the camera. I flipped the photo over and my heart throbbed when I read the name written on the back.

I struggled to catch my breath. "I'm… Holly?"

Ichirou gently rubbed my shoulder.

"You wanted to know where you came from. That was the first picture of you in the orphanage, after you left the hospital."

"What happened to me?"

"You were found in the woods, near the Holly Hills National Park. It's a days' drive away from here."

"What was I doing there?"

Ichirou fell silent and leaned against the seat.

"I don't know," he said, lowly. "You were found buried in snow and covered in blood with a nasty head wound. It was a miracle that you recovered, but you couldn't remember your name or where you came from."

"I couldn't talk?"

"If you can call biting and snarling at the people, 'talking.' That head injury might have caused your seizures, but that's speculation."

I stared at the photo, questions stirred in my mind. "If my name was Holly, where did Mayu come from?"

"Mom, who else? She thought naming you after the place where you nearly died was in poor taste. Dad suggested Yukiko, but she argued it would've been inappropriate given the circumstances. Your memories never recovered, and mom wanted you to have a fresh start. So, she named you Mayu. Do you remember what that means?"

My cheeks warmed up. 'Mayu' had a couple of meanings depending on how it was written in Kanji. With the characters Mom used, "Ma," meant true and "Yu" was gentleness. Together it meant...

"Compassionate," I smiled at my younger self. "I guess the picture didn't come without a favor."

"Mom and Dad want you to call them at least once a week. Are you alright with that?"

"Yeah..." My eyes narrowed at a little detail in the photo.

"Something wrong?"

"The walls behind me. I could've sworn they were grey."

"Nope. Puke green and piss yellow," he chuckled. "What made you think they were grey?"

"Must have remembered it differently." I slipped the photo back into the envelope. "Thank you for getting this."

"No problem, Runt." He messed with my hair. "Let's get you to Isa's."

Ichirou put the car in drive, and it cautiously trudged out of Union Circle and on to the main road. We drove down the street and passed John Carter high school, a castle of glass with wide windows reflecting the white world.

"Still a piece of shit," Ichirou grumbled.

"At least we didn't have dumpster fires." I watched the school as it shrank away behind us.

"You did pretty good," Ichirou said, slowing down at the red light. "You think you'll be ready for spring? It won't be long before it gets back to being crazy again."

"I think I can handle it."

# About the author

Devin Thornton is an aspiring author and artist with an unyielding love for mythology and fantasy. When she isn't writing, she spends her free time drawing or daydreaming about legendary creatures walking among humans, and mystical worlds hidden in plain sight. An avid reader herself, Devin hopes to see her debut novel amongst the stories that inspired her wild imagination.

I write this in honor of the late Akira Toriyama (1955-2024), creator of my favorite series, *Dragon ball Z*. From its manga and anime to the video games and parodies, Toriyama's story had brought me great joy and comfort throughout my life, while teaching me many morals that I carry to this day: complexity in its simplicity, finding strength in myself and striving for improvement over empowerment.

I loved *Dragon ball Z* so much, I would daydream about it. And I daydreamed about it so much, I wrote about it, created my own characters and adventures that branched off into stories of their own. And through many revisions, rewrites, edits and workshops with friends, family and a myriad of editors, it brings me immeasurable joy to share my story that was inspired by my love for *Dragon ball Z*. All because many years ago, nine-year-old me looked over my brother's shoulder when he was watching TV and I asked, "Why does that boy have a tail?"

www.ingramcontent.com/pod-product-compliance
Lightning Source LLC
Chambersburg PA
CBHW031926280626

47169CB00017BA/126